Reali

Disclaimer Notice

This book includes explicit content, depictions of violence, the use of alcohol and drugs and sexual references. This book is not suitable for persons below the age of 18

Please note that the content contained within this book is for entertainment purposes only.

This book is a work of fiction. Names, characters, business, events and incidents are products of the authors imagination. Any resemblance to actual persons, living or dead, or actual events is purely coincidental.

The cultures involved within this story are purely of the authors imagination, taking much inspiration from real world ancient civilisations. Although cultures may closely resemble those it was inspired by, they are not a direct or historically accurate representation.

''Though our realms have never crossed, you are a brother to me.

Let us charge the faceless together, and channel our darkest rage into our greatest weapons.

Give in to the anger that pulls us deep into the void.

And at the edge of darkness, we shall be our brother's keeper and bring each other back into the light.'' - D.B.

Legends of Altharn
Realm Walker

Zack Smithson

1: Fanara's Cradle

Altharn, Darogoth, Ard. Somewhere in Fanara's Forest, Year 4AB 282

Nightfall coats the land in shadow, the sound of a cricket's chirp echoes vastly throughout the everlasting darkness of the forest, the ambience is peaceful, tranquil.

A blanket of mist cast within Fanara's Forest swallows the oak and beech, a grey sea that laps up against the trunks and lurks within the bushes.

Numerous footstep's part the way, trampling through the shrubbery, snapping twigs and fraying through the dense leaves. The moonlight glow shines bright, revealing several figures donned in white hooded robes carefully making their way through the forest, accompanied by armed soldiers and battlemages alike, their chainmail armour clunking and rattling with each vigilant step.

They are druids, religiously and politically important figures in the world of Altharn, specifically to their native Kingdom of Darogoth. They are a revered and sacred people, held in high regard across all Darogoth, their words are absolute in the ways of politics, medicine, magic and belief. For where kings rule, druids guide.

Parinos, Arch Druid of Seers Crossing, leads his companions to their destination with haste, the group open up a small enclosure buried deep within the night washed thicket of this ancient forest, lost to the ages.

''Here we are my brothers and sisters, Fanara's Cradle,'' he extends his arms proudly before a large stone structure nestled within a disproportionate grove.

The druids and mercenaries continue to fumble their way into the dark opening, illuminating the ancient stone with torchlight. The structure was in moderate condition aside from the excessive overgrowth.

It was surrounded by many pillars of stones, large megaliths with mysterious otherworldly markings imbedded deep into the cold rock, within the centre of the circle was another circle of pillars notably smaller, and finally nestled in the very middle of this vast structure, a stone floor, coated with withered leaves and flakes of mud impacted all around. The markings are only just visible, lying adjacent to each other as they twirl around in an everlasting enfold presenting a beautiful yet eerie aura of something ancient and lost.

''What in the world… I've never seen this before, and so close to the village? It's not like the others, those glyphs….'' says Lucotorix, the arch druid's apprentice in amazement, rustling his shaggy brown hair. ''Has this been kept from us?''

''This one was built by Fanara and her seers, where she herself bore her ethereal magic within… her nature cloaks it from us, sealed thousands of years ago out of sight just before the Gods were banished, and now… I think now is the time to put it to use.

Although I fear using it may destroy it, that's the risk we must take. Besides, that's probably for the best,'' replied Parinos sternly, brushing his wispy beard. He turns to his followers behind him who stood in awe and anticipation. ''You all understand what we must do? I'm truly honoured by those of you who have put themselves forward for this to work, especially considering the risks… life energy may be the key to unlocking power to this extent. When the energy of life mixes with that of the endless void… the most remarkable things are said to happen, I can't tell you which one of you may die, but your death will be for the good of Darogoth, for the good of Fanara. You will always be remembered by your sacrifice, the void works in mysterious ways… and the life it chooses cannot be comprehended, we have little choice, this is what the mother of life teaches us, this is what she put in place, this circle.''

Lucotorix scrunches his face in confusion. ''Are you sure you still want to go through with this Parinos… the high king advised against this… he said the wa-''

''The war cannot be won by man alone,'' Parinos interrupts. ''The high king is stubborn… you know this Lucotorix… look to the north, it's beginning to fall under Venethari control. If Kastrith truly is the vessel of Vistra as so he claims, then only Fanara can stop this. Vistra is no tyrant, he knows only love for our lady. We have to try, try and breach the veil of our worlds to bring back Fanara… or at the very least one of her seeds, we must rival whatever it is Kastrith is forging within himself, he threatens the very heart and soul of Darogoth. If he prevails… we lose our way of life, for what is Darogoth without its druids?!'' Parinos fumbles with his beard again, he straightens his weary back, ready to speak in confidence. ''Yes, we also have absolutely no idea what we could bring forth. Her seers? A beast of the void? That's why whatever it is that does come forward is hostile, we have the mages to restrain it and the mercenaries for… well… you know,'' Parinos looks down to his feet in concern and then back to Lucotorix fixing his wrinkled face. ''But this is of her making. We must trust in our lady, all we must do is unlock it, and now… we have its key.''

''He's right Lucotorix, the Venethari will continue to overrun our homelands… It's already begun, us druids will be put to the slaughter if we do not obey his command to abolish our practices. We have to try, brother. He's playing a smart game, the high king won't have any of this nonsense, until when he does finally see what's going on… it'll be too late,'' replies Orthunus, Lucotorix's younger brother, patting his shoulder attempting to ease his brother's discomfort.

Lucotorix nods silently, avoiding eye contact, nervously scratching at his moustache giving a breathy sigh of unease. ''Orthunus, you're but a boy, you shouldn't even be here! What if something happens to you?!''

Parinos steps forward. ''We spoke about this. You know Orthunus will not participate, he is standing with the mercenaries tonight. Lucotorix, we're druids young one, we're the hand of Fanara, everything including our lives and our legacy is at risk if we do not try… only we can do this. When our fellow countrymen are blinded by the world and its many perils, they seek us for vision and this is what we do. This is no mere circle, with luck we may break through to Fanara's realm that's cast aside from our own and bring forth a being of purity if not the mother of life herself, if this is what it takes then we must do our duty as her loyal hands. We could change history, bring back the days of old under the God's embrace.''

''And what if whatever comes through is hostile and it can't be killed? You said it yourself; it'll be drenched in the power that surrounds our world, what if we ourselves release another monster into this world? One worse than even Kastrith,'' replies Lucotorix, his jaw beginning to visibly shake from his tender heart.

''We'll be able to subdue any being coming through the circle regardless of its drenching… because whatever does come through won't know how to harness it. Stay strong my friend… remember what you are, they're times in our lives where we as druids must make decisions as frightening and outlandish as this, our ancestors have spent their lives unlocking the secrets of the Gods and this circle,'' he looks to the centre of the ancient structure. ''Fanara's Cradle… the gate of life,'' he gives himself a moment to appreciate its mystical and foreboding aura, he turns back to Lucotorix. ''So, my apprentice, will you stay?'' He raises his bushy eyebrow in concern.

''By Fanara… you know I will, Parinos. Am I not wrong to question such uncertainty?'' Lucotorix replies in angst, adjusting a brave face.

Parinos gives a gentle grin as he takes a step back to address the others who were waiting anxiously. ''Let us waste no more time. To your positions. Remember, on my call focus every inch of magic you possess onto the central platform. Once the markings on the inner circle illuminate with your combined magic, extend your hands to the druid next to you and connect to their power. Once the outer circle illuminates you can relax and you'll feel the flow take hold of you. Once that flow is steady it will move throughout you all on its own accord, but DO NOT break that flow. As I stated before, this could take hours, even days if we're unlucky. Once the magic has bound to its source it may disconnect one of you from your life… or… it may not, but the warning is there. No matter what happens, keep focus. You'll find yourselves in a peaceful stasis once everything is set in place. Keep it and embrace it my druids… I believe in you, Darogoth believes in you… I'll give you all one last chance to abstain from this… reckless attempt at tearing through the void,'' he sighs. ''What say you, druids of Seers Crossing?''

A silence sweeps the group as they look to one another, a mutual agreement was forged, signed in silence.

The druids move to surround the circle standing a metre apart, the mercenaries move away to keep their distance along with Orthunus, who was to observe.

Parinos gives an uncertain sigh as he enters the centre and extends his hands to the floor drawing out a field of magic from his very essence for the druids to feed off as they focus their energy. Parinos's umbral eyes shudder into a dazzling magenta as he casts his magic, reflecting the power of the world through his soul.

A faint aura emits from Parinos's very being, as it flutters about, the other druids then begin to focus their magic towards the centre.

The inner circle illuminates, as it does, Parinos removes himself, visibly exhausted from the cast in just those few precious moments. He moves to wait behind the south side of the cradle to gently channel his energy to his fellow druids. ''Now, extend,'' speaks Parinos calmy, not to break the druid's concentration, they obey.

A low frequency humming begins to slowly vibrate through the air. ''The voice of nature itself… It's working,'' Parinos inner voice gasps.

The druids continue their spell for many more minutes, then hours. Some of the druids begin to start appearing gaunt in the face. Parinos, observing the ritual, becomes concerned. Deep-down he was unsure of what to do, was this going to kill or seriously injure all the druids? Magicka exhaustion was prying imminently. He felt confident the magic bound to the cradle will keep them in a secure stasis.

The spell's humming intensity reaches a high-pitched buzzing, shaking the very fabric of the air itself. The mercenaries begin to feel it on their skin as their hair's raise.

Upon noticing the change in the frequency, Parinos cast his thoughts aside. He walks forward ever so gently weaving underneath the druids arcane energy, pulling out of his rugged satchel what appeared to be a small stone etched with an ancient glyph that he grips tightly amidst his large callous hands. ''The final piece of this everlasting puzzle, generations of work and restoration, by the Gods, let this work… and if this be my last moment upon this world… then so be it,'' he whispers to himself.

The stone's glyph begins to glow in his hand. The energy of the druids begins to weave around erratically towards the runestone on its own accord. Slowly the runestone disintegrates into nothing, materialising into thin air as the energy attacks it, vanishing from existence.

Camula, a young and promising druid woman, begins wincing in pain but remains as strong as her body will allow her.

Noticing the faint noises, Parinos snaps his head toward her in immediate concern and approaches cautiously. He inhales a deep breath through his broadened nostrils as he places both his hands to hover over her aura, emitting his magical energy onto her, helping sustain her magical connection, and her life.

Camula realtors her posture, silently signalling to Parinos that she's okay. Parinos takes a gentle step back and glares intently at her for a moment as he catches his own breath from the cast, her face a sunken gaunt, her skin now pale and dry, almost cadaverous. She was showing severe symptoms of magicka exhaustion, much more than the other druids.

In an instant her eyes pry open, an entrenching look of terror washes her youthful yet shrivelling face, she winces forward still withholding the connection. Parinos readies himself to aid her but is halted by Camula's cold stare.

She was staring at him, lifelessly. She appeared as if she was attempting to scream at the top of her lungs but couldn't push out even a single breath, her arms frozen amidst the force of magic, paralyzed by the flow, crucified by the very essence she herself helped sustain.

But something was different, looking deep into her hazel eyes engulfed by the purple ensemble of magic, was the vision of a voice, the image of a sound. Parinos couldn't for the life of him explain what he was seeing, or feeling. She wasn't dead, but she wasn't even breathing. She then spoke as if not even speaking at all.

''I see it, the endless void!'' She strains tightly.

Frozen by what Camula just said, Parinos stood in complete awe, hypnotised by Camula's stare.

Her eyes dimmed of all magic, back to her natural hazel colouring as she flopped forward, face first into Parinos's arms. The connection she held was beginning to buzz around her body, the aura danced around her for a few seconds, only to fade into nothing.

Tears began to well in Parinos's frail old eyes, flushing out uncontrollably as he embraced her delicate frame. Stilled by her initial fall, he felt her very life being taken away by a mysterious presence that haunted the enclosure.

He takes a brave gulp as his legs begin to shake; he flutters his eyes to fight off his tears. After a few moments of realisation and acceptance, he places Camula to the floor. He kneels down and props his frail hands on her neck to check her pulse, she was no longer living.

Whilst down on the ground he drags poor Camula to his lap, where he embraces her like a child of his own. The humming's frequency changed again, this time peaceful and soft. All that could be heard now was the tranquil hum of magic, glistening over the night washed forest. The druid's focus was not broken, they were men and women of stern will, as all druids are.

From here onwards the ritual remained unbroken, all they could do now was wait.

Despite the emotional hardship Parinos was enduring, he had to remain strong. Generations had sought this kind of power and he knew now was the time to use it. It had been a mystery that was lost to the ages, it was Parinos's duty as arch druid to execute what was to come, he knew this and would remain as strong as possible.

To ease his suffering, he would embrace Camula, whispering to her that everything will be okay, just like a father to a sick child. ''I'm sorry, my dear. I'm sorry,'' he whimpers mournfully.

As he ran his fingers through her raven black hair he knew at this moment he would never forgive himself for the loss of her young life. She was an astounding druid and loved by many, she was always inquisitive and truthful, she loved and revered the Gods as much as she did life itself. He knew the image of this day, the feeling of those cosmic powers taking her life away would haunt him for as long as he drew breath.

More hours passed by, then two days. The druid's stasis was now acting as a life-support as well as their demise, if something wasn't going to happen soon It would surely kill all who are stuck within. Magic is internally dangerous and takes an incredible amount of time to master.

Parinos as well as Orthunus are the only druids not within the stasis, he knelt there on the floor, gently stroking Camula's hand with his thumb wondering if this was all for nought. Only he could stop the ritual before it did any more damage, but he had to wait it out.

And so, he did.

2: Gordon

Earth, United Kingdom, Middlesbrough. 2010 AD

Middlesbrough, a place where the sun doesn't shine, or so the local saying goes, primarily due to the amount of smog that spews out into the atmosphere from the local industries scattered across the coast of Teesside where this low to working class industrial town sits, under the grey skies of north east England. Hence the nickname of the local populace, 'Smoggies'.

It's a chilly December Friday evening at a murky backstreet bar named 'Mickeys' shackled between a few dingy alleyways in the centre of town.

Muffled metal music can be heard echoing in the alley outside of the bar as it shudders against the tatty brick walls that enclose the area, the band 'Blood Winter' are performing their weekly set inside for their local fans and friends.

The music is loud, the crowd drunk and rowdy, it's the perfect environment for Gordon Barker and his band mates.

Gordon was a twenty-five-year-old bass player and metal enthusiast, he lived for his music. If he wasn't listening to it, he was playing it, if he wasn't playing it, he was writing it, and if he wasn't doing any of those, he was probably at work. He had a simple life, he lived with his long-term girlfriend Helen in their small home in Middlesbrough, by day he would work as a shelf stacker at the local supermarket and by night, he was living his own fantasy as a metal musician.

The mosh pits opened up as the band descended into a brutal breakdown. The people barged and jumped around as they became enthralled by the power of Blood Winter's rhythm, they were quite a well-known band in the local scene, the crowd always gave a little extra for Blood Winter.

Grasping his bass, strumming furiously and slamming his head side to side to the rhythm of the music, Gordon's carefree nature oozes amongst the band and into the crowd, feeding their energy as he sings along with the vocalist through the night in metal melody.

Chains hanging from his baggy cargo trousers. Tattoos of skulls, tigers and wolves decorate the entirety of his arms, he's quite the alternative man. Gordon was never not seen dressed in black, short dark spiky hair with a blonde tipped front, and a small soul patch hanging from his bottom lip. A very averagely built fellow, with a developing beer belly.

Although appearing quite intimidating on the outside to some, Gordon was a soft and caring soul and that's why so many people took a natural liking to him, be them his loyal metal fans and friends, or just your everyday person, Gordon always resonated a positive energy and was quite the joyful person in general, even in his downtimes.

The crowd grew wilder, Beer was sloshing around all over the place making the floor even stickier than it already was as the crowd moshed away with the band, the lights were flashing as the guitars shredded, the soundwaves of the drums smashing could be felt rattling in the chest. A night of great vibes and good times, a night that every single Friday was for Blood Winter.

They played their final song of the night and then packed away their instruments, Gordon picked up and chugs the rest of his pint that sat upon the stage, throwing the remainder of the plastic cup at the crowd for their pleasure, quite the showman he was.

''Thank you everyone, as always, you're all fucking legends, have a great night! We've been, Blood Winter! Thank you!'' Slurs Jeb, the band's vocalist through the mic as he makes his way off stage clutching his band mates and patting their sweaty backs.

The drummer Dan forcefully wrangles Gordon's neck as they step down from the stage and kisses him on the head. ''Good fucking show, mate!'' He bellows with glee; Dan is Gordon's lifelong best friend. He was a large man, chubby and joyous, sporting long brown hair that hung down to his thighs with a scruffy neckbeard to complement it with.

''Yeah! Great night as always!'' Replied Gordon, stumbling through the crowd, many of whom would grab and shake the band's hands and pat their backs, congratulating their stellar performance.

As they made their way down, Helen was waiting in the crowd to greet Gordon off stage, her exuberant grin beaming across her face as it always does. ''Well done babe!'' She pounces into Gordon's arms. ''The new stuff you guys have got is amazing, as always!'' She says as she looks upon him in admiration.

‘’Cheers babes!’’ Gordon kisses her forehead, the scent of hairspray enough to plant a taste of it in his mouth.

‘’Sorry am I not important anymore, Gordon?’’ Jokes Dan.

‘’Fuck off, Dan!’’ Gordon replies with a drunken smirk as he tightens his hold on Helen.

Insults as a term of endearment were always common amongst the people of the north.

‘’Alright, dickhead. I’ll go find myself a new husband, shall I? You aren’t Gunna find these love handles on her,’’ howl's Dan, punching Gordon in the arm.

Dan and Gordon's relationship was a loving bromance filled with verbal abuse, good times and a brotherly bond that could never be broken, the two had known each other the longest out of the whole band, since their early years in secondary school.

‘’Mine!’’ Helen grabs Gordons face and kisses him.

‘’Bork!’’ Shouts Pete, the band's guitarist. A skinny man with a face full of metal and a freshly shaved head that he was always keen on topping up, another one of Gordon's good friends.

‘’I know, right?!’’ Replies Dan.

‘’Alright, alright... soz ‘ard boys, soz ‘ard! Right then, who’s wanting a drink? I’ll grab this one,’’ Gordon announces as he loosens his loving grip on Helen.

‘’Nah mate, don’t you worry yourself, I’ve got this,’’ offers Dan.

‘’Fair play, buddy.’’

They huddle by the bar, awaiting to be served.

‘’Coming out for a cig?’’ Pants Dan the sweat visually dripping from his head, sticking his hair to his face. He passes Gordon and Helen a beer.

‘’Well aye… were has Jeb end gone?’’ Frowned Gordon, referring to their vocalist, Jedediah. Nicknamed ‘Jeb end’ or more appropriately ‘Jeb’ by the boys.

‘’He just went straight to that new girl he’s seeing near the bar. Pete will grab him, come on,’’ replied Dan hurrying Gordon along.

The three exited the bar and headed outside to the smoking area. As they leave, they are met with the biting cold that tears at their exposed skin, they all retract their shoulders as the freezing air tightens its grip.

‘’My God, I can finally breathe,’’ Helen says as she lifts two cigarettes from her pack and pushes one in Gordons mouth and lights it for him.

‘’Cheers babes,’’ he smiles, warmed by her affection.

‘’She says, as she lights up a stick of death that literally clogs up her lungs,’’ Dan jokes.

She tuts and smiles, turning to Dan to light his unlit cigarette hanging from his mouth whilst he pats around for a missing lighter.

‘’Thanks Hel,’’ he says, happily.

Helen was a caring person, always thinking of others over herself. She was always seen as the mothering figure in her friend groups. Looking after the drunks and being the shoulder to cry on. She was utterly stunning and usually caught the attention of many men, golden blonde hair with black dip dyed tips. Heavy black makeup that complemented her style. As a couple, her and Gordon couldn't be better aesthetically matched. ''I can't bloody wait for next Friday!'' She expresses.

''I know! It's going to be our first Friday not playing at Mickeys! Fucking mental!'' Muffles Dan with his cigarette hanging from his mouth.

Gordon places an arm round Helen underneath her jacket to warm himself up. ''It's the start of a new era for us, mate. Let's make this Friday one to remember and celebrate, yeah?''

''One hundred percent, supporting War Chant, a well-known band like them at fucking Manchester… I still can't believe it man, Pete was actually being legit, I thought he was talking shit at first, not going to lie man, you know what he's like.''

''Really? I believed him? I know he's a little eccentric, but he's never lied to us before,'' Gordon puffs.

''I know mate, but it just seemed too good to be true, you know?''

''But it is true! And you're going to do great! Finally get the traction you all deserve!'' Smiles Helen.

A loud rowdy noise came from inside the bar, it was Pete and Jeb followed by a few friends as they marched out together arm in arm, chanting.

''Oi Oi, Oi Oi!'' The chants get louder. The bunch were clearly in high spirits knowing they had made a huge step for themselves to support a big band and propel their name forward in the metal world. The three each cast a smile as they watch them dance through the doorway.

The band embrace one another once again in a masculinised brotherhood way as they grasp hands and pat backs. Jeb then introduces his new girlfriend to the group.

''Lads… and Helen, this is Stacey, we're official now,'' Jeb announces, flicking his hair to the side as it constantly falls into his eyes.

Stacey lowers her head shyly, laughing off the awkwardness.

"Official now? Just testing the waters, were we?" Sniggers Pete.

''Blink twice if you need help love!'' Laughs Dan ''Hah, jokes… jokes,'' Dan leans in to hug Stacey. ''Nice to meet you, love! He's a good man, our Jeb! Treat him well, will you?'' He smiles.

Stacey responds with a drunken grin, narrowing her glazed eyes. ''Thanks, nice to meet you,'' she parts her fringe out of her eyes.

''Nice to meet you!'' Responded Helen and Gordon in sequence.

A cheeky grin expands across Jeb's face. ''So yeah? Friday?!''

''I know mate, we were literally just talking about it!'' Replies Dan.

''Hey Stacey, I've only just noticed, nice shirt!'' Gordon shouts out.

Stacey proudly presents her shirt, the bands own merch which was also sold on a small stall within the bar, it was their band's name etched across the breast with the logo, a white wolf's head on the front, snarling viciously as its teeth dripped with fresh blood. ''I know, right? Jeb actually got it for me.''

''Surprise, surprise, for free I bet?'' Laughs Gordon.

The group chuckles amongst the bustling crowd of people outside smoking, Pete gives the group a drink each and they have a toast.

''To Blood Winter!'' Screams Pete at the top of his lungs.

''To War Chant!'' Shouts Jeb. ''If it weren't for those guys, we'd be going nowhere!''

''And finally, to Pete!'' Gordon adds, spilling out a few drops of beer as he clinks his bottle a little too hard.

The group drank to their small success, supporting a big band like War Chant in a big venue was sure to gain them a lot of followers online and more listeners in general. Exciting times were ahead for this little bunch of head bangers.

They made their way back inside to make the most out of their last night at their local, prancing around amongst the crowd like there was no tomorrow. Band after band would come on stage and the mosh pits would grow wilder and wilder as they partied on.

When the night drew to a close, the band, Stacey and Helen made their way back to Helen and Gordon's home and sat in the kitchen to carry on their Friday celebrations.

Gordon is the first to burst into his kitchen, turning back to Dan, continuing his conversation they were having in the taxi. ‘’You know what I mean though?’’

‘’Yeah, fuck him,’’ Dan responds to Gordon.

‘’He was a dick in school as well, nothing’s changed man,’’ said Gordon.

‘’Remember that time he tried to act all hard in the toilets and I walked in on him trying to get money out of you, so I just got some wet some paper towers and pinged them off his head?’’ Howl's Dan as he reminisces on old school shenanigans, stumbling his large frame around Gordon’s kitchen, knocking over a few old mugs.

‘’Hah! Yeah! He never really bothered me again after that… he didn’t have the balls to throw shapes with you, did he?’’

‘’I’m a big lad, my G,’’ Dan lift’s his shirt, patting his exposed flabby belly.

''He used to think he was untouchable because he hung around with all the hard chavs, but even they thought he was a twat as well,'' Gordon plonks himself atop his kitchen counter. ''Tell you what, I do not miss those days….'' Gordon looks back, his voice trailing off.

''Yeah, but does anyone miss school? Like, really?'' Says Pete as he opens a bottle of beer on his belt.

''I did! I loved school!'' Helen chips, taking a seat next to Gordon.

''Of course, you would, Hel,'' laughs Jeb.

''Didn't you go to an all-girls school?'' Asks Pete, taking a swig of his bottle.

''Yeah.''

Pete downs his whole bottle, giving a satisfied ''Ahh,'' as wipes his chin. ''Surely, that must have been worse than a regular comprehensive?''

''Not from what I hear... you guys all hated it!'' She smirks.

''Touché… what was so good about your school then?''

Helen raises an eyebrow at Pete. ''Well, for starters, there were no boys.''

''Ha… ha, funny funny…'' chuckles Pete, rolling his eyes sarcastically.

‘’But girls are more bitchy and just as bad to each other, if not worse. You must have been surrounded by loads of posh wankers,’’ Gordon playfully nudges her.

‘’Doesn’t matter where Helen goes, you could find her in the gulag and she’d still be happy as Larry,’’ says Pete.

‘’Explains why she’s with Gordon then,’’ Jeb butts in.

Gordon picks up an unopened loaf of bread nearby on the counter and throws it at Jeb. ‘’Oi, cheeky cunt!’’

Jeb swiftly dodges the load of bread. ‘’Whey!’’ He shouts, Impressed by his own tipsy dexterity. ‘’Hey mate, haven’t you got work tomorrow?’’

Gordon jumps down from the counter making his way to the fridge. ‘’Yeah, don’t remind me,’’ he groans as he grabs another beer.

‘’You’re brave!’’ Jeb remarks.

‘’You know me, always pushing my luck,’’ Gordon stumbles

Pete squeezes past Gordon and steals a beer from the fridge. ‘’Cheers to that,’’ he laughs.

The night goes on flowing with alcohol and laughter, as does a usual Friday night for this hearty group of friends. The morning eventually began to illuminate the horizon, which spilled into the windows of the house, the group dispersed, said their goodbyes and went their separate ways, apart from Dan who slept on the sofa.

Gordon knew he'd only be getting a few hours of sleep, he also knew he couldn't escape the entrenching reality of adulthood responsibilities, and so he set his alarm with a large sigh of regret before his night came to an end.

Hours later, the sound of Gordon's phone alarm vibrates through the murky bedroom air. Helen, who's asleep next to him wakes first, rubbing her eyes as they adjust to the morning haze that glared through the window netting, she nudges him, attempting to wake him. He bats her off as he continues his peaceful slumber, grunting his way back into his personal paradise. Helen then steals the bed sheets and slaps Gordon's behind.

''Wake up! Work, Gordon….'' Helen blurts as she turns back over to attempt to drift back off to sleep.

Gordon slowly rises from his rest, head still spinning and ears still ringing from the night before. ''Fuck's sake man, why do I keep doing this?'' Gordon mutters to himself, regretting his decisions of heavy drinking the night before work, something he had a habit of on the weekends. Regardless, Gordon sluggishly gets up and dawdles over to his drawers where his uniform lay, dumped atop his cluttered drawers. A simple pair of navy-blue cargo pants and navy-blue shirt with the supermarket's logo imprinted in the breast. He brushes his teeth whilst attempting to fix his messy hair that still stood on end from the previous nights over embellishment of hair gel.

He made his way down the stairs, upon opening the door to the living room he sees Dan already awake, playing on his phone.

''Morning princess,'' Dan smiles.

''Now then… you're perky?'' Replied Gordon, still squinting from the morning light with a cigarette hanging from his mouth.

Dan throws the makeshift quilt of jackets and blankets off him as he shuffles off of the sofa. ''Aye, someone's got to bring the energy, right? Anyway, want me to make the cuppas?''

Gordon sighs with relief. ''You are an actual legend. Go on then, you want some toast or out? I'll do breaky if you do cuppas,'' Gordon offers as he fights with the flint of his lighter.

''Well aye, mate,'' replies Dan.

Gordon gives up with his lighter and quickly dips his head above the stove in the kitchen, pressing the end of his cig into the metal coil and lighting it successfully.

Dan flicked the kettle on as Gordon put four slices of bread in the toaster.

''Time you finishing today?'' Dan asks as he leans into the counter, carefully moving aside the mountain of empty beer bottles littering the kitchen.

''About four? I think?'' Gordon rubs his head sluggishly, still feeling the weight of the beverage hammer against his skull from the night before. ''How about you?''

''Well, I'm only on a three-hour shift today, starting at twelve and finishing at three, I can come meet you after work if you like? Could try that fucking solid raid,'' says Dan referring to a game they both play together, Golden Sword.

‘’Aww mate I’d love to, but me and Helen are watching a film and grabbing a takeaway tonight, can do tomorrow though?’’ Replies Gordon following up with a yawn.

‘’Fair enough! Yeah, tomorrow is grand, I got nothing on. Want me to meet you after work tomorrow then? You’re working tomorrow, right?’’

The Kettle finishes boiling and Dan prepares the Coffee’s.

‘’I’m not actually, I got Sunday off! So, it can be an all-day gaming session if you want! Still need to show the Archdemon of Thurindale a thing or two,’’ Gordon winks.

Dan Chuckles ‘’From our last session it seems he’s showing you a thing or two. You need to remember to position yourself better, using backstab on his knees isn’t going to do much is it? You silly cunt,’’ he winks back.

Gordon scoffs. ‘’Yeah well, I wouldn’t have died if someone would keep the other enemies taunted,’’ teased Gordon, referring to Dan’s sloppy game play.

Dan chuckles and snorts. ‘’Yeah well, I’m working an eight-hour shift Sunday, but come over after and we’ll play some Golden Sword mate.’’

The toaster pops and Gordon prepares the toast, the two retreat to the living room with their coffee and toast.

‘’Got a work social on Monday, not sure if I’m going to go yet. The only reason I’m considering is the free booze,’’ Gordon scoffs.

''A work social... on a Monday?'' Dan scrunches his chubby face.

''I know, right?''

''Want me to come by?''

''You got caught out last time trying to guzzle the free beer... I got a right bollocking for that, why bother again?''

''Worth a shot mate!'' Smiles Dan.

''This place has a little beer garden in the back. How about you go in on your own and wait in there... and then I'll bring some drinks out?'' Suggests Gordon raising his eyebrows deviously.

''Yeah! Not bad, not bad... I'll see what I've got going on, then and I'll get back to you about it,'' laughs Dan.

Before even finishing his toast Gordon had to rush out, realising his time was cutting short.

Accompanied by Dan, they both make their way out and walk to Gordon's workplace together, the two then went their separate ways at a road crossing, hoping to see each other soon.

Upon entering his workplace, Gordon's mood instantly wavers, emotionless and uninspired by the place. This is just a job to keep him secure, to earn something, his day job so to speak.

Gordon wanted to work with his music, or at least have a job in the music industry but he lacked any form of qualification, he dropped out of college and his only musical experience was with his band, so getting a job in the industry would prove somewhat difficult, sometimes he felt all he had to hope for was his band being signed.

He would do anything to get away from his job, he despised it, the rude customers, his weird boss, even his colleagues annoyed him. Gordon didn't hate his work colleagues, but he certainly wasn't fond of them, say for two, Sam, a girl a little younger than him who was a little overly fond, and Dean, the quiet man who doesn't really speak much and avoids the rest of the crew due to their mild bullying, but he spoke often to Gordon, who he felt comfortable around.

Although he wasn't keen on his environment, his job wasn't too bad, or so he kept telling himself, stacking shelves was the easy part, he didn't have to speak to the customers he just needed to stack, or for the most part at least.

''Have you got any more of those limited-edition Prosecco bottles that were on that stand over there?'' Spoke out a middle-aged woman in a lavish faux fur coat, looming over Gordon who's knelt down working on a bottom shelf of confectionery.

Gordon takes a second to boot his memory. ''Erm, the limited time ones of the display stand?''

''Yes, that's what I said,'' she sternly responds.

Gordon sighs in the recess of his mind, he already knew what he was in for. ''Oh… yeah because they were limited… the only ones we had were the ones on display, sorry.''

''Can you check in the back?''

''There isn't any in the back, the only ones we had were put straight out on display.''

''Can you not go and check though?'' She insists.

Gordon rises up from crouching down at the shelf. ''Look, there isn't any in the back, the only ones we had of that bottle were on the display stand. If there's none left, we definitely don't have any stocked in the back… sorry, love,'' he gulps back his patience.

The woman's posture changes aggressively. ''I said, you can at least go and check for God's sake, it's all you lot ever seem to say these days, well I'm not falling for it.''

Gordon wasn't backing down. ''Us lot?'' He spits. ''Falling for what? You think I can't be arsed going to check? I'm telling you how it is. I'm not going to stop doing my job to go in the back and stare at a fucking wall just for you am I?''

''Excuse me!'' Her voice raises. ''Who had the audacity to even employ you? No respect. None at all. Where's your man-''

Before the woman can even finish her sentence, Gordon's manager who had overheard the raised voices approached the situation swiftly.

''Manager? That would be me madam, how can I help?'' Steve, Gordan's manager, turns his head to Gordon looking down on him, unimpressed.

''This young man has been treating me awfully, when all I asked was a simple bloody question.''

‘’And she got a simple bloody answer. I told you that there was none of the limited edition in the back and you tried to get me to go anyway? I’m not your lapdog,’’ Gordon bites back.

‘’Right, Gordon, ease yourself down. Be careful how you speak to your customers. Apologies madam, this is Gordon’s first day and he’s only just adapting, he will correct his behaviour if he wants to keep this job, won’t you?’’ He scowls. ‘’Now is there any way I can help?’’ Steve adds.

‘’I asked him politely to double check the back to see if the limited-edition Prosecco bottles were in stock, he refused and gave me a pathetic excuse to be lazy, and he bloody swore at me!’’ The woman snaps.

‘’He is in fact correct, when we were given the limited-edition bottle for the display stand all available stock was put out on display and none was kept in the stock room. That display stand will be filled later today with a new weekly item.’’ Gordon’s manager explains with a calm nature.

‘’See….’’ Gordon sneers.

‘’Gordon, office,’’ says Steve, in a snappy response.

The woman raises her eyebrows in delight.

Gordon scoffs and shakes his head at her as he dawdles towards the office, awaiting the wrath of his boss.

Steve arrives with a march, his endless number of keys dangling from his belt jingling to the beat of his pace.

‘’What in God's name is up with you lately lad? This is the second time I’ve pulled you up this month about verbally abusing customers!’’ Steve rants.

‘’I didn’t abuse her; she wasn’t having anything I was saying?! I was repeating myself over and over! You should've seen the way she was speaking to me.’’

‘’Why couldn’t you just humour her instead of letting it escalate like that? Come on son, use your head, professional environment here you know?’’

‘’Because I’m not her lapdog, Steve. I’m telling her how it is, if she’s getting narky with me how else am I supposed to respond?’’ Gordon pleas, rubbing his forearm in a beta stance.

‘’By humouring her. Look, I know some customers can really grind your gears at times, but you have to bite your tongue, Gordon. Come on, you’re a good lad and you work hard, but bloody hell, get a grip. Don’t let some pissy customer get to you like that, it makes you look silly, and it makes us look even worse. If I have to pull you into the office again like this I’m going to have to start dishing some serious disciplinaries to you, or worse if the area manager catches wind of this, sort it out Gordon.’’

Gordon dips his head in submission.

‘’Now, have five minutes to calm yourself down and get back on the floor, you still have the meal deals to get out before twelve.’’

‘’Righto,’’ Gordon responds blankly.

Steve pats Gordon's shoulder reassuringly and promptly leaves the office without saying anymore.

Feeling defeated and rather humiliated, Gordon scrolls through the social media on his phone for a good five minutes, muttering obscenities about the situation under his breath until getting up and continuing on with his job. The day goes by and Gordon continues to work, the alcohol section was looking bare, so Gordon took it on himself to restock. Sam, his co-worker was operating the till nearby, the shop was quiet.

''You going to the social on Monday?'' Sam asks as she twiddles her long black hair tied off to the side in a long ponytail.

''Erm… I don't know to be honest, Sam. I might do… are you?'' Gordon responds as he scours to find the right place for a crate of brown ale.

''Yeah, can't pass up the free house, can you?'' She grins.

''True,'' he bluntly replies.

''I heard about that woman earlier today,'' Sam adds.

''Don't get me started, she was a fucking nutter.''

''I'm glad Steve let you off a bit though… he's always soft on you! So… come out Monday, we can laugh it off!''

Gordon grunts.

''Aww come on! It'll be great, we always have good banter,'' she smirks.

''If I do come it'll only be for a little bit, can't really be arsed if I'm honest, I'm sure I'll have plans with Helen,'' Gordon winces as he lifts a heavy crate of beer.

Noticing no customers are around, Sam leaves her till to approach Gordon, leaning on a pillar next to him. ''So how was your gig yesterday? Feeling the burn today, are we?'' She chuckles. ''You look like you've been dragged backwards through a bush, did you even do your hair when you woke up?'' She teases as a mischievous smile grew across her face of heavy foundation.

Gordon was getting agitated at the flurry of awkward small talk and preferred to do his job in peace, but he did like Sam as a person, she was witty and funny, almost childlike. She was goofy and bubbly and didn't ever seem to talk down to him like the others did, so he would always humour her out of respect.

''Aye, was a banger... got another one coming up Friday but in Manchester this time, so things are going quite well for us,'' he says proudly, quite lightened up by Sam's interest.

''I need to come and see you guys play still, I can't believe we've worked together for a year and I still haven't been to one of your gigs.''

''I say this every time, it's not your thing,'' Gordon sniggers.

''I like all kinds of music, me! It must be good if you're going places now, eh?''

''I mean, feel free to come down to Mickeys on a Friday night, that's when we usually play. You already know that.''

Sam's face brightens. ''I think I will… Friday after next yeah? I'm not working the day after so I'll drop by to see what 'your' kind of music is about.''

''Metal, Sam. It's called Metal.''

''Yeah, yeah… whatever,'' she laughs.

A customer approaches the till and Sam scurries off, leaving Gordon to finish his Job. A somewhat stressful day at work ending with a slight sigh of relief and a surprisingly quiet shop floor.

As soon as Gordon leaves the building, he throws on his hoodie, and instantly his natural 'out of work' mood returns. Walking home now with a smile on his face knowing his time was up and he could go home and relax.

''Ahh, Pizza tonight, bit of weed, what else?'' He ponders to himself.

Realising he had smoked all of his weed last night, he rings Pete, Pete being a dealer as well as a guitarist. ''Ehy up, got any twenty bags in?''

''Yeah mate, you free now?'' Pete replies.

''Yeah, just got out of work, can you drop off at mine?'' Gordon proceeds to light up a cigarette whilst balancing his phone on his shoulder.

''No bother bud, I'll be there in about an hour, is that okay?''

''Sound as a pound, cheers Pete,'' Gordon chirps.

Arriving home Gordon finds Helen in the kitchen emptying a shopping bag.

''Hello babe,'' Helen says in a quirky manner.

Gordon walks in and kisses her on the cheek. ''What've you been buying?''

''Just some milk, washing up liquid and some girl stuff.''

''Girl stuff?''

Helen gives an obvious gesture.

''Oh… you know you can just say tampon, I'm not freaked out by them, come on Hel how long we been together now?'' Gordon laughs. ''So does that mean…?''

Helen laughs. ''No, I'm due soon though.''

Gordon grips Helen's waist, pulling her into him ''Well, best get to it then!''

''If you're a good boy, maybe!'' She teases, bopping his nose.

''I'm always a good boy! Right then, Pete's dropping a bag off soon, I think Jeb's working tonight so we'll probably get a cheeky discount on the Pizza, any idea what you fancy watching tonight?''

''That reminds me! I saw The Mist in the shop going cheap, I bought that today!''

''Oh, fucking perfect! I watched that with Dan when it came out, but we were so stoned we fell asleep at the opening.''

‘’Typical,’’ Helen sarcastically replies.

‘’Well at least you actually decided on something to watch,’’ he sniggers.

‘’Oh, shut up you! I’ve had a good day today actually, hung out with that Stacy girl Jeb is seeing, we went out for a coffee, she’s so lovely!’’

‘’Oh really? You must be mates with everyone in Middlesbrough by now, you can’t walk down the street without stopping to say hello to someone,’’ chuckles Gordon.

‘’Well, it doesn’t hurt to be friendly! I like having lots of friends! How was your day at work?’’

‘’Dogshit, had another asshole customer, got a warning from Steve to stop talking back to people,’’ Gordon rolls his eyes.

‘’Oh Gordon… you need to watch yourself at work, are you okay though? What happened?’’

As Gordon proceeds to tell Helen about the altercation at work, they’re both interrupted by the door knocking five times in a rhythmic pattern.

‘’Oh, that’ll be Pete, hang on,’’ Gordon rushes to the door.

‘’Ello ello, drug delivery,’’ says Pete.

Gordon hands Pete twenty pounds as Pete passes him a bag of weed.

‘’What’s the plan tonight mate? Just having a chill smoke?’’ Pete asks.

''Yeah, me and Helen are going to drown the remainder of this hangover with some pizza and weed, going to watch The Mist as well.''

''Bang on mate, bang on, enjoy! I'll probably see you on Friday then!'' Pete bounces.

''I know man, we need to organise a practice beforehand though, maybe two this time? Just imagine how many more people are going to be listening to us after this gig, we're going to need to sound extra fresh for it!''

''Hell yeah, man!'' Pete shoots Gordon a high five. ''Anyway mate, got a few more drop offs to make, if this gig goes well, I might be able to pack all this in before the inevitable police raid.''

''Let's hope, eh? Although I'd have to start buying off Fat Andy and his weed is shit man, plus I can barely understand a word he says, but it is what it is.... Anyway, I'll see you soon mate.''

Pete leaves Gordon's front garden performing an estranged and humorous walk as he exits the gate, making weird noises.

''Go on, fuck off, you weird little cunt,'' laughs Gordon as he closes the door.

''Fuck you, G!'' Pete shouts back as he raises his middle finger.

3: The Light

The majority of Gordon's Sunday was spent with Helen, they went out for lunch together and got their weekly shop in, re-stocking their cupboards for the week ahead. Returning home Gordon practised on his bass until heading out to Dan's flat, the two would smoke and play Golden Sword for the remainder of the day just like they would as teenagers, laughing and joking the day away as they drop their responsibilities away without a care in the world, nothing but bliss between the two as they relished in their time together.

Monday arrives as quickly as they revelled in their joy, with yet another boring work day. Gordon slogs through, stimulated by day dreaming and planning the evening to come within his head, and as fate would have it, the day went by slowly.

He met up with Dan on his break to discuss a plan of action, they both planned to meet in the beer garden in hopes of taking advantage of the free alcohol, Gordon even persuaded Dean to join them both, Dean was rather reluctant to attend but was soon convinced otherwise by Gordon.

The time arrived, seven o'clock. Dan was strategically placed in the back of the garden below the canopy of the smoking area, amusingly wearing a scraggly fishing hat and sunglasses. Gordon was making his way inside the bar, upon his arrival he could see two large tables populated by his fellow colleagues who were all in deep chatter, laughing amongst themselves. He was then greeted by his manager Steve, who gave him two tokens for his free drinks. Gordon hastily made his way to the bar and ordered two pints of lager, snuck outside and made his way out the back to greet Dan.

''There he is! The man with the booze!'' Says Dan, slamming his palms on the table in delight.

''Yes mate! Not sure if work is going to be bothered about this, but whatever... anyway I only got two tokens….'' Gordon pauses as he scans Dan. ''Nice disguise,'' he scoffs.

''Thanks,'' Dan tips his hat to Gordon. ''Ah, don't worry about it, I'll get the first round in after the freebies. Hey, didn't you say your mate was joining us?''

Gordon passes Dan his pint as he sits down adjacent to him. ''Aye, he should be arriving soonish? He's a sound lad is, Dean.''

''Cool, Sounds good to me.''

''Anyway, I don't want to be here too long, abuse the booze, have a few after and then I'm going to be heading back.''

''Fair enough G, any plans afterwards?''

''I don't know… probably just chill out? It's all life is as an adult, work, chill, work, chill,'' Gordon groans.

Dan notices something is up with Gordon. ''Tell me about it, just think of the band though yeah? That'll keep you chugging on through! You okay bud? You seem a little off.''

''I'm fine, I just don't like being around my work folk, they suck the life right out of me.''

''Hey, they're inside and we're outside, but it's understandable,'' laughs Dan. ''Get some of this down you and you'll be right as rain, I know what you're like pal, few pints and you'll be bouncing of the fucking walls.''

Gordon cracks a smile from the side of his cheek as he takes a drink, smudging the white froth into his nose.

Gordon's phone bleeps as a message comes through from Helen. *''Hi Hun, do you know what time you'll be back? Could you pick up a pack of cigs from the shop on your way home for me, pretty please.''*

''It'll be around ten or eleven I reckon, of course, I'll text you when I'm on my way back,'' he responds promptly, he also notices he has an unread text from Dean, telling him he won't be coming.

Gordon looks back to Dan ''Ah, seems Dean has bailed… fair play I guess, I know these aren't his sort of thing, oh well, I tried,'' he sighs.

''Ah well, just the two of us suits me better anyway,'' says Dan.

''It's a shame though bec-'' before Gordon can finish, Sam walks into the beer garden interrupting their conversation.

''Well, well, well… what do we have here,'' she smirks. ''You not joining us inside, Gord?''

Gordon jokingly rolls his eyes to Dan. ''Erm, nah… think we're just going to chill out here.''

''Oh, come on! Who's your friend? You look familiar....'' Sam replies.

''I'm the beer goblin,'' smirks Dan proudly.

''Oh yeah! You… I didn't recognise you for a second there….''

Dan nudges Gordon. ''See, it works.''

Gordon rolls his eyes again.

''I remember now, Gordon got a right telling off for that,'' she laughs. ''I must admit, I admire your spirit,'' she continues as she takes up a seat next to Dan. ''Them lot inside are boring me, plus Steve is being a little creepy so I thought I'd come find you.''

''He's being weird again, is he? Ugh, well… welcome to the cool club, I guess?'' Gordon replies, gesturing with his hands.

The three continue to laugh and drink, eventually more of Gordon's work colleagues spill into the smoking area outside and Gordon reluctantly joins in on being somewhat social, whilst Dan and Sam flirt away in a corner.

Gordon started feeling a little left out, almost like he was being third wheeled, although it made him happy seeing Dan and Sam together, he couldn't help but think they made quite a good couple despite their drastic differences. Then again, Dan always had a way with words and a shining personality.

After sinking his last pint, Gordon realised he was starting to spend more and more time on his phone as the two just continued chatting away amongst themselves, so he decided he may as well announce his departure.

''Right, you two,'' he slaps his thighs as he stands up. ''I'm going to be heading off home now. Got to pick up a few things for Helen.''

''Okay mate! I'm gone stay here, this Sam girl is alright I suppose,'' winks Dan.

Sam punches his arm. ''See you at work tomorrow, Gord. I'm on the evening shift with you.''

''Aye, God help me,'' laughs Gordon.

''See you later mate!'' Says Dan.

Gordon gives them both a friendly hug goodbye as he collects his jacket that hangs off the back of a chair.

He leaves eagerly with a spring in his step, he never really wanted to go in the first place. After leaving the bar Gordon begins his journey home, he decides to give Helen a ring instead of texting her, he always preferred that, he enjoyed hearing her voice.

''Hello you!'' She chirps as she picks up.

''Hello babe! Just on my way home now, anything else you need from the shop or just some cigs?''

''Hello! Yeah, just cigs. I mean if you want to get me a little treat that's totally fine too!''

Gordon laughs. ''I'll have a look see and what they have.''

''Thank you, babe, see you soon, might have a surprise for when you get back.''

''Oh, really now?! Well, I look forward to it… see you soon, yeah?''

''Bye!'' Helen says, heightening the pitch of her voice.

Gordon makes his way into his local corner shop he frequents often, he buys two packs of cigarettes, one for himself, and one for Helen, he also grabs her favourite chocolate bar after spotting it by the till.

He leaves the shop and immediately sparks up a cigarette for the remainder of the walk home, he takes the cut through the local park to make his journey shorter.

It was quite a large park, with huge open fields, known for its bothersome youths on a weekend that would get drunk and trash the place with litter and vandalism, making it almost impossible for any children to play in the playground due to all the shattered glass and urine coated slides.

The park was gloomy that night, a faint mist had settled upon the grass like a large grey blanket, the blackness was rather intimidating, making Gordon feel slightly uneasy walking through, especially at night.

He couldn't hear anyone around and decided it was safe enough to continue. After all, he'd done this for years, he knew all the people who knocked around these parts, he'd be as safe as home would allow, but it never hurts to be cautious.

While making his way through the ghostly mist, he notices a faint glimmer of purple light that seemed to increase and decrease rapidly in exposure in the distance on a patch of grass just a small way off from the groundskeeper's hut. It was incredibly eye-catching as well as bizarre, constantly shimmering in Gordon's peripheral vision.

He steadied his pace as he walked down the path trying to make sense of the purple glimmer, curiously puffing away on his cigarette. Was it a lost phone? A new light installed on the floor? It would be a weird place to install one. His curiosity was taking hold, he decided to investigate.

Initially he was confident that someone had dropped a phone and it was ringing on silent, but the light that was emitting was far too large to be a simple phone, the bushes surrounding the light illuminated alongside it.

''The fuck is that?'' He murmurs to himself.

He edged slowly towards the light, as he got closer his pace slowed even more as he cautiously approached, looking around and behind frantically to see if anyone else was nearby. Nothing, no one.

He was now just metres away from the estranged light, it didn't seem to come from anything at all, it seemed to hover above the floor, there was nothing beneath it that seemed to be causing it. It was just… a light?

''What… the….'' he stops in his tracks, halting all movement as he lurks by, dazzled by its beautiful mysticism, trying to figure out what in the world it was.

Gordon swipes underneath with his hand, nothing. He then anxiously reaches for it ever so slowly, there was no heat coming from it, nor any temperature for that matter. He edges even closer toward the light.

A small faint humming noise was coming from its centre, it was like a ball of energy that was nestled amongst the weave of the air.

He tries to give the light a quick flick of his hand, but within a split second of having his hand within the light, it disappears instantly, faster than Gordon could even blink, quicker than he could possibly comprehend.

A loud deafening roar lasting not even a fraction of second screeches through the night, shuddering the air around him which appeared to physically vibrate, it halted immediately into an eerie silence.

''Shit!'' He shouts out in shock; dropping his cigarette as he jumps.

Something was not right.

The air felt weird, the atmosphere had shifted, his senses had heightened in the snap of a finger, smells were more pungent and stronger, sounds were clearer.

A strange surge of energy vitalises his body, a sense of calming and confidence flushing around his entire body.

An invisible aura pulsates from within, before he can take note of what's happening, his newfound hearing picks up on some new noises, noises that now surround him.

Dumbfounded by the overwhelming surge of changes, Gordon refocuses his vision on his surroundings as his eyes adapt to the darkness.

Stone pillars are scattered all around, imbued with a strange glow, the pillars crumble to the ground creating a loud thunder clap as they topple, the glow they emitted imploding violently.

In front of him, an elderly man in white robes holding what appears to be an unconscious woman dressed similarly, the man was sobbing, he looked up noticing Gordon standing there in confusion, the man's face snapped from sadness to surprise, his jaw hit the floor followed by his tears of sorrow.

There were more people around, all dressed in these peculiar white robes, all of them looked as if they had just fallen down to the floor, all of them panting and gasping, making a huge commotion amongst themselves.

''Akilenios balas!!'' A harsh and gruff voice screams from Gordon's side as men and women armed with swords surround him, their armour rattling and clanking loudly, followed by more people in robes and staves.

Gordon winces in fear and confusion, totally dismayed by the number of bizarre things going on at once.

His eyes widened in absolute fear. ''The fuck!? The fuck?! No… no, Wait!? NO,'' he backs up, holding his hands out in front. ''What is this?!'' his voice shakes.

The elderly man gently rises as he carefully places the woman to the floor stroking her gaunt cheeks a final time as he settles her down, whispering to her in a strange language Gordon was not familiar with. The elderly man shifts his gaze to Gordon, mesmerised.

He stared intently, utterly bewildered; he extended his arms to the armed men and women easing them away from Gordon, the whole area fell silent. ''Bek roe al eseli bek roe… ella fanagos sin Fanara?'' The elder man speaks in confidence, wiping away the last tear that clung to his wrinkly cheek.

''Oh my God, what the fuck!? Who are you? I'm not in the park?! Where am I?'' He begins to cough out of panic as his heart kickstarts a fearful beat, dizzy spells attack his vision and perception but Gordon keeps a hold of himself by the sheer force of will, his blood pumping vigorously with adrenaline. ''What? Err… w-wh…what's happened? Wh… who are you? Where am I?'' Gordon stutters as he attempts to string out a calm sentence shaken by the fear that grew and grew each passing second.

''Stay calm,'' an alien voice from within Gordons' head echoes. Gordon slaps his hands to his head in confusion from the voice. ''Woah!?'' He responds as he cocks his posture.

''Alaminoros gurinfertal,'' says the elderly man.

''I don't understand,'' Gordon shakes his head erratically, signalling his distress. ''Erm….''

The elderly man slowly approaches, raising his hands in a submissive manner whilst pointing at himself ‘’Ek alamos, Parinos.’’

Something seemed to click in Gordon’s confused head, almost like he was starting to understand this strange language already, although vaguely.

A warm feeling flutters down Gordon’s spine unexpectedly. ‘’Focus,’’ the voice echoes again from within, it trails off with an echo almost like it was nearby.

Again, Gordon slaps his hands forcefully onto his head in a poor effort to dull the voice. A feeling of warmth and safety takes hold of him.

Assuming the man had just given his name, Gordon attempts the same.

Placing his hand on his chest and another outward as if to protect himself from the wall of swords pointing his way, he speaks shakily. ‘’Gordon.’’

A silence follows along with whispers amongst the people around him, many of them now rising to their feet, staring at him in bewilderment.

Gordon then points to Parinos. ‘’Parinos….’’ he takes a nervous gulp. ‘’What’s going on? I need to go home… where am I?’’ Gordon starts panicking again, a strength deep within kickstarts yet again, his feelings were a rollercoaster, constantly fraying back and forth, naturally he would panic but every time he did it was almost like his own brain was fighting back on its own accord without his consent. ''What's happening? Why do I feel so fucking strange? Why do I feel… so… alive? Am I dead? I don't get it….'' he thinks to himself.

''Gordon?!'' The elderly man points to him. ''Ruwyth ahir kilanoleren ekron, Gordon? Neh sin Fanara, rue kan erlofikos wyth wyr?''

Upon hearing the man speak his name, Gordon realises this is an accent he's never been familiar with, it almost sounded like a German language with a strange mix of Italian, combined as one.

Confused, he collapses to the floor in a wave of emotions, unable to make sense of anything. The world feels like it could crash any moment, an overwhelming feeling of existential dread clouds his mental vision, weighing heavy on his heart and his mind, Gordon can no longer hold back his fear, he now feels truly lost.

How? Not five minutes ago he was walking home, and now stranded in some forest, with people carrying weapons, swords? The confusion was too much.

His stomach winces, his heart rate raises yet again, he struggles to get out a breath.

The elderly man places his hand on Gordon's shoulder and forcibly lifts his chin. ''Neh Fanara… nehki… ekhar duna werlunyr, Gordon unginaros emtarios. Doc enus furen.''

Instantly Gordon felt calmed by the elderly man's voice, one thing he did understand was that he didn't feel threatened by the man. It was clear that this Parinos was in charge of the people around.

Although confused and scared, the man's piercing eyes settled something within Gordon.

''Whatever he is, he looks very much human to me, but something's not right… he speaks a strange language, and his appearance is… quite otherworldly to that of any human of the Altharn. Look at his clothes… those black markings coming from his neck… and his hair? It's two different colours… he cannot be from Fanara's realm, nor our own. One thing's for certain, he's clearly unsettled, and I can't say I blame him. We need to get him to the village right away and try to help him make sense. There's a serious language barrier between us, but he does seem to understand us to some extent. We need to find out where he is from and… what he is,'' Parinos declares, still holding onto Gordon.

Gordon mumbles in his native tongue.

''What do we do?'' Lucotorix attempts to catch another breath as he supports his stance by the side of his brother, Orthunus. ''Will we take him back? Are you sure?'' He pants steadily, hunched over supporting his weight with his hands on his knees.

''Yes. He may not know it, but he has been drenched. It's strange… but we-'' Parinos stops in his tracks noticing the mercenaries puffed up in fear with their weapons pointing closer and closer to Gordon, Parinos barks out an order. ''Sheathe yourselves! I know this entity to be no threat… follow us for a while though….'' Parinos shifts his focus to his druids. ''Everyone who's able, gather up your brothers and sisters who have suffered the most, we make our way back now… Lucotorix, Orthunus, please pick up Camula if you have the strength too… we will mourn her upon our return.''

''Are you sure, Arch Druid? What if it snaps and attacks?'' Says one of the mercenaries closest to Gordon, his arm relaxed but sword extended.

''You don't see what I see young man, you have to trust me,'' Parinos returned his sight to lock onto Gordon's eyes, his eyes were frantically darting up and down, left to right, there was a lot going on inside him that even he wasn't certain of. ''Gordon… Gordon, look at me. We… we… are… going to leave. Come,'' Parinos says slowly in hopes Gordon can understand anything at all, he then signals Gordon to rise on his own as he takes a gentle step back from him.

Partly ignoring Parinos's request at the behest of their own safety, the mercenary's back off but keep their weapons firmly drawn.

Gordon stares on in confusion as he catches a breathing pattern, the more this man speaks the more Gordon feels familiar with the words that escape his chapped lips, hearing the rattling and clanking of armour and weapons brush further away from him, Gordon finds a flicker of confidence and rises back to his feet slowly, watching those around him very carefully… he then takes this time to soak in his surroundings once again.

Rubble litters this small clearing amongst a sea of beech and oak, looking around he can't understand how or why he is where he is, he notices everyone in the area staring at him with the same confusion he has for them.

''I need to go home,'' he says calmly. ''Home,'' he points behind him, unsure of where he is even pointing.

Parinos frowns in pity and attempts to repeat Gordon's words. ''Home?''

Hearing Parinos repeat his English, his eyes widened with hope. ''Yes Home! I need to go home!''

Parinos steps forward. ''Dosillia foriganus, 'home'?'' The language barrier is persistent.

''I think he's wondering where he is?'' Says Lucotorix, brushing forward nervously, fixing his gaze on Gordon. ''Maybe asking to return to where it… sorry, he came from?''

''Yes… that would be the more natural thing he would ask, we should get underway quickly,'' replies Parinos, his eyes still locked upon Gordon.

Lucotorix nods in response.

''You're safe,'' the voice in his head echoes again within Gordon, his stomach flushed with a calming warmth.

Parinos whips his hands signalling Gordon to follow, he pats down the mercenary's swords vigilantly to reassure Gordon he is in no danger.

Delirious and desperate to return home, Gordon felt he had no choice but to follow.

He steps forward cautiously and looks at Parinos for assurance, Parinos nods and smiles as he continues to signal his hands to Gordon, then placing one arm gently around his shoulder to comfort him. ‘’Gordon, Ek emor esrios anfalagrim gorma essios’’

Bizarre as it may seem, Gordon felt familiar with Parinos, his calming nature, his friendly face. He trusted him, to some extent at least.

Gordon didn’t know what to do, he needed answers, as did the druids.

And so, he follows.

4: The Druids of Seers Crossing

The druids fumble around as they help each other up, the mercenaries aid Lucotorix and Orthunus with Camula's body whilst Lucotorix recovers from his exhaustion. The rest of the mercenary's scowl at Gordon viciously, holding onto the hilts of their weapons with an anxious grip.

A few druids are still unable to stand, one or two are even unconscious, most of them however, seem fine. Exhausted, exasperated, confused, but fine.

The group cut through the way they came in, through a mass of shrubbery, most of it now disturbed, creating a little pocket for an exit. Gordon sticks to Parinos's side, wearily scanning around at his environment and the people in it as he dawdles along.

''So, It's a Gordon? That what it said?'' Orthunus asks.

''No… it's his name,'' replies Parinos.

''How do you know that?''

''I can't explain, Orthunus. Something strange is going on,'' says Parinos, a look of concern drowning his face.

Gordon glanced at Parinos curiously, he understood a few words that were spoken. The words rattled within his mind over and over.

Name. His. It.

‘’Why are they starting to make sense? I’ve never heard this language?’’ He thinks to himself. ‘’Name, Gordon, yes,’’ he speaks out feebly in desperation.

‘’He spoke our language?!’’ Lucotorix jumps forward to Gordon with little energy he has remaining.

Gordon looks to Lucotorix in confusion. ‘’Language?’’ He repeats the word.

‘’He seems to be learning rather quickly, he must be quite intelligent? A human male… of another world it seems? Is this going to work for us? This is strange,’’ says Orthunus in curiosity.

Gordon reaches for his phone in the back pocket of his jeans in hopes of reaching Helen, or at least any kind of help. As soon as his phone screen lights up to be unlocked the mercenaries move in with impressive haste.

‘’Arch Druid, move!!’’ The mercenary commander shouts.

Parinos leaps to the side, Gordon drops his phone in shock as the mercenaries surround him, raising their swords to his back and his neck, Gordons stomach drops like the weight of an anchor.

An awkward silence sweeps the crowd, the sound of Gordon’s intensified breathing coats over the silence of the night air as fear escapes through the fog on his breath.

‘’What is it?’’ Parinos mutters.

One of the guards moves Gordon aside whilst his comrade pokes at his phone carefully with the tip of his sword. ''A weapon?''

''No, no,'' Gordon shudders. ''No… weapon.''

The guards, suspicious of Gordons words, look to Parinos for an order.

''I've not seen anything like it… let me see it,'' Parinos asks.

The mercenary bends down slowly picking up the phone, his gaze switching between Gordon and his phone consistently. After giving it a quick inspection, he hands it over to Parinos.

Parinos plays around with the casing trying to make sense of the object. ''I'm unsure what this is… I trust him though, for the love of Fanara lower your weapons! Gordon, what is this?''

Gordon mumbles in and out of his native tongue in fear. ''It's my phone! Erm. Neh rukin, look… flario cura. I'll show you what it does,'' he stretches his trembling hand out to Parinos as he takes a deep breath trying to regulate his racing heartbeat.

Parinos takes note of Gordons excessive trembling. ''He's scared out of his mind, stand back from him, Iskarien damn you all. He's no threat!''

The guards, disapproving of Parinos's trust, size up Gordon like a piece of meat. Regardless, Parinos gives Gordon back his phone.

Upon opening his phone, he notices there is no signal, no data.

To avoid any misunderstandings, he decides to immediately show Parinos his phone and try to explain what it was with the limited language capabilities he has, he shows Parinos the text messages from Helen.

''It appears to be some form of book? It has strange glyphs on it that move as he touches it… a type of scroll maybe?''

The druids give a small sigh of relief, followed by mutters of intrigue.

''An interesting item indeed… it seems wherever he is from is quite… advanced? Or is this his form of magic? This is very intriguing, once we get him to the village, I'll focus on teaching him our tongue. He seems to be grasping it unnaturally well, it may not take not long for us to get some answers.''

Looking back at his phone a sadness washed over him, seeing again that there was no signal and no data means he had no way of contacting anyone. Despite this, he attempts to ring Helen, the mercenaries watch on, utterly baffled by Gordons actions as he places his phone to his ear.

Nothing.

What has happened? Where was he? Right now, he was walking through a forest with men and women dressed ever so strangely. A large group of people in white hooded robes and others in chainmail armour and leather padding, wielding swords and staves. It was like something from the stories and movies he'd seen over the years.

Gordon needed to find out how to get back home, he felt there was no choice but to listen and follow on.

But something was off. He himself felt very different, he reflected on the moment that light disappeared trying to establish a connection between it and what was going on now. He feels energised, his sight seems clearer and the noises around him are sharp and loud, the years of damage to his ears from music just seemed to have vanished, and the strangest thing, the language. Gordon had already picked up words the people around spoke and recognised them enough to use them in speech himself, the words would resonate in his mind constantly, deciphering with ease. Although still very unsure of the language, he felt confident that soon there would be an answer to all of this.

His initial panic upon arrival to this place was subdued by a deep comfort inside of him which he couldn't explain. Surely a situation like this would have driven him mad? But something didn't feel right, was it a dream? Was he really dead? He couldn't be dead, because he never felt so alive.

Gordon attempts to catch Parinos's attention. ''Home,'' Gordon speaks in his native tongue. He then repeats the word in the tongue of the druids. ''Halio, home… halio….''

Parinos's ears prick at the words, ''Home….'' he frowns, saddened by the word.

Gordon sighs as he pulls at his hair.

''Deh calam er tu, halio?'' Parinos speaks.

You. To. Want. The words resonate.

''Er tu? Home? Halio?'' Replies Gordon.

''Ekahnuden, Gordon.''

Gordon attempts to string a sentence in the strange language. ''I… want… go… home.''

Parinos stops in his tracks, staring upon Gordon mournfully. ''You want to go home… of course… it's a little complicated Gordon… but we shall have much to learn once we reach our village.''

Discuss. Village. We. Learn.

Gordon's eyebrows were buried within a complex frown, so much was overwhelming, but so much was being handled. But how? By what?

To add to his confusion, Gordon can't help but notice the lifeless woman being carried by the mercenaries alongside Lucotorix and Orthunus. Why was she like that? Was she dead? If so, how? Gordon tried to ignore it, but couldn't help but glance over to her from time to time, especially when Lucotorix and Orthunus would take breaks from carrying her.

The group had walked for two hours, within that time Gordon would hear nothing but this strange language being spoken amongst the people, as alien as it sounded, he was picking up words the more he heard them being spoken, as if they had been spoken to him before.

Gordon felt more and more distressed about walking so far from the site they had left, feeling that the area he came from was his only way home, except it wasn't even there in the first place.

He had to press on, follow the group and see what is to come. Hopefully soon he might find a way, maybe soon his phone signal would return.

As they exited the forest, they were now in clear view of a dirt road, and in the distance a faint glow of light flickered through the lining of the forest, smoke could be seen spewing from atop the silhouette of some large trees past the clearing, this must be the village they spoke of.

Approaching the clearing, houses were now becoming visible, roofing made of thatch that dipped over intricate stone cobbled walls, the houses were rounded and quite large, they were everywhere, the footpath also cobbled, decorated with many beds of otherworldly flowers, large lantern posts with a dazzling emerald fire dancing within iron castings were scattered throughout the village, giving the night time vibe a beautiful green hue.

‘’Why is the fire green?’’ He thought to himself, another question upon the many gathering in his fragile mind.

Within the village centre was a large statue of two creatures, one of them seemed to have what seemed to be branch-like antlers spouting from its head accompanied by pointy knife-like ears. It appeared to have a feminine body shape, naked, except for what appeared to be roots twisting all around its body; its arms were outstretched as if to offer a motherly embrace. The being next to this one was more recognisably a person, or so he thought.

This one was quite different; it was of a woman wearing a crown or a tiara of sorts. She wore a dress of animal pelts and furs, one of her arms was entirely skeletal, as was her leg and a small portion of her jaw. This statue was slightly more harrowing upon initial view, aside that, it was a beautifully crafted statue, the details were exceptionally fine, master crafted to say the least.

‘’Gordon, welcome to our home,’’ announces Parinos.

‘’Home,’’ Gordon repeats.

‘’This is Seers Crossing, home of the druids.’’

‘’Druids… fanaseeren… druids…’’ he repeats again, still mesmerised by the statue in front of him, dazzled by the spectacle of the village.

He took note that it was quite similar to that of a Celtic village in his own world's history, except it seemed… very different.

The village was abundant in beautiful well-kept flowers of all kinds, kinds he’d never even laid eyes on before. Finely trimmed hedges, iron fencing, and the houses themselves, although appearing in quite an old primitive style, had a lot of intricacies about them, such as framed windows and wonderful swirly patterns etched into wooden beams.

Lucotorix dawdles by, still supporting Camula’s lifeless body alongside Orthunus. He notices Gordon’s gormless expression as he stares upon the statue. ‘’Gordon… that is, Fanara and Iskarien,’’ Lucotorix smiles proudly at the statue. ‘’Our Gods,’’ he pats Gordon’s back.

Gods. Fanara. Iskarien.

Even the structure of the words spoken to him began to connect and make sense.

Gordon turns to Lucotorix but is distracted by the woman's body he was helping carry.

''What, her?''

''She's gone, my friend,'' Lucotorix gives a sorrowful smile, his face returning to a blank state as moves to place Camula's body beneath the statue, moving the body into a position of comfort. Gordon watches on as they hobble along with her, laying her out across the base of the plinth.

''Now my druids, please see to yourselves, your work has been… successful, despite how uncertain things may seem,'' Parinos addresses his druids.'' Tomorrow we will see our beloved sister Camula handed to the Gods. Let us rest now,'' he gives a moment before turning to Gordon. ''Gordon, come,'' he shuffles him along.

The mercenaries depart and the other druids go their own way. Lucotorix walks with Gordon and Parinos leaving Orthunus with Camula at the statue.

The village is quiet, its serenity was unmatched by anything Gordon had ever seen, his head arches all around in amazement.

Parinos and Lucotorix usher Gordon to a large roundhouse further into the village.

It was well decorated with animal pelts and woven tapestries alike, in the centre of the house sat a large fire pit with two cauldrons rested atop, around the fire pit were benches carved with exceptional craftsmanship. As he looked around, he noticed more furniture, a desk, cupboards, seating of impressive design, he also noticed that upon the desk were many books and papers scattered all around. ''Books?'' He wondered. As ancient and historic as this place seemed, he knew that ancient civilisations such as the Celts never had books, or furniture of such intricacy for that matter, things weren't adding up.

Parinos sit's Gordon down upon the bench.

Lucotorix and Parinos sit opposite Gordon across the fire pit, gawking at him in astonishment as they allow their heavy hearts of the day's work to settle.

Parinos holds his hands toward the fire pit, his eyes glow a purple hue, a fire illuminates from nowhere underneath the cauldron, Gordon jumps at the sight in surprise.

''What the fuck?'' He shouts, shocked by the sudden roar of the fire.

''What did he say?'' Lucotorix asks.

''I'm unsure, it was similar to what he was saying when he arrived, I assume it's a form of expression in his tongue, he's clearly never seen magic before, or fire?''

''He's in for a treat....''

''We must not disclose that to him yet, Lucotorix,'' Parinos mutters.

''Must not to me?'' Gordon speaks out in Urosi, the native tongue of these people.

Lucotorix smiles awkwardly. ''Forgot that he was catching our language so quickly for second.''

Parinos laughs in embarrassment. ‘’Yes…’’ he turns to Gordon. ‘’Gordon, do not worry yourself, all will be revealed.’’

Gordon nods in confusion.

‘’Is learning our language so quickly part of the drenching?’’ Asks Lucotorix.

‘’No… that wouldn’t make sense… or would it? Honestly Lucotorix, I’m quite stumped,’’ he glances back at Gordon. ‘’Gordon, where are you from, where is your home?’’

Noticing the speech patterns, Gordon understands the sentence. ‘’My home?’’ He gestures to himself.

Parinos nods. ‘’Yes… where is your home?’’

‘’Middlesbrough,’’ Gordon replies.

Parinos and Lucotorix look at each other in confusion, folding their eyebrows at the name of the place, a word they’ve never heard in a dialect unbeknown to them.

‘’Never heard of it… another realm of humans?’’ Says Lucotorix.

‘’Hmmm… a high possibility, Fanara teaches us that the realms of the void are infinite, and possibilities of all forms of life are endless, this is a perfect example of that… look at his clothing, his hair… those markings on his skin, otherworldly is exactly that.’’

Gordon nervously laughs, knowing full well they were talking about him, but not entirely what it was they were saying.

''Don't worry, Gordon. We've just… never seen anyone like you before,'' says Lucotorix comfortingly, giving a friendly smile.

Parinos stands and begins to fumble with one of the cauldrons. ''Are you hungry, Gordon? Would you care for some food?''

Gordon shakes his head, raising his hands.

''Don't worry, Gordon. It's just a stew, Parinos was preparing it earlier, it's good!''

''I go home?'' Gordon asks.

Parinos gives a deep sigh, ''Listen to me Gordon, take in every word I say. The way back… to your home… is no… longer… open,'' Parinos's jaw judders in pity for Gordon. ''I promise you… I'll try and help you… find your way home, but… it may take time… and it won't be easy.''

Although Gordon didn't completely understand the words spoken, he understood their meaning, he was aware Parinos was speaking slowly for him.

That panicking feeling started erupting from within his stomach again, he started sweating, he felt a choking feeling wrap around his throat.

''Home, please, home!'' Gordon begs. He stands abruptly, not knowing what to do with himself, the grasp of fear tightening.

''Gordon, Gordon, listen! Look at me,'' Lucotorix rushes to him, almost tripping over his robes. ''We will try and find a way for you to return home… okay?''

Strangely reassured, Gordon begins to settle but remains standing, something inside begins soothing him again.

‘’I just… I just… I don't understand… where… I… am,’’ Gordon speaks out as clearly as he can.

‘’You’re in a different world… our world, Altharn. You came through a world gate,’’ says Parinos.

World. Gate. Altharn.

Suddenly something snaps in Gordons’ head, the light.

‘’I’m not… no… dream?"

‘’No Gordon, this is our world, you have been brought here by an ancient power that has pierced the veil of worlds,’’ Parinos says as he continues to stir the cauldron.

‘’I… need to go home.’’

‘’We know Gordon, and we’ll find a way for you to get back home,’’ smiles Lucotorix as he anxiously takes a glance at Parinos.

Parinos turns to Lucotorix as he prepares the stew. ‘’Tomorrow I’ll sit with him and teach him as much of our language as we can. I want him to know the truth and how he got here. I feel it may give him some clarity and ease, for now we’ll eat together and rest. Let’s get acquainted.’’

Lucotorix agrees, and aids Parinos in preparing the stew.

Parinos hands a bowl to Gordon. ‘’Gordon, have some food, please sit with us and eat.’’

Gordon double takes Parinos and the stew, slightly paranoid, but reluctantly accepts the stew in fear he may offend them. He sits and takes a deep breath, watching Parinos and Lucotorix as they blow on their stew and eat it as they would any meal. As he takes a gentle sip, he soon realises there is no threat, he then swallows a whole spoonful.

It was amazing, the textures, the composition, the taste was extraordinary, still on edge he continues to eat slowly trying not to let the excitement of the taste take over.

''Good stew, yes?'' Lucotorix says stuffing his face, drips of the stew staining his white cloth.

''Good,'' he replies, tapping his wooden spoon on the bowl.

Parinos smiles. ''Gordon, you will sleep here with us tonight, we'll keep you safe and tomorrow we shall learn the common tongue of our people.''

Gordon nods, but then pauses as he realises something.

''Sleep? Sleep? Sleep… here?''

''Yes, we have a spare bed,'' replies Parinos pointing to a wooden balcony structure that touched the roof of the roundhouse with a crooked wooden ladder leading up.

Gordon didn't want to stay here, he wanted to go home. Helen must be worried sick by now, it's been hours since his phone call with her, he checks his phone again. No signal, no data.

Is what the two men say true? Did Gordon really walk through a 'world gate' and end up in a different world? The idea itself is ridiculous, but given the current circumstances, what other explanation was there? Gordon couldn't quite wrap his head around the idea.

He knew if he was to stay here, he wouldn't sleep, with all the stress going on he was certain he would not sleep well tonight. Regardless, he humoured the men and reluctantly agreed to stay the night knowing no other way around, at least he felt somewhat safe.

With all the questions and confusion weighing down his mind, his smoking cravings kicked in. He reached into his jacket pocket and realised the two packs of cigarettes were still there.

Parinos and Lucotorix look on inquisitively.

''Go… outside?'' Gordon asks nervously, pointing to the door.

Parinos and Lucotorix share an uncertain glance.

''Does he want fresh air? What is that thing?'' Asks Lucotorix.

Parinos shrugs. ''You want to go outside?'' Parinos asks Gordon.

Gordon nods.

''Show him outside, Lucotorix,'' Parinos pulls Lucotorix in by the scruff of his sleeve. ''And stay with him.''

Lucotorix guides Gordon outside, back into the majestic view of Seers Crossing.

Gordon rests a cigarette into the fold of his lips. Lucotorix looks on, baffled by the object. Gordon then lights it with his lighter.

''Woah,'' Lucotorix's gawks in curiosity. ''What contraption is that? Does it use magic to emit the fire?''

''Magic?'' Replies Gordon with angled brows.

''It seems all your otherworldly possessions emit some form of magic?''

Gordon grunts awkwardly as he begins to puff on his cigarette.

''Ah, so that thing is like a pipe of sorts? I like to smoke too!'' Lucotorix reaches into his rugged satchel that's attached to one of the many belts of his robes, producing a wooden hollowed out pipe, displaying it proudly with a strange bag of herbs. He fills the pipe showing Gordon every move he makes.

Humoured by Lucotorix's enthusiasm, Gordon extends his lighter to Lucotorix's pipe.

Lucotorix backs off slightly, but gives in to the trust that filtered the moment. ''Incredible....'' Lucotorix says in awe as he watches the small flame spark from the lighter. ''Hmm, you have your own ways with magic, and we have ours.''

Gordon gives a dejected smile.

Unknowing how to respond, Lucotorix looks off into the starry night sky as he puffs his pipe. ''It's funny isn't it, we're so different, yet so similar. We'll figure all this out, together,'' he smiles. ''I must say, you're quite a peculiar one.''

''Your… name? Luc… ot… or…ix,'' Gordon drags out his name, signalling for approval.

Lucotorix chuckles. ''Yes, that's my name.''

The two continue to puff away their smoking devices. Otherworldly to each other, yet connected as one.

Feeling his stress subside and his craving halter, Gordon takes a deep breath as he takes in the scenery. His disastrous emotions burning away, yet staying ever vigilant in the recesses of his mind. It just made no sense, it was one place, then another? That kind of desensitisation, he couldn't comprehend it. He was still so perplexed at himself for remaining as calm as he was.

''An eventful night indeed… one moment my life is on the line for a magical ritual that activates some of the only power of the Gods left upon our world, the next I'm sharing a smoke with an otherworldly being, ridiculous to say the least. But it's true… otherworldly humans do exist, so it seems. I'd only ever heard the lore of Fanara, never once saw a glimmer of its truth… Fanara says all manner of life walk throughout the void, some unique, others very similar, and few exactly the same.''

Gordon smiles awkwardly.

''I know you can't understand everything I'm saying… but Camula would have loved this… she was always into learning and educating others of the Gods, and whatever other creatures may harbour in the infinite worlds that scatter the endless void. When Parinos told us of the ritual to open a world gate, half the druids declined instantly. Camula was one of the first to jump at the chance to join, regardless of the cost… Hmm, I'm sorry

Gordon, I need to air my feelings… but… you are here and she is not, as a druid I cannot blame you for her death, any other man might… but you had no idea, did you? You were just… taken. You walked the bridge of realms without even knowing.''

Gordon stares at Lucotorix, understanding a connection between his words and the woman he was referring to.

''She was a strong druid, a quiet girl, very balanced in her mind, and also very adept with her magical sustenance. If you ask me, she was a better contender for the arch druid's apprentice than I… just very confused that it was her life that was consumed by the void. She could have outlasted any druid's magical capabilities who were participating. Maybe she gave a little too much of herself to the void? Who knows.''

Gordon places his hand on Lucotorix's shoulder. ''I'm sorry,'' Gordon thinks back on the woman, Camula.

Gordon had never seen a dead body before but looking back now, he knew she was dead. There's a strange aura that fills the air when death is present. An emptiness like no other, he just didn't want to believe it.

He felt bad for Lucotorix and the other druids for losing their friend, he felt it may have been his fault, but not all of Lucotorix's words were all too clear for Gordon to make assumptions and estimations. He was aware an alleged ritual took place and a world gate supposedly brought him here, he just couldn't for the life of him believe something like this had even happened at all, let alone take someone's life in the process.

''I'm sorry, Gordon. Camula was a sweet girl, it's just a shame we've lost her. Her poor father…'' he looks down to his feet. ''But as Parinos would say, her existence will now be embraced by our Gods amidst the endless void. By Fanara, I hope that's true. Enough of this talk, we want you to feel welcome here, come Gordon, are you finished?'' He signals to the house with his head.

The two dawdled back into the house, Parinos was at his desk, carefully documenting the eventful day.

''Everything okay?'' He asks, lifting his neck from his frigid slouch.

''Yes, Gordon has his own way of smoking would you believe.''

''Interesting… may I see?''

Lucotorix signals to Gordon about his cigarettes. ''Show Parinos your smoking pipes!''

Gordons produces and shows Parinos his cigarettes and lighter.

''That thing there,'' Lucotorix points at the lighter. ''It produces fire!''

''You surprise me more and more each time with your trinkets, Gordon,'' Parinos shakes away his interest. ''Anyway, we should sleep, Gordon you must be overwhelmed beyond belief, let me show you your bed.''

Parinos guides Gordon up the small balcony that looms over half of the interior, supported by beams entrenched into the foundation. Upon the balcony were four beds, to Gordon's eyes they were just small wooden frames laden with the pelts.

Parinos and Lucotorix both undressed and entered their own beds. Feeling quite awkward, Gordon removed his clothes underneath the pelt covering. He lay there for a few minutes, staring at the ceiling still trying to make sense, wondering why he was going along with all this, frustrated. He wanted to go home, maybe if he slept, he'd wake up normally? Maybe it was some crazy dream? Maybe someone spiked his drink and he blacked out? A sudden feeling deep within urged him to sleep. His eyes became heavy, a forceful comfort swept over him, almost like he was being put to sleep by force, he didn't feel he had much control, like being put under by anaesthetic, he couldn't resist the urge to sleep, and finally his eyes shut.

A slumber like no other.

5: Missing

Middlesbrough, 2:30am.

Dan's phone vibrates, the ringtone blaring out one of Blood Winter's own songs. Dan reaches over to it. ''Who the fuck's ringing at this time?'' He moans to himself. Looking at the caller ID he sees its Helen, his eyebrows raise in surprise.

''Ello poppet,'' he answers.

''Dan? Are you with Gordon?'' Helen frantically asks, the concern in her voice unsettling him.

''No… is he not with you?''

''He's not come home; he should have been here hours ago now… his phone's off and everything!''

''You're joking? He left us around ten, said he was picking some stuff up for you and going home?''

''He's still not back Dan, I'm starting to worry now! He rang me before going to the shop and then nothing… I'm a little on edge, this isn't like him,'' her voice shakes with uncertainty.

''Hang on, Hel. I'll be right over,'' he drops his phone without hanging up as he frantically scouts around his cluttered flat for a pair of jeans.

Something wasn't right. Gordon should have returned by now, two thirty in the morning and nothing but radio silence, anything could have happened.

Had Gordon been jumped by a gang of unruly yobs looking for a fight? Unlikely, but the chances were never zero. Had he been robbed or worse, stabbed? Kidnapped? All these scenarios run through Dan's head as he rushes around his flat.

Despite what Helen had told him he tried to ring Gordon's phone. Nothing, it went straight to the answer phone.

A rushing concern hits Dan, he runs out of his flat and jumps on his moped, thrashing the speed limit to reach Helen and Gordon's house just a ten-minute ride away.

Helen anxiously awaits by her living room window for Dan, or Gordon. She returns to pacing up and down the living room with nothing but a slew of scenarios running rampant throughout her head. Every minute that went by with nothing from Gordon only fed the anxiety brewing inside her.

The sound of a large motorised chugging noise disturbs the peace of the street. It was Dan, on his clunky moped skidding onto the path outside, almost tumbling over as he came to a stop.

She opens the door and before he even has a chance to get off of his moped, he catches her as she begins to tremble with worry.

''I have no idea where he is! He should be home!'' Helen cries. ''He's never done this! He wasn't too drunk, was he?!''

''No, he only had a few. Calm down Hel, he'll be fine! He's a smart lad, he won't be in any bother, it's Monday night and there won't be any trouble out on a Monday… have you rang the police?''

''Yes, and they just told me to wait and see if he comes back… it's too early to file a missing person's report.''

''Fuck off, what the fuck! It's late at night though?!'' Dan ponders for a moment, attempting to decipher where Gordon could be or have gone. ''Wait… you said he went to pick up some cigs? Does he still buy them from the same shop? Maybe we can ask to see if they saw him? Is it still open at this time?''

''Yeah, the corner shop, it's open twenty-four hours.''

''Right, jump on then,'' Dan signals to his moped.

Feeling rather unsafe by the looks of his shoddy vehicle that could probably fall apart at any time, Helen declines. ''I'd rather walk, what if we miss him on the roads?''

''Fair enough, good thinking, gives us chance to cover some ground I suppose.''

Helen quickly runs back inside and grabs her bag and jacket.

As they walked, their heads snapped in all manner of directions looking out for Gordon or anything that could lead to him but they saw nothing. They walk through the gloomy park together, the mist adding to the dread that haunts their subconscious thoughts, scouring around and calling out for him on occasion as they stroll through.

After an unsuccessful scout, they arrive at the shop.

‘’Ello bud,’’ Dan greets the cashier, a young Malaysian man by the name of Umar, who knew his locals quite well.

Umar smiles in response. ‘’Hi Dan, are you keeping well? What can I get you?’’

‘’You haven’t seen Gordon at all have you?’’

‘’Yeah, he came by a while ago, everything okay?’’ Umar replies with a raised brow.

‘’He’s not returned home, we’re getting a little worried about him,’’ Helen splutters.

‘’Damn?! Well, it’s not busy tonight, want me to check the cameras or something?’’

‘’Please buddy,’’ Dan says in angst.

Umar could tell this was serious, Helen’s face was slightly smeared with makeup that still ran down her eyes and Dan had an unusually unsettling tone.

Umar knew the group well, Dan would always be cracking jokes with Umar, and Helen was always smiling and overly polite as she always was. Not once in the years that Umar had worked in that shop had he never seen these two in such a worried state.

Umar offers Dan and Helen to follow him round the back of the till and into the side room where the camera and TVs are located, he spends some time fiddling around finding the right time frame until, ‘’Bingo, there he is, yep… comes in at exactly, ten forty-two.’’

Helen pushes afront. ‘’Oh my God….’’

Umar lets the footage play out, they watch as Gordon buys his cigarettes and a chocolate bar and then leave the shop.

''Right… outside camera now,'' Umar switches the main TV to the outside Camera, watching Gordon leave, nothing seemed suspicious at all. ''He headed towards the park by the looks of it… you live by the park, don't you?'' He comments as they all watch Gordon head into the park.

''Yeah, we do… I don't understand,'' says Helen, defeated.

Dan comforts her. ''Shall we check the park again, maybe?''

''Wait… the park has cameras, doesn't it?'' Asks Helen.

''Not sure, we'll go have a look, but the place that manages the park shuts at nine… so if we want to see their CCTV, we might have to wait till tomorrow….''

''Dan, I can't wait until Tomorrow, no chance… I'm not going to sleep tonight until he's home.''

''We'll figure something out. Umar, thanks bud, appreciate it.''

''No worries, Dan, hope you guys find him safe, if you need me, you know where I am,'' Umar replies, shaking Dan's hand.

Dan and Helen leave with haste as they cross over to the park. Looking around, they don't see any cameras near the entrance.

''Bullshit! They should have cameras here?! All sorts probably go on when the little shits are festering it on a Friday,'' Helen rages.

‘’It is dark though… hang on, look,’’ Dan notices a large metal pole next to a building that has two cameras attached at the peak, one pointing near the entrance and another pointing away toward the playground. ‘’We’ll come by the moment the management opens their little building… that’s unless Gordon’s come home already? You never know.’’

‘’Right… fine,’’ Helen replies. "GORDON!" She shouts. "GORDON!" Her voice breaking on the scream. She buries her hands in her face. ‘’Where could he have gone? Everyone we know literally lives on the other side of town, if he came this way he must have been coming home,’’ Helen catches her breath in a nervous sigh, her voice visibly shaking. ‘’Dan… I’ve got a bad feeling about this, something’s happened in the park, hasn’t it? He's been attacked?!’’ She runs her hands through her hair grasping her scalp in emotional torment.

‘’It’s starting to worry me more and more as well now….’’ replies Dan. ‘’Let me try to ring him one more time,’’ Dan quickly flips his phone from his pocket to dial Gordon. Again, it didn’t even ring, it went straight to the answer phone. ‘’Fucking hell man,’’ Dan grunts in frustration. ‘’Let’s head back to yours, see if he’s come back?!’’ Dan Suggests, holding Helen firmly by the shoulders in comfort.

Helen nods softly. ‘’And if he hasn’t?’’

‘’Then we’ll try the police again, we’ll try and convince them to come out or something.’’

Helen, feeling hopeless, agrees.

They rang all their friends who were possibly still up, most of them didn't pick up, and the ones who did answer, had no clue.

Returning home, Helen and Dan pondered around the living room discussing all possibilities, trying to figure out where Gordon could be.

They waited and waited… still nothing, the hours went on by.

''Where the fuck is he, Dan,'' Helen murmurs leaning into her arms on the kitchen counter, heavy with sleep deprivation. '' It's five in the morning, Dan. Can we try the police again?''

''You know what they'll say and it'll just piss you off even more,'' he stops pacing. ''Look, the park management opens at six, that's an hour away, just wait until then and we'll find out more, okay?''

''Dan, every minute feels like an hour!''

''I know… I know,'' he runs his hands through his greasy hair. ''Come on, Hel. Pull through, we don't know what's happened, you haven't even rang his mother, something could have happened?''

''Weronika's in Poland, she's looking after his grandmother.''

''Exactly, what if his grandmother has… died or something and… he's gone to get the next flight?'' Dan stutters with uncertainty.

''Dan the thing is… if anything happened with his family, I'd be the first to know. Besides, we don't even have the money for a sporadic flight to Poland.''

''What about his dad?''

''Dan! Come on… I'd be the first to know! He wouldn't just disappear like this!''

''You don't know how serious it could be!?''

She slams her hands down on the counter. ''Dan, for fucks sake!''

Dan jumps at the bang that rattled the nearby cutlery. ''Sorry Helen, I'm just trying to shed some light on it all….''

''I know! I'm sorry… I'm really sorry for snapping, I'm losing my head here… oh my God, can it just be six already.''

''Hey, I get it, okay? I've never seen you this distressed, it's alright, love. He'll be fine… okay?'' Dan consoles.

The next hour went by just as slowly as they expected it too with still no word from Gordon.

Ten minutes prior to the hands of time striking the twelve and six, Helen and Dan leave for the park having no sleep whatsoever.

They were a few minutes early, the door was locked to the shoddy little outhouse centred within the park and no one was inside, until the grounds keeper arrived, ever so slightly late for his shift.

A man adorned in scruffy mud-stained garb and dusty flat cap approaches, whistling his way toward the building without a care in the world. He notices the two standing impatiently outside his office, his approach becomes weary. ''Oi oi… can I help?'' He grunts in a thick accent.

Helen is the first to answer, stepping forward towards the Groundskeeper. ''Hi, look, my boyfriend is missing and the last known place he was seen was walking through here last night. Can we check your cameras?! Please?'' She grovels.

The aged man ruffles his flat cap scratching his scalp underneath. ''Have you not rung the police, love?''

''They won't take it seriously with him only being gone for a few hours… he's not come home all night, he's not like this, I'm worried something has happened as he's come through here, we live just on the other side, he cuts through the park all the time.''

''Bloody pigs. I swear they're getting lazier by the year, they just don't bloody care, do they? '' He gives a moment to reflect on the situation as he scans the two intently. ''Alright love, come on in, we'll have a gander.''

Helen waits awkwardly as she watches the Groundskeeper fumble around with his keys to open the door. Her stomach dips as she is hit with a musky smell of coffee mixed with a stale odour of an old dirty ashtray upon entering the building.

In the corner of this room was a desk with a computer. The Groundskeeper sat down and turned it on, scouring through the CCTV footage.

''You want a cuppa or anything?'' He kindly offered.

Dan and Helen both politely deny the request, quite put off by the smell of the place.

''Right then… what time do you reckon he came in?''

''About quarter to eleven,'' Dan remembers.

''Okey dokey, let's have a look then,'' he slowly scans through the footage, narrowing his ageing eyes, until… ''Is that him?''

''Yes! Oh my God!'' Helen squeals. Her stomach tightens again in fear, worried she may witness something happen to Gordon. She grips the sleeves of her coat tight in anticipation.

They all watch as Gordon enters the park.

As he walks out of frame the Groundskeeper switches camera to another nearby. They watch on as Gordon stops to peer over to something out of shot. A light can be seen flickering faintly in the corner of the screen.

Gordon walks toward it very slowly, coming away from the path and out of view of the camera. After a few minutes, the light disappears. The camera's recording enters a field of disturbances that shudders the screen of the recording until returning to normal. Gordon doesn't return to view and the park is dark once more.

''What the… fuck.'' Helen whispers in fear.

They fast forward the footage carefully and nothing else unordinary comes forth.

''A car?'' Dan suggests.

''That is bloody strange… hang about, I'll have a look at the other cameras to see if anyone else could have been around. You see… there's not a great deal of CCTV here, the kids tend to knock it all down, little bastards.''

Helen's heart begins pounding at an alarming rate. She stands there in silence, chewing on the sleeve of her coat.

''Could a car get in here?'' Asks Dan.

''No… there's no bloody space in those gates for a car, I mean… the council can get in, but they have keys for the bigger gates further up, but they haven't been here in about a week,'' the Groundskeeper replies. ''I don't think there was anyone else who entered or even left the park around the time your feller came by.''

''Impossible… somethin-'' Helen stops in her tracks. ''I'm going to see where he went,'' without warning, Helen bursts out of the building and toward the gate Gordon entered, she followed his footsteps carefully, using memory of the footage to aid her navigation.

After a few minutes of careful pacing, she finds the spot where Gordon left the path and onto the field and follows it off trail.

Taking very small steps, she scours the ground for any kind of evidence of his presence. It didn't take long until she found something, something that was only a short walk out.

By some bushes was a patch of ground that appeared burned, as if they had been a bonfire of some kind.

She stands there, confused by what she was looking at. A bonfire made by the troublesome youth? Or something that could connect to her missing lover.

Dan and the Groundskeeper catch up.

''Helen?!'' Dan shouts.

''Dan....'' she mumbles as she peers around the blackened floor. She takes note of a burned-out cigarette resting by the grass.

''Looks like the remnants of a bondy,'' Dan comments.

''That's not from a bonfire laddie. I've worked here long enough to know what they look like, trust me. That? That's....'' the Groundskeeper pauses, scrunching his face as he tries to fish out an answer. Even he was confused. It was just black grass. Black grass that spiralled out in a circular motion. He bends down to touch the area, picking out a blade of the grass. ''Strange... it's not actually even burnt. It's as fresh as any other blade of grass.''

''That cig... could that be his?'' Whimpers Helen. ''It's the only thing here apart from the weird grass....''

Dan's demeanour suddenly changes, he could feel something strange in the air. It grasped tight at him and squeezed hard; a wave of dread lurks.

''I... I don't know Hel. Look, we need to get back on it with the police, something weird is going on here... don't touch anything!'' Dan orders.

She slowly lifts her head to take in a view of the surrounding greenery. She could only see the bushes and trees surrounding this part of the field that enclosed the area, the only other place Gordon could have gone was back toward the path.

‘’I… don’t understand… Gordon….’’

6: The Drenching

His eyes open, everywhere around him is a black void, the floor has no texture and no material sense or feel, yet he could feel himself firmly grounded.

In the distance a white glow offended his vision, it seemed to be calling out to him or signalling something, he wasn't quite sure. Everything felt so real just like when he touched the light.

The glow was calling out but he struggled to hear its voice, it was muffled, like being submerged in water.

He tries to focus but the voice is still dulled, echoing throughout this endless void. As he focuses harder, the voice becomes ever so slightly clearer.

As the glow edges forward, it appears to morph into a human shaped silhouette.

''Gordon,'' the voice is distinctly female. ''You… are safe,'' the silhouette speaks, her voice shuddering through his body invasively.

''You speak my language?'' Gordon asks.

''No, you speak mine.''

''But… I… what? I… I need to see Helen!''

''The way to your realm is no longer open. Listen, you must understand those around you, take in these words, nurture them, they can help you-''

''NO!'' He refuses to give the voice a chance. Frustrated, he loses himself. ''Get me out of here! For fucks sake!'' He whines.

''Gordon, you must remain in balance. I can't help when-''

''Please!'' He screams, trembling in fear. ''What is this!!?''

''I'll be here with you, embrace,'' the ethereal light shudders violently as Gordon continues to yell at the glow as it materialises into the void, still speaking but the words unreachable to his ears, until it finally fades into nothing.

The void begins to rumble.

Gordon screams as he pleas for his life. He screams in pain, he screams and screams but the only response is the echoes of his own suffering.

''PLEASE JUST HELP ME!'' He screams as he shoots up from his bed, drowning in a clutch of purified dread. ''HELP ME!!''

Parinos leaps from his bed in an instant, disturbed by Gordon's wails. He disregards his fragile frame as he darts to Gordons side. ''Gordon!? It's okay Gordon! Calm down!''

''No, no! I need to see Helen, where is she?! Helen! HELEN!''

''Wha! What's going on! What's he saying?'' Lucotorix rises up in shock.

''I don't know, he's speaking his native tongue,'' Parinos tries to get Gordon's attention. ''Gordon! Look at me!''

Gordon didn't take notice of Parinos, he continued to scream in terror, shouting and flailing. ''I don't know where I am! Helen!''

Stumped, Parinos watches on as Gordon fights away the reality surrounding him. Thinking quickly, Parinos wraps his arms around him, pulling him into his half naked body, embracing Gordon like a child. ''Gordon, Gordon Listen, it's okay, you're alive, you're well. We will get you back, we just need time.''

Lucotorix watches on with a hanging jaw.

''Helen....'' Gordon cries, he begins to sob uncontrollably into Parinos's arms.

''This is awful, Parinos... what have we done?!'' Lucotorix gawks in regret.

''Quiet down, Lucotorix. This was not in our control,'' Parinos snaps.

''Look at him, Parinos. Look at him! What have we done to this poor being?!''

''Lucotorix! I appreciate your concern but right now it isn't helping, please just remain calm or remove yourself.''

Lucotorix gives in to Parinos, he slips into his robes and ventures down the ladder.

Gordon begins to settle, he tears himself away from Parinos in embarrassment, hiding his saddened face, looking around discreetly. He wasn't living in a dream, this was real.

He takes some breaths as he wipes away at his snotty nose and looks up to Parinos who's sitting at the edge of his bed. ''I'm not going home, am I? I'm stuck here?'' He speaks in Urosi.

Taken back by the instant improvement in his language, Parinos takes a minute to soak in Gordon's speech. ''Erm, no… that may not be the case, Gordon.'' A smile of false hope masks him.

Lucotorix can be heard rustling around, he then makes his way back up, poking his head above the ladder. ''Want to smoke with me, Gordon?''

Gordon understood every word.

''Yes… yes,'' says Gordon, drained.

As Gordon puts back on his clothes, Lucotorix catches a glance at his tattoos, looking intently upon them, only to realise how perverted he must look, staring at Gordon as he dressed, he gives his head a shake and awaits Gordon outside.

Parinos shuffled out of the way, he felt incredibly concerned for Gordon and was unsure of how to tell him that they may not be a way home. He sighs and walks over to his dresser, picking out some fresh robes for the day ahead. He was due to wake in a few hours' time but since Gordon had woken them earlier, he decided he may as well start his day now.

''Are you okay, friend?'' Lucotorix asks, as he prepares his pipe. ''Sorry… stupid question.''

''Your language? I feel I can… almost….'' says Gordon as he lights a cigarette.

''It's very strange indeed, but it's nice to speak with you, we will help you, Gordon. I can't even imagine how hard this is for you.''

Gordon stressfully brushes back his hair. ''Sorry Lucotorix, I'm still grasping words… but less… does that make sense?''

''Your progression of common Urosi is astounding to say the least, friend. Look, I just wanted to smoke with you, it seemed to help you a little last night. I even got a smirk out of you. Thought it would help you calm down from that nightmare or whatever it was.''

''It's strange, I feel like this is a nightmare, but it isn't. I did have a dream though, and… it wasn't scary… no? It was? I don't know….''

Lucotorix's eyebrows raise in surprise at his speech. ''Elaborate?'' He asks, twiddling his moustache.

Staring upon the morning dew, Gordon takes an extensive drag of his cigarette as he reflects his dream. ''I was… standing in… nothing. A woman approached… told me I was safe.''

‘’You’re right, that does sound quite… ominous. Still… you woke up shouting in your native tongue, what were you saying?’’

‘’That I wanted help, to go home… to see, Helen, my girlfriend.’’

‘’That's very sad, friend. That explains why you woke up the way you did, with everything that’s happened to you so suddenly, I’m not surprised. I’m sorry if I seemed brash back then… I just woke up and I felt bad for you, this is our fault. We didn’t mean to pull you away from your home, we expected… or hoped something else to break through to us.’’

‘’...Okay?’’ Gordon replies, deciphering Lucotorix’s words.

‘’We will help you as much as we can, Gordon. You have to trust us. Well, you don’t have much of a choice really,’’ he scoffs. ‘’But we will help you… okay? Work with us, and we can work with you, take in this place, Gordon. A man of virtue must embrace all, even the darkness, only then may he have power over the light, or so Parinos always tells us.’’

Those words alone made Gordons arm hairs stand to attention, he thought back to his dream of the woman.

‘’You can understand me? Gordon?’’

‘’Yeah… sort of,’’ Gordon could definitely feel an understanding of the language, known to him now as Urosi, it was unlike anything he had experienced.

‘’You boys talking about an old man behind his back?’’ Parinos interrupts as he creaks open the door.

''Well, your hearing is still with us at least…. Just teaching Gordon here the ways of… Darogothic druidism.''

''Of course you are…'' replied Parinos, smirking. ''I've brought you some breakfast, boys. Chin up, Gordon.''

''You never make me breakfast, special occasion?''

''Shut up, Lucotorix,'' Parinos replies, pulling a face and handing them both a bowl of broth. Mushrooms could be seen bobbing around alongside some other herbs and meats.

Lucotorix laughs as Gordon stands there emotionless, still puffing on his cigarette.

Gordon could feel the carefree and happy atmosphere of these two druids' lives and wanted to chuckle along with the banter, but couldn't bring himself to. Regardless, it was nice to actually speak with these men properly for a change. He felt lucky he was lost with friendly folk at least.

''Hey, I noticed those markings on you. What are these? They look like some kind of war paint, are you a warrior?'' Asks Lucotorix.

''No, I'm not a warrior, it's a… Tattoo,'' Gordon says. ''It's… like… a… painting, that stays on your skin… forever?''

''Okay… I got some of that, Interesting. Here we have a paint that stays on the skin for a few days or so, many wear it to battle or for festivals, some even just wear it for fashion. But nothing as intricate and so finely designed as these… woah, look, it's a wolf! it's almost life like!''

As Gordon produces his bare arm for Lucotorix, he thinks on Lucotorix's words. It reminded him of the history of his own world, the Celtic warriors who donned blue paint for battle, it seemed to be quite a similar thing. A lot about these people seemed quite similar to the Celts of his own world's history. Similar, but not quite the same.

Lucotorix gawks upon Gordons tattoos, a beautiful mix of images, wolves, skulls and fire that brandished upon his arm. Lucotorix prods and strokes then carefully. ''So, they don't come off?! At all?''

Gordon shakes his head.

Lucotorix rubs at them slightly. Astonished, he returns to holding his pipe. ''Well… that's extraordinary. Do all your people have these? How do they stay on?''

Gordon finishes his cigarette kneeling down to the floor to eat his food. ''Not everyone,'' he struggles to find the words in Urosi. ''A needle goes to the skin… underneath.''

Lucotorix's face shifts into horror as he awkwardly stuff's his face with food.

''When you're finished Gordon, meet me inside will you?'' Says Parinos sternly. ''Lucotorix… prepare yourself for today, you'll be assisting me in Camula's afterlife ritual.''

Lucotorix nods and mumbles inaudibly with his stuffed cheeks.

''What do people do here?'' Asks Gordon.

Lucotorix quickly swallows the food in his mouth and prepares to speak slowly for Gordon. ''Well… this is Seers Crossing, home of the druids. Many people come here to live and learn amongst us. Me and my brother Orthunus came about ten years ago. Us druids work as… personal advisors, physicians, herbalists, arcane advisors and offer religious insight to our fellow countrymen in higher positions. Seer's Crossing has its permanent residents that tend to the village, like what myself and Orthunus are doing now… most only stay here to study until they're picked up by a lord, it's a peaceful life here.''

''Lord? Picked up?'' Gordon shrugs at his own lack of knowledge. ''It is a beautiful place… but I must leave,'' he adds, taking in the morning view as the horizon shifts from a blanket of darkness into a glorious hazy sunrise.

''You think? We shall try, friend… I wonder what your home is like, Gordon.''

Gordon looks down to his feet.

''Sorry… I didn't mean t-''

''No, no, just… you know.''

''I know,'' he pats Gordon's back then promptly rises from his squat, stretching himself out. ''Well… I have a lot of preparations to make… oh, do me a favour would you? Take this bowl inside for me? I'll see you later, Gordon.'' Lucotorix props his empty bowl on top of Gordons and wanders off toward the village centre waving as he walks off.

Gordon rises giving a deep sigh and wanders back inside the house.

''Parinos, you wanted speech?'' He asks awkwardly while holding the bowls.

''By Fanara! Did he just dump those on you?'' Says Parinos, referring to the bowls.

''Erm… yes?''

''Lazy little bastard, put them down by the stool. I'll wash them myself,'' Parinos grunts as he corrects his posture. ''So… I was unsure of how long your stay with us would be, so I rummaged around and found these spare robes, Lucotorix's old ones I believe. Don't want you stewing in your own clothes now do we?'' Parinos gestures to some neatly folded robes hanging over the bench by the fire pit.

Gordon laughs awkwardly, grabbing the robes and holding them up to look upon them, they were quite intricate considering how simple they initially appeared. He was unsure how he would even get into them; they were layered around the waist and had a set of wraps to tighten up the large sleeves, they also had a hood that drooped over the shoulders, all of it a soft cotton white.

''You don't have to wear them now, they're just here if you need a change of clothes,'' smiles Parinos. ''Do you understand?''

''I do… I understand almost every word, I don't know how. I swear since I slept, I've learned a lot of new words I feel I already knew… but didn't… It's a language, I've never heard it before.''

''I have allot to explain to you.''

Gordon places the robes on his arm. ''I'm just glad I can speak to you… sort of, I hope I can get home soon.

''We should sit down and have a little lesson on language. Let's see how well you are really fairing with it. Come Gordon, take a seat.''

Gordons sits aside Parinos upon a rickety stool. As soon as Parinos gave a word to Gordon he repeated just as well, even explaining its meaning.

''Okay… can you say 'north'.''

''North.''

''Now, north is this, a direction,'' he points at a crinkled map that's laid across the table.

Gordon took note of the map, realising none of it was familiar with Earth, oceans and landmasses that he'd never seen before, was he truly in a different realm?

''So… north of Darogoth is this country here? Venethar?'' He points out.

Parinos widens his eyes in disbelief. ''…You can read that?''

''Yeah… the markings, the letters… they just sort of… make sense," Gordon ponders. ''I stare at them for so long and it just comes to me. It's like when I hear the words for the first time and they stick."

‘’Of course, of course… hmmm… hear me out, maybe your language abilities are good enough for you to hear what I have to say, I was going to sit down with you and teach you but I don't think there's much need if you're learning this quickly."

Gordon leans in, ready to listen.

‘’This may be much to take in considering you just got here… If you don’t understand what I tell you, just say so, yes? I feel the more we speak the more you begin to grasp.’’

‘’Okay.’’

‘’Please take in everything you can, I’ll speak slowly for you, but this is a lot to explain….’’ Parinos takes a deep breath and clears his throat. ‘’A while ago now, the location of an altar known as Fanara’s Cradle was discovered, it’s said that some of Fanara’s old magic was imbued within, the secret was kept and passed down only to the arch druids, which in turn that knowledge eventually came to me when I became arch druid here. After continuing the work to restore the altar and finalising its… ‘activation’ we had hoped the altar would pierce the veil into her realm and free our God, letting her return to our world, or at least bring forth one of her creations. I knew the cradle could act as a portal, a world gate of sorts, something our world has only heard stories of… until now. We activated the magic within, we were unsure if it was actually working… until you, you just appeared. A being that resembles any other man, but you're different… your appearance, your language, the only explanation is that you are from some other realm of humans, we thought you were of Fanara's realm, but she does not model her creatures after humans, we are completely uncertain to how you came to us.''

''I think... I think I understand. Before I was... here, I was walking to my house, I saw a light, a strange light... something was very different about it. I touched it and it disappeared... and then everything changed. The world around me, the way I felt. Everything.''

''Well then. It appears our ritual did open a gate, and into your world. Clearly, we knew it would to a degree, but where would it open? We had no way of pinpointing that. Most of my druids were scared it would lead to a realm of evil and monsters,'' he chuckles faintly. ''We had only trust for our God that Fanara's magic would lead to her realm, naturally. The magic that flowed through that altar was of cosmic origin. A kind of magic alien and unpredictable as the void itself, as our mother teaches us. Perhaps that was her intention, or perhaps we misguided ourselves.... However, this ritual cost a young druid her life.''

Gordon doesn't respond, a sad look washes over him.

''Do not blame yourself, Gordon. Out of everyone involved in this, I am to blame. She knew her life could be taken to activate that altar; she was aware of the consequences and carried on regardless. Any one of us could have perished.''

Everything Parinos was saying was so bizarre, unbelievable. Gordon almost felt like scoffing at his words at how utterly absurd all this sounded, but there was no explanation as to why this place even existed in the first place, if any explanation made sense to where Gordon was standing right now, it was what Parinos was telling him.

''But… why? Why did a woman die for me to be here?''

''You have a lot to learn about this world, Gordon. We sought out the power of Fanara's Cradle as an act of desperation. Our kingdom, Darogoth, is at war with its former ally, Venethar. Their king… Kastrith Mundur, something isn't right… he is wielding a strange power… many have come to naming him the 'Vessel of Vistra', Vistra is another God much like Fanara who once walked this world before they were all banished, just over four thousand years ago.''

Gordons brows perk at his words. ''Gods again, huh? Hmm… you talk about your own God as a sort of… God of life, is Vistra… evil? A God of death or somthing?'' He humours as he scoffs to himself. Gordon was not a religious man.

''No, actually the God we revere for death is Iskarien, she is not evil, she is a part of life. The only Gods ever seen as 'evil' are the three cannibal Gods of The Paw, but that is subjective to its people I suppose. Vistra is seen to represent virtue and fate, like Fanara he teaches a balanced way of life and to always better one's self, to live within the now, to sow the present and reap the future. We're struggling with Kastrith because he claims to have been gifted power by Vistra himself, despite how impossible that is, and then he took it upon himself to force the knees of everyone around him under this new found power. He orders Darogoth to abandon its druidic way of life, it's tyrannical considering Venethari culture. They're supposed to believe in the free will of all beings, regardless of worship and race.''

''So… he's started a cult?''

''Not exactly… but yes you could say that. The thing is… Kastrith was never like this, but his power… It's come from seemingly nowhere and he's displaying such a tremendous amount of it, the people around him are convinced Vistra is actually to return to our world, and through him. They want to do his bidding, they want to please their God, and therefore have been driven to heinous acts under Kastrith's rule, other followers of Vistra are convinced Kastrith is blaspheming Vistra's name in efforts for power, which to me sounds more believable. But that begs the question…. What is this power and where is he getting it from? How is it he's so powerful he's actually convincing people Vistra himself, a banished God is to return? I'm unsure… it's frightening, and he's demanding Darogothians to even drop the worship of Fanara, and so a war breaks out, the first war with Venethar since the first age. Three thousand years of peace, and then this. Kastrith is playing a smart game… he's a man of sound word… we have information suggesting his source of power, but I don't want to fry your mind with the details just yet, you've only just arrived and have to deal with the fact you're no longer in a world you recognise.''

Gordon sits, squinting at his words, quite overwhelmed by the information Parinos has given. After an awkward moment of staring at nothing, taking in all the information, something clicks in his head. ''Vistra… Vistra?''

''What is it?''

''It just all feels weirdly familiar.''

Parinos freezes in thought. ''Interesting….'' Parinos slaps his balding head as he rises from his seat and paces around the house.

''What's wrong?'' Gordon asks.

''Nothing, just… leave all the details to me, Gordon. There's so much more I have to tell you, but I'd rather you settle in first.''

Gordon tilts into a brief surge of frustration. ''You're acting like I'm going to move in!? Parinos, I appreciate what you've done for me… but your story… It sounds like total fucking bullshit to me.''

Parinos's eyes snap open in shock at the sudden change in Gordon's demeanour.

''This is the craziest shit I've ever heard in my life… I want to go home! I'm not aiding your political crisis; I can't even believe I'm having this kind of conversation!? And in this language?! What the fuck is this language?! We focus on me getting out of here, okay?!''

Parinos lowers his head with a heavy sigh. ''Gordon… there's more you need to know.''

Gordon rises from his stool forcefully, knocking it to the ground. ''Then fucking tell me!'' For the first time Gordon raises his voice at these peaceful people, his body language rapid and excessive, he instantly felt remorseful acting in such a way but he was getting desperate, he'd had enough, he needed to get back home.

''You, have been drenched.''

''What?'' Gordon spits.

''Our world, its force, is surrounded by magic. It is known that if a being were to pass through the veil, they would become drenched by its ethereal path. This means you have a natural control over its magical force, far greater than the average magic user… people train hard for many years to just cast the simplest of spells, but you, you….''

Gordon begins to chuckle manically. ''You're taking the piss?''

''No,'' Parinos frowns defensively.

''I think I'm going mad… I've heard it all now, fuck….''

Angered by Gordon's outrageous behaviour, Parinos snaps back. ''Gordon, stop it! I know you're distressed, and I can't apologise any more to you for all of this, but Camula's life was taken away from her for you to be here! Don't you dare laugh and mock me and my beloved druids. You spit at their efforts and passing like it means nothing! This is real, Gordon. We didn't expect another human to appear before the Cradle, we didn't know what to expect, but here you are. I beg you Gordon, have some respect, at least for the poor woman who died… for you!''

Gordon's face drops. Remorse flushes his spine. ''I'm… sorry… I'm sorry, okay? I… I didn't mean to say it like that… I just… I'm confused. I'm fucking scared! My family and my friends will be worried about me, I need to get back home. I don't belong here!" He buries into his hands, ashamed of his outburst. ''Do you have any idea what this is like?! I can't even believe this is real!?''

''I know… and I said to you I'll help you find a way back home, but the way you came through is gone, we need to find another way… I just needed you to hear me out about our plight, our intent was to have whatever came through the gate to help us, you may not be from Fanara's realm, but I needed to know if you would… help. I feel stupid asking because you're clearly not fit for what we need, despite the potential you harness within. But our people are running out of options, I did what I did for the good of my people, please Gordon… don't let Camula's death be in vain.''

Gordon sits back down on the bench in submission. Feeling nothing but a flow of unwelcome guilt. ''So, this magic? That I'm apparently a natural at… could that get me home?'' Gordon felt himself wince knowing how selfish he sounded.

Parinos scoffs. ''Not that I'm aware of, only cosmic magic or magic of the endless void as it is formally known, that is the only magic capable of tearing through the void, the veil of worlds. It doesn't naturally sit in our world as our native magic does… that is the magic of Gods, you were not drenched by cosmic magic, if you were… you'd become a God yourself. You were drenched by the natural magic that filters our world… the power if the Altharn itself.''

''Of course,'' Gordon replies sarcastically, doubtful.

''Look,'' Parinos stretches his arm out.

Gordon looks up and jumps in fright at the sound of a crackling roar as Parinos produces a ball of fire that emits from the palm of his hand, roaring fiercely. And just as quickly, it disappears.

''You can also do this but you don't need the years of mental training it takes to weave this kind of magic through your body.''

Gordon's jaw had dropped from his face, he thought he saw Parinos use magic to light the fire in the firepit the night before but passed it off, Gordon sat there looking on in bewildered silence.

''Follow me outside, I'll show you, don't want you burning down my house now.''

Perplexed, Gordon follows Parinos outside, he takes him by the river just a way out from the village.

''Hold out your palm toward the sky,'' Parinos orders.

Gordon was sceptical, but humoured him.

''Focus, and feel the energy of the world around you, feel the atmosphere manifest in your body, and imagine the force and infusion of flame.''

Gordon obeyed, but nothing happened, he shut his eyes and tried to think of a flame, but nothing. He opens an eye to look at Parinos.

''Focus,'' Parinos sternly orders.

''Focus,'' that familiar voice from before echoes in Gordon's mind, hearing the voice he slipped into a second long trance.

A gigantic roaring inferno exploded from his hand, frightened by the explosion Gordon subdued it as fast as he could, the shockwave flung Parinos and Gordon to the ground.

''FUCK! Holy fucking shit!'' Gordon gasps.

''You see! Now imagine you learned to control that kind of power?'' Parinos coughs.

''Are you okay?!'' Gordon rushes to help Parinos up.

''I'm fine, just a stumble.''

''Wait… this feeling,'' Gordon holds his hands up to his face. ''This is magic? I felt strange when I arrived here and the world shifted… as if I was buzzed with energy… this energy! What?''

''Yes Gordon, you can feel the magic of the atmosphere and pick at it. Let's try again, now that you know how it feels to unleash such power, try controlling it… don't close your eyes this time.''

Gordon obliges and focuses on the palm of his hand, attempting to manipulate the energetic feeling that buzzes in the air. A small light the size of a candle begins to materialise. Shocked, he tries not to lose focus.

''Make it bigger,'' whispers Parinos.

Gordon obeys and grows the flame in his hand into a ball of swirling element with ease, he couldn't believe his eyes, it was magic, he was casting real magic. ''What should I do with it now, Parinos?''

''Throw it in the river.''

Gordon slowly moves with the ball of fire that dances elegantly from his hand, becoming familiar with its feel. He then pivots himself to the river and throws it outward. A roar blisters through the air as it smashes into the water, steam sizzling on impact.

''What the... fuck... I can't... I can't believe it... how... how is this real?'' Gordon has a small reality check, seeing and using magic now made all this and what Parinos had said much more believable, in the strangest of ways. However, the question still begged in his weary mind, how does he return home?

''Be careful, casting too much will cause you to suffer an affliction known as magicka exhaustion, which if you overdo yourself it can progress to magicka sickness, you'll feel it drag heavily on your very soul the more magic you use... be mindful to take breaks but you must also practise, meditate and weave the essence. Although, your control is absolutely astounding. You know, manipulating a flame like that takes people well over a decade of training, even they get exhausted by it quite easily.''

''So, anyone can do this?''

''Yes, but magic isn't practised as commonly as you may think, it's very difficult to master. In Darogoth, druids are usually the main bulk of magic practitioners, many druids that don't become advisors train to become what we know as war seers, a battlemage of sorts under druidic influence. You may run into a few magic users from time to time... maybe they can teach you a thing or two. However, you can accomplish much with your kind of power. With magic, you can manipulate your own perceptions and the elements around you, as well as force. I'm showing you this because this is what we needed from you... or should I say what we needed from whatever came through Fanara's Cradle, that now being you. Do you see now, Gordon?''

''As amazing as that is Parinos… I still have to go home,'' Gordon speaks out sadly, still staring in awe at his hand.

''Well Gordon, I don't want to talk down to you, but you're here with us now. Embrace everything around you and yourself in this world, for I feel the only way out is to put yourself to use. Sitting around and crying about it isn't achieving anything now is it? I'm sorry Gordon, I'll try my best to find a way back for you, this I wholeheartedly promise, but in order for me to do that, I need your help too.''

Gordon begins to glum. ''What am I even supposed to do?''

''Nothing my boy, at least not yet. Learn of this place, we shall hold your hand in this world and guide you as much as we can, it's what we druids do. Just remember Gordon, please… think of Camula, I know you didn't know her, but it's her life that this has cost. We will try our best, if you do too.''

Gordon glances down to the floor and gives a subtle nod.

''Now I've shown you what you're capable of, I do ask you to be careful. Magic can be volatile at the best of times, although I trust you in your drenching, you still must learn to control, it doesn't hurt to be overly careful, train, meditate, allow yourself to become one with its flow. Now… speaking of Camula, I'd be honoured if you would join us in seeing her off to our Gods. Of course, if that makes you uncomfortable… you don't have to.''

''No. I'll come,'' Gordon responds fleetly in respect.

Parinos gives a warming smile. ''We'll head to the centre of the village by nightfall, Lucotorix is already making preparations there… and Gordon, I swear by Fanara, we will get through this, together.''

Gordon delivers a hopeful smile, still shackled by the torment of his lost soul.

For the remainder of the day Gordon spends it alone, he plays around with his new found abilities by the river. He would stand by the river's edge moving the water with his magic and casting odd flames here and there to spin around and play with. He also discovered he could manipulate his perception of time, making everything seem to move slower, after his initial use of magic it just seemed to click for him instantly, It really did come naturally, as natural as even breathing.

After a few hours, Gordon started feeling the effects of exhaustion as he tampered with his magic sporadically. It was much like overdoing a physical activity, he became breathless and weak, although he would soon regain his strength.

He was curious how much power and effort he could really put into magic and felt keen on learning more. For the time he decided to stop and sit by the lake to ponder what he'd been through, he wanted to accept this but all he could think about was Helen, his band, he was still trying to make sense of the world and everything around him. His language skills had exploded in just a day, he was almost speaking fluently now, a few mistakes here and there but even his dialect felt natural. His accent remained drastically different to others in comparison. This was all too incredible, he still couldn't believe everything that had happened was real, he was sure he must be dead.

He fumbles around in his pocket to find a cigarette, he hears the crispy noise of a wrapper in his pocket and pulls out the chocolate he bought for Helen from the shop, a single tear streams down his smooth clean-shaven cheek. Would he ever return? He didn't know, but Parinos's words would echo and repeat in his mind.

'Sitting around and crying about it isn't achieving anything now, is it?' And it was true, if there was a way back, he had to find it and Gordon felt a lot more confident, especially now he could cast magic. It changed everything, he had to adapt and overcome it all.

He pulled out his phone, still no signal or data and his battery life was getting lower, forty four percent left. He decided to flick through a few images of his life to reattune his sanity, to hope he wasn't actually dead. He scrolled on, selfies with his friends, with Helen, the holiday they all had in Amsterdam last summer, videos of drunken nights. It was all getting too much for him, he closes his phone down and forcibly pushes it back in his pocket, he gets up and marches his way back to Parinos's house, he grabs the druidic robes Parinos gave to him and decides to put them on, seeing as he stuck out like a sore thumb in this place.

After a few awkward moments of fumbling around with the fastenings and layers, he manages just fine.

Lucotorix and his brother Orthunus arrive at Parinos's house. ''Gordon? You here?''

''Yeah,'' Gordon reveals himself from the bed balcony.

Stunned by his appearance, both Lucotorix and Orthunus freeze in sync. ‘’Wow… look at you! You’re truly one of us now! You look good!’’ The two brothers chuckle amongst each other.

‘’Things have really come on well with him?’’ Says Orthunus.

Orthunus had a similar look to Lucotorix minus the mutton chops and moustache. They could almost be mistaken as twins despite the obvious age difference.

Orthunus had quite an awkward looking moustache with short curly brown hair and a youthful face of puppy fat, his overall appearance and stature would suggest he had only just begun blooming into manhood.

“Oh Gordon, I never introduced you properly, this is my brother, Orthunus,” Lucotorix presents.

Gordon nods in greeting. "Hi."

“A pleasure… Gordon. Lucotorix has told me so much about you today.”

Gordon gives a friendly smile, dimly lit by his dull eyes of emotional drain as he makes his way down the ladder.

‘’Druid Gordon, I love it… let me formally re-welcome you to Seers Crossing, Druid Gordon,” Lucotorix jests.

Gordon Scoffs.

‘’Parinos said you would attend the afterlife ritual for Camula? That’s really good of you, a symbolism like no other, quite beautiful If I say so myself,’’ says Orthunus, quite chirpy in nature.

He was like a softer, more mature version of Lucotorix, despite being younger. He was a happy go lucky kind of fellow, naive and innocent.

''Ignore him, although he's got a point," Lucotorix nudges Orthunus with the end of his elbow.

Gordon noted again how happy these people seem to him. Even in the event of a death they seem relatively unhindered by it emotionally, perhaps it was their way of life, their seemingly obsessive worship of life and death.

Gordon knew of druids in his home world's history but he never knew much of it, in fact, he'd always be brought back to thinking of how the world around him seemed to resemble his world in the past, but the designs of the houses were quite a feat of architecture to seem 'old' in comparison to a traditional Celtic roundhouse, some of the houses weren't even round, some triangular. He did notice there was no sign of electricity, or any modern appliance, the world or at least the area he was in had that Celtic vibe to it, lots of intricate patterns etched in woodwork, robed druids? It was odd to say the least, but there was definitely something that wasn't so Celtic about them, these Gods they spoke of, the furniture in their homes, books? Magic? Something still seemed off.

The three dawdle onward to the village centre toward the statue of Fanara and Iskarien. The sunset illuminated the sky projecting a glorious orange hue upon the horizon, filtered by the stretching of the clouds. A small crowd had gathered around the plinth of the statue, all chatting and drinking, Gordon felt incredibly awkward in the robes, he felt almost insulting.

Parinos notices the three approaching and shuffles toward them. ''My, my… look at you, Gordon.''

Gordon smiles painfully.

''I'm glad you've come, you don't have to do anything, just be here with us, for her….'' Parinos turns respectfully to Camula's lifeless body, placed elegantly on a wooden bed-like structure that mounted the plinth, fixed below the statue.

She was decorated head to toe in flowers, herbs and small trinkets alike. Her face was leathery and pale, her eyes shut tight, it was eerie at first glance, yet the aura around her body danced in a peaceful light.

Gordon watched on mournfully as Lucotorix and Orthunus approached her to pay their respects.

''Is this it?'' A gruff and shaken voice bellows from Parinos's side. Gordon's head diverted away from the enigmatic sight of death to the voice directed upon him.

It was an older man, his eyes so sunken into his sockets that his skull was just barely visible from the transparency of his selfcare. His skin was dirty and his robes stained and murky.

''Excuse me, Albin?'' Replies Parinos, somewhat startled.

''Is this it?! The thing that cost me my daughter's life. Is this a joke?'' Albin replies sternly.

Parinos wasted no time with his honesty. ''Yes, Albin. This is the being that Camula's life brought forward.''

Albin barges past Parinos and stumbles toward Gordon, twisting his face and sucking in his cheeks. ''Bah! A mere man? A skinny one of that, my daughter died… for this!?''

''Albin….'' Parinos pleas for peace.

Albin sways slightly as he turns his glare to Parinos, a single tear trickles down the man's face, racing through the lumps and bumps of his disgraced skin at great speed, he wipes it away just as quickly as it left his tear duct. ''You even dressed him like one of us?'' Albin scoffs as his voice begins to crack.

''I'm sorry, I never wanted this,'' Gordon squeaks.

Albin and Parinos both tilt their heads to Gordon.

Albin marches upto Gordon, pressing his face unto his with a fury burning in his eyes. The stench of poor body odour now very present as it lingers into Gordon's nose forcing him to wince at the unpleasantry.

''Listen, I don't ca-'' Albin halts his words, losing himself in Gordon's crystal blue eyes, his face drops.

In this moment he sways ever so slowly as he stares on, mesmerised. His face slowly shifts from a drunken red to a ghostly white.

Gordon is frozen in fear and confusion. Not knowing what to do, he looks to Parinos for some indication but Parinos too just stands there, watching on.

Albin's eyes begin to well up, tears begin streaming down his blotchy face, the ghostly white reforms back to the intoxicated red it was. He grabs Gordon and pulls him into a clutched squeeze. Gordon wrenches from the smell.

Gordon reluctantly approves the moment; he is aware this man had just lost his daughter and was willing to console him. He humbly welcomes Albin and pats him on the back. ''I'm sorry,'' Gordon whispers in comfort.

Albin breaks down into a gush of tears, muffling out a wail of mourning into Gordon's shoulder.

After a few intense minutes, Albin tugs away, returning his view on Gordon. ''Sorry, I....''

Gordon smiles, giving him a reassuring arm pat as he holds his breath.

Parinos steps in. ''We understand, Albin.''

''No... No... it's, it's....'' Albin points frantically at Gordon.

Parinos steps closer. ''I know.''

Albin rears his head to the sky. ''By the light of our lady and the shadow of Iskarien, please, please be worth all of this,'' he gives a forced smile to Gordon and promptly wanders off back toward his daughter's body, still looking back over his shoulder to Gordon every second or so with a curious expression painting his face.

''What was that all about? Is everything okay?'' Says Lucotorix, who had witnessed the event from a short distance.

''Everything's fine, he's distraught, Lucotorix. He's just working out his emotions in relation to Gordon, that's all. We must allow him to validate himself in these troubled times,'' says Parinos. ''We'll begin shortly.''

Gordon, still quite taken back by Albin, couldn't help but feel such pity and guilt for the man. Albin's soulless stare remained imprinted in Gordon's mind. This was a face he'd probably never forget; the intensity of that stare had seethed into him greatly. He gives out a breathy sigh, rubbing his face and stretching back his eyes, still subconsciously trying to make sense of all of this.

As Gordon tagged around Lucotorix and Orthunus, he couldn't help but notice the gapes he was getting from the other druids. They would whisper amongst themselves whenever Gordon was nearby, they would double take a glance, their faces blank, others more screwed up. It made him feel even more uncomfortable and exposed.

He felt responsible for taking Camula's life, although in reality he did nothing to her, let alone even know her. He felt the other druids had some form of grudge for him. He thought that they must be disappointed in him for not being what they expected him to be. He felt alone, the only simmer of comfort he felt was when he was with Lucotorix, Orthunus and Parinos.

Parinos took a stance in front of Camula's rest. ''Druids of Seers Crossing! Gather around, gather around!''

The druids shuffle around all with their heads fixed on Parinos, Albin rises and stands aside as does Lucotorix. Gordon hides away at the back of the crowd with Orthunus.

‘’Today is the day we say our final goodbye to a fellow druid, a druid whose enthusiasm for herbalism, magic, and devotion to our beloved Gods was embraced and loved by all who reside here within Seers Crossing. Camula here, gave her life for a cause. The cause though uncertain… Is yet to be fulfilled. She gave her life as a druid for her people, for our Gods. To spiral our efforts in our favour to continue to live under the love of Fanara. In years to come, if we still stand here as druids of Fanara, then it was all because of this young lady here. For she gave her life in hopes we can continue ours,’’ Parinos lowers his head.

Albin could be heard sniffling profusely. Other people amongst the crowd could be heard sobbing faintly, quite similar to a funeral in Gordon's home world.

‘’Camula Ard-Garrius. Daughter of Albin Ard-Garrius will join her mother, Aoife Fen-Garrius to be embraced by our lady. Iskarien has cast her shadow upon you and Fanara guide your soul into a new life amidst the endless void, Camula.’’

A shiver shudders through Gordon’s spine.

‘’Fanara guide you,’’ the druids shouted out in unison and in absolute passion.

‘’Fanara guide you….’’ Gordon whispered under his breath in respect.

Orthunus smiled to himself upon overhearing him.

The druids began moving around and shuffling about, Gordon stood awkwardly, still trying to cling onto Orthunus's side.

''You,'' Albin's voice bellows from across the crowd.

Gordons' head snaps up, slightly frightened by the spotlight now hanging over him in front of all the druids.

''Will you help me… please?'' Said Albin to Gordon, gesturing toward the wooden structure that Camula lay upon.''

Gordon's eyes widened in shock.

Parinos also froze on the spot.

Gordon dawdled carefully toward Albin. ''Yeah… I'll help.''

With a few other druids, Albin and Parinos pick up the structure that Camula lay on, they wriggle it off from the plinth, Gordon makes his way around, being signalled by Albin where to go.

After a small count, six of them lift the structure together. Parinos and Albin both at the front and Gordon positioned at the back.

The druids move to create a formation behind those carrying Camula and walk steadily alongside each other. The ones carrying Camula lead the formation all the way to the end of the village by the river. There was a large platform set up just for Camula in which she was to be placed on top of, a pyre of sorts.

Gordon couldn't believe what he was doing and was very surprised Albin had even asked him to help carry his daughter, but he soldiered on for Albin's sake, regardless of his own concerns. Gordon had always been a respectable man.

They placed Camula atop the pyre and stood back. Albin grabbed Gordon by the arm dragging him afront, Gordon was now starting to feel very uneasy about Albins handling. He glanced once more into Gordon's eyes, staring on for an uncomfortable amount of time. He gives Gordon a single pat on the shoulder and ruffles his hair until turning to Parinos, who was holding a torch he had infused with his magic.

Albin takes the torch. ''Goodbye, my girl. I love you; I'll always love you. Soon our souls will meet in the aether of life and death, and we'll never lose each other again. Thank you… thank you for being the perfect daughter to a broken man. Fanara guides you my dear,'' he breaks down erratically as he tosses down the torch in total despair, mourning the loss of his only child, his daughter.

Everyone takes a step back as they watch the flames grow and grow into a whirling inferno, the crackling and roar of the engulfing flames snap violently off the gentle blow of the wind, Consuming the body of Camula Ard-Garrius, Druid of Seers Crossing.

7: Investigation

Middlesbrough.

Twenty-four hours had come and gone and there was still no sign of Gordon, his phone still wasn't receiving calls and he still had not turned up anywhere. Helen was quick to get in contact with the police like she had done multiple times in desperate efforts to try and get their help. Eventually, after a painful and anticipating wait, they came to take details about Gordon and his mysterious disappearance.

Helen gave them every inch of detail they needed to know, many things, like the fact he wasn't in debt with anyone, he had no 'enemies' and that he was happy with his life and didn't really have a valid reason to go missing at all.

She explained that he was at a bar with work colleagues on the day he disappeared and how it was completely out of the ordinary for him to just vanish without saying a word. She also mentioned how they found camera footage of him the night he disappeared and found some strange things that might help aid the investigation. The police took their notes and went on their way. They scoured through the CCTV and turned the park upside down in their efforts to search for the missing young man.

Even at the start of this missing persons case, the police were left stumped by the oddities.

Noticing the strange black grass and the cigarette resting beside it, they decided to send samples to the forensics team. In the meantime, they would begin interviews with all the people who knew Gordon in an attempt to connect someone to a reason as to why he'd vanished and how.

Helen reached out to Gordon's parents. Weronika, his mother who was currently in Poland caring for his grandmother, and William, his father. The two had been separated for many years but had always been on civil terms. Before meeting Helen, Gordon lived with his father when his grandmother became ill with dementia, forcing Weronika to move over and take full care of her.

Upon hearing the news of her son's disappearance, although shocked and very clearly concerned, she was sure Gordon would be somewhere safe and would turn up soon. She told Helen she had to remain in Lask until further news.

His father took the news just about the same. He was a little worried but was certain Gordon would show up soon but as Helen described what she had found since his disappearance William's voice became evermore weakened by concern.

Dan had informed the band of what happened.

The band decided to have a meeting about the situation and all agreed to meet at Mickey's Bar during the day, to seat themselves down to a casual pint.

Dan entered the bar to find Jeb already sitting alone, waiting. The bar was rather empty aside from a few regulars here and there, he promptly orders a pint and joins him.

''Where's Pete? Wasn't he coming?'' Asks Jeb, lifting his head to Dan.

''He said he was… I'll give him a ring in a sec,'' Dan replies as he slumps down on a crooked stool.

''Any news then?'' Jeb asks in concern.

''No mate. Let's wait for Pete first, yeah?''

''Fair enough… honestly mate… I don't get it….''

''Yeah Jeb, no one does. It's-''

Pete barges through the main door with a ghostly look on his face. Dan and Jeb's heads both dart over to see Pete, looking rather unhinged. ''Lads!'' He shouts.

The whole bar snaps to his highlighted entrance. Noticing this, he immediately reforms his demeanour.

''Pete?! What's up?'' Dan rises.

Pete scurries to the table. ''Lads….'' he leans in whispering loudly. ''The fucking police!''

Dan and Jeb share a glance as their ears prick up. ''Have they found something?!'' Ask's Dan.

''No! Thankfully Ian had the gear moved before I let them in… could have sworn I was about to get done. Honestly, never come so close to actually shitting myself.''

Dan shakes his head as he slumps back into his stool. ‘’For fucks sake Pete. Gordon!’’

‘’Yeah, I know! I was getting to that! They just wanted to interview me about him. Asking me all sorts of questions.’’

‘’You prick. Did it go well?’’

‘’Standard as anything… they just asked me when I last saw him, what my relationship with him was like. You know, all that malarkey. You two heard anything yet?’’

‘’No… I haven’t heard anything from Helen,’’ Dan replies, his face reflecting his exhaustion on the situation.

‘’Same mate, I've heard nothing,’’ says Jeb.

‘’What the fuck boys. What the fuck!?’’ Pete rubs the back of his neck vigorously as he grits his teeth in angst.

‘’Sit down Pete man. You’re making me anxious,’’ moans Jeb.

Pete slides a stool out from under the table, plonking himself down.

‘’You not getting a drink?’’ Asks Dan.

‘’No mate, not in the mood.’’

‘’Wow….’’

‘’So, what’s the crack then? What do we do?’’ Says Jeb.

‘’Well, we obviously need to find a bassist for the gig on Friday…’’ scoffs Pete.

Jeb rests his elbow on the table, palm to his face. ''I know… I feel like shit even talking about this. It's not right replacing Gordon like this… but what are we going to do? We can't miss this gig.''

Dan takes a long sip of his pint and slams it down on the coaster. ''I know what you mean man. It's not right… but come on. This is literally a once in a lifetime opportunity. With a bit of luck, he may show up before then, but we obviously need a backup.''

Jeb snaps back his posture. ''Dan… I know, but we can't just do it without him….''

''What else can we do?! He'd only kick us for not doing it, he'd want us too.''

''You sure?! It's a big thing for him to miss, mate.'' Pete adds.

''Of course it is. It's also a big thing for all of us to miss, at the end of the day mate, if he turns up after the gig, he's still in the band! We're not kicking him out! We just need a temp for the day just in case he doesn't show up by then… doesn't hurt to be prepared.''

''Okay… yeah,'' Jeb begins to reason with Dan's words.

''Hope to fucking God he's okay though, boys,'' Pete mumbles.

Jeb peers down his pint sorrowfully. ''Aye….''

The three all give a sigh of discontent, worrying for the safety of their good friend.

Jeb lifts his head slowly, his red fringe flops back onto his face. ''We're doing this for Gordon, not without him.''

Pete gives a soft smile of respect. ''Yeah man!'' He gives Jeb a brisk slap on the shoulder. ''So… Dan, what is it you said you and Hel found? Black grass?''

''Yeah! Weird fucking grass, looked burnt at first but when you pick it up it's just… black? On the cameras he's seen walking in that direction as well… proper weird.''

''Guessing you didn't see much on the cameras?'' Asks Jeb.

''Actually… yeah… a weird flash of light.''

Pete leans forward in interest. ''Okay….''

The three share an eerie silence amongst themselves as they all glance at one another.

''A… flash? He couldn't have been… shot?! Could he?'' Jeb suggests.

''In this country?! Come on mate,'' scoffs Pete.

''You never know! Gun crimes do happen!''

Dan folds his arms as he himself ponders. ''Maybe… I don't know lads. You need to see it for yourselves. Look… I filmed it.''

Jeb's face lights up. ''You what?!''

''Yep. I got it on my phone. Here, look,'' Dan opens his phone and skims over to the videos he had stored. He produces footage of Gordon in the park. Jeb and Pete lean in to watch eagerly.

''See, there he is… walking in… now we switch to the other camera here… now he stops… he's looking at something… and then,'' they all watch as Gordon walks out of frame, the light in the corner of the footage brightens to a flash.

Jeb and Pete jump back to their seats. ''Woah, fuck!'' They both exhale in shock.

''Okay… now I need a fucking drink,'' Pete wastes no time making his way to the bar.

''Exactly. It's weird, too weird,'' Dan responds.

Jebs' eyes darted around, searching for an explanation in his head. ''I'm stumped mate… and he's just gone after that?''

''Yeah, that is literally the last place, the last known possible thing about him. This was literally the last time anyone had heard or saw of him. Few hours later, Hel rings me asking where he is because he hadn't shown up at home.''

Jeb shakes his head in frustration and confusion.

Pete returns. ''Call me mad, but I have a theory and don't laugh! I'm being serious.''

''Aw, here we go, go on….'' Jeb's eyes narrow.

''What if… what if… it's….'' Pete takes a moment to find a way to release his words without sounding crazy. ''Aliens… an abduction! I'm sorry boys! but that's too fucking weird! None of that looked natural!''

To Pete's surprise, Dan and Jeb's faces didn't even inch.

‘’At this point mate. I’m not even going to deny that possibility,’’ groans Dan.

‘’I’ve heard all sorts about abductions… that dude in America that went missing for like a week?’’ Jeb leans into the table. ‘’Same kind of shit as well! Weird lights… a flash with no explanation, no trace of him… it’s all too similar, especially after watching that.’’

‘’Can’t fucking believe we’re all sat here talking about this shit,’’ Dan says as he slaps his hand across his face.

‘’I know man, but you have to admit… it’s too much of a coincidence!’’ Pete says sternly.

Pete was always known to be quite eccentric and wacky, even paranoid, most would say it was the drugs, he was quite a heavy user, but for those who’ve known this metal faced man the most, they’d just call him Pete.

But for once his weird ramblings and suggestions actually made some sense to the boys. They didn’t want to believe it, but they had no idea what to believe. They sat and drank a few more pints together before leaving the bar. The search for a temporary bassist for Friday's gig would begin.

Sat at home, constantly watching her phone, yet always attempting not to, was Helen. Her eyes kept fixating on her phone, always glancing over, always hoping.

Helen had invited her long-term friend Emily to come stay with her and support her during this hard time. Emily was the polar opposite of Helen yet they were the best of friends. She was a 'girly' girl always dressed colourful and was all about the 'girls' nights' her makeup always pristine, her fashion always to date. She was loving and supportive just as Helen was. Whenever Emily was around, she'd always have Gordons friends ogling her and giving badly attempted pick up lines with awkward small talk to win over this brunette beauty.

As the two sit idly on the sofa, Helen's phone rings. The two stand up just as quickly as each other.

''Hello?!'' Helen's voice squeaks.

''Miss Bainbridge?'' A professional sounding voice responds on the other end of the line.

''Yes, speaking.''

''Just updating you on our investigation on your partner, Gordon Barker?''

''Have you found something?!''

''It's quite complicated actually, the cigarette does in fact have traces of his DNA on it. It contains remnants of his saliva and the prints on the filter do match those of the items you provided. The grass however… it's hard to explain, the forensic team cannot pick up anything unusual about the grass that would indicate anything sinister towards Gordon's disappearance.''

''I don't understand? It's black… that isn't normal.''

''Yes, correct… but on closer examination, the properties of the grass are completely normal. there isn't even any pigmentation of the ‘blackness’ through a microscope. It's quite unusual, so we don’t think this is any of our concern.’’

Helen gulps back a plethora of disappointment. ‘’But isn’t it a coincidence that the grass is discoloured and is near his last known location?’’

Emily tilt’s her head at Helen’s conversation as she attempts to listen in.

‘’I’m sorry Miss Bainbridge, we can’t answer that right now, we will however consult other professionals on this matter.’’

‘’Is there anything else?’’

‘’Yes actually, we have made some attempts at tracking his phone. Our systems allow us to track the phone of an individual even when the battery is gone… but… we have had no luck. It’s almost as if he doesn’t even own a phone according to our system… but he is on the database as being the owner of this ID, so we are unsure what is happening there. However, we can confirm the cigarette we found was his, so this was definitely the last location he was known to be at, and our team now have a ground to go off.’’

‘’Yeah… thanks,’’ she rolls her eyes.

‘’We will continue our investigation thoroughly and will update you as soon as we can.’’

‘’Okay….’’

‘’We do have a support team that could help you in these trying times, would you like the number for them?’’

‘’No… thanks….’’

‘’I understand you’re distressed and we are incredibly sorry. If you need any support please get in touch.’’

‘’Okay….’’

‘’Goodbye Miss Bainbridge, have a nice day.’’

Helen hangs up without responding.

‘’Well, the police are fucking useless,’’ she tosses her phone sluggishly to the sofa.

Emily perks up from her slouch. ‘’What did they say?’’ She leans in toward Helen intently.

Helen gives a belated sigh. ‘’Basically, just to confirm that the cig on the floor was his… oh and their shitty system can’t even track his phone,’’ she exclaims in utter frustration.

‘’That’s it? What about the grass?’’

‘’They don’t think there’s a connection.’’

‘’Strange….’’

‘’I know!! Oh Emily… I want to rip my hair out.’’

Emily shuffles over to Helen and consoles her. ‘’They’ll find him! Just let them do their job!’’

‘’Don’t say that… I don't like this Em… something’s not right. I think something bad has happened, I know it!’’

‘’Don’t think like that Helen! I know it must be so unbelievably hard for you, but you need to stay positive. You’re going to drive yourself insane!’’

As Helen stares longingly over Emily’s shoulder thinking of all the things that could have happened to Gordon, her eyes begin to swell and glisten as her chin jitters like a child who’d dropped an ice cream. She breaks.

‘’Helen!’’ Emily brings Helen back into her caring hold.

‘’I can’t believe this, Em! He’s gone! He’s fucking gone! Where is he!?! Where?! I can’t take it! I can’t!’’

‘’Helen, Helen! I'm here, okay. I'm here! I'm not going to leave this house until he’s found,’’ Emily strokes Helen’s hair. ‘’Just let them do their job… we’ve done all we can, okay?’’

‘’I just don’t understand! I don’t get it!’’

‘’None of us do! It’s fucking horrible! I know!’’

Helen pulls herself away, sniffing away the mucus of her nose. ‘’I swear to God… I will find whoever’s hurt him,’’ she begins to pace. ‘’But why?!? What's he done?! Everyone loves Gordon!’’

‘’Are you sure he doesn’t owe anyone money or something?’’

‘’I swear Emily! We share our money in the joint account, I know how much he gets with his wage and where he bloody spends it! He smokes a little bit of weed… but he buys it from Pete. He doesn’t owe Pete anything and I know he doesn’t dabble in other kinds of drugs.’’

‘’Are you… sure?’’

''Emily....''

''I'm just saying! He might of been hiding something from you...''

''Well, if he has, he's done a good job. He's terrible at hiding anything,'' she collapses back into the sofa, weary of pacing.

Emily gives a sigh.

Helen does the same. ''I don't know... I'm going to try and look through his things... I've been stopping myself from going through his messages and stuff because I'm not like that... but....''

''But you need to do what you can to make sure he's safe. Don't the police have access to his social media and stuff?''

''They do... but they haven't said anything, yet.''

''It's worth a look, Helen. Just do it.''

Helen gives a small indication of agreement to Emily.

The longer Gordon was gone, the more Helen's mind became haunted by uncertainty. The idea of sinister things happening to him, had he been robbed? Kidnapped? Had he run away with someone? Had he killed himself? Had he been killed by someone else? Emily was right, she was driving herself insane.

8: The Oathsworn

''In the days of old during the age of the Gods, the continent of Uros was a very different place, for Darogoth was naught but an unsettled haven.

Fanara resided west within The Glade and Iskarien in the south, in what we now know as one of Darogoths modern day provinces, Dun. To the north in Venethar, the dreaded God Ushkaru festered with her Var'kesh, a ferocious matriarchal horned folk, hellbent on power through strength and conquest.

Aside from Ushkaru, the two Gods, Fanara and Iskarien, had a bond like that of sisters, both representing the same principles, yet on completely different spectrums. Where Fanara would shine light, Iskarien would cast her darkness, for without darkness, there was no light. Where Fanara gifted the breath of life, Iskarien would embellish the sweet release of death. The sisters of the cycle.

The two shared a mutual love and respect for the magic of the world and the life it inhabited, they welcomed Uros the cycle of the void. Fanara guided her elves, whilst Iskarien led the mountainous human tribes of Dun. The rest of Darogoth was a haven of life and death, where it would start and end as naturally as the world allowed. The forests were lush and the rivers ran a plenty, by the two Gods' law, no man or elf would settle upon

Darogoth for it was the sacred hunting ground of their peoples, a place where nature happens, a place in between life and death.

Trouble from the north would always upset the balance, Ushkaru took advantage of the sacred haven. She would send her Var'kesh south, burning the forests and culling the animals within the lands out of spite, using it as an advantage against Fanara and Iskarien in an attempt to invade their respective homelands, for years the two Gods attempted to hold out from the almighty force of Ushkaru, but her power was far too formidable.

One fateful day, a series of events would change everything. Men and women came to Darogoth fleeing a terror from the neighbouring island of Osforth, washed up ashore in what is now known as the province of Ard, The elves found and held the pitiful humans captive for Fanara's judgement, Fanara however was always more lenient than her loyal elves, it was this judgment that forged the foundations of the Kingdom of Darogoth from the days of old. Fanara granted these humans land in Darogoth, so long as they held a promise to help protect it from the Var'kesh. Over the years they held true to their promise to Fanara, fighting alongside her and Iskarien, eventually coming to worship them both as their own Gods. They would even interbreed with the tribes of Dun, flourishing the human race on southern and eastern Darogoth.

As the fighting went on, Fanara and Iskarien decided now was time to end the law of the sacred lands and formally granted it to the humans who had spread out and amassed a large population, forming the provinces of Glaen, Ard, Fen and Dun. United, they became the Kingdom of Darogoth.

Although now all forces had a strong footing to keep the Var'kesh at bay, they never were successful. Ushkaru devastated much in her path of destruction, Glaen was nothing but a military front, populated by elves and men holding out for their dear lives until yet again another great change would befall the lands.

More humans would land ashore, this time in Venethar, these were the nomads of Kuria, led ashore by their very own God, Vistra. A man whose appearance took the form of the night sky. A walking void in the shape of man that glistened with the beauty of the stars, they fell right into the heart of Var'keshi lands, and their steps were painted in blood.

This time it was Ushkaru's lands and people whose balance was to be offset. The Glade and Darogoth saw their chance and launched a full-scale invasion, a bloody campaign lasting many years, the Var'kesh were being attacked by all sides.

The elves of the Glade in the west, humans from Darogoth in the south, and now even more humans from the eastern shores of their own home. With the combined power of Vistra, Iskarien and Fanara, they brought down Ushkaru and sent her people fleeing for their lives, with Vistra personally ripping Ushkaru's horns from her head, creating the legendary war horns of Kasidor that sit atop the castle to this very day.

From that moment onward, the three Gods formed a pact upon the spire of Oldwood in Glaen, a pact of unity, the pact of Uros. Peace befell the lands for many years to come, until the day our Gods were taken from us.

– Ulderin Dun-Formus, Arch Druid of Seers Crossing. Year 2AB 12 – The Ancient History of Uros.

''Please, there has to be a way home, where are you?!'' Gordon's voice echoes into the peerless void.

Nothing responds.

''You said there was an answer?! Please. Helen will be fucking distraught; I've been gone for days now!'' He begins to cry.

A powerful gust of wind ejects from above his head down onto him, a beaming light flashing woefully like an erratic storm. ''I can't… sometimes it's….''

''What! What?! For God's sake, just fucking tell me!''

''You need to keep… control.''

''Please, just try,'' he whimpers.

''He's dying….''

''Who's dying?! What the fuck am I supposed to do about that?! Does this mean I can't get back home?!

''I need you to calm yourself Gordon, I can't reach you like this,'' the voice echoes, becoming quieter as it tries to continue speaking.

''No… no!'' He screams at the top of his voice. ''Come back! COME BACK TO ME!''

Gordon rises from his bed in terror. ''Come back! COME BACK!''

Lucotorix, who was down the ladder eating, jumped out of his skin upon hearing Gordon's screams. ''Shit! Gordon are you okay?''

Realising he was dreaming again; Gordon wipes the sweat dripping down his forehead ''What... no?'' He gasps.

Lucotorix races up the ladder, ''It's okay my friend, another bad dream,'' he holds himself on the ladder as he peers over to Gordon.

''Lucotorix, Luke... I'm sorry, they're so vivid....'' Gordon struggles to get his breath.

''Catch your breath, Gordon, then we can go have a smoke, that'll calm you down? Yeah?''

''Aye,'' he replies.

''I'll wait outside for you, maybe you can try some of the herbs I smoke? They're good!''

Gordon nods as he continues to wipe down his forehead giving a thumbs up in the process.

Out of curiosity as he's done every morning, he checks his phone, still no signal, or data, no messages, nothing. His battery was low, now at only seven percent.

''Still here....'' he silently mutters.

He had reframed from using his phone as much as he could to preserve its battery life, in case it started receiving a reception. Seeing the percentage run further down each time was making him feel more conscious of the fact he was not going home any time soon.

He gives a heavy sigh as he reaches for his robes to join Lucotorix outside. It had rained through the night, enhancing the dew that sparkled throughout the village.

''I have a gift for you, I made it myself,'' Lucotorix proudly proclaims.

Gordon glances at Lucotorix curiously as he places one of his cigarettes in his mouth.

Lucotorix produces a wooden smoking pipe with impressive little weaving patterns etched into the handle.

Gordon takes out his cigarette in astonishment. ''Wow… you made this?''

''Well yeah, I know how much you love to smoke and I thought since this was how we got bonding in the first place it would make a good gift, just a little something to make you feel more welcome. I know you're going through alot in that head of yours, it's silly… but I noticed you're running low on your otherworldly… cigs? Figured it might be time to take up Darogothic smoking now….''

Gordon takes the pipe, inspecting and appreciating the craftsmanship. ''Luke… thanks… this is really cool,'' he chuckles gleefully. ''Aye… you're right, I have about six left actually… I even started smoking from the pack I got for Helen.''

''I'm sure she'd understand,'' laughed Lucotorix.

''Hah… yeah,'' Gordon's face returns to a blank stance.

Lucotorix reaches into his satchel. ''Here, try these. Put them in your pipe, light them and puff away. They burn really slow so you don't have to keep lighting like most smokable herbs.''

''What is it? Will it make me high or something?''

''No… they are herbs, we call it rust. It's the crushed stem from the rustos reed from the river, you crush it in a pestle and mortar and add del flower nectar, then you dry it out for an hour and leave it out for about a week or so and it creates a smokable compound. It's good for you, we give it to our warriors as part of their rations but they get the chewable version which is easier to produce. It calms the nerves; this one doesn't make you high like the ones the warriors get… theirs has other ingredients involved.''

''Ahh, so it's like shit weed?''

''Shit weed? Is that a herb from your world?''

''Yeah… sure,'' Gordon gives a strained giggle.

''I'd like to try some shit weed, especially if it's similar to rust,'' smiles Lucotorix innocently.

Gordon chuckles to himself as he lights the pipe conjuring a tiny flame in the bowl from his hand, putting his magic to good use.

''Where's Parinos?'' Asks Gordon.

''He's giving a induction to some of the newer members of the village.'' Lucotorix pauses for a moment as his eyes whisk around at the sky. ''Oh yeah… I'm going to show you some herbalism today if that's okay with you? Take you into the forest and show you what we do, Orthunus is going to join us too. Trust me, herbalism is a skill you can't pass up, especially with the benefits it can reap, you can make potions to heighten senses, lower senses, cure ailments, create useful compounds and so much more! I don't want to make your head explode but I thought it would do you some good to get out after days of being stuck in with Parinos learning words and reading books all day long.''

''Sure, sounds good.'' he responds lightly. ''Wish there was some kind of herb that would charge my fucking phone,'' he jokingly mumbles.

''Sorry?''

''My phone… it's dying.''

''Dying?''

''Sorry… I mean it's running out of energy, power… charge?'' Gordon produces his phone from his satchel.

''Oh, that thing… why don't you use magic?''

Gordon's eyes widened. ''You think I could?''

''It's an idea… you said it requires energy? Magic is a form of energy, is it not?''

''Would you be able to give it a try?'' Asks Gordon.

‘’Gordon, I have no idea what that thing is, I don’t want to break it, I know how important it is to you.’’

Gordon stares at his phone for a second, thinking.

Clamping his pipe in his mouth, he removes the battery and grips it within his right hand, he focuses for a second, feeling the weave of the atmosphere. He feels the power inside the battery almost like it has a weight. A spark flickers and snaps from his hand and attacks the battery at great speed, feeling the power encase itself within, he stops his magic out of caution and places the battery back in the phone, he turns it on.

Lucotorix looks on in intrigue.

The phone turns on, sixty seven percent.

‘’Fuck me! It worked?!’’ Gordon screeches in surprise.

Lucotorix laughs at Gordon’s expressive words.

‘’Luke, you fucking genius.’’

‘’Hey, I’m not the arch druid’s apprentice for nothing now.’’

Gordon chuckles but quickly suppresses his delight upon a constant subconscious reminder that he is stuck in this world, an awkward silence falls flat amongst the two.

Lucotorix rises from his seat on the rough outdoor bench that rests against the house. ‘’Let's go find that little brother of mine and get going, yes?’’

Gordon gives a lazy nod as he puts his phone back in his satchel and rises with Lucotorix.

The two walk over, swerving through the many roundhouses, flower beds and herb patches that are scattered across the village, all the way over to where Orthunus lived.

Orthunus lived with two other druids of similar age, Lucotorix rattled the door a couple of times. ''Brother! You in? Come, we're heading out,'' some noises can be heard coming from inside, the sounds of many objects rattling and clanking, suddenly the door bursts open with an eager Orthunus, looking scraggly and worn. ''Lazing around for once, are we? Well… this is new.''

''Sorry brother, I was drinking with the others last night, I feel awful today.''

''Drinking? You? Well, you are growing up after all. Don't make a habit of it, Parinos will have both our heads,'' Lucotorix responds with a mischievous grin.

''Not to worry, so… what's the plan again? Showing Gordon the world of herbalism?''

''Exactly that, show him the basics, let him get a grip of the world and what it is we druids do and since we're starting with the basics maybe we could brew up a potion for that hangover of yours, eh?''

Orthunus chuckles. ''Perfect!''

''Come now,'' Lucotorix signals.

The three venture out of the village a short walk away into the density of the nearby surrounding forest, the forest is remarkably thick and full of all kinds of life, Gordon notices small animals similar to that of his home, rabbits, voles, pheasant, was everything so similar, how could this be another world? He took note of the flora as he dawdled, many of it looked alien and strange yet others looked remarkably familiar, as he trudged through the shrubs he noticed a little rat-like creature squeak and scurry by his feet, shocked by the creature, he jumps, It wasn't a rat, It looked like some form of small dog with a large puffy mane but with a rat's head? ''The fuck was that?!'' He yells.

''That was a ferin. Don't worry, they're harmless, they make good pies,'' laughs Lucotorix in jest of Gordons fright.

After a few steps forward, Lucotorix stops in his tracks and scans the area. ''Here, there's a small weed that grows underneath the many rocks, given a certain time and temperature, we call it 'dry marsh' since it resembles a marshy moss, but you'll see it has a stem also, quite a unique plant. It plays a vital part in most of our concoctions.''

Gordon seemed perplexed at the descriptions Lucotorix was giving, Orthunus rolls over a large boulder nearby as Lucotorix watches on, the boulder gives a thunderous thud as it flattens out on its back, a flurry of insect's scurry from the exposure, scuttling around frantically.

Orthunus grabs his sickle that was sitting on his belt and begins scraping through the other greenery and mud. ''Dry marsh tends to bury itself underneath, just a few inches down. I think this one is barely a sapling… you can usually see its leaves poking out from the rock. Once the dry marsh reaches maturity its leaves escape from underneath the rock to start taking in the light to deliver back to the root, before it matures it relies solely on nutrients provided by the insects, you know, excrement and such…. Hmmm,'' Orthunus rises back up, rubbing his chin, appearing as if he was looking around for something. ''Ah! This one,'' he finds a smaller rock with some spiky leaves jutting out from the bottom. ''Here, Gordon, look.''

Gordon bends down to give a closer look at the leaves.

''Those are the leaves, that means this one is quite mature,'' Lucotorix adds.

''Here, Gordon. Take my sickle,'' Orthunus hands Gordon his sickle, a crescent shaped tool made for reaping flora, a tool all druids are given and use often. ''Now come down with me, and move the rock.'' Orthunus and Gordon both lift the rock out of the way. ''Notice how the stem comes from beneath the dirt? Dig it up a bit… not too vigorously mind… we don't want to ruin it.'' Orthunus aids Gordons inexperienced hand in moving the bits of plant matter and dirt. Eventually, a small green moss presents itself, it looked like any other moss that grows just about anywhere, but was certainly different.

It had its own bulb that it was sprouting from, not only that, the moss had a weird looking consistency, Gordon's face scrunched at the sight.

Lucotorix leans over like a teacher watching his students. ''Now all we have to do is shave off some of the moss, but not all of it. We don't want to kill off the plant, if we take all the moss away from the bulb, it withers and dies. We usually take a small amount and move on to the next when we collect this stuff, we only collect it from mature growths, the younger ones don't produce the correct alchemical base that is required for usage and dry marsh is impossible to keep allotted, so we always have to go out into the forest to get it.''

Gordon nods despite not really knowing anything about herbalism as he carefully shaves off some of the mossy growth from the plant, collecting a handful to present to the two.

''Yep, now you place it in the herb pouch and you're done,'' smiles Orthunus.

''Wait… then what?'' Lucotorix adds, testing his little brother.

Orthunus's eyes search for an answer then quickly return to his brother's judging gaze. ''We replace the dirt and the rock!''

''Good, little brother. We always leave dry marsh as we found it, otherwise it may not grow back.''

Gordon looked confused. ''I'm not the best gardener, but why is it so hard to keep allotted? Why does it die if its leaves are already getting its nutrients at maturity?''

''It's the bulb of the plant, the bulb relies on darkness and condensation, as well as the natural work of the insects around, when it matures the leaves gather separate nutrients that aid in giving the moss its alchemical property when everything is mixed up. It's a sensitive plant, but that's as far as our knowledge goes, it seems to just kill itself when we try to farm it and we don't know why… so the best option is to collect it from the wild and aid it to regrow.''

''I see… so this is what's used in potions and stuff?'' Gordon replies.

''Not all of our potions, but definitely the most useful.''

''What like?''

''Well, we use dry marsh in a concoction for wound treatment, if you sear a wound shut with heat and then apply a dry marsh mix on top, you get an astounding healing effect, it fights infection and it's also used to cure some illnesses, headaches, belly aches, constipation… they all have different names and mixes and we'll eventually get into that, but yeah… dry marsh is the generic base of it.''

''Cool….'' Gordon replies slightly disinterested but kindly keen to learn.

''So, Gordon. Can I rely on you to search around for some more dry marsh? I'll gather some yellow selanis and blue selanis, Orthunus could you get some stritchen?

''Sure,'' Gordon replies.

''You keep hold of the sickle for now Gordon, you'll need it for dry marsh, it's a lot rougher and more finicky than stritchen, I can just pick that with my hands,'' says Orthunus.

The three continue to search throughout the small grove, Gordon finds success in finding a few handfuls of dry marsh and really felt this was a lot easier to do than Lucotorix's long winded explanations made it seem. Lucotorix was collecting yellow and blue selanis, a sort of sap produced by some of the local trees, Orthunus had the hardest job of the three, looking for stritchen, a grey grass not entirely rich in the area they had chosen to forage in, nor was it largely abundant in Darogoth at all, but without a problem Orthunus eventually found a small patch of stritchen by a murky overgrowth just a way off from where they were foraging.

The whole ordeal of looking for herbs felt quite peaceful for Gordon, herbalism or any kind of botany was never in his interests but it helped distract him from his despair for those small precious moments.

The three would converse and throw banter at one another, specifically Lucotorix and Orthunus being the brothers they are. Gordon would try to join in with the jokes and laughter but always found himself holding back from even having the slightest bit of fun, all Gordon wanted to do was go home, most of the time all he could think about was Helen, his band mates and family. He wondered if they were searching for him, what they were going through.

His head felt like it could burst at times with the amount of stress that would bleed into his mind, to combat it he had to keep himself busy, there was nothing else he could do. Having the sudden ability of magic was definitely somewhat distracting for him, it was incredibly mind blowing to say the least, but even still, It was never enough. If anything, being aware of his magical prowess made him feel more like he could actually be dead, it was just too bizarre for him to comprehend.

After an hour, Lucotorix calls them all back together, he tells them they are to return to the arch druid's home and prepare some basic mixtures, and so they return back to Seers Crossing with their herb pouches fat and full to the brim.

''So then, we have what we need. Very basic stuff but it's the good stuff! Still got that headache Orthunus?'' He pelts Orthunus's head with a wooden spoon he found lying on a nearby table.

''Ow! Bastard… yes!''

''Good, then we can start with a little hangover cure. Orthunus, could you refill the cauldron quickly? Gordon, would you do the honours of lighting the fire underneath?'' Lucotorix says cheerfully.

''Parinos doesn't want me using magic in the house whilst I'm still learning,'' Gordon remarks.

''Ahh… it'll be fine, you have a good grasp of your control, I've seen you do it… go on, I'll take the blame if it all goes to shit.''

Gordon shrugs, the nature of his care for everything slowly seeping away.

Orthunus returns with some water and adds it to the cauldron. ''There we go.''

''Thanks, brother.'' Lucotorix smiles, turning his gaze back on Gordon signalling him to light the fire.

Gordon reluctantly approaches the cauldron's base and stretches out his hand to the fire bowl beneath, he takes a deep breath and focuses, feeling the power within. The invisible force gathers to his being like a glass of water being filled to the brim, he forces out his magic with as much precision as he could.

A small crackle ripples from the palm of his hand onto the fire bowl, igniting the fire and slightly blowing outwards to the other side. ''Shit! Shit, that was a tad too much!'' He panics as he subdues the flame.

Lucotorix laughs. ''It's fine Gordon, it's not like the house is on fire!''

''Wow, he really does have this amount of power?'' Orthunus comments, looking on in amazement. ''You did that with such ease? I start feeling faint emitting a mere candle flame… I've been practising since I was ten.''

''I told you!'' Replies Lucotorix in excitement.

Gordon brandished an awkward smile, feeling quite exposed.

The fire was crackling underneath the cauldron healthily. Lucotorix instructed to Gordon that the water must be at boiling temperature before starting, once the water bubbled vigorously he placed the dry marsh scraps into an infuser that dangled over the cauldron until the green moss formed into a dingy yellow, after that he added both of the saps he had collected and stirred them all into a mix.

''This one has to be one of the simplest mixes, '' Lucotorix explains. ''This is what makes the base of most tinctures for health, or anything to do with the body.''

After a vigorous stir, the liquid turned a dirty brown. Lucotorix extinguished the flame and waited for the mixture to cool, once cool, Orthunus dipped a small bowl and took a giant gulp wincing his face in disgust. ''Rancid taste… but does the job within a short span of time,'' he says, giving a slight pant of relief.

''Okay, now that's done I'll show you a basic healing mix that does wonders for any kind of physical injury. First, we place the dry marsh in the cauldron at boiling temperature again, this time we don't need an infuser since we won't be ingesting it,'' Lucotorix boils the dry marsh awaiting the colour change. ''Now we take a handful of stritchen, and chew it for a few minutes until it feels all mushed.''

Gordon becomes somewhat enthralled.

''When you chew stritchen, our saliva reacts with its properties, releasing its potential and creating a sort of bonding agent. When it's mixed with the dry marsh it creates a little paste that can be applied to minor wounds and even more severe ones too, to fight infections,'' Orthunus adds while Lucotorix gnaws away at the stritchen.

Lucotorix fishes out the boiled dry marsh from the cauldron, he cools it down by fanning it out and spits out his mouthful of mush into his hand. ''Also be careful not to burn yourself, this bit can be tricky,'' he says as he wraps the two reagents together, mushing them into a thick paste. ''And there we have it; all you do is apply it to where it needs to be. It tends to go off within a few days and becomes dull, but we create a liquified version that our warriors can carry in vials, it lasts longer but it's not as effective as the raw thing,'' says Lucotorix proudly.

''Interesting… but I can't see myself using it,'' replies Gordon.

Suddenly the door swings open, Parinos stumbles through, tired and worn. ''Good day, boys. Good to see you all working hard here. What is it you are teaching him? Lucotorix, would you mind cooking today?''

Lucotorix gives a breathy sigh. ''Just simple healing concoctions, and of course Parinos, I'll get right on it.''

''Good lad! That's my apprentice right there, hah,'' laughs Parinos. ''So, Gordon, how's the reading?''

''Better, I read The History of Uros today, very interesting stuff! I grasp it really quickly. When I look at the pages. The symbols… they just keep making more sense, it gets easier to read every time.''

''I noticed… It must be part of your drenching? A good skill to be blessed with If you ask me. Fanara knows how long we'd be teaching you the language and reading… months maybe? Even years? Shall we have another look at some more readings? It's good for you to read with me, you'll learn more and more of this world.''

''Sure,'' Gordon replies.

Gordon takes a seat near Parinos aside a small table while Lucotorix and Orthunus make food together.

Parinos produces a book and the two begin flicking through, learning more words and structuring sentences. Although Gordon was battling the inner turmoil of not returning home, the world he was in was very alluring to him, he was quite keen on learning more.

At times Parinos would lecture Gordon about the politics of the world and other pieces of Altharn's lore, he felt it necessary for Gordon to know. He'd give small lessons testing his knowledge.

''So, the Venethari are from Venethar, and that's the country north of Darogoth… they are ruled by a dynasty, the… Mundur Dynasty, their ruler is, Kastrith Mundur?'' Gordon speaks out slowly as he digs out the answer from within his head.

''Correct,'' replies Parinos ''And who is it that rules Darogoth?''

''High King… Vocorix.''

''His full name?''

''Erm… Vocorix…. Fen… Drosii?''

''Correct, very good! Vocorix Fen-Drosii, the word Fen means he hails from the province of Fen, where he received his torc, and Drosii is his clan name. Darogothic names are meaningful to the individual of where they are from and what clan they belong to. Identity plays an important role here. Mine for instance, is Parinos Glaen-Furius. I was born in Glaen and I received my torc there too. Glaen is the northern province of Darogoth and my clan is the Furius clan, which in my case, my younger brother is clan lord, and lord of Ollus, I denied that responsibility of clan lordship when I became a druid. Clan lords, or chieftains as some of the older generations call them, are usually the eldest member of the family, any member of a clan can be a lord of a holding if you're part of the right clan of course, try not to get confused by the two, remember, clan lords are different from lords.''

''I see, it makes sense. So, a torc is that metal necklace thing around your neck... and there's four provinces in Darogoth? All have their own style of torc?''

''There are four provinces, yes. Glaen to the north and north east bordering Venethar. Fen to the west bordering The Glade, Ard, that is central all the way to the eastern coast which is where we are now, and finally Dun, that takes up the southern peninsula. All these provinces make up the Kingdom of Darogoth, all each have their ruling clans that govern each province and swear loyalty to the high king.''

''Okay... that's quite easy to grasp, Luke, Orthunus where are you two from?''

''Ard, quite close by actually, our whole clan are typically druids, it's a family practice,'' say's Lucotorix as he stirs the food cauldron.

''What about you Gordon, how do names work where you are from?'' Asks Parinos.

''Well, quite similar actually. Except we don't call them clans and we don't add a place name at the beginning of our second name, my full name is Gordon Jozef Barker, sometimes we are given middle names that are usually names of our grandparents or other family members. Barker is my family name, sort of like your clan names? Jozef was my grandfather.''

''Two forenames? How exotic! I like it,'' smiles Orthunus.

''What are your full names?'' Asks Gordon.

''Ard-Grenwalda,'' the two brothers replied in sync.

''It's nice that you name yourself after your loved ones, do you ever run out of names in smaller families?'' Asks Lucotorix.

''No… If that was the case, we… we'd name a child after a family member that had passed, an ancestor? Or just give a name that we like or something. It's different all over the world I guess.''

The men would chatter for hours exchanging stories, especially of Gordon's home world, Gordon seemed keener to talk more about his home of late. He was even able to show them all what his home world was like through pictures and videos on his phone, the druids were truly mesmerised by the technology Gordon produced, blown away by the fact that everyone in his society had access to this kind of technology, Gordon's world was so alien to them, just like Gordon, they couldn't even comprehend his world even existed. Their evening of chatter would come to an abrupt end with a hard knock at the door.

Bang! Bang!

''Arch Druid! Arch Druid! Urgent!'' A voice yell from outside.

Parinos's face sharpens into a frown as he hovels toward the door. ''Yes, yes… coming!'' He glances at Lucotorix in concern.

Gordon catches wind of the looks the two had exchanged and begins to feel uneasy.

Parinos opens the door to find a young druid. ''Arch Druid… oathsworn have arrived. They're asking permission to enter the village and see you,'' he exclaims to Parinos timidly.

‘’Allow their entry,’’ Parinos looks back over to the boys. ‘’I’ll return shortly… I’ve a feeling I know why they’re here,’’ Parinos leaves the house after giving a lasting glance to Gordon.

‘’Oathsworn?’’ Gordon asks.

‘’They’re an elite type of warrior, loyal to lords and clan lords, they’re warriors selected by the lord personally to act as their personal guard and as representatives of their military. They’re high-ranking officials, basically,’’ Lucotorix explains.

‘’Oh… why does Parinos seem so nervous? Why do you all seem nervous? Is this bad?’’

‘’Erm… maybe? We’re not too sure… you’ll be fine! Trust me,’’ Lucotorix smiles.

Despite Lucotorix’s attempt with calming words, Gordon couldn’t help but feel very uneasy.

Parinos returns quickly.

‘’Boys… let me introduce you to, Brennus. Oathsworn Commander of Carsinia to High King Vocorix.’’

‘’Oh… shi-’’ Lucotorix falls over scurrying from his seat. ‘’Greetings… Oathsworn, a pleasure!’’ Jumps Lucotorix.

‘’So, where is he?’’ Brennus asks, wasting no time with his questions sternly in a deep stoic voice. He was an incredibly stocky man, massive to say the least, standing easily above six feet. Gordon could see how well built this man was even with all his armour on, he was donned in chainmail mixed with leather, with many a buckle laden all over, more notably the boss-like buckle in the centre of his chest that held up his green tartan cloak, it was etched with a symbol of a patterned wheel, one Gordon had seen in one of the many books he'd read, it was representative of the city of Carsinia, capital of Ard.

Brennus was a fiercely handsome man, a strong face that was scarred and dented by battle, powerful jawbones and glorious golden hair which he tied back to keep out of his eyes. He had a very impressive moustache that trickled down his jowls, decorated with coloured beads. The most imposing feature of Brennus other than his stature was his missing eye, shadowed by a leather-bound patch.

''This… this is Gordon, the one that Fanara's Cradle brought forward,'' Parinos announces.

Gordon rises from his seat in respect and also in a slight tatter of fear.

Brennus sizes Gordon up like wounded prey.

A silence washes over the room as he stares him down. ''You're joking?'' Brennus shimmy's past Parinos toward Gordon, his chainmail rattling with each thud of his steps, looking upon him intently. He grabs Gordon's arm, pressing down hard with his thick coarse hands, inspecting his physique. ''This is the being that will oppose the hordes of Venethar? The beast from Fanara's realm?'' He shakes his head. ''He's just a… man, I think?''

''He's not from Fanara's realm, he's from a realm of humans, humans unlike me or you… but he has magical capabilities, that is certain. He was drenched by the veil,'' Parinos exclaims.

''Face the hordes of Venethar? I'm no soldier,'' Gordon murmurs.

Brennus gives a bellowing laugh. ''Arch Druid… Is this what your devastating ritual cost you? Please tell me there's more to this? High King Vocorix was against your little plan and you went and did it anyway, I personally understand your motives, but how will this help?''

''Oathsworn Brennus, he's still recovering from being torn away from his home. He is completely bewildered by the event and we are helping him recover, please have some consideration for him and his mental wellbeing. His magical prowess is immense, that I can promise.''

Without a word Gordon storms past the men to go outside. Lucotorix follows in concern for Gordon.

''Fucking hell! I'm not here to fucking stay! How many times, Luke?! I don't need to be reminded about how fucking useless I am, I got that enough in my own world!''

Lucotorix says nothing as he allows Gordon to express himself.

''I felt like a fucking sheep being sold at a market in there! You're all treating me like a friend, but you're just fucking using me to get out of this mess you're all in, I bet you all know how to get me back don't you?! You just won't allow it!''

Lucotorix stands still, listening carefully.

''I'm not fucking staying, I've got a life I need to get back too, God… I can't… I… miss Helen.''

The door of the house swings open, Brennus steps out with a proud posture, clutching one of the many belts that laden his chained armour. ''So… little… Realm Walker.''

''Fuck off you, you cunt,'' Gordon shouts out recklessly in blind anger.

''Aha! Now there's the fire Darogoth needs!'' Laughs Brennus.

''Seriously, fuck off. I'm not helping you or anyone with this, I want to go back home, you tore me from my fucking home! I had enough with Parinos telling me all this and all that! What's so difficult?! This is a place of magic, yeah? No?! I don't fucking know anymore. Fuck you all and fuck you more, walking on in here making me feel this big?!'' He gestures with his fingers. ''You don't even know me man, what the fuck do you want?!?!''

Brennus's face straightens out. ''Calm down.''

Noticing Brennus rest his hand on the hilt of his sword, a fearful sigh escapes Gordon. ''I can't fucking cope anymore.''

More oathsworn clad in chainmail, who were waiting nearby, scurry over to investigate the commotion. ''Brennus? Everything okay?'' One of them shouts over.

Brennus raises his hand in signal. ''Everything's just fine, leave us.''

''Apologies, Oathsworn Brennus. He gets agitated easily and rightly so; he's been torn away from his home. His place is nothing like ours, he's confused, very confused. We've been helping him adapt and he's been doing exceptionally well at it.'' Lucotorix fixes his attention to Gordon. ''Gordon… Gordon, look at me, friend. The reason we're teaching you so much and helping you meld into our society is not because we want you to fight our battles, it's because you're lost. You're not home anymore, we're here to HELP you, Gordon. Yes… we wanted someone or something to aid us, but you don't have too Gordon, no one is forcing you… the problem is we have no idea how to get you back home. The only thing we can do now whilst we figure that out is to make you feel welcome. We're trying Gordon, why do you think Parinos is so tired every evening when he returns home? He's not doing his arch druid duties much anymore; he's been in the grove and the library, looking for answers. For you.''

''I'm here on behalf of the high king. We were told to investigate the being brought forward to see what exactly you are and if you are a potential threat to us. Arch Druid Parinos performed the ritual despite the high king's denial to it. It's our duty to ensure safety in Darogoth, And… yeah… I can be a bit of a cunt,'' he smirks. ''People get used to it though.''

Gordon buries his face in his hands.

''You want my advice, Realm Walker?'' Brennus adds.

Gordon lowers his hands looking upon the hearty warrior towering over him. He couldn't believe he snapped at such a man, he was utterly terrifying, what even came over Gordon?

Was he really that distraught to start picking fights with beastly men like this?

‘’From my knowledge, the interference of realms is something to do with the magic of the Gods… a rare form of magic not found in this world much anymore. But I know of something that holds such magic, or at least claims to have it.’’

‘’What?’’

‘’Kastrith Mundur.’’

Gordon Sighs.

‘’You already know of him, eh? So, what the fuck have you got to lose?! Show me what you got, Realm Walker. Show me this power… or are you going to sit here and cry like a lost little piglet, hmm? Or… are you actually going to get off your arse and fight for it!? Because as far as I see it. If you’re helping us, you get what you want anyway.’’

‘’I said I’m not a soldier, I'm no fighter.’’

‘’I can help with that; I’ve been tasked to oversee you. Anyway, what have you got to be scared of? You have power, yes?’’

‘’But I….’’

‘’But nothing. You want to get home? You have to fight for it, simple.’’

‘’You want me to kill people?’’

‘’Well, yeah.’’

''No deal, couldn't bring myself to kill anyone, it's not who I am.''

''So, you want to live the rest of your days as a druid in a world you don't know? Stop for a second and think, Walker. How badly do you want to get back home?''

Gordon says nothing, defeated.

''Look. You're practically living amongst us now, this world isn't so precious outside this dainty little village, trust me. Let me see what you can do and maybe we can work together a little bit. I'll show you how to defend yourself with a weapon, how to deal with real situations, hmm? Then if you're really feeling up to it, you join us. You fight for your desire to return to your home, these druids will find a way with some magic bullshit, and in the meantime, we will acquire what harnesses it, yes?''

Gordon says nothing.

''You can even have a couple of swings at me, you know… because I'm a 'cunt'?'' Laughs Brennus menacingly.

Gordon, feeling no other way around this, agrees. Lucotorix gives a nod of leave as he re-enters the house leaving Brennus with Gordon.

Brennus led Gordon to a small clearing nearby away from Parinos's house.

‘’Right, this should be okay,’’ He murmurs to himself as he ponders around. ‘’Show me how you do the magic shite, I want to see this power.’’

Gordon says nothing and finds his weave.

Focusing as he looks upward to the sky, his eyes form a purple glow as magic flows through him.

He throws his hands to the sky and ejects an immense roar of flame hurling upwards into the red lit sky of the setting sun. Gordon puts even more energy into his blast, feeling the magic around him fiercely shimmer as it rebounds from his soul. The flames grow large like a giant tree of flaming oak, he thinks back on how angry he is, how frustrated he is, that he can’t return home, he's lost. The flames grow wilder, reaching out even further.

Letting out his emotions he screams with all his might, with all the air compact in his lungs. A visible shockwave thunders toward the heavens, decorated by the inferno Gordon unleashed as he lashes out his frustration in one more enormous blast of magical might. He was determined to prove he wasn’t weak, especially to one as intimidating as Brennus. He was determined to return home.

The roar of the blast was deafening, a ringing noise began to rattle through Brennus’s head. ‘’Fuck me!’’ He shouts out, bewildered like a child, his eyes drawn in awe. ‘’Well….’’

Parinos, Lucotorix and Orthunus rushed out of the home fearing Gordon may have hurt someone or himself.

''What on Altharn was that?! What's going on?!'' Parinos shouts, breathless as a result of his age.

Gordon stood drenched in sweat.

''The Realm Walker here....'' says Brennus, still astounded by what he had witnessed.

''Gordon, was that magic? You did that?'' Parinos asks.

''Yeah... yeah, I did.'' Gordon replies. ''Everything's fine, just showing Brennus what he wanted to see.''

''It's okay, Arch Druid. Leave me with him,'' Brennus asks politely.

Parinos nods and brings the others back inside, warding off all the other druids who had come to investigate the disturbance on his way back, the few oathsworn warriors come to linger by Brennus.

''Unbelievable... you really do have power, Realm Wa- Gordon? You need to utilise this strength; you have no idea, do you? Do you know what you're capable of? You could even use this to return to your home.''

''I don't know how.''

''Then we'll find out how. It'll take time without a doubt, but like I said before, what else are you going to do? Sit around and complain? Or fucking do something about it?''

Gordon sees clarity in Brennus's words, noticing his hardened outer shell had a friendly touch to it. Gordon felt more obliged to act more civilly for him. ''You want me to help with your problems? You want me to kill people?''

''Those people will only end up trying to kill you, Walker.''

''What do you mean? I've not done anything to anyone!?''

''Word spreads about you, you're on the tongues of everyone in Carsinia, no doubt Venethar will catch on and try to take you out themselves, you're a threat, a very dangerous threat with a lot of power. This is serious… we're trying to help you.''

''Fine, FINE,'' Gordon shouts, overwhelmed by the battles in his head. ''Look… I know you're right… I can't just piss and wine about it… it's hard man, it's hard. So much strange shit has happened since that day, so much is happening to me. I… I feel great inside… everything is weirdly clear… things like your language, at first I couldn't understand a word, but within a day I was almost fluent and now… I basically am. I have so much energy, I can't explain it. I can only go off what Parinos tells me, but whatever it is you need, I need to get back home… but know this, that the moment I find it, I'm gone.'' Gordon says sternly as he holds his head in frustration, struggling to find the right words to make sense of how he now perceives things.

''Fine by me, lad,'' Brennus extends his arm vertically toward him, Gordon responds with a confused face. Brennus smirks and grabs Gordon's hand and fuses it with his forearm. A friendly gesture of greeting. ''You'll get used to me.''

''I'm sorry for being a dick to you… It's ju-''

''Say no more of it, words don't pierce my skin,'' Brennus laughs ''Ever held a sword before, Walker?''

''No… never. I mean, a toy sword when I was a kid?''

"How about a quick taste? Hashna! Come over here… can he borrow your sword quickly?"

An oathsworn comes forward, a towering woman with arms like tree trunks. Her frame was bolstered by pure muscle, donned in armour akin to Brennus. She had rather masculine features that she carried valiantly, a square jaw and a broad nose, long luscious auburn hair all thrown back into a beautiful weave of war braids. ''Here,'' her voice, gritty and fearsome. Gordon felt a lot more comfortable in this one's presence. She had a kinder face than Brennus, her aura was soothing.

''Thanks,'' Gordon replied sheepishly. He takes a moment to inspect the intracity of the swords design, it was beautifully crafted like most things were in this world, it looked to him like a bronze handle that was strapped with high quality leather, both the pommel and the guard had the same design as one another, both pronging outwards, Gordon felt familiar with its design.

Brennus demonstrated a few basic swings and guards, as well as stances, Gordon copied him well enough, they would practise slowly so Gordon could grasp the hang of it and adapt to the weight of a real sword. Already he was feeling the strain in his forearm.

''Alright, how about we really put you to the test hmm?''

''Okay?''

‘’Hashna, grab a couple of those sticks over there,’’ Brennus points toward a rubble of branches that lay beneath a nearby oak.

‘’Sticks?’’ Gordon sniggered.

Hashna obeyed, handing them each a large branch. Brennus’s face lit up quite deviously.

‘’If we’re teaching you how to fight, we’ll start with the old-fashioned way, eh?’’ Laughs Brennus. ‘’Don’t hold back, Walker. I can take a hit, especially from a stick, I’ll go easy on you since you’re only wearing robes.’’

‘’Okay….’’ Gordon readies himself.

‘’Now, show me how you block. Remember what I just told you.’’

Brennus instantly takes a swing from the right, only putting a small force behind it. Gordon knocks it out the way effortlessly, feeling a little more confident Gordon gets a little riled up.

The warriors share a laugh upon Gordon’s confident stance, as does Brennus. ‘’Fair enough,’’ he chuckles.

This time Brennus again swings from the right but with full force, he feints his attack switching the directions. Gordon misses the block and becomes winded by the blow.

‘’Fuck!’’ He splutters. ‘’Okay… you’re fucking strong.’’

‘’You want to carry on, Walker?’’ Brennus smirks.

A strange feeling began swirling inside. ‘’Again!’’ Gordon shouts as he brings himself up.

Brennus feints an overhead swing into a left swing, full force.

Things seemed different; Gordon felt a weave of magic not brought on by himself. Everything was moving slowly, he watched as Brennus's stick switched its position in slow motion as he again fainted his swing. Gordon goes to block with force and succeeds. As soon as the strike finished, so did his slowed perception and the grasp of magic. Brennus breaks through Gordons stick, striking him in the ribs.

''Ah… fuck!'' Gordon winces.

Brennus laughs. ''Sorry… I don't know my own strength sometimes, but a nice block! Okay then, Walker….'' Brennus kicks Gordon's leg, obscuring his balance, following up with a heavy swing, Gordon quickly springs himself into a position to block effectively with now two sticks, everything moving slowly as he weaves his magic, altering his perception of time once again.

''Good. Always expect the unexpected,'' says Brennus, narrowing his only eye.

''Especially from Brennus, he's a dirty fighter,'' laughs Hashna.

Brennus Scoffs. ''Quite an agile one, aren't you?''

Gordon found a new use for his magical abilities, it seemed he could bend his perception in the midst of combat but it required a lot of strain, he was unsure how much he could perform this little trick, but he was certain it would come in handy if need be. Being aware of this he focused hard on the remainder of the session, he enjoyed it allot, being able to vent his frustrations like this.

''I think that's enough, I just need to see your natural form and how you learn. Good job, little Realm Walker. Right, so I'm to return here a few days a week to oversee you and train you. I'm uncertain what is actually going to happen with you… I'm just following orders, any information I gather, I'll let you know,'' Brennus nods to his warriors. ''Mount up, we return to Carsinia,'' he glances back at Gordon as he climbs atop his trusty steed. ''Give the arch druid my regards, and keep your head up.''

Gordon returns the nod in respect.

Days went by, more days not being home, he would help with the day-to-day activities among the druids, making potions, collecting herbs, fetching water, fetching firewood, cooking, everything. Gordon was living in Altharn.

Every night without fail he would run through his phone, looking at pictures of him and Helen, him and his friends, the videos. He felt a great sadness wash over him every time but also it filled him with motivation, motivation to learn of this world, to meld with it, and use his newfound abilities to find a way back home. How long would it take? He had no idea, so he did the only thing he could, and pressed on.

9: A Sight to Behold

''I thought I'd start writing, in my own language of course. At least if anyone from this 'world' finds this book, no one can read it.

I've been here a while now, two months? I find it hard to count the days now, especially with the way people do things here. They have like ten days in a week or something? I can't even be bothered to keep track of that.

Everyone back home must definitely think I'm dead by now, who knows. One moment I'm walking home from a night out, the next I'm in a forest surrounded by people out of myth and history, or so it seems.

If I was to explain this to anyone back home, they'd think I'm crazy, smacked out on hard drugs, but no, is this real? Magic is real, I can do magic, I feel weird even writing these words.

So far, I've not stepped away from this village, Seers Crossing. I've been living amongst them whilst they teach me everything they can about the world and their life.

I wake up every day hoping to wake up next to Helen and breathe a giant sigh of relief that it was all some crazy dream… but it isn't, I still find myself getting overwhelmed with distraught daily, little things keep my mind at ease, learning of the world, hanging out with Luke and Orthunus, those guys seem chill.

On the bright side everyone here is friendly and comforting, it helps. Thinking about what's happened, I'd say it's enough to send a man crazy, I'm told I crossed a barrier between realms... it's bat shit insane if you ask me, took some time for me to come round to the idea but honestly, I can't even comprehend this shit in words. It's fucked.

It's funny actually, since living here I've noticed a massive change in myself, I feel great. My skin is looking great too, might have something to do with all the good food I've been eating since being here, proper fresh meats and veg, everything organic.

The people here are interesting, they call themselves 'Darogothians', a 'druidic' kind of folk, their language resonates with me and I instantly decipher their words and meanings with little effort. This has happened since day one and now I'm basically fluent in this weird language. It doesn't even feel weird anymore at this point.

They have an interesting dress code, these people all dress the same, white layered robes, bits of fur here and there, I noticed a lot of jewellery amongst the many i've met, the people here really like their jewellery and on top of that they say all Darogothians all wear a large metal necklace or neck brace thing called a 'torc'. It's part of their culture, a symbol of identity.

They're granted a torc when reaching around four or five years old, and depending on which part of Darogoth you live, the torc's style differs, it also affects their surnames too, which I find interesting.

This world is a world of magic, it's the type of shit you read in a fantasy book, play in a game or watch in a movie. Casting magic myself... that is a feeling like no other, I feel the world around me vibrate within, it's fucking bizarre man. Once I did that, I felt how fucking real this really is... I'll do whatever it takes to return home, I'll use the magic somehow, we'll figure it out, but right now I'm stuck, with no way home.

So, I spend my days now being tutored by Parinos, the Arch Druid. He's a great man, very serious about his work, he does his best to accommodate me and takes good care of me. I appreciate him more and more every day, kind of reminds me of my grandad. I tend to hang out with Orthunus and Lucotorix most of the time, I call him Luke since it's easier, some of the names of these people are such a mouthful. Luke is the apprentice of Parinos and hopes to take his place as arch druid someday. Orthunus is his younger brother, about fourteen? Something like that. He's a good lad, very sensible and intelligent. It's odd hanging out with a kid that age, but he's pretty mature. Luke reminds me of myself alot, he's a bit of a joker but knows when to be serious, me and him click just like me and Dan do, he'd fit in well with the boys.

Then there's Brennus, the warrior... or 'oathsworn'.

From my knowledge the oathsworn are an elite force of warriors, kind of like a knight or something? He's a burly fucker, very rough and ready kind of guy, but he's kind enough to get on with, he's showing me how to fight with a sword, I'm doing well I think, especially when I use the magic to aid myself. Brennus comes by every now and then and spars with me, he's not allowed to stay in the village since it's 'sacred ground', he can only visit on duty, I guess I'm an exception?

But these people are my only ticket home as far as I'm aware. I question whether they already know how to send back but are refusing to let me leave.

Helen, I'll get back to you, Dan, Pete, Jeb, Mother, I'll return, I fucking swear I'll find a way, I'm not dead, I'm coming home, however long it takes."

- *First entry, Journal of Gordon Barker, Year 4AB 282*

Two months since Gordon arrived in Altharn. He has learnt much of the world, but not enough. At the behest of the high king, he is to remain with the druids so they can properly educate Gordon about his magic, the world and the kind of things druids do best.

Brennus would visit twice a week and train Gordon in melee combat for the entirety of the day, Gordon was doing well. In his spare time, he would read the many books Parinos kept, further strengthening his reading abilities, communication skills and expanding his knowledge of the world. Everything was going great for him, his motivation to return home really fuelled him, as well as haunted him.

it was overwhelming and Gordon struggled to see straight from the stress whenever he thought about it too much, it affected his sleep greatly. He'd dream much of home and wake up in sweats most nights, sometimes he'd cry out, other times he'd just stir violently, and there was something else going on whilst Gordon slept. He'd have vivid dreams of a black void and an echoing voice that seemed to stalk him, he could never quite explain it, nor escape it, but then again, he couldn't explain a lot of the things he'd experienced, in his time in Altharn, his hair had grown quite messy and his little soul patch and grown into a rugged mess, he was looking quite dishevelled to say the least.

Gordon was outside, smoking his pipe with Lucotorix and looking upon a frail map of the world, talking about the countries and cultures of the people. Gordon enjoyed learning of all the cultures, and seemed rather eager to see it all for himself.

''Is there anywhere that is really dangerous? Like somewhere where no one ever goes?'' Gordon asks.

''Yeah, there's a few places actually, see here down at the bottom?'' Lucotorix points to a large stretch of land in the far south of the world. ''That's Rekali, it's a desolate waste land, there's a jungle next to it but the people who live there are hostile to anyone who walks that land.''

''There's a city to the north peninsula, is that right?''

''Ah yeah, that's A'desh, I don't know much, but I do know that they aren't a part of Rekali, there's a border around A'desh's peninsula that's just a huge wall, you could call it the smallest country on Altharn. I heard that everyone who crosses over the border never returns, either the heat will kill them or the natives and beasts will….''

''Where else is off limits?''

''Murk and Deep Swamp are quite ominous places and have always had some kind of hostility with Aventium… I think that might be personal though, no one outside of Murk has ever set foot in as far as my knowledge goes. I know it's inhabited by murkith and that the swamp is so thick that even breathing is difficult… or so they say.''

''What are murkith?''

''Swamp folk, kind of like us… but have leathery skin and quite freaky eyes.''

Gordon leans back in disbelief. ''Fuck.''

''Hah, you'll probably never see them so I wouldn't fret.''

''What's this island far to the southeast of Darogoth near The Paw? It's huge,'' Gordon remarks.

''That's Duosh, they isolate themselves from the politics of the other countries, not too long-ago Mavros Avir attempted to invade Duosh, they failed miserably. Duoshi warriors have the most fearsome reputation for their discipline and honour, they are a rich and mysterious nation, and quite peaceful too from what I hear. Their land is a great desert, they're a dark-skinned folk, not as tall as your average Darogothian, but they could probably punch you twice as hard as one. Some of them migrate around, but you don't see very many Duoshi people around here, although there was a Duoshi lad who had a Darogothic mother, he came here to train as a druid, he got picked up by the lord of South Crag in Dun about a year ago or so, he was a nice guy.''

''Wow….'' Gordon takes a quick puff on his pipe as his eyes scour the map. ''What about that island up north? It's almost the size of all of Uros, just above Venethar.''

''Oh, that's Dakiva. Although it's large, it's got a very small population. It's essentially just a giant snowy tundra, not easy to live in.''

''What are the people like?''

''It's hard to tell with the number of furs they wear to keep warm. We usually only ever see their eyes, they're humans, that much is certain,'' Lucotorix chuckles. ''They tend to have narrower eyes and paler skin than Urosi folk.''

''This is so cool… and that country west to Aventium, on the other continent, that's Mavros Avir? Yeah?''

''Correct, a very… interesting place to say the least, it's rich, filthy rich. Their little empire is not very popular amongst its continent of Loria. They have enslaved many Kurians, you see they are renowned for their slave trade. They take magic extremely seriously as part of their core as an empire and even in their politics. Their imperial nobility is currently married into Ventheri royalty, which may complicate things… Kastrith's mother was of Mavros Avir, one of the emperors daughters I think?''

Parinos emerges from inside his house. ''You boys seen my sickle?''

Gordon looks up to Parinos. ''Sorry, Parinos. I used it yesterday when I went out with Orthunus to gather some stuff, I left it with the cutlery.''

Parinos chuckles. ''Cutlery?! Gordon, sickles aren't for prepping food.''

''Well, technically you could....'' Lucotorix smirks.

''Quiet you, right then... I'll go and grab it. Speaking of food, can you boys go hunting today? Get some fresh meat in for the dryers since we're running low.''

The two smile and agree.

Just as Parinos was to step back inside, a strange thunderous rumble began to erupt in the sky. Parinos is the first to notice and looks up. ''Strange... clear skies, a few clouds here and there but it doesn't look like a storm is coming... I swear I can hear thunder?''

Lucotorix and Gordon look around in confusion.

The noise continues, growing louder and closer, the two stand up curiously.

Lucotorix notices something beyond the clearing up a nearby hill in the distance.

''Parinos....'' he says nervously, his voice giving a slight break.

''What is i-'' Parinos face drops as he stares on in terror. ''No....''

It was a galloping horde of Venethari Cavalry. The crashing of hooves smashing into the ground was the thunderous sound they had heard and it was about to rush right into Seers Crossing.

''No... Impossible?! How?!'' Lucotorix shouts. ''Why would they come to sacred ground?! How did they get this far?!?!''

''What is it?'' Gordon speaks out timidly.

''The Venethari...'' a thought storms Lucotorix's head. ''Orthunus!!'' He shouts out, bolting towards Orthunus's home in panic.

Parinos grabs Gordon urgently by the arms in fright. ''Gordon, there's nothing we can do, Seers Crossing has no defences, this is sacred ground, you need to get out of here, those people will only be here for one thing. You.''

Gordon's eyes widened in shock. ''What the fuck, Parinos?!?!''

''LISTEN! They're coming, and fast. Get to Lucotorix and Orthunus and get out of this village, you look like a regular druid, you might just get out in time.''

''What?! But... I... What about you?!?''

''I'm going to help the others to escape, quickly now after Lucotorix, GO!''

''Parinos I can't ju-''

''Yes, you can, Gordon. You have to, do you want to return home?!''

Gordon stood defeated and started to tremble in fear as his sight darted over to the hill that shifted like a great wave. The hill was moving with little black specks that grew larger and larger with each passing second, their hoofs kicking up a visible dust. Truly a sight to behold.

''Gordon! You must live, GO!'' Parinos shouts.

Gordon gives Parinos a quick hug, patting Parinos's back before sprinting off after Lucotorix. ''Please, Parinos. Stay safe!'' He shouts back as he runs off.

The thunder was growing louder and louder with each passing second. The sound of galloping hooves was becoming clearer, the terror was now beginning to hit him the louder the noise grew. His legs began to feel like jelly from shock, his stomach was churning. That gushing sensation of adrenaline being forced into his bloodstream was taking hold, he wanted to throw up but his body forced him to run and push on.

As he ran through the village, he noticed the fright in all of the other druids, they were also running around frantically trying to gather what they could of their belongings.

Gordon could see Orthunus's house in the near distance and the door was wide open, he rushed to the door as quickly as he could. ''Luke?! Orthunus?!? You here?!

''GORDON! Come on! We need to leave now!'' Lucotorix shouts as he scrambles from inside the house, packing his satchel desperately. ''Orthunus, hurry!''

Orthunus drops his things and barges on out with haste, leaving behind most of the stuff he was attempting to pack.

''What is it?!? What do we do?! Where do we go!?'' Gordon shrieks as the thunder drowns his words.

''I don't know… I don't know how they got this far into Darogoth, or where we are going, but we need to get as far away from Seers Crossing as possible!''

Seers Crossing had turned from a peaceful haven of druidic tranquillity, to a frantic mass of panic and fear. Parinos screamed at the top of his lungs, alerting his brethren that danger was fast approaching. People were scurrying all over, some disappearing into the folds of the forest, others busy gathering their belongings.

Gordon, Lucotorix and Orthunus were just about to leave the house until they were halted by the relentless charge of Venethari Cavalry bursting their way through the village tearing down fence posts and smashing through the many beds of flowers.

The sounds of horses neighing viciously and men screaming with the thirst of blood became overbearing. The raiders began to manoeuvre around the village with expert horsemanship, cutting people down without a second thought and firing barrages of arrows into every white robed druid they could see.

The three stood in horror, unknowing what to do. More and more Venethari poured in, the three could do nothing but wait for an opportunity to carry on escaping without being trampled on by a warhorse as the remainder of the raiders charged on through. Gordon looked back towards Parinos in concern, Parinos was stumbling around attempting to avoid the stampede of horsemen and druids alike.

A horseman gallops by Parinos, rearing his hearty stallion, only to send it forward onto him, burying its hooves deep into Parinos's chest, slamming him to the ground before Gordon's eyes.

''Parinos! NO!'' Gordon wailed in utter disbelief.

Parinos's body was limp like a ragdoll the instant the hooves struck his chest. A visual scar seared into Gordon for eternity, seeing someone he cared about so much being forcibly relieved of their final breath in such a catastrophic manner.

Orthunus places his hands gently on Gordon's shoulder in support as the three crouched down in submission behind the rickety fence of Orthunus's home.

Gordon looks away from Parinos, only to see more druids being slain, cut, stabbed, shot. It was everywhere, no matter where he looked to avoid the bloodshed, his eyes couldn't evade the slaughter.

The raiders had all arrived fully in force within the village, many of them started to dismount and break open the doors of all the houses, capturing or killing other druids.

Lucotorix saw his chance to run for the forest behind. ''We need to move! Now's our chance! Come on!''

The three leapt up and ran as fast as they could, Gordon considered using his magic, but was nervous. The horse archers scared him the most and they seemed to make up the bulk of the horde. If he was to cast his magic, he would certainly become the prime target. So instead, he decided to just run, run as quickly as he could hoping not to feel a sharp pain strike his back.

Lucotorix directed them toward where the raiders had come from, the clearing that was surrounded by the thick forest, the three bolted into the forest knowing the cavalry would struggle in the terrain. Orthunus stopped running and came to a dawdling walk.

‘’Orthunus?! What are you doi-‘’ Before continuing his sentence he noticed why Orthunus had stopped.

An arrow head was protruding from the front of his neck, blood gushing and pulsating as he frantically gasped for the breath that was escaping through his pulsating wound. Orthunus fell to the floor, revealing behind him a mounted archer with his composite bow drawn and a face as blank as death itself.

‘’Brother….’’ Lucotorix rushed to Orthunus’s side without a care for himself.

Gordon’s skin turned white at the sight, he felt sick looking upon Orthunus’s fatal wound, he then noticed the horseman behind was dismounting. ‘’Lucotorix… Luke… what do we do?!’’ Gordon’s eyes fixated on the soldier.

‘’Go, Gordon… just go, I’m staying… he’s just a boy. I… I….’’

‘’I can’t just leave!!’’ Gordon pleaded, his heart racing to such a degree his chest was uncomfortably tight, watching the Venethari soldier casually walk towards them, drawing his axe.

‘’I’m here brother, I’m not going to let you die alone. I promise,’’ he mutters as he strokes Orthunus’s coarse hair, Orthunus stares back in fear, woefully fixed upon his big brother's eyes that glistened in a sorrowful comfort, terrified, so terrified he soiled himself in the moment, trying to speak but only erupting more blood from his throat. ‘’Gordon, for the good of this village, for Orthunus’s sake. Please, leave!’’

''I! No! I can't! Come on! Argh!?'' Gordon's feet scurry back and forth as he pulls at his hair.

Lucotorix snaps. ''Gordon!''

The Venethari man grabs hold of Lucotorix's shoulder, readying his axe in the other hand ever so casually, Gordon prepares himself to cast magic, until he notices something.

The soldier's grip was calm… he was keeping hold of Lucotorix whilst he waited with Orthunus, allowing him to be with his brother in passing. The soldier looks up to Gordon and the two lock eyes.

''Listen to your friend, druid.'' The soldier speaks out in a thick accent, notably different to that of anyone else Gordon had spoken to since arriving.

Gordon turns and runs into the forest, skimming past the many trees, breaking through the bushes, the leaves scraping and batting his face, refusing to look back. He'd never ran for such a distance in his life. The sound of Lucotorix's scream echoed through the forest and shuddered through him as he fled in terror, pushing him to run even faster, tears streamed from his eyes uncontrollably, yet he still did not look back.

The horror, it was all too much, eventually Gordon had to stop. His heart was racing so quickly he felt he was about to faint. Once he stopped, he looked back, no one was nearby. The sounds of the raid were still bound in the distance, men and women screaming, horses whinnying, Gordon jolted over his front vomiting violently all over a marshy bed of moss and grass.

He felt his world shatter before him, all over again, everything he had left since coming here was what Seers Crossing was.

Gordon had nothing left, and now he was truly stuck in this perilous world.

The tears would follow with anger, once he finished vomiting, he punched the nearest tree repeatedly until his knuckles couldn't take it anymore, his fists gushing with blood whilst he screamed through his clenched teeth.

After a brief moment of emotional breakdown, Gordon took a hold of himself, looking around still hearing the noise of the bloody carnage. He needed to keep moving, he had to survive.

He started to feel weary and anxious about the distance he'd made, fearing he may not find his way back, so he decided to set up a makeshift camp in a secluded little grotto.

He slumped down, repeating the images of the event. The view of the horde making their way down the clearing, the horse that trampled Parinos kicking its hooves right into his chest and Orthunus, that scarred him the most.

Watching a poor innocent young boy have his life taken in such a gruesome manner, the arrow protruding from his throat, the blood, the pure look of fear and horror that plastered his face, watching him squirm in his brothers' arms as he tries to breathe whilst wincing in pain, crying and pissing himself.

To see it for real, was truly a harrowing trial.

And so, Gordon sat, and cried. He wailed, he collapsed to the floor, he thought of ending his own life there and then, this was it, he couldn't cope, he'd endured enough.

He stood back up and removed his belt, as his satchel thumped to the dirt floor his phone fell out, lighting up and revealing his lock screen, a picture of him and Helen.

Helen… home.

10: Survive

''Wake up.''

The black void beckons once again.

''Gordon, wake up.''

Gordon stood in stasis. A blank face, staring into nothingness. The air… it was cold.

''Gordon,'' the woman's voice calls for him again, the voice echoes throughout the void just like before.

A small white light appears off to his side, the air becomes warmer.

''They're dead….'' Gordon mourns, his eyes drained of all innocence.

''I know.''

''They're all fucking dead, and I couldn't do anything. I couldn't do it!''

''Our sacred land….''

''What do you mean? Our?''

The light drew closer, revealing a humanoid silhouette, still too far away and too bright to make out what it really was trying to be, a guardian angel? An ancestor? A God?

''You're giving up. It's easier to reach you… but Gordon, you must not fall further back, do not allow yourself to succumb to the void.''

''There's nothing left. I'm lost….''

''Go back to the village.''

The light flashes and Gordon instantly awakens. He springs up from his slumber, hitting his head on a low hanging branch.

''Fuck! Fuck!'' He yells, still drenched in sweat. As he collects himself, he realises how groggy and dizzy he's become from the sudden movements.

He was hungry, to the point where just standing up made him light headed. He took a moment to sit back down and rub his head whilst he caught his breath.

Gordon had spent the night in his little grotto resting beside a small dancing flame of magic he had conjured up, he had fallen asleep out of emotional exhaustion, despite the only thing he saw when he closed his eyes was Orthunus's face.

He was sure he might not even wake up at all, but to his surprise here he is, again. It was Autumn in Altharn and the cold in Darogoth was setting in slowly, the sky was clear and the dawn casted its crystalline blanket over the land.

His stomach grumbles reminding him of his hunger, so he decides to search for some food. Thanks to his time with the druids, Gordon felt confident about foraging and hunting, so he left his shady grotto and searched around for berries and signs of any rabbit or deer, anything.

Memories of the day before would beat at him repeatedly as he scoured dew rich grass, he tried as hard as he could to shake it off, putting his own survival first. He would mourn when the time was right.

He knew Lucotorix wanted him to escape, he knew he had to get back home, he knew he had to find out what to do, to do with his magic, to do with himself.

First things first, food.

He eventually finds a lone doe; it hadn't spotted him yet. He charges up a tight flame in his palm and brings it down with a nimble bolt of flame to its head.

He removes the doe's hind leg with a small knife he had attached to one of the many belts that rest upon his robes, it took some time due to his inexperience, it was gruesome and bloody, but he managed.

He proceeds to prepare it, cook it and eat it.

''Go back,'' the voice in his head echoed as he chewed through the thick and slightly overcooked venison.

He remembered his strange dream; it gave him an idea.

Brennus was due to visit again soon, he might be able to catch him at Seers Crossing, it just meant he had to go back and witness what was left of the once peaceful village. Would he be putting himself in danger again? Would the raiders still be lurking nearby?

Gordon trekked slowly, still eating pieces of the doe he'd slain as he dawdled through the forest retracing his steps, he was incredibly lucky that his water skin was still attached to his belt which thankfully had a day's supply of water in, he always filled it up every morning. He trekked and trekked until Seers Crossing came back into view.

There was an eerie silence coming from the village, once in plain view he ran toward it, carefully checking his surroundings.

A faint mist was tangled throughout, remnants of flame and death lurked amidst the uneasy atmosphere, he crept up by a house that stood by the edge of the village, in his peripheral vision he could see bodies still lying on the floor, scattered all around, at first he refused to look, but then he fought his fear and walked right into opening of the village where Fanara and Iskarien stood, watching over.

The houses were broken beyond repair, some of them burnt, none had doors attached anymore.

Bodies were all over, still as the air itself. He looked around to find the area he had escaped from.

Orthunus, he was still there, lying in a pool of dried blood. Gordon winced at the sight.

Lucotorix was nowhere to be seen, he may have been taken, or even escaped. Gordon could only hope.

Gordon approached Orthunus's corpse, looking over it for a moment. Tears began to erupt down his face as he peered upon the body of his friend.

''Orthunus... you're just a fucking kid! Why do this to someone like you?!''

Orthunus's eyes were directed off to his side, wide open in a disturbing stillness, no expression on his lifeless face, his skin a blueish white, the arrow still poking out from his neck.

Gordon bent down and stroked his hair.

''Rest in peace, mate....'' he sobbed uncontrollably. ''I'm sorry. I'll do something about this, I swear to fucking Go- '' he readjusted himself for a second, thinking upon his words. ''By Fanara, by Fanara! I'll do it, whatever it is, I'll do it!'' He leans over and attempts to remove the arrow from Orthunus's neck. Gordon sealed his eyes shut in disgust; the tension of the arrow only made things worse as he pushed it through.

Once he removed the arrow, he looked upon him for another moment, allowing the good memories to trickle in, remembering this once chirpy, polite, happy go-lucky druid boy.

Gordon removes Orthunus's torc from his blood-soaked neck. ''Fuck... man....'' he winces, he gave Orthunus's torc a small wash with his waterskin and placed it in his satchel. ''Hope you don't mind... I'll keep this to remember you. Goodbye Orthunus,'' he rolls his hands gently over Orthunus's eyes, shutting them forever.

He then made his way over to Parinos's house. Lying limp and lifeless just a few feet from his door was the body of Parinos, his robes scuffed with dirt and hoof prints.

Gordon slows his pace, looking mournfully upon the man who held his hand in this world.

''Parinos, what's happened? What is this world? You've shown me so much, taught me so much and all I ever did was piss and moan that I wanted to be anywhere but here… and look at this shit, look what's happened… because of me? People came here for me, they should have had me, but I know you, even if it was for a short time. You'd give anything for your Gods, your people… even… me,'' he takes a deep breath. ''Well, I'm not going back anytime soon now that's for sure! FUCK OFF GORDON!'' He shouts at himself, hitting himself in the face. ''I fucking swear! I'll do it Parinos, what have I got to live for now!? FUCK ALL, that's what. No… no… you… you can't die like this!'' His tears stream so much his nose begins to run.

He bends down and takes Parinos's torc, kissing it in love for the man who took good care of him in his darkest moments here in Altharn.

In that moment he remembered Parinos embracing him when he woke up screaming after his first night here, he remembered how warm he was, how just being around him calmed him so deeply, the love Parinos had for life and those around him, Gordon embraced Parinos, just as he did him, picking him from the floor and wrapping his arms around him tightly.

''Goodbye, Parinos,'' he whispers.

Gordon arose, seeing all the people flee all over again, hearing all the screams, the horses, the thunder.

He spends the rest of the day gathering up every single dead druid and collecting them all together on a makeshift pyre he had constructed with parts of the village that now stood in ruin, he places Parinos and Orthunus in the centre next to each other; he stood back, staring at this estranged effigy.

''I don't belong in this world… then again sometimes I felt I didn't belong in my own one,'' he scoffs at himself. ''Yet here I am. May Fanara guide you all, druids of Seers Crossing. I'll never forget you, for as long as I live….'' Gordon holds his hands out to the pyre and sends forth a mighty blaze, lighting up the corpses of everyone who'd perished that fateful day.

He lies down on the dirtied floor, watching the flames engulf all he'd ever known, he falls into a slumber, exhausted, drained, depressed.

He wakes the next morning, the pyre is out, nothing remained but ash and memory, the wind carries away the silence, howling through the trees around, the skies are dull today.

He looks to the house he lived in with Parinos and realised some of his possessions may still be there, the house had been burnt badly, its roof had fallen through but some of the furniture and beams were still intact, he rummaged through finding his old clothes, they were damage beyond repair, he picks up his leather jacket and places his hands in the pockets pulling out the chocolate bar he bought for Helen.

He gives a sad sniff as he removes it, it's squashed and torn, his jacket that he holds is in tatters.

Upon closer inspection he then notices his jacket had been pulled apart at the seams. If it had perished with the house, it would have been burnt or even still fully intact, but it was ripped apart just like the rest of his clothes, his house keys were missing, the keys that had a keyring with a picture of him and Helen.

''Ello there,'' a gruff voice spit from behind.

Startled, Gordon jumps.

There stood three men in roughed up looking leathers, one of them a sword drawn, it was Darogothian in pattern, a poor looking sword but Darogothian nonetheless, it was the first thing Gordon noticed. The men looked rough, their faces were pox marked and unkept, none of them clean shaven as their facial hair brushed out in all manner of directions. The two men at the side seemed rather young, the middle man was well aged, late thirties or so.

''What you doing?'' The younger man to the left speaks out.

''My village, raided… who are you?!'' Gordon stutters.

The three men glance at one another in a smug manner.

''What have you got in that satchel, druid?'' One of them speaks out.

Gordon was confused, he felt intimidated by these men, weren't the people of Darogoth meant to revere their druids?

''Herbs,'' Gordon answers hastily.

''Looks rather heavy to just have herbs in,'' the older man says, edging forward, chipping his sword through the rubble carelessly. ''Let's have a look then, eh?''

The man holds up his sword to Gordons chest, poking it forcefully enough to sting, but not enough to draw blood.

He tears off Gordon's satchel and passes it to the man on his right.

''Look, I don't want any trouble, my village… was raided by Venethari, this was my house.''

''Hang on a minute… speak again, druid,'' barks one of the younger looking ruffians.

''What do you mean?''

The elder man's eyebrows perk up. ''Yeah, what the fuck is that accent? You're not from Darogoth,'' he approaches Gordon and yanks at his hood, looking upon his bare torcless neck. ''No, he's not. What kind of 'druid' is torcless eh? Where are you from? Speak.''

''I… erm….'' Gordon stumbles on his words.

''What the fuck is this?!'' One of the men rummaging through Gordon's satchel produces his phone, staring at it in confusion, he throws it to the eldest man who inspects it intently. ''And two torcs?! In here? Looks like he's trying to find a disguise if you ask me? A foreign thug preying on a recently raided village? Wouldn't be surprised if he was one of the raiders.''

''Aye… couldn't tell you what this is thing is though, could fetch a price maybe?'' The eldest man looks back to Gordon. ''Tell you what 'druid' you tell me what this is and let me have it and I might let you live.''

Gordon's stomach churns heavily as he takes a nervous gulp before speaking. ''Okay… okay… just point that away from me… please. I can show you? Okay?''

''Fuck off, do you think me an idiot? You fucking degenerate,'' the man slaps the flat end of his sword against Gordon's arm.

Gordon jolts in response. ''Okay… erm… so… if you press that button on the side, it will light up… with… magic, it's a small device… that contains magic.''

The three men glance at one another.

The eldest presses the button and the phone lights up, he drops it in shock. ''Woah!''

Gordon sees a chance, there's no other way out of it.

He throws a shockwave of force toward the three men, throwing them to the ground. Without hesitation he readies his right hand with a powerful flame and runs it through the eldest man's face before he could return to his feet.

''Fuck off! Fuck off! Fuck off!'' Gordon screams, repeating a barrage of inferno directly into the man's face, sending bolts of flames like a flurry of punches.

Once Gordon realises he's gone too far he steps back in remorse of his own actions. His emotions had burst through attempting to take control. He had incinerated the man's face down to the bone with the intensity of the blasts, his skull visible and charred.

''What the fuck have I… Oh no….''

One of the men tries to get up and run for his life, Gordon snaps back into a fury, using a magical force to stop the fleeing brigand in his tracks before he can escape. ''No! No!'' Gordon shouts as he drags the man toward him with the force of magic, he grapples his neck tightly, the other still bound to the floor in submission next to his dead comrade.

''Don't fucking move, you cunt!'' Gordon shouts, his teeth protruding in anger.

''Okay! Okay!'' The man begs.

Gordon uses his magic to direct the dead man's sword to his hand, brandishing it to his hostage's throat.

''Now, who the fuck are you?'' Gordons' confidence soared now knowing he was in full control of the situation, speaking through his teeth, his voice distorted.

The man on the floor shuffles backward onto his forearms in fear. ''We're just a bunch of folks who look for things of value… we're poor… we have nothing. Come on, please don't hurt him, we're just trying to get by. I swear, we wouldn't have really hurt you!?''

''Why would you do this, druids are sacred to your people?!''

‘’I know… but these are desperate times. There’s a war raging, the Venethari, they… they raided us too. We’re just trying to survive!’’.

Before anyone can say anything else, a monstrous thundering noise can be heard battering the dirt floor coming from outside of the village.

Gordons head snaps to the noises. ‘’No… not again!’’

‘’Stop right there! You!’’ It was Brennus accompanied by Hashna. He was shouting from a distance and hadn’t noticed Gordon yet. ‘’What the fuck is going on?! What’s happened?! The village!! Wait… Gordon?! Gordon!!’’ Brennus shouts in surprise as he dismounts his horse by swinging his leg over and off with haste.

His sword was already drawn knowing full well the village was in disarray, he walked up to the man still on the floor, analysing the situation. ‘’What’s this? Bandits? Robbing druids? You got the wrong one lad, he’ll fuck you right up, just like your friend there,’’ Brennus snarls as he remarks on Gordon's fatal work, kicking the dead man’s head.

Hashna grabs the man in Gordons arms and casually slits his throat with the rim of her blade.

Gordon jumps back in shock.

Brennus points his sword toward the man’s neck on the ground.

The man raises his hands in desperation. ‘’Please, please it’s not what it se-’’

Brennus ignores the man's pleas and gently pokes the edge of his sword through the young man's throat with ease. He bursts a glorious spray of blood from his neck and mouth as he succumbs to Brennus's blade which lunged in deeper, slowly.

''Crimes against the druids is a death penalty, cunt,'' he glances back to Gordon. ''Gordon, are you okay?'' Brennus asks.

''No.''

''What the fuck happened here Gordon? Was this all you? The Brigands? What happened?!''

''Venethari....''

''HOW?! Bastards... fucking bastards!'' Hashna shouts as she kicks the dying man on the floor.

''By Fanara, look at this place,'' Brennus murmurs as he stares around in disbelief at the destruction of Seers Crossing.

''I got away, but came back because I knew you were coming, then these guys jumped me. They're all dead Brennus... everyone. I collected the bodies and I burnt them on a pyre....'' Gordon breaks down.

Hashna squeezes Gordon in her stocky arms. ''You've been through enough, little Realm Walker. Come with us, you'll be safe and we'll figure this all out. Then we'll make them bleed for this.''

The dying man gurgles as he desperately tries to breathe through the slit in his neck.

''SHUT. THE. FUCK. UP,'' Brennus stamps on the man's face repeatedly putting him out of his misery, frustrated by the carnage of Seers Crossing, the sacred land of Darogoth.

Gordon backed off as he attempted to recollect himself, the amount of violence he had witnessed in such a short span of time was too much, the suffering, the death, taken back by even his own sporadic act of self-defence, he couldn't process it. ''Brennus… did you really need to kill these men? They surrendered,'' Gordon speaks out, his hands gripped firmly onto his hair as he regulates his fear induced breathing.

''Like I said, Walker. Crimes against the druids are punishable by death.''

Gordon says nothing.

''We need to get him back to Carsinia, Brennus,'' Hashna states.

''I know, we should move now. I can't fucking believe this… Seers Crossing….'' Brennus was wrought with fury. ''Walker, with me.''

Gordon followed on and mounted Brennus's horse, saddling up to gallop all the way to Carsinia, the Capital of Ard and all of Darogoth.

Gordon glanced back longingly as he gripped Brennus's waist upon the horse, watching the torn village become smaller in his view, leaving behind Seers Crossing, forever.

11: Friends in High Places

''The banishment. A word that holds much uncertainty in all the people's hearts. An event that happened many thousands of years ago that separated the people of Altharn from their Gods. No one knows why or how this happened but the Gods themselves felt it in their bones just days before this world changing phenomenon.

All beings counted the passing of time in different ways until the banishment occurred.

The banishment of the Gods was so significant, we now add 'AB' or 'After the Banishing' into our dates, and the number that accompanies the letters calculates each thousandth year that has passed since and thus our ages become ordered as such.

For example, In the time of writing this book we sit in the year 4AB 115, 4,115 years since the banishment occurred.

Not a lot is known before the Gods' age, most estimate the Gods' age lasted about ten thousand years, others say longer. The Gods' age was a time of much mystery, although few records still stand.

Before the Gods' age there was a period scholars call the 'Ancient age' legend says that mysterious beings walked upon the Altharn, beings of immense power and once the Gods started propping up, those entities promptly disappeared for unknown reasons, there are many theories, but no proof. Maybe it's best little mysteries like this remain unknown.

The Gods themselves derive from mortal beings like ourselves, at some point in their life they came across something that ascended them beyond the power of the Altharn. To this day the people still speculate, all that is known is that they share a form of magic, magic of the endless void itself.

The Gods shadow such information and rightly so, some say they themselves don't even know as some would suggest they were blessed by the core of Altharn itself, but this has never been proven.

But what we do know is that one fateful day all God entities that walked the lands of Altharn vanished without a trace. Many have dedicated their lives to uncovering the incident but none have prevailed in seeking answers.

Records suggest the Gods knew what was to come, like this account written down by Vistra's followers, said to be In Vistra's own words.

His words are as follows.

''Soon we will be gone, those of us that have adhered to the void, something is resonating within us, a darkness like no other. I don't know what I can do, but what I can do is try. Fate guides us all, yet only those true to themself guide their own. I'll bind my soul to this world and I will reach back from where I am shackled. If this fails, then maybe fate has decided I'll surely perish in the abyss of the endless void.''

Vistra excavated himself underground and tore out a part of his very essence embedding it as far from the surface as possible, it was said those above the surface could hear his screams of pain, the sheer power of his cries causing a great quake in the heart of Venethar. The location became secret amongst his most trusted and then forgotten forever.

Vistra did this in hopes of reconnecting himself to the world, shackled by invisible chains that tugged harder and harder. He tried to evade this by keeping himself firmly aligned with the Altharn putting all his power into separating his very core, but unfortunately for him his efforts were vain, for no one can escape the void, not even the Gods, for they are but reformed manifestations of its power, that much we know.

Fanara however was more accepting, she addressed her people moments before she was torn away.

''All that lives, must die. Even the immortal will perish. Everything is created and everything is destroyed, the cycle is everlasting. This is the way of life, what I teach you all every day and now. Time pushes forward and worlds will shift, live on people of this beautiful world, live on.'' Moments later she disappeared into thin air, followed by a rumble that shook the very surface of the entire world at once. Then the first age began, and it began with bloodshed.''

– Hjathfire Hirend, Year 4AB 115. - Where are our Gods?

Somewhere in Fanara's Forest, Ard, Darogoth.

''Urskull Olm, I'm not sure what it's worth to us… seems to be a key? Look at what's attached to it.''

Olm, Urskull of Venethar, a high-ranking officer, gently takes the key from his fellow soldiers' hands, Gordon's keys.

Olm is a giant of a man, shaven bald with a fearsome braided beard to compensate, he towers all he stands by. A face worn by conflict, his soul a hardened shell. ''Is it a painting? Looks like a painting? No… it's too real… too… strange to be a painting… Why would someone attach a miniature painting to a key? And this is all we salvaged from the Arch Druid's home?'' Olm bellows in a voice so deep it vibrates the air that escapes his mouth.

''Yes, Urskull… there were some clothes too, odd looking clothes, I've never seen any clothing quite like them… I can only assume they were from the being they brought forward?''

Olm inspects the picture on the keys intently. ''Good work, you can go now….'' he ponders the keys intently. ''Human? I don't understand, they brought forward another human to our world?''

Another urskull, Fenrith, a much younger man, steps forward, overlooking the picture on the keys as he rests his hand on the neck of his axe. Fenrith was a shorter and softer looking man in comparison to Olm. But his youthful soft looks should never be taken lightly, Fenrith was renown in Kasidor as possibly the most skilful fighter in all of Venethar, known to be swift and precise, a famed combatant before his rise to military service. ''It's clearly otherworldly… I saw the clothes myself, Olm. If it is human, it's a human of another realm. Hyphal told us that no matter what passes through the veil it becomes drenched in the magic of the Altharn. If you ask me, a human becoming drenched in such magic is far worse than any beast.''

''You think that's possible?'' Olm hunches as he squints his beady eyes at the picture.

''Fanara herself brought forward her 'oaken seers' through that same stone circle, although they are extinct now. That's the only instance I know of beings being brought forward from another realm….''

''But humans, other humans? Really?''

''They say the number of worlds is infinite, if that's true then we shouldn't be surprised, but this is what we salvaged from the pockets of the clothes we found… it was the only item we thought that held any kind of value. We didn't see anything else.''

''I suppose. Will the druids talk?''

''No,'' Fenrith scoffs as he fixes his long black hair that he tied back tightly in a bun.

''Of course, they won't cooperate with us, they don't fear death,'' Olm sighs. ''Okay… do what you will with the remaining captives then. Actually… Fenrith, take the key to Kasidor and one or two of the captives, we'll split the party here and move out, I'll see what I can find out about this being. I'll try and track it down,'' Olm orders as he hands the keys to Fenrith.

''It probably escaped to one of the nearby villages, no doubt it'll be accompanied by druids if some have escaped… if you lay low you might be able to get some gums flapping, hah,'' Fenrith belts as he struts toward his horse.

As he mounts up he takes another look at the picture on the keys. As he stares upon the picture, he notices something, something he clearly overlooked. ''Olm! Come here….''

''What is it?'' Olm marches over to Fenrith.

Fenrith narrows his eyes. ''The man on this painting….''

''Yes?''

Picturing the events of the raid, Fenrith's memory jigs with alarm bells. ''One of the druids I killed… his brother approached to mourn his death… but there was another druid with him… it couldn't be? No, yes! It was him! He was the other druid… the man in this painting, he had two hair colours, just like this!''

Olm stands befuddled. ''So… you found the being?''

''I swear, it's the same face!''

''Well, where is he? Is he dead?''

Realising what he did in the moment when he allowed Gordon to escape, he tries to sugar coat his story. ''He ran, into the forest!''

''You just let him run off?''

''He looked just like any other druid! I thought we were hunting some kind of otherworldly beast, not some peasant in robes.''

Olm shakes his head at Fenrith in embarrassment. ''Fucking idiot, can you at least tell me which way he went?''

''He ran south west; he was alone too.''

''Fuck me, fine. I'll take my party south west, you get back to Kasidor and bring word to the king, see if you can shake some heat off our tails while you're at it,'' Olm leaves Fenrith's side. ''Mount up!'' He shouts in his terrifying voice. ''We're moving out, back to Seers Crossing and then southwest, all those under my command!''

Fenrith gathers his own party and the two urskulls separate.

Eastern Road of Carsinia, Darogoth, Ard.

The man's face, charred and burnt, the way his body thrashed as Gordon's flame obliterated his face, the way the skin peeled back into a bloody mess, erupting as the burns consumed, the smell of burning flesh, so strong.

The images flash in and out, Orthunus's bloody neck, the arrow, the look on his face, the terror in his innocent eyes.

Gordon wakes with a small gasp, he keeps drifting in and out of sleep yet finding it difficult being mounted upon Brennus's horse that bounced him out of his slumber. He couldn't get the images of the slaughter out of his head. He killed someone, burned him alive, he never thought he'd bring himself to do it, he had no idea what even came over him, he knew at times his temper got the better of him, but never like this.

The scene will never leave his head, he'd repeat the events over and over every time his eyes closed, for they were never truly closed, they would open to the horrors of those fateful days.

Gordon readjusted his hazy vision, the great city of Carsinia can be seen in the distance resting against a crashing shore beside the expansive River Os. The city was huge, cobbled stone buildings with thatched roofs can be seen poking out from behind the outer wall and just off to the right atop a small climb of cliffs stood a humongous castle, firm within its own walls. He'd seen castles before back home, but never one that isn't in ruin and so glorious in view.

The walls of the city stood tall, decorated with many banners bearing the symbols of Ard and the clan of the high king. A patterned wheel on a yellow backdrop representing the province of Ard and separated atop this section on a green background was the crest of the Drosii clan, four bronze horses all entwined and tangled amongst each other.

Brennus, Hashna and Gordon had travelled for just over a day to reach the city, Gordon's clothes were rancid from the day's riding and the tribulations he had endured, sweating and stewing within them.

''I'll grab you a fresh set of clothes before we head up to the castle. We can't have you walking in there stinking of shit now,'' Brennus remarks.

Gordon gives a lazy grunt.

The huge gates of Carsinia are open wide as people tottle in and out. A piece of raised ground creates a ramp-like feature that leads up to the city, the outer walls being almost level with the ground once inside. Gordon was dumbfounded to see such bio architecture.

The place is bustling, the people donned in colourful woollen tunics and dresses, many wearing little plaid cloaks and shawls, others in fur and leathers. The people of Darogoth were rather vibrant in their dress, particularly over accessorising in jewellery, almost everyone he looked at was covered in golden bracelets and rings, this was the first time Gordon had ever seen anyone outside of Seers Crossing aside from Brennus and the oathsworn, it was quite pleasing on the eyes to such vibrancy amongst the people, even the common folk.

The guards of the city all carried spears and swords with huge oval and rectangular shaped shields, all with the same design as the many banners painted on the front of the shield, all of them cloaked, battle-ready in chainmail and bronze helmets.

Brennus stops at the market to purchase some cheap clothes for Gordon and takes him all the way to the inner keep beside the castle where the oathsworn reside, right by the castle gate.

‘’There’s a little shed we have that’s attached to the garrison just here, it has a spare bed in there and a table and some other clutter. It ain't pretty, and definitely needs a clean but it’s better than nothing, Walker. That'll be where you stay for now, take these clothes, have a rinse from the barrel toward the back, don’t worry it’s fresh, it gets changed daily. Now that you’re here that'll be your job now,'' he jests. ''Meet me by the castle gates when you're done, but be quick, let's just get this over with, okay?''

Gordon, feeling quite confused, agrees. He dismounts Brennus's horse and walks on into the shack, he opens the door expecting the worst but it wasn't as bad as Brennus made it out to be, the floor was of stone and looked rather cold with clumps of straw strewn across, there was some tools thrown around cluttering the place, a small bed and a table both equally as messy.

Gordon just assumed it to be a spare room or tool-shed and felt completely fine with the place. After all, at least he had somewhere of his own to sleep now.

He strips himself of his dirt, sweat and blood-stained clothes and quickly dips into the water barrel by the back, it's freezing cold. He uses a small amount of magic to heat it up and quickly rinses himself down, running his now coarse hands through his shaggy hair. The water of the barrel soon changed into a murky brown, gathering all the filth.

He gives himself a moment to relax in the warmth of the barrel, thinking of all that has transpired, he shakes his head at the images of slaughter, he needs to keep himself distracted.

After bathing, he takes the clothes Brennus handed him. A navy-blue tunic with a small embroidered trim around the neckline, plain tan pants, some leather boots, a belt, and a simple short brown shawl to keep warm in. Gordon quite liked the look of it all once he had it on, it definitely felt comfortable. He looked just like the many people he had seen coming up here, except not as colourful and glistening with gold.

After drying out his hair he steps out of the shed, attaching his druid satchel to his new belt that fit tightly around his waist, he marches to the gates of the castle toward Brennus who stood with Hashna. ''All done,'' Gordon exclaims.

''You look good… bet you're glad to finally get a wash, eh?'' Says Hashna. ''Glad to see the clothes fit too, knowing Brennus I thought he'd pick something oversized just to take the piss.''

Brennus didn't even flinch at Hashna's light joke.

''Right then, I'll get back to the garrison, have fun, Brennus. Gordon,'' she nods a goodbye as she guides her horse toward the stables.''

Brennus hitches his horse on a nearby wooden pole. ''Right… come on then,'' Brennus says, ushering Gordon toward the castle.

The two Journey on through another giant gate that led into a massive oval courtyard with many extravagant flowers and plants plotted around, some Gordon now even recognised. They approached the main doors, doors so thick even a battering ram might have a lot of trouble. Gordon wondered how such doors were even opened.

''Morning Brennus, doing well?'' One of the guards calls out from aside the doors.

''Aye… could be worse, where's the high king? Do you know?''

''In his chambers I presume, he's not left the castle today. Who's this?'' The guard clocks Gordon.

''This is Gordon. He's... an unfortunate one, urgent news from Seers Crossing. The high king will want to speak with us.''

''Interesting name, where ar- wait... did you say Seers Crossing?''

''Yes... It's been- ''

''Raided, aye, we know... a druid came by yesterday and told the high king everything. Venethari bastards, didn't think they'd stoop so low personally.''

''Can you open the gates? There's more to it, it's urgent.''

''Of course, friend,'' the guard gave a great knock into a panel on the side of the wall, the doors opened slowly from a pulley system controlled by another guard from inside, the doors gave a loud rumble as they opened up.

Gordon and Brennus walk on into the castle.

''He said a druid from Seers Crossing came by, someone survived?!'' Gordon speaks out in hope.

''Yeah... we're going to find out who, don't worry.''

The two walk around many twists and turns marching down the many halls that stretch throughout the castle. Gordon peered around in amazement like a lost puppy as he looked on at all the beautiful tapestry and ornamental statues that blessed the stone halls.

Servants and soldiers alike can be seen pottering around their daily business. Brennus greets a few he knew on the way until they arrive down the final hall, a beautifully carved oaken door stands before them etched with all manners of swirls and loops.

''Let me do the talking, don't speak unless spoken too… although I'm certain he'll want to speak to you,'' Brennus knocks three times loudly.

A booming voice echoes from inside. ''Who is it?''

''Oathsworn, Brennus.''

''Brennus! Come in!''

Upon entering, High King Vocorix can be seen rising from his writing desk, to Gordon's surprise the high king was also quite a well statured man, smaller than Brennus if not a little porkier, he was clearly a man of military experience and noble gluttony. He had long flowing red hair and an extravagantly long moustache that dropped to his breast, decorated with gold and silver braids and beads. He had a handsome face of prominent structure, although clearly a little cursed by the over embellishment of alcohol, which was present in his red cheeks and nose. Just below his sharp jawline sat the most beautiful golden jewelled torc he'd seen. The fabled torc of unity, resting upon his clavicles, the symbol of the high king. Vocorix's warm expression instantly drops once he sets his eyes on Gordon.

''Is that?''

Brennus nods.

''Well….''

Gordon bites his tongue, expecting a barrage of insults.

Vocorix edges toward Gordon. ''You speak our language I hear?''

''Yes.''

''And you have… power?''

''Yes….''

''So, might I ask why didn't you stop the attackers at Seers Crossing?''

''I would have made myself a larger target, I'm new to this world, I don't know what they were capable of… they would have killed me. I'm not stupid.''

Vocorix wheezes a raspy snigger. ''Fair enough... Realm Walker,'' he readjusts his position and takes a deep breath. ''I'm not going to lie to you, Realm Walker. I was very displeased with Arch Druid Parinos when he went against my orders… but druids are druids after all, their words mean as much as mine in Darogoth, especially those such as Parinos, a respectful man to the very core he was. A fine druid and a finer man, I mourn his death, Realm Walker. I really do. The Venethari have desecrated sacred grounds and slaughtered innocent men and women, men and women who aren't even akin to combat and why? To find you? I can only assume Kastrith Mundur has gotten word of your arrival and wanted to eradicate any major 'threats' as soon as he could.'' Vocorix clears his throat. ''Now, when I heard that the almighty being drenched by the magic of the Altharn was nothing but a mere man who barely even had skin on his bones I was quite concerned by it… but Brennus's reports tell me you have exceptional magical power and you're not even half bad at your training. You use your magic to aid yourself in melee combat, making you already quite the combatant… isn't that right, Oathsworn Brennus?''

''Yes, High King,'' Brennus responds.

Gordon takes note of Vocorix's expression, he appears sorrowful yet intently stern with Gordon, he felt as if his very existence being presented before him was somewhat offensive, especially in the tone he spoke in. He couldn't work out if he was being spoken down to because he was a king or if he was just displeased with his presence.

''Interesting. Well, I'm deeply sorry for what has happened to you, Realm Walker. It must have been… awfully enduring. Forgive me, I don't quite understand you, but it sounds like you've experienced a lot of heartache already in the short time you've walked upon our world.''

''The guard said a druid came by who survived the slaughter, who was it?'' Gordon asks.

''Ah… yes, a druid by the name of Albin, he's not here now, he left as soon as he delivered the news from the village… but… I heard a report just before your arrival… that he took his own life,'' Vocorix dips his head in respect.

A pulse of dread and pain surges throughout Gordon, he holds his head in distress at the sensation taking hold.

''I also understand you're desperate to get back to your 'home' Realm Walker.''

Gordon nods painfully.

''I'm afraid there's no known way as of yet. I'll make sure my druid works on finding a solution as soon as possible. It'll be her priority for you this I promise. But in return I want your service.''

Gordon squeezes his eyes shut in a flurry of emotions, he felt grateful Vocorix would help him, but still disheartened to the fact he had to work for him, kill people, or so Gordon assumed.

Gordon nodded excessively. ''Yes… High King.''

Vocorix cocks his head in surprise. ''Again, I'm sorry for your losses, my deepest sympathies,'' he studied Gordon for a moment. ''Oathsworn Brennus, I wouldn't usually order this, but I want you to take him on as your ward, in these circumstances I feel I must and besides, you've had the most experience with him… we'll see how he gets on and what we can do later down the line. Yes?''

''My ward!? Y-yes, High King,'' Brennus says in shock.

''I tasked you with overseeing him in Seers Crossing. Besides, it's quite fitting.''

''I agree.''

''Right, you best be off, get him settled and make him feel at home. I have some business that needs tending to up at Glean so I need to make some travel preparations.''

''Yes, High King. Come, Gordon.''

''Oh yes... Gordon, your name,'' Vocorix chuckles. ''Farewell... Gordon.''

Gordon gives a forced smile. ''Thank you.''

Gordon and Brennus leave Vocorix's chambers, Gordon is especially eager to leave.

''That went a lot better than expected....'' sighs Brennus in relief. ''Fancy a drink? I bet you'd love one after all you've been through, eh?''

''Fuck it, yeah, let's do it.''

''You're going to love the stuff at the tavern, much wider selection than all the fucking chouchen the druids drink,'' he sniggers.

Gordon and Brennus wander off into the centre of the city, Brennus chooses the tavern he frequents with his fellow warriors.

It was a glorious and impressive looking building, large and rectangular with a thatch roof that dripped over the walls, supported by large circular beams with much artwork carved into the frames.

Upon entering, the cleanliness of such a place was astounding, Gordon expected something drab and filled with rowdy locale. It wasn't too busy this time of day, small groups of folk were evenly spread out, a bard could be seen in the corner playing an instrument that could only be described as some form of drum, the noise similar to that of a bongo.

Brennus sat Gordon down at a corner table as he made his way to the bar. ''I'll get you some real good stuff, hopefully it'll be easy on your otherworldly belly, hah,'' he chuckles as he walks off, his chainmail rattling with his motion.

Gordon shifted his eyes around feebly, no one seemed to pay him any extra attention, or gave the concerned glances like in Seers Crossing, maybe they didn't know who he was, it was quite freeing.

Brennus returns with two large tankards both frothing at the brim. ''There we go,'' he announces proudly, seeming much more relaxed than before.

He slides Gordon a large wooden tankard of frothing cold broth.

''Thanks, Brennus… you've paid for so much for me….''

''Oh, you have money?'' Brennus jests.

''No….''

''Then don't trouble yourself, just settle yourself down first. You heard what the high king wants, yes?''

''Make me your ward? What's that?'' Gordon takes a sip of his drink. ''Wow… you know this isn't half bad at all… I've missed drinks like this.''

Brennus smiles. ''Before we continue, here,'' he holds up his tankard to Gordon. ''To the druids of Seers Crossing,'' he mutters plainly, his face matching.

Gordon lifts the corner of his mouth in a half smile as he clinks Brennus's tankard. ''To the druids,'' the two pull back into their seats.

''Yes, you're my ward. A ward is usually picked out by the oathsworn to take on as a sort of apprentice, usually close friends… family… people like that tend to become wards, basically… You're working to become an oathsworn too? But I can't see why the high king would just drop that on you especially since you're so desperate to get back home, being oathsworn is a lifetime commitment unless released of their oath, quite the achievement for someone who's only existed here for a couple of months… but if you ask me, I'd say you just knew the right people,'' he sniggers.

''Oh….'' Gordon's face droops.

''Oi,'' Brennus playfully barges his tankard into Gordon's shoulder splashing a small amount of his blackened stout. ''Remember, you're fighting to get back home, I don't think the high king will make you an oathsworn, like I said, that's a life commitment, hence the title. I'm sure he's just trying to find a way to legitimise you to the people. You'll be fine with me, Walker. I sure as fuck will be fine with you, especially with that power!'' He takes a glorious gulp, the stout filtering through his upper lip hair. ''Stop fucking thinking about it, Gordon. How hard am I going to have to rattle your head to help you see straight, eh?''

''I know, I know….''

''Would it help if you talked about your home? I'm quite keen on learning more about you actually… go on tell me of your home!''

''No… if anything has helped, learning more of this one has.''

Brennus gives a sorrowful smile. ''You're doing well here, you even have your first kill now,'' he winks deviously with his only eye.

''Not proud of it….'' Gordon snaps back.

''We all get pissy the first time we kill. But you need to remember something very important, if they were given the chance, those fuckers would of gutted you without a second thought, they were robbing a druid, by Fanara, you really think they wouldn't kill you? No one in this kingdom commits harm onto a druid unless you're a complete and utter fucking scum bag. You're lucky, Gordon. Your instincts kicked in and saved your sorry little arse.''

''Yeah… I suppose you're right.''

''I'm always right, get used to it.''

For the first time since leaving Seers Crossing, Gordon's face lights up a little, smiling. He gives out a weak laugh, enough to make him feel just that little bit more alive.

''How do you find Carsinia? Big, isn't it?''

''Yeah, it's actually incredible… it's beautiful, these clothes are pretty cool, comfortable too.''

''There's a whole world out there for you see, and I'm sure we'll be getting about it soon enough.''

''Yeah, that does sound nice… I learned a lot about the countries of this continent. I know that we sit on a continent named Uros… we are in Ard, a part of Darogoth. To the north is Venethar, and to the west is The Glade, where elves live… elves!'' Gordon's eyes light up greatly in disbelief at the thought of an elf. ''Also, I found out that Darogoth and Venethar hold some sort of weird treaty with The Glade? I didn't fully understand though.''

''Those fucking elves… yeah 'the divine pact' it's called. Basically, means we have no interaction with them out of respect for our Gods or whatever. It happened after some wars took place not long after the banishment when everyone was blaming each other for the Gods going missing. I don't know… never been too fond of those elves myself. Cowards, that's what they are, and then they form the pact when Uros turns into a bloodbath, instead of resolving anything or defending themselves they come up with some bullshit to 'respect our Gods' so they get an easy way out,'' he repositions his posture. ''They never liked humans, they got famously jealous when Fanara gifted Darogoth to us in ancient times and then the Venethari came and she formed a bond with them too, so yeah. There are a few elves that live in Darogoth, they're nice enough, but the Glade elves are always usually stuck up their own arse. The divine pact even stops us trading with them, every form of cooperation and communication was nullified, now us and Venethar have nothing to do with them. The only thing we can do is join forces if a foreign invader from another continent lands on our shores, then they have to step in and aid us. But… with the current war with Venethar? If their allies join the war, they can technically set foot on Urosi soil because they're allies of Venethar and The Glade won't do anything about it… because it doesn't affect them, we're fucked.''

''So… wouldn't this Kastrith man benefit from warring with The Glade rather than Darogoth?''

''Good question, but no, he's not an idiot, he's trying his best not to seem overly tyrannical, he's trying not to make too many harsh decisions… I mean, he is,'' Brennus scoffs. ''But he's being careful trying to justify whatever it is that he does. He's playing the game carefully and he's always been a man of sound mind, he's well known for it… or at least was. He needs to gain the trust of his people and he rightly did so after his cunt brother died. His people even named him 'the redeemer'. He used to be a great man, Gordon. I even cheered his name when he took up the throne of Venethar. Something strange is going on, something really strange… I don't like it,'' Brennus stares upon the windowsill by their table, lost in translation. He gives a quick shake of his head and takes another sip of his drink. ''Anyway, he's trying not to stoke up a civil war with all the shit going on at the moment. His sister Tarna recently escaped their capital city, Kasidor. Some say she's joined or started a rebellion? I've not heard much else, this is all new, I can only assume she'll be found dead sooner or later.''

''So Venethar were good allies with Darogoth?''

''Very much so. The best of friends, not anymore though, the past few years have been very tense, I'm sure you can see that.''

''Do you really think he's actually the herald of a returning God?''

''He's the herald of being crowned another cunt rather than a king! No, Kastrith is surely using that line to justify himself. He was known to be quite fond of learning magic, he was never good at it mind, but I reckon he's found some insane way to power himself and it's probably all gone to his head or some shit, you know the usual stuff that happens to people like him? It's just strange, he genuinely was a good man.''

''I guess this is what we're all trying to figure out then.''

''Basically, and then relieve him from it.''

''What would happen if Kastrith dies?''

''Then Tarna would take the throne, she actually was supposed to take it instead of Kastrith, they crown their monarchs by the age of their heirs and she's older than him. But I'm sure he swayed her to fuck off somehow? Probably why she's been on the run… Venethar rule their country through a dynasty, you understand?''

''Yeah… what if they both die?''

''Well… they both don't have any children, so the lords of Venethar would probably figure something out, I don't know Gordon, I'm no politician,'' laughs Brennus.

''But surely as an oathsworn you deal in politics to some degree?''

''If you mean politics as in, 'here's a cunt, kill him' then yes.''

''Fair point... so, Brennus, you probably get asked this allot, but... what happened to your eye?''

Brennus gives a mighty roar. ''Hah, nothing heroic, did it when I was a lad, slipped on the floor at this very tavern, drunk out of my mind, I smashed my head of a table, my eye got gouged by a loose piece of wood, didn't work after that, Daxos, the druid here in Carsinia removed my eye, said it would have gotten infected, so she just took it out. Aye, that was back in my ward days. I was a ward to Gulvatorix, he was my uncle, he's gone now, Fanara embrace his soul.''

''Does it bother your sight much? Like, does it hinder your fighting?''

''At first, yeah... I got used to it after a while, but the ladies love it, that helped a lot,'' he winks.

The two continue drinking, Gordon begins to get rather tipsy from guzzling down tankard after tankard. He starts opening up a little more as his confidence begins to shine through the alcoholic mist, revealing his true nature.

He produces his phone, showing Brennus the many impressive things about his home world. Technology, concrete buildings, cars, the people and the videos of him and his band mates drunk. Brennus is mind blown about such an advanced piece of equipment and even disregards what he sees in front of him, but that was the drink talking.

As the evening starts settling in, Brennus escorts Gordon back to his little shed. Gordon, quite clearly intoxicated, slumps into his stool staring upon a blank dusty table, scouring his new environment in his drunken state. ''Books… I need some more books man, yeah that's what I need!'' He slurs. ''Books helped a lot in Seers Crossing… yeah! Brennus was right… my instincts kicked in! I didn't mean to, they made me… yeah?'' He slams his head into the desk. ''I'm fucked man, I need a kip,'' he attempts to raise himself up, tumbling over into his new bed, passing out peacefully.

12: Ard-Barker

''Elves are peculiar beings, their most unlikely trait is that of adaptation and that's saying something, considering they're only known to inhabit The Glade.

During the Gods' age, the Gladian elves began loading up their criminals and deporting them to a land In Loria, far west of The Glade across the Silent Sea into a desolate and dangerous swampy marshland inhabited by murkith, bog stahls, and many other ferocious beasts as well as deadly plants that spewed poison and rot into the air.

A land once called the Exiled Marshes, we now know this place today as, Aventium. The elves who were left to rot on this foreboding land quickly adapted to it. In fact, it's noted by Gladian druids that it only took them just a few generations to change completely.

Their skin turned a dull greenish grey and thickened like a strong hide. Their eyes became more rounded, their noses flattened to their face giving their nostrils a larger flair in comparison to your typical Gladian. However drastic and beastly their appearance had differed, they still held the glamorous poise of their Gladian brethren, standing tall and slender. They became known as 'marshland elves' to the outside world but the Gladians always shunned them as exiles, and then, when the famous marshland elf 'Khan' came forth, their entire world changed forever.

Khan was a marshland elf hell bent on disowning Gladian ancestry and bringing the marshland pride out from the bogs, riddled with pure hatred for the mass atrocity his old kin committed to him and his people.

He was born an innocent man into a world of misery and torment, constantly fighting to survive against the clashing tribes of desperate elves, the wrath of the murkith and the jaws of the land itself. Little to all of Altharn's knowledge, Khan was to establish a new world within this swamp that he himself named, Aventium.

Khan forged a kingdom and a religion, an anti-religion, abolishing the worship of God entities; the marshland elves would worship no one but themselves.

He created a civilization that thrives on his legacy to this very day. The newfound tribes fighting to survive in Aventium were united. Khan became the founder of Aventium and the Gladians had inexplicably forged a rival unlike any other.

Khan's name was of his own choice, abandoning his former elven name of Ilfranyos out of disgust for anything Gladian, even giving his title of leadership the same name. Khan. Quite similar to the khans of Kuria, but this Khan had other plans.

'We are no longer fighting to survive; we survive to fight!' As goes the famous words all the marsh landers abide by, the words Khan himself screamed atop the Black Stone Keep, when he successfully drove off the murkith.

The Gladians had no idea how well adaptive their anatomic designs were to outside lands. Still to this day they refuse to leave their precious Glade, never attempting to take advantage of this obvious positive trait. The world watched as the marshland elves developed a kingdom that gloriously rose from swamp and ash.

And now the world recognises the Aventium Khanate.

Who knows what else the elves could be capable of if they inhabited other parts of the world.

It is said they lay an entire kingdom under water of the elves who fell to the sea during the mass deportation, but this is only mere rumour. Although, seeing what had transpired in Aventium, the notion itself it's very plausible.''

– Uthran Elran, Head Scholar of Mysticia. Year 2AB 476 – The peoples of Altharn.

Venethar, Vul march, Kasidor.

Stood atop the tallest tower upon the battlements of castle Kasidor, lifelessly staring toward the vast and beautiful Mountains of Muuranth. The moonlight glimmering, his eyes glowing a purple hue from within his gold-plated mask.

Kastrith Mundur, King of Venethar, stands patiently waiting, meditating, harvesting the ethereal shroud of arcane energy.

Urskull Fenrith barges through the door to the outer battlements. ''My King, news.''

The purple glow dims from the eye sockets, his eyes now shadowed away by the depth of his mask, a mask that resembles the face of a man. ''Speak, Urskull,'' his voice somewhat strained in his adoring tone.

''We recovered this item from Seers Crossing, we believe it to belong or have an affiliation with the otherworldly being brought forward by the druids.''

Kastrith turns to Fenrith and gently takes the key from Fenrith's hands.

He looks upon it briefly, taking note of the picture attached to the key. ''And what of the being?'' He asks calmly.

''Urskull Olm is tracking it down as we speak. We believe it to be human, or at least similar to human form, we also believe it to be posing as a druid, it slipped our grasps during the attack.''

''Worry not, you knew naught of what you were hunting… I'm happy to hear of your progress. Now… let me take a proper look at what we have here,'' Kastrith takes the key and squeezes it hard. His eye sockets glow vigorously once again, silence shattered by the hum of magic. ''Human he is. His world… astounding….'' the glow dimmers. ''I hope Urskull Olm makes haste on his hunt, taking this 'man' out now at his weakest moments would eradicate the threat of treachery and hedonism it could be capable of. We must act before it masters it's drenching.''

''Agreed, my King.''

‘’That being is a threat to Vistra’s return, Darogoth will stop at nothing, but we ourselves must understand this man, but I wonder… what of his neutrality?’’ He tilts his head to his flag that rippled against the wind by the edge of the tower, a black flag with the head of a golden sabre cat sewn in the centre, the symbol of the Mundur Dynasty.

‘’I don’t follow?’’

‘’His time here was spent within Darogoth, nestled into the druidic teat as they spout their lies. He knows nothing of this world and only of what they tell him with their forked tongues. I wonder… is he a being of reason? With free will and consideration, or one of martyr and obedience to a single cause? His existence in this world does not have to be narrowed to just Darogoth,’’ Kastrith peers over the picture attached to the keys. ‘’Look at him. The glee and carefree happiness upon his innocent face, this must be his lover…. A key of sentimental value, I wonder what it unlocks.’’

‘’Do you think there’s more than one, he came with another being?’’

‘’No, there’s only him, I felt but one interference that had pierce the veil, he is lost.’’

‘’Any other orders my King?’’

‘’No, you and your men should rest, you must be tired after a perilous journey so far into enemy territory. You’ve done well, all of you. I must return to my gaze within Vistra’s realm. His strength grows with each passing day and I must aid him.’’

Fenrith glances off. ''Of course, my King.''

Kastrith pivots back in view of the mountains, his eyes glow once more. Faint dust-like particles shimmering in the moonlight begin materialising from the air, floating toward him. His essence consumes the particles one by one as they vanish from existence. The blissful hum of magic eloping with the gentle breeze of the northern winds.

Darogoth, Ard, Carsinia.

Carsinia was a breath of fresh air, physically and mentally. The air in Altharn was always notably more fresh and purer than what he had lived in prior to his arrival.

Gordon spent the majority of his time in Carsinia training with Brennus and Hashna, the consistent exercise and sword training really helped Gordon to follow a straighter path within his fragile mind, his lifestyle had gone from a careless young adult, woefully scorned after being torn from his home, a man who barely gave much care to his physical health even prior to his arrival, to now eating real organic foods and exercising regularly. For the most part he'd wake up every day sore, his hands were rough like sandpaper, his shoulders and forearms constantly ached, his muscles were tight, like being bound by girthy ropes.

This rapidly affected him, bolstering his mental fortitude by unleashing his frustrations through his sword arm was always a good form of therapy, but he knew this was not enough. After all, he still wasn't any closer to home.

From time to time, he would venture out of his little shack and wander the streets of Carsinia, he enjoyed people watching in the market, watching people go about their daily life as people did in his own home, comparing the differences of lifestyle, noting how old fashioned this world was in comparison to his own. He would Hang out in the tavern, browse items in the market. He was earning money now that he began officially training as a 'warrior' despite not really taking the ordeal as seriously as he should.

Vocorix would pay Gordon just as a regular oathsworn ward would be paid.

He spent his money on food, drink, and small trinkets here and there. He decided he'd spruce up his little shack to keep him busy, he replaced some ill-fitting panels, cleaned the place up and added a few decorations here and there, bits of furniture such as cupboards and a stand next to his bed. he even installed a small window by the door above his bed. all this handyman work he never truly experienced back home, and he was enjoying it. He was offered a bed in the barracks, but politely declined feeling comfortable where he was, enjoying the shack as his own special home, he didn't want to give up this kind of privacy.

He would tend to the daily jobs, changing his bathing water, tending to Brennus's armour, sharpening swords, mucking out the stables, he'd feed and take care of the horses and he even learned to ride them, he'd never even rode a horse before. The experience was immensely thrilling, apart from the chaffing, he loved horse riding so much he even vowed to take it up when he eventually returns home.

Aside from the typical hard labour jobs he'd also accompany Brennus on his duties, he watched and learned a lot about the life he was now forced to live. Brennus would take Gordon on patrols through the city, debt collecting, arresting criminals, patrolling the main roads and escorting the high king's family from place to place.

Although he knew his position amongst the oathsworn would be very different, especially knowing of his 'realm walker' status, Gordon actually was enjoying this new life, he felt as though he was appreciating all the small things he couldn't back home, he always yearned for a fresh start in life doing something completely different, something abstract and thrilling, he never expected this though.

Gordon still suffered quite badly from his night terrors, dreams of his old world, dreams of that voice. He'd wake in sweats, and as a result he always appeared quite puffy around his eyes that drooped with bags. The dreams were so surreal, he couldn't comprehend them, some of the dreams were of home, he'd wake up in bed next to Helen often, believing Altharn to be nothing but a simple nightmare, but every night he would be proven wrong as he woke in puddles of his own sweat, his heart racing to the point he felt he could collapse, sometimes it felt it was beating so fast it would burst right out of his chest, he dissociated reality for brief moments quite often as a result of being pulled through the realms, this weighed on him the heaviest. Sometimes even during the day he'd have dizzy spells and would have to adjust himself as he recuperated to his new reality. It was scary, but the cure was distraction, he needed to be distracted at all times to combat such grasping fears.

''Even after all I've been through, I feel a lot more content than I did in Seers Crossing, I guess it's because I'm busy all day every day and I'm surrounded by people I can meld with a little easier, everyone is quite nice to me, they respect me and just generally find me quite interesting. When people learn who I am it's constantly followed by a barrage of questions regarding home, and honestly, I don't even mind much now. It's always so funny to me, to see the disbelief on their faces as I try to explain how my world is compared to this one.

I still have days where I spend looking at my phone, it hits harder every single time I think about it, but distraction is key. I have a goal, not sure how to accomplish it, but I need to just put my head down and keep pressing on, it's been so long now, four months? Five months? Yeah, probably about five now... I should make more effort to keep track, but the more I realise how long I've been gone the more it hurts, so I try not to bother, I'll just focus on living in the now, trying to find the answers.

I've been reading a lot in the castle's library, looking for this 'magic of the endless void' still nothing. All I know is that when these 'Gods' were banished, the things they imbued with their magic did not disappear with them, I know that Fanara's Cradle was imbued with her magic and she no longer exists here, once it was used to bring me here, the magic eradicated itself, I just need to find some kind of artefact or something that's imbued with the magic of the Gods, just like Fanara's Cradle, so far, no luck, I have heard of artefacts left over by the Gods, but they're not charged with the right kind of magic, It has to be magic of the void, or the universe? I think that's what these people mean by that. Is the universe itself a form of magic? Could be something for the scientists to look into back home. What am I saying? It's crazy.

I'll find a way, I feel I've grown a lot since being here. I've even noticed my weight, I'm looking so lean these days. Honestly, I've never felt so comfortable in my own skin! I look great. If only Helen could see me now, my hair is quite long now too, I've started tying it up, never in all my life have I had long hair, it's quite something, and my beard... it's a little scraggly but it's kind of my way of trying to fit in I suppose, but I like it.

It's a cool world, honestly, beautiful. I just hope that soon I'll be able to sleep without having nightmares and flashes of that day. It's seriously overbearing.

I should write more, I never really keep track of this journal but I'll try and commit more to it, there's so muc-''

- *7th[th] Entry, Journal of Gordon Barker. Year 4AB 282*

Bang! Bang! Bang!

The door to Gordon's shack shakes, Gordon jumps in freight of it.

''Gordon, Gordon!'' It was Hashna's voice, she sounded unnerved.

He lunges toward the door, swinging it wide open. ''Hashna?! What is it?''

Hashna stood with a menacing grin, much like a Cheshire cat. ''We found them.''

''Who?''

''The raiding party, they haven't left Darogoth yet. The ones who slaughtered Seers Crossing! We assume they're still looking for you… Brennus asked me to come get you. We're preparing to leave within the hour, we're taking a small unit of Cavalry and Charioteers,'' she announces, almost tripping over her own words in excitement.

A rage boils deep inside, the craving of vengeance presents itself to Gordon. ''Fuck! Oh… but… I… I don't even have any armour of my own yet, or a sword.'' Gordon starts bouncing, trembling with the lust for blood. He wanted nothing more than to satisfy his urge. He questioned why he felt like this, he wasn't even sure anymore. They must pay.

''I'm taking you to the armoury now, we'll get you kitted out. You'll be riding in the chariot with me, you'll be on the back so you can cast from there and you can jump down with your sword if you need to.''

Gordon's stomach churns in fright and uncertainty, but then a flashback of horror returns to haunt the recesses of his mind, reminding him of the carnage, the death of his friends and all the innocent people who suffered by Venethari hands. ''Okay… let's go,'' Gordon steps outside. He wanted revenge, he wanted it now.

Hashna walks Gordon to the barracks. ''They're camped out near the river Sen, someone in the neighbouring villages spotted them and we had scouts track them. They're moving around as much as they can but our scouts are keeping us posted.''

''How do you know it's ones who raided Seers Crossing?''

''Because no unit of Venethar has any reason to be this deep in our territory, let alone even make it this far. We thought they would have gone by now, but they've been trying to pose as civilians and asking a lot of questions about you. Anyone asking too many questions about you in a Venethari accent is far too suspicious, Idiotic in fact. I heard they even kidnapped an innocent farmer to try and get information. Take a right here, this is the armoury,'' she points as she marches through the barracks' many rooms.

Hashna began digging through all the spare parts of armour, there were a lot of variants of chainmail and leather, even some plating here and there. ''Okay you'll probably want to be quite light on your feet, I'm guessing you won't need a shield since you'll need one hand free for casting. How about this? Chainmail, layered around the chest, lighter around the belly, there's some leather chaps there and some plated boots that might be ideal for you, don't forget the bracers… oh and here's some strapping for a short cloak, is there anything else? Oh helmet, of course… there's some good enough helmets here. Do you think you'll need extra protection on the shoulders? Or is the layered chainmail enough do you think?''

Gordon shrugs. ''Erm… I'm relying on your judgement here.''

Hashna Scoffs. ''I suppose this is kind of new to you,'' she smirks. ''Okay, that should do, standard protection, not too heavy, not too light, now let me just grab you a sword,'' she dumps all the armour in Gordon's arms and moves on over to the weapon racks, inspecting them for a brief moment until picking out a good length blade. ''Here, how does this feel for you?''

''Give me a minute, just getting this gear on,'' Gordon can't actually believe he's putting on armour and readying himself for a fight, he halts himself half way into slipping into his chaps as he allows a few seconds to remind himself how unbelievable this all is.

Hashna studies him as he places all the armour on himself. Thanks to his experience working around armour of late, he managed well enough fitting into all the complicated parts. He felt slightly drowned by it all once he was kitted up. ''Is this the right fit?''

''Not exactly, these are the spares… move around a bit.''

''Yeah, I think this is fine….''

''Don't just think it's fine Gordon, know it is. You're going to battle! Not a fucking festival.''

''No seriously it's fine, I can move.''

She throws Gordon the sword, he catches it by the handle and gives it a few test swings. ''Yeah,'' He nodded eagerly.

She returns the nod in agreement and the two exit the armoury.

He felt surreal donning armour, it wasn't the flashy armour the oathsworn wore, after all he wasn't an oathsworn, he was a ward. But he felt like a real warrior, it was immensely bizarre.

Gordon and Hashna marched back out from the barracks, their armour clinking as the chains rattled at the force of their hastened steps. Brennus can be seen barking orders here and there whilst he fastens a few belts onto his horse.

''Brennus!'' Hashna shouts.

Brennus turns to see a battle-ready Gordon. A smile washes over him as he adjusts his eyepatch. ''Gordon,'' he lowers his head in respect. ''You'll be with Hashna on the chariot, she's a phenomenal charioteer. We're taking in the horses to get there as fast as we can, once there, we will dismount and wait while the chariot unit will charge in and cause a little bit of disarray, then we'll face them head on. Gordon, I want you to cast from the chariot, you can jump down from it if you need to manoeuvre or engage in melee. I planned this out to be easy for you, I'll keep an eye on you and will be next to you the whole time once we get into the thick of it. Hashna will too, and she'll be firing javelins at the bastards whilst she's on the reins, trust me her shots always count. They're cosying up somewhere by the river Sen, if we catch them off guard the chariots will be enough to scurry them and stop them from organising their archers efficiently, if the archers become too much for you, just duck within the chariot,'' he places an arm on Gordon's shoulder. ''Once you're in the heat of it all, remember to focus and breathe, panicking will end your life faster than an enemy blade. Just remember what those cunts did to you, show them who the fuck they're messing with,'' he turns off, shouting at the other warriors. ''Why the fuck is that horse still not got a saddle?!''

Gordon takes a deep sigh as he adjusts his clunky helmet.

''Come, let's get the chariot ready,'' says Hashna.

Hashna brings Gordon to a large wheeled chariot with huge deathly spokes poking out from the side of the wheel, the chariot itself was big, it stretched right up to Gordon's chest once he stood inside, Gordon aided by setting up the reigns and placing armour upon the two horses breasts and head.

It was time to go.

Brennus and Hashna alongside another oathsworn, Gaeliun, were leading the attack. It was a small army of about thirty warriors and twelve chariots. Gordon remembered how many raiders there were. He was scared they might be slightly outnumbered, Hashna assured Gordon that the numbers won't be a problem, Venethar are known for their horse archers, but Darogoth are famed by their charioteers and infantry, she told him chariots work well against horse archers if steered correctly, especially the way Darogothian chariots are built.

The warband sets out and leaves Carsinia in thundering haste, Gordon stands in the chariot alongside Hashna as she grasps the reins, many pockets of javelins by her side at the ready, her large oval shield hanging from her back, he'd never seen the oathsworn properly suited for battle, it was a truly fearsome look, their helmets a glimmering gold topped with a beautiful black plume, their armour a mix of chainmail, leather straps corrugated with small pieces of scaled plating.

The roar of the warband shook Gordon's heart as they sang songs of glory and conquest throughout their journey. Directions and plans had to change from time to time as scouts would come to and from the location of the raiders, keeping Brennus and Gaeliun informed of their movements.

The raiders had made their way into a cave by the river Sen, as they approached near the location, Oathsworn Gaeliun ordered a halt.

''Gordon, with me, we're going to scout ahead,'' Brennus orders.

Moving through the bushes Gordon grasps his hilt anxiously as he readies himself to draw his blade. Brennus slaps his hand, ''Calm it.'' he whispers loudly.

They poke their heads through the bushes about a mile out from the cave, there were people here, men outside the cave who appeared to be cooking some food and fishing in the river, none of them wearing anything that would specify them as Venethari.

''Is that them?'' Gordon asks.

''Not sure… could be, there's a few horses that are hitched up but I only see three… hmm, could be some hunters from Lunarum. Let's wait it out for a bit,'' Brennus begins rustling around in one of his pouches. ''While we wait, here,'' Brennus produces a small wooden container of blue powdery liquid.

''Is that warpaint?'' Gordon asks.

''Yeah, we never got a chance to paint up as we needed to leave so soon. But I feel it's important for you, I want you to feel the true morale of a Darogoth war party,'' Brennus grins, displaying his teeth.

Gordon thinks for a moment. ''I mean… I've seen regular people wear it in the street, it looks like it takes some skill, I'm no painter….''

''Yes, people wear it casually… but its original use is for battle, it's tradition. I'll put it on for you,'' Brennus digs his hand into the mixture and gives a single hard swipe to Gordon's face. ''It's not meant to make you look pretty,'' he laughs quietly as he reaches for more to use on himself. ''The others will be doing the same.''

After around an hour of scouring upon the men around the cave, they finally see something.

''Brennus, look,'' one of the warriors pipes up.

A large man had exited the cave, he was wearing the fearsome armour of the urskulls, a plated helmet with a visor to shield the nose and eyes, and attached to the visor was chainmail that hung from the helmet, drooping onto the shoulders to create a form of chainmail veil, the man's shoulders were engulfed by thick bear hide. The rest of his kit is of hardened leather coated with metallic rings. The Urskull uniform is famously iconic.

''An urskull, that's them. Gordon, back to the chariots. There's enough space outside the cave for about six chariots? Once the infantry joins in the chariots will dismount. The rest will wait on the perimeter of the clearing to aid if needs be. We have them in the palm of our hands! Head back and give Gaeliun the information, be quick… I think their making some preparations to move again.''

Gordon ran all the way back to the warband as quickly as he could, he used some magic to improve his speed along the way, zooming past trees, propelling forward with impressive momentum.

He gave Gaeliun the information he needed and the warband was to make its move, Gordon jumped onboard with Hashna.

''Draw your blade, Gordon. In moments to come you're going to paint it with Venethari blood!'' Hashna shouts valiantly.

Gordon draws his sword as he holds on to the rim of the chariot. Time was moving slowly, the anxiety was beginning to hit him only to be suppressed, suddenly washed away, that feeling inside, another flashback of Seers Crossing. Parinos, Orthunus.

The chariots carefully ride up behind some large bushes and form up into an orderly fashion on the perimeter before charging on through, ''Brace!'' Shouts Hashna as she snaps at her reins, plummeting through the shrubbery and into the fray, the chariots sways violently as they trample through uneven land, the spokes of death ripping up all manner of plant life.

The men outside the cave already heard the noises and had their weapons drawn, walking toward the noise to investigate.

Chariots burst from the bushes with malice, the soldiers ran back to the cave in fright. ''CHARIOTS!'' They screamed.

''There's more of them… look, down the stream!'' A soldier next to Brennus points out.

''What?! Where the fuck did they come from?! Their mounted and ready?!''

''I don't think they know just yet; they haven't got their weapons drawn.''

''Well, they're about too! We need to get in there before they get overwhelmed, good thing our shields are fucking huge, eh lad?'' Shouts Brennus as he punches his comrade's shoulder. ''Let's form up, quickly!''

Hashna grabs a javelin and with the tremendous force of her giant ropey arms, lofts it toward the fleeing men, it hits directly into a soldier's calf, pinning the man's leg into the murky ground, she lets out a horrific blood curdling war cry as she allows the spokes of her wheels tear the man to pieces as she runs him down.

She reels the chariot into a U-turn, other chariots follow the pattern as they barraged the cave entrance with javelins.

Men scurry into the cave; others scurry down the stream of the river trying to take cover.

One chariot follows the men fleeing to the river, before it even reaches the bank, mounted Venethari unexpectedly arrive into the fray, crashing into the chariot, killing the horse and throwing the riders into the shallow stream.

The horsemen were just as surprised to see the charioteers as they were the horsemen, they were galloping to the cave before the warning shouts occurred.

The battle ensues, the Venethari cavalry draw their bows and begin returning fire in defence.

Feeling the morale rapidly shift as the bulk of their force returns to camp, the soldiers who took refuge in the cave rally out armed and eager.

Seeing the enemy rally out, Gordon seizes his chance, he forges a dreadful pressure within the palm of his hand and sends it toward and into the cave, his ball of fire screeches deep into the cave at incredible speed, exploding from within, giving out a ferocious roar as the cave lights up from the inside, burning fiercely. Many Venethari pouring out of the cave become ignited in the blaze, falling to the ground meeting their fiery demise.

''Yes Gordon!'' Hashna shouts valiantly.

As the men pour out and the horse archers attempt to out manoeuvre the chariots, Gordon ducks within his rigid spot, shaking left to right within the chariot vigorously as he watches arrows skim above him.

Hashna lets out even more screams as she rushes to grab more javelins mounted on the inside and hurling them all around, the deafening whiney of a nearby horse takes frontal force of Hashna's incredible throw.

Then suddenly, another cry of warriors can be heard. It was Brennus and Gaeliun leading the charge of infantry. Their mighty screams deafening that of the current clash.

Gordon cautiously pokes his head from the chariot, he sees a mounted arched reel into his open point, he rises holding on to the edges of the cart, keeping his balance, he ejects a powerful wave of force toward the horseman, the surrounding area ripples with a violent shockwave. Gordon tears him and the horse down to the floor.

''Gordon, take him out, jump! Go to Brennus, I'll keep them busy!'' Hashna shouts as she halts her chariot.

Nervous yet eager, Gordon jumps from the chariot, sword in hand. The vibrations of the chariot still resonate in his thighs and feet.

He runs toward the downed soldier who was desperately trying to scurry to his feet. Gordon doesn't think twice and goes to thrust his sword to the man's ribs, the man sees it coming and propels himself backward, avoiding the thrust and fleetly rolling onto his feet.

Gordon brings back his sword arm and propels his casting hand with a blast of fiery hell directly to the head, a direct hit. The man propels back to the ground, screaming in agony.

''Gordon!'' Hashna shouts from behind.

A mounted Venethari had swerved past Hashna and now aimed directly for Gordon with his axe held high ready for a fatal swing. Gordon manipulates his perception and gracefully dodges the blow in mere seconds. The horse comes to a halt and the soldier jumps down with a swift landing.

He runs at Gordon, yelling ferociously. An overhead swing comes into play, the soldier is testing Gordon's strength.

Gordon parries the blow with a small knockback to himself and his attacker, Gordon's heart begins to pound hard.

The Venethari soldier swings relentlessly, Gordon dodges and blocks the swings just as he had trained too, along with magical aid.

He needs to react back to the attacker but he can't focus. The attacks are quick and fierce. The fear striking Gordon was suppressing his focus on magic, he remembers Brennus's words and forcefully grounds himself, eventually he manages to manipulate his perception again, blocking a swing and connecting it with his hilt, disarming the attacker in a swift and skilful manner.

Gordon sees his chance and swings toward the attacker's head as quickly as he can, carelessly putting all his strength into this one swing, he slices the leather flap of the man's helmet covering the neck and face, and penetrates the man's cheek with brutal force. Gordon's eyes widen in astonishment at what he is looking at. Blood spurt outward, Gordon winces back his sword hastily and stabs it into the man's kidneys where his armour is weakest. Gordon pushes the man back, retracting his sword. Realising the chaos was growing around him he had no time to take in and ponder on what happened, he needed to keep fighting. He couldn't help but feel the man's blood run cold upon his hands as he watched the life of this soldier slip away slowly from his fatal strike.

It seemed that the initial plan was not going as well as it should have. Everyone was attacking relentlessly; the field of battle was erratic and chaotic.

The chariots had all dismounted now, and only a few horse archers remained mounted trying to get shots from the outside of the skirmish; they were quickly taken down by the chariots on the perimeter waiting to act as back up. All that was left was a melee that stood firm outside the cave.

Gordon glanced toward Brennus, who was just a few feet away. Brennus was absolutely maniacal within the heat of the fight, his roars piercing the hearts of men around him, his face painted in blood spray, his swings ruthless, fast and ever so powerful.

Gordon sees a soldier pick an axe from the floor behind Brennus, he charges him by lifting the axe above his head to strike Brennus in the back.

''Brennus!'' Gordon shrieks.

Brennus glances over, Gordon fires a shock wave knocking both the attacker and Brennus to the ground. Gordon darts toward the man, stabbing him through the open part of his helmet over and over again in a flurry of bloodlust.

Brennus springs back to his feet. ''Fuck me, Walker!''

Another charges onto Gordon, knocking him back, almost tripping him to the ground, the two lock their weapons as they stumble around in a frenzied race of might, their swords scrape against each other fiercely, cutting into Gordon's chin.

The soldier reverts his weapon and raises his pommel, breaking the stalemated stance and striking Gordon in the nose, busting it open. Gordon tries to maintain focus, pulsating more magic to keep the fight under control but he was becoming exhausted, he was struggling to keep up his magic consistently.

The soldier's blade was not far off after the initial pommel strike, swinging diagonally towards Gordons throat, Gordon lunged backward to avoid the hit.

Brennus becomes locked in combat unable to assist.

Gordon throws a punch to the man's face as a nimble counter, his attacker is too fuelled by adrenaline to even react.

Gordon repositions himself, readying his sword. He then drops his stance, lifting his casting hand and propelling a hellish inferno, engulfing the man, effortlessly blowing him away into the clashing crowd.

Gordon takes a second to wipe the blood pouring from his bust nose, spitting out some that had trickled into his mouth. Looking upon his hand smeared in his own blood, he feels a rush, a rush like no other.

He bellows out a cry of battle, curdling the very winds that blew by, blessed by Iskarien's breath.

He charges into the crowd, stabbing away furiously at unsuspecting victims, using his magic to force the enemy to the ground and blow them away, a group of Venethari attempt to collect themselves together as the battle now edges heavily in Darogothian favour. This only created an opportunity for Gordon, sending yet another enormous blast of fire into the centre of them, bringing them down ablaze in a blistering inferno.

Many of the Venethari soldiers try to escape, many cut down by chariots and picked off by the back up on the perimeter, the battle comes to a swift and victorious end.

Gordon collapses to his knees into the dirt, bewildered, scared, furious and blood drunk. The pain of his nose, now very present.

Brennus approaches the surrendered urskull. ‘’Get the fuck down!’’ He kicks the man's knees inwards, producing a horrid snap. ‘’You’re coming with us, Urskull,’’ he darts around looking for Gordon. He spots him nearby, noticing his gormless and spaced-out expression as he kneels to the floor. ‘’Gordon, Gordon?’’ He calls out.

Gordon doesn’t respond as he stares at the clear skies above, his eyes empty.

‘’You did well, lad,’’ he gives a gentle kick to Gordon’s ribs to grab his attention and then extends his hand, assisting him to his feet.

Gordon locks his eyes to Brennus. ‘’Fuck, Fuck….’’ his voice shakes.

‘’It’s over… savour yourself.’’ Brennus says proudly, holding him firmly by his shoulders.

Gordon collects himself, feeling disgusted, proud and overwhelmed all at the same time.

Hashna approaches with a rag of torn cloth. ''Clean yourself up, warrior,'' she smiles, her face also speckled with blood.

Gordon cracks a smile as he takes the rag and cleans his bloodied face, trying to be gentle around his bust nose, all the cuts on his face stinging away as he dabs around.

Brennus returns to the urskull he left with the other warriors, tying him up and throwing him into a wagon they brought along with them. ''Gordon, with the prisoner, if he escapes cook him, will you?''

Gordon obeys and jumps into the wagon, the other Darogothian warriors scour over the bodies, looting them dry.

Vengeance had been done.

The urskull glared Gordon up and down, his eyes fixated. It started making him feel uncomfortable.

''Problem?'' Gordon spits.

''You....'' the urskull speaks. ''I saw what you did... are you, him? ''

''Depends what you mean by him.''

The war party begins moving back to Carsinia, the cart thuds and sways with the bumps of the ground.

The urskull tries to balance himself in his beaten state as the cart knocks him around. ''The being, the one not of this world,''

''Maybe?'' Gordon glances off to the treeline, refusing to look the urskull in the eye.

''My men recovered something, your face… your face is on it, there's talk that the realm walker is human.''

''And?''

''Just interested,'' the urskull winces in pain.

''You lead the raid on Seers Crossing?''

''Yes, me and one other urskull.''

''Why? To find me?''

''Correct… just following orders laddie, just like you do.''

Gordon's head snaps to the Urskull. ''You wanted to kill me, so you slaughtered an entire village of innocent people? Fuck off.''

''I didn't kill a soul that day, I captured two druids, my men did the slaughtering.''

''And you ordered that.''

''No.''

''Whatever, cunt.''

The urskull laughs from his belly, giving out an ugly smile, exposing his blood-stained teeth matted amongst his fiery beard, the wrinkles folding upon his bald head. ''I didn't know what I was looking for, something that didn't belong here? That's all I had to go off, and it was summoned at Seers Crossing. My men were afraid, you understand?''

Gordon's face scrunches.

''If the druids have that kind of power, what else are they capable of?! My men cut them down out of fear, nobody ordered it... maybe Urskull Fenrith did? He's quite a bloodthirsty one is Fenrith,'' the urskull gives a hideous snigger. ''We had to take you out, do you have any idea what a being drenched in magic is capable of? Long ago this happened once, and many suffered and died at the beast's hands. We obeyed for the good of our people and 'the safe return of our God' or so our king says.''

Gordon says nothing.

''And here I am sitting adjacent to you, incredible. I'll likely die anyway, Realm Walker. I don't care much for what you think of me, or these lot, I know the laws of Darogoth. My life is forfeit. So, tell me, where is it you are from?''

''Not important now, is it?''

''Well, no. I'll die, anything you tell me isn't going anywhere. Come now, this is going to be one awkward fucking journey for the both of us, at least make my last moments on this world interesting.''

''How about you tell me who you are?''

''Okay, we can play it your way. After all, you're the victor here. My name is Olm, Olm Uldur. I'm one of the five urskull to the seventh horde of Kasidor.''

''What is urskull?''

''Someone who's attained standing and rank within the hordes of Venethar, quite similar to your oathsworn, I lead that band of men, as you already know.''

''How did it feel, watching your troops cut down all those innocent people?''

''I didn't feel anything, as is so in the ways of battle, even your oathsworn will tell you the same.''

''How are you so… calm?''

''How? I'm an urskull of Venethar, we yearn for the noblest of deaths, death in battle. I knew the dangers of this quest. Afterall, the pay-out we were offered was a rarity. I couldn't turn that down.''

''Ah so you did this all for money? Of course….''

Olm Scoffs. ''You have a family, Realm Walker?''

''Hmmm,'' Gordon mumbles.

''You'd do anything to keep them safe, content, fed, happy? In my world I need money to do that. I could of fucking retired with that kind of money. Me and my wife, Ilda, we planned to buy a ranch… live out the rest of our days in the steppe and watch the children grow, that's all any real man wants.''

Gordon's brows raise. ''You have children?''

''Two girls, twelve and seventeen, the eldest is a fierce little shit so she is,'' his eyes glisten with a single tear, he blinks it back.

Gordon felt pity for Olm.

''Don't try to sweet talk me so you can try and escape,'' Gordon barks.

''And how would I do that with a broken leg? You're oathsworn brute fucked it right up,'' Olm gives a breathy sigh. ''I'm not trying to escape, I'm trying to embrace my final days, I thought it was quite something, you know? Sitting with the 'beast' who's to make a mark on our two kingdoms.''

Gordon refrains from being brash and allows himself to lower his guard. ''This world… I… I never killed a man before, until I arrived here. You think I'm to make a mark on these kingdoms? I'm gone the first chance I get; I won't be making marks anywhere other than on your men, it was good to get revenge on you bastards.''

Olm smiles. ''We do what we must to survive. You're simply obeying your instincts, if you had to kill someone in battle, better you kill them than they kill you, doesn't matter who you are… we all have the same notions,'' he sits up from his pain induced slouch. ''Do you think you can do it? Take down Kastrith Mundur, Kastrith the Redeemer?''

''I don't know.''

''He's changed, that's for sure, but without him Venethar would cease to be, families would have starved to death, the famine his brother caused set in a poverty that swept my nation. Kastrith corrected this.''

''Why is he doing this? Why is all this bloodshed on Darogoth? On me?''

''He has his reasons.''

Gordon feels something in Olms words. ''Is he crazy?''

''Only the Gods know.''

''Why do you fight for him.''

''I just told you.''

''So, what do you think about him then? You don't seem too confident in your king.''

''I don't think about him, I think about myself and my girls.''

''Fair enough.''

Olm gives a light grunt. ''You have children?''

''No… just a woman I left behind when I was torn away from home and dumped here.''

''Hah, now you see, you don't seem to be too confident in Darogoth,'' Olm gives a smug grin.

''I'm trying to find a way back, Darogoth is my only hope.''

''Maybe so. Maybe not, but do you see? We all have our reasons.''

''Yeah, I suppose we do.''

''I may have taken Seers Crossing away from you. But the druids took your entire life and put a sword in your hands, remember that. Now, the real question here is, what are you going to take? the lives of thousands of Venethari because of what Darogothian druids did to you?''

Gordon looks off to the base of the cart feeling a truth in Olms words, he gives a vigorous shake of his head. ''The druids had no idea what they were bringing forward or what this would cost. They were scared, scared of you, and from what I know, Kastrith is the one putting swords in his people's hands because he's claiming to be the herald of a God, that's fucked.''

''You see? We all have our reasons.''

Days pass, and they finally arrive back in Carsinia. Olm is taken to the dungeon below the castle for interrogation, Gordon watches on as he is carried off, hobbling along on his broken leg.

''Careful of that one, urskulls are vicious bastards and ruthless fighters. Don't underestimate him,'' Hashna says as she joins in on Gordons view of Olm.

''Aren't the oathsworn?'' Gordon replies.

''Only if you're a blonde bastard with one eye,'' laughs Hashna. ''No, we don't kill innocent civilians, let alone men and women devoted to their Gods who'd not spent a single day with a sword in their hand. I heard you two talking, don't listen to the words falling from his forked tongue.''

''Gordon,'' Brennus shouts. ''Get yourself cleaned up and rested, we'll have some business to attend to shortly.''

''What business?''

''You'll see.''

Confused, Gordon pats Hashna goodbye and promptly returns to his shack. He was scared to be left alone, knowing he would do nothing but re-picture the events of battle over and over.

Brennus headed straight into the castle to seek Vocorix. Vocorix was dining with his family as Brennus knocked for his attention outside the feasting hall, Brennus knocked lightly.

''What?'' Vocorix says bluntly, clearly aggravated by the disturbance.

''It's Oathsworn Brennus. We've returned….''

''Get in here!'' Vocorix swallows what's left in his mouth. ''You're back from the attack, I'm assuming all went well since you're stood here breathing?''

''Yes… although not entirely to plan, we still came out on top. We have an urskull awaiting interrogation in the dungeons.''

''Brilliant, how did Gordon fair?'' Vocorix continues to dig into his food.

''Yes, he did fine… I actually wanted to talk to you about him for a brief moment… if I'm not interrupting….''

''Oh? Is there a problem?''

''Well… yes.''

Gordon lay in his bed, staring blankly at the crooked roof, reminiscing the fight, he couldn't help himself. The lives he took, watching people draw their final breath, it was harrowing. Something else stirred within, he felt proud, Parinos, Lucotorix and Orthunus, they can rest in peace now, their deaths were avenged, but at what cost? Was it really worth it? Or was he just as bad as the raiders?

Olm's words repeat in his head, echoing over and over like a broken record, even the flashbacks of the disaster at Seers Crossing, Orthunus, Parinos, the man's face searing with the heat of Gordon's flame, Lucotorix's screams. It picked at him, scratching at the surface of his sanity. He slaps his head, holding it in frustration.

''Just take me home,'' he mutters. ''Please.''

A gentle knock at his door cleared away the cloud of uncertainty.

He opened the door to Brennus, the rain pelting off his armour as the skies opened up, washing away the blood and dirt that he was still proudly smeared in. ''May we come in?'' His face was barren.

''We?''

Brennus barges in with a druid that follows with their hood covering their face. Gordon ogles the druid intently.

''This is… Daxos. Druid to the high king.''

Daxos removes her hood, revealing a frail old woman, even older than Parinos could have been, she looked incredibly fragile and almost ready to drop dead at a moment's notice. Her eyes sunken so much that the outline of her skull was clearly visible. She had a surprising amount of hair for her age, all tied back into a messy bun. ''Greetings, Realm Walker Gordon. We haven't had the pleasure as of yet,'' she croaks as she gives a warming smile.

''Hello?'' Gordon responds, somewhat concerned

Brennus clears his throat. ''So… I… have something for you, Gordon,'' he signals to Daxos, she produces a wooden box, patterned and pretty.

''What is it?'' Gordon asks.

''May I, Daxos?'' Brennus adds.

She passes the box to Brennus; he opens it slowly. Inside sat a golden torc with a twisted arch, its heads representing two wheels, finely crafted, resting upon red velvet. ''I didn't know how you'd feel about this, but I wanted to welcome you formally and officially to our world… as one of us.''

Gordon is speechless, a single hard shiver scuttles down his spine.

''Gordon?''

''Brennus… I… can this even happen? I'm not even from here, I'm….'' Gordon stops himself.

''Yes… I asked permission from the high king, Daxos is here to witness and present to you your civilian-ship,'' he hands the box back to Daxos. ''So? Will you accept this? I'm not binding you to us, it's just… I thought it'd be… nice… you know… all that shite. You can still return to your home. I just thought it would be nice to have… and… to… remember us, you know?'' Brennus stumbles on his words.

''Yes Brennus, I accept….''

Daxos takes the torc from the box, she stands before him lifting the torc above his head and behind his neck. ''Under the eyes of Fanara's hand. I, Daxos Ard-Lun. Druid of Carsinia under High King Vocorix Fen-Drosii, grant you this torc to become one under the lands of Darogoth. Be Faithful to yourself and the world you walk, and of course… your own world. Forged in the lands of Ard, from this day, you are reborn, Gordon Ard-Barker,'' Daxos gently places down the torc to rest amongst his collarbones.

A tear sheds slowly from Gordon's eye, he attempts to hide it. ''I….''

''You did well back then, you deserve this, and also… It helps to not be torcless in Darogoth.''

Gordon scoffs lightly in jest. ''Shut up Brennus, you're a big soft arse really, aren't you?''

''Fuck off, Gordon.''

''Oathsworn! Language!'' Daxos snaps, hitting Brennus in the stomach. ''Congratulations, Gordon. May your future bring you happiness and the answers you seek. Might I add, I am looking into your… issue. I'm studying Parinos's notes that we salvaged on Fanara's Cradle. It'll take time, and I warn you, it's not going to be easy.''

‘’Thank you… Daxos.’’

She gives a small bow and leaves Gordon’s shack, shuffling out of the door and slowly disappearing into the pouring rain.

Brennus slaps Gordons arm as he smiles and follows her out, escorting her back to the castle.

As soon as his door slams shut, he places his hand on his torc, running his fingers over the curves and swirls of the arched frame and feeling the bulk of its weight.

He stood in silence

A golden torc, a symbol of the people.

13: Brother

A light beckons in the distance. ''Gordon,'' its voice quakes around him.

He stands once again, observing that alluring white light within the blackness of nothing, staring, captivated. ''I can feel you again,'' he mutters as his entire body shudders with warmth.

''Gordon.'' The light echoes as it floats overhead ever so calmly toward him.

The overbearing shine dimmers as it comes in closer, softly placing itself before him, revealing a white robed woman, her hair, black like the feathers of a crow, her face beautiful and young. ''You're growing well, it's pleasing to see.''

Gordon looks upon her in awe, she resembles those of the druids, he is warmed by her sight.

''What... are you? Why do I feel this so... intensely?''

''I am a part of you, Gordon. Bound to you when my existence forfeited.''

''That didn't really answer my question, this place though... it feels different than before.''

''That's because this void is you.''

''What?''

''All beings exist within the endless void; in turn the endless void exists within all of us. Endless possibilities with endless forms of everything. When you came here, I could break through to you but you severed my reach many times, you were startled, panicked, broken beyond recompense. I'd try and try again; I'd use all of my strength to simmer the chaos you once were. Yet my influence was as just as I intended, thankfully.''

''Have you got something to do with the reason I'm here? You can… help?''

The woman stares intently for a moment. ''I'm that feeling deep inside, I'm the voice of your reason, I'm your guide to our world, I was the one to soothe you in your most frightening moments. My life force opened the gate and my soul bonded to the magic surrounding it and my world. When you stepped through… I was born again.'' She pauses for a moment as she looks upon Gordon's feeble face. ''And no, Gordon. I cannot take you back, that my dear is an impossible task. You know what will take you back, you just have to find it.''

''Then how did I come here in the first place?''

''You were brought forward by such magic, that of which has been exhausted and from my knowledge it was the only known source of it left, left over by the Gods that once walked.''

''I never truly believed it. I did… sort of,'' he glances up at the woman, catching her eye in a mutual hanging of silence, then it clicks.

''Hang on… you… you're….'' Gordon's inner memories flashes. Images of a dead woman being carried and rested amongst the statue in Seers Crossing, his heart begins to race, his breathing weighs heavy. ''No, no… you're….''

He wakes in sweats, swallowing a large gulp of air to sate his starving lungs.

''Camula!'' He shouts out as he wipes his sweat drenched forehead. ''Camula….'' he gently pats his body, checking himself over as he eases down from the shock of waking.

A sensation of purity and love gushes down his spine, tingling into his arms and legs making his arm hairs stand firmly on end. ''Camula?'' He shakes his head and rubs his eyes, he reaches for his torc of gold, placing it around his neck and giving it a soft stroke.

His head snaps around scanning the shoddy walls of his shack. ''This is fucked up.''

After his exasperated wake he readies himself for the day of his usual work load and leaves his home.

Flashes of Camula's face flicker in his head, memories of her lifeless body, her empty eyes, her ethereal being that stalks his slumber… followed by another warm sensation flushing throughout, he smiles to himself in comfort.

Walking toward the stable Gordon notices Olm, tied to a post and half naked, it seemed as if he was no longer bound to the dungeons of Carsinia Castle, now left to rot in a muddy patch of ground where everyone can see him. He was black and blue with bruises, his face smeared with a mixture of dried blood and dirt, his eyes puffed from the swelling, the two shared a glance in passing.

''Realm Walker… Gordon. Or should I say, Gordon Ard-Barker, the Realm Walker,'' he splutters and slurs feebly.

''Olm…'' Gordon stops in his tracks. ''What are they doing with you then?''

Olm gives an unsettling grin. ''Death, in the coming days I presume.''

''May your God be with you then,'' he continued on his way.

''Walker…'' Olm strains.

Gordon double backs to him.

''Die with a blade in your hand, don't die with piss in your breeches,'' he laughs pitifully. ''May your otherworldly Gods smile upon you, Vistra willing….'' a friendly smile breaks out from under his pain, he nods Gordon away.

Startled by the comment Gordon nods back and carries on toward the stable leaving Olm to his demise, before he makes his first step another voice beckons from behind.

''Gordon,'' a familiar ruffled voice bellows from behind. It was Hashna.

''Morning, Hashna, I haven't seen you since the Sen,'' Gordon chirps.

''Good day to you, ah yes… duty calls….'' her eye's become drawn to a golden sparkle around Gordon's collar. ''You're no longer torcless?!'' She remarks.

''Yeah… Brennus and Daxos came and gave me my civilian-ship.''

''Good on him, eh?'' Olm interrupts.

''Get fucked, Urskull.'' Hashna Spits. ''He didn't mention anything- oh never mind, it's Brennus… of course. Well anyway, you deserve it. I'm proud of you, little Walker,'' she punches his arm lightly.

Olm gives a snigger. ''A beast like you with a heart of gold? I didn't think women like you existed,'' he scoffs faintly.

Hashna delivers a hard kick to his already beaten and scuffed face. Olm collapses coughing profusely in agony.

Taken back by Hashna's kick, Gordon attempts to continue the conversation. ''Aye, should have seen the look on his face when I thanked him,'' Gordon laughs, his eyes glancing away from Olm's suffering.

''Next time he tries to do something nice, just punch him square in the face, I'm sure he'll appreciate it more,'' she chuckles. ''Oh, the high king wishes to see you by the way, he said to find him when you're free in the day, he'll be in his chambers until sunset.''

''Oh? I could go now?''

''And who's going to muck out Brennus's horse?'' Hashna folds her arms sarcastically.

''The guy who did it before me?''

Hashna gives a roaring laugh. ''You're getting far too comfortable here!'' She punches his arm again, numbing it.

''Yeah… right, well I'll sort the horse out once I've seen the high king, don't worry.''

''Relax, I'll see you soon,'' she winks, propelling a spit of phlegm over Olm as she walks off.

Gordon gives a casual sigh as he rushes toward the castle, he glances back to Olm shackled to the post. He wasn't conscious, his head was dipped into his chest as he lay limp suspended by his arms, a pitiful sight to say the least. Regardless, Gordon pressed onward.

After passing the guards and entering the castle Gordon gets slightly lost winding through the endless cobbled halls, eventually he finds Vocorix in passing.

''High King…'' Gordon gives an awkward bow.

''Gordon… or should I address you as… Gordon Ard-Barker?''

Gordon awkwardly laughs at the comment. ''You wanted to see me?''

''Yes… come to my chambers, we'll speak there.''

Vocorix and Gordon march off through the winding corridors and enter Vocorix's chambers; as soon as the door behind slams shut, Vocorix immediately turns to speak.

''I have two things to speak with you about. Firstly, about your position. I've heard nothing but good things, especially from the fight by the river Sen. Taking out those raiders was a sort of test for you. I can't lie... I wasn't exactly confident in you at first but I wanted to see how you fared. Brennus, Gaeliun and Hashna assure me you performed to an outstanding degree amongst the other warriors, especially for your first fight. You know these two to be oathsworn, and ideally, I want you to join them... but becoming oathsworn means you swear your life to your Lord and in this case, it's me. But I understand you're eager to return home... so you won't exactly become an oathsworn, but I'm granting you the same reputable standing, the perks and all that. The Realm Walker can't just run around as Brennus's ward, the war presses on and we need you, besides I'm sure Brennus doesn't want to be outshined by his own ward... I'm offering you a unique position in urgency. I'm grasping at straws here because personally I don't fully trust you or your abilities. But I do trust my oathsworn, for they have sung your praises... please... don't make me regret this Gordon, Darogoth is in dire need. Half of Glaen is already under Venethari occupation. The city of Shem was taken from us just two weeks ago and we don't have any time to waste... what say you?''

''Erm... yes, High King.''

''Good. Now the second thing... I received a rather... peculiar letter.''

''Oh?'' Gordon cocks his head.

Vocorix gestures to his writing desk. He walks over and picks up the letter in question and begins to read it out.

''High King Vocorix Fen-Drosii of Darogoth.

This bloodshed between our nations is tough on both our people, with the fruitful past of being the closest allies of Uros and the wonderful history we both share. I wanted us to speak on the terms of recent conflicts. I'd like to propose a standstill with a formal discussion, upon the Spire of Oldwood, the place where our Gods formed their pact of peace, Fitting is it not? Perhaps we can do the same.

Call off your hostilities on my people and I shall do the same, Your Lord of Shem is still alive and well. I implore you, High King, consider the offer.

I also have taken interest in the being your druids have brought before us all from the other worlds. I know more about him than you think. Bring a large contingent of your loyal if you wish, I understand our relations of recent are somewhat sensitive. I can assure you there is nothing malicious to fear of me in my offer.

Kastrith Mundur, King of Venethar.''

Vocorix throws the letter back to his desk carelessly. ‘’Arse licking prick.’’

‘’He wants to make peace?’’ Gordon asks.

‘’No… my bet is that he wants to size you up and then maybe assassinate me.’’

‘’Okay… so what are thinking of doing?’’

‘’It would be foolish of me to agree, but it would be foolish and cowardly of me to disagree.’’

‘’So, you’re going to meet with him?’’

Vocorix scoffs. ‘’Of course, no high king of Darogoth is to be seen as a coward, and you will come too, I don’t for a second doubt that the war will continue, but if there’s a chance for something, I want to know the terms and the reason to why he’s decided to ask for this meet… he’ll likely spurt some tyrannical speech as he did before when all this first began, asking us to abandon the druids and halt their practises. I know that’s what he really wants.’’

‘’Why?’’

Vocorix takes a seat at his writing desk. ‘’He claims the druids are plotting to stop him and his ‘awakening’ he feels the druids grow jealous that Vistra is the one to return and not Fanara, he claims they’re preaching false information about Vistra and himself, leading the Darogothic people to disregard him. He wants control, and he knows he can’t control Darogoth if the druids are present. He calls us and the druids blasphemers.’’

‘’Sounds delusional, the druids never spoke badly of this Vistra when I lived in Seers Crossing, they were peaceful people.’’

‘’It is delusional… considering our Gods formed the unbreakable bond and lived in harmony for thousands of years. You know that we are primary worshippers of Fanara because we live under her will, she granted the Ardites their home here in Darogoth and we must always revere her for her kindness, we’d never disregard Vistra, for he too saved our arses back in the God’s age, but this… this is maniacal.’’

‘’Yeah… I read much about those times… so, when will this meeting happen…?’’

‘’In the coming weeks I presume, I’ll keep you updated, for the meantime enjoy a pay rise.’’ Vocorix produces three small bags of coins from a drawer inside his desk. ‘’You'll be paid by me personally, same wage as the oathsworn. Here… get yourself some fitted armour and a reliable weapon, this bag here is your standard pay, the other two is an investment from me, for your weapon and some armour. You're a warrior of Darogoth now, I can’t really give you the big façade the oathsworn usually get, there’s a lot of uncertainty in these troubling times for our people, just know you’re no longer Brennus’s lackey, you fight for me now,’’ his eyes peer of to the side as if to swallow his own pride.

Gordon gives a silent nod.

‘’Do you feel you got your just revenge at Seers Crossing?’’ Vocorix asks, returning his glance unto Gordon.

‘’I don’t know… yeah… I suppose… I try not to think about it.’’

‘’Never killed anyone before, have you? I remember the first time I killed someone… It was a filthy little ruffian that raped my sister. I still remember the look in his eyes when I shoved the knife in his gullet… I never could wipe it from my head. But the thing is, I watched my sister smile for the first time in years when I told her what I did. Her smile… will always be the cure. The world is a terrible place, you need to keep your priorities on those you love, your survival. You kill because you must, I don’t know what it’s like in your realm… but here….’’

‘’I understand… I think back to the day I watched everyone I care about die. I think back to waking up by my girlfriend's side in bed and I realise that whatever this place is… I have to fight it. There’s… something inside of me… something suppressing a lot of the negativity in my head. It happened the moment I arrived here… without it… without her… I’d probably die. I still struggle though… you know?’’

‘’Maybe our Gods have blessed you when you walked through the veil, who knows.’’

‘’I never believed in Gods and stuff… but here it actually seems too real….’’

‘’Our Gods are real, Gordon. They walked the very surface of Altharn many ages ago.’’

‘’I hope they are… High King. I best be leaving… don’t want Brennus to find his horses not mucked out yet.

Vocorix exhales a relieving smile. ‘’Oh, give it up, don’t bother with all that peasant nonsense. Now, begone. For the first time in months, I’ve got a day free to myself and I’d quite like to enjoy it,’’ Vocorix laughs as he dawdles toward a nearby cabinet of bottles.

Although Gordon felt he was adapting to this world well, he wondered if he ever will make it back home, but if there’s one thing he did know he was going to die trying. The stride in his step as he marched down the halls of Castle Carsinia said everything about his motives.

He will fight.

Venethar, Vul March, Kasidor.

Urskull Fenrith had been called to Kastrith’s quarters of Kasidor Castle, Kastrith waited patiently as peered upon a jewelled ring that once belonged to his father, Arkhuul Mundur. He twists and turns the ring, inspecting it, remembering his loving father and wonderful memories he shared with him in those happy days.

Knock Knock Knock.

‘’Come in.’’

Fenrith steps in, wearing his casual garments, a belted cotton tunic with a sabre cat’s pelt strapped around the shoulder and some leather trousers, he’d been mostly off duty since the raid.

''Urskull Fenrith,'' Kastrith blurts. ''Have your men reported anything on my sister?''

''No, my King. She seems to have vanished, although activity within the rebellion is growing, I can only assume she plays a part.''

''Tarna... Tarna... with any luck I can solidify a non-aggression with Darogoth whilst we deal with the pests of our own lands,'' Kastrith places the ring back inside a small wooden chest atop a dresser.

''There were rumours of her being smuggled throughout The Heart by some of Kasidor's own. My guess is she'll make her way to The Borderlands, there's no doubt the rebellion will harbour around the borders, Tarna may even try to escape Venethar all together perhaps?''

''I will find her... send out the gryphons to scour The Heart, and secure the borders of Darogoth, make sure our units on the frontlines are made aware to keep an eye out, just be careful around the Faceless Forest, and make sure patrols in Vul March are heightened.'' Kastrith pauses as he takes a few steps toward Fenrith who stood regimentally with his hands folded behind his back. ''I need her alive and well, she is my sister, you understand?''

''Yes, my King... What if she is to fight back and gives us no choice?''

''I need her alive.''

''Of course, my-''

''If I find out anyone has harmed their princess. I'll tak-''

Before Kastrith can continue a gravelly voice interrupts him from outside the room. ''My King! Message from High King Vocorix,'' spoke Hyphal, the court wizard and long-term friend of the Mundur Family. Hyphal was an incredibly tall and crooked man. He tutored Kastrith in the arts of magic as a boy and has served the Mundur family since the start of Kastrith's father, Arkhuul's reign.

''Finally…'' Kastrith sighs. ''In you come, Hyphal.''

Hyphal enters the room handing Kastrith the letter, bowing as he passes it into his hands.

''What's your bet, Fenrith?''

Fenrith Smirks. ''He's agreed, he's too predictable, Darogothians are too proud a people…''

Kastrith opens the letter, reading slowly, giving suspense. ''Correct,'' he pats Fenrith's back. ''High King Vocorix has agreed to a small moot upon The Spire of Oldwood and… we get to see this 'Realm Walker' in the flesh.''

''Are you going to kill him, my King?'' Hyphal says sternly.

''No. Why would I?''

''He opposes you, does he not? He is the result of druidic hedonism. He does not belong here, isn't that why we orchestrated the attack on Seers Crossing?''

''He has only lived coddled by their means, if the being is smart, he will listen to me. Killing him as he entered the world can be justified through the fear of our nation, it was merely an act of caution. He will see clearly that I do not mean to harm him. Besides, I have a gift.''

''A gift?'' Hyphal frowns.

''Yes. A Gift.''

''What does this entail?''

''Naught of your concern as of yet, my friend.''

''Yes, my King,'' Hyphal backs away slowly to the door.

''He may be the result of druidic hedonism, but he is still a living being that fate has guided; he had no choice in the matter, much like the birth of an innocent child… It was fate that brought him to us. A fate we must control, by Vistra.''

Darogoth, Ard, Carsinia.

Back in Carsinia Gordon is traversing the market, he happens upon a shop laden with books and scrolls, he'd never actually visited the place as he only relied on the books that he had recovered from Seers Crossing to gain the knowledge of the world.

He learned allot from reading books but he wanted more, and more importantly he was now trying to find something… something that led to this 'magic of the endless void.' A lead, a clue… something buried deep within the lore of Altharn.

‘’Good evening… ‘’ Filindril, the shop owner greets, scouring Gordon with buried brows, noting the faint blonde upon his black hair.

‘’Hi…’’ Gordon replies awkwardly, as he proceeds to loom around.

Filindril watches him carefully noticing small foreign mannerisms. After a few minutes he breaks the silence. ‘’Where do you hail from, friend?’’

Gordon gives a slight laugh. ‘’Not from here, it’s… complicated.’’

Filindril smiles warmly. ‘’Wouldn’t happen to be the Realm Walker, would you? That word is on a lot of folks' lips these days. I can’t say many people with two hair colours and skin markings such as that pass by my shop on the daily.’’

‘’Yeah… that would be me….’’

‘’Well… what a pleasure it is, my name's Filindril I run this place… I couldn’t imagine what you’ve been through, I've heard a few stories indeed… I won’t bore you with the talk you probably here on the regular, are you looking for anything in particular?’’

Gordon smiles in thanks at the consideration of Filindril. ‘’Just anything that can help me understand more of Altharn, the history, the cultures, old magic? The Gods?’’ He contemplates for a moment, comparing Filindril’s appearance with his current knowledge. ‘’Filindril… that’s not a Darogothic name, is it?’’

Gordon takes a look at Filindril, scanning his thin frame and tall stature.

Filindril stood very tall, well over six feet, he appeared to be in his thirties? Medium length Greying hair and a single long braid hanging from his chin, his eyes seemed slightly more exaggerated in their oval-like protrusion and then he spotted his ears, pointed.

''That's because I'm from The Glade, I'm an elf. Have you met an elf before?''

''No… I haven't,'' Gordon stares in amazement. ''Sorry.''

Filindril Laughs. ''Maybe you'd like to read about us? Or maybe some of the other races of man, elf and beast folk alike? I know of a book written by a famous Gladian druid that really goes into detail about the culture of elves in comparison to the people of Darogoth.''

''Perfect! I did read very briefly about elves, not a great deal though… a friend of mine had a book from a scholar in Mysticia that mentioned the creation of Aventium and its elves?''

''Ah yes… that old tale… those elves had a tough time to say the least, they have turned their backs on Gladian elves since their beginnings. My home nation has had quite the controversial history.''

''What nation doesn't?''

Filindril snorts. ''Of course…'' he agrees. ''Yes, the swamp folk… Khan's legacy they follow. Made a stand in the dreaded swamps and formed a civilisation, over the years they spent warring with the natives and living amongst the bogs and marshes, they changed to adapt, quite remarkable. I also have a book detailing their initial formation as a separate nation and the trials and tribulations they faced, written by one of their own actually. It's handy that they kept the Urosi language alive whilst in Loria! Quite an accent though, can be hard to understand them, even in their writing.''

''Great, I'll take it! Do you have anything related to the Kingdom of Venethar? I've only ever read small details about them too; I wanted something more focused about the Venethari as a people.''

''Of course, they are our neighbours after all. The Venethari, a race of nomads escaping their homeland in order to settle for the first time as a people. It's a beautiful story actually. Especially when Vistra came into the picture and helped Fanara and Iskarien rid Uros of Ushkaru the Horn Mother,'' Filindril glanced off to the floor. ''So, something more detailed… about their current lifestyle and cultural practices, how they mobilise their armies? I see what you're doing. Very wise of you,'' he winks.

''Hah… yeah. How do you feel about this war?'' Gordon asks.

''It's a bloody tragedy, given our past. Personally, I don't even know what to believe anymore, Kastrith saves his people from tyranny and exposes his brother to his crimes stopping potential wars at the time and now he's starting them. Claiming to be 'the vessel of Vistra' and preaching his return, it's quite extreme. I've heard of his power, I've heard of what he's capable of and it frightens people, even me, then years later the druids bring you forward. Could you, do it? could you rival the power of Kastrith? Or better yet, a God.''

''No. But here I am… I want to go home… wait… do you know what the magic of the endless void is?''

''That's the magic of creation, correct? Forgive me, I'm not much of an arcanist. All I know is that it was the Gods who had access to such magic. Why do you ask?''

''I just thought you might know, they say it was what brought me here in the first place and it's my only way back, if I want to go home, I need to find this kind of magic.''

''I can't help you there, friend. I didn't even know Fanara's cradle even existed until you came about, let alone house such magic. Fanara did work in mysterious ways.''

''Worth an ask…''

''Of course it is, I want to say I understand your pain but… I don't.''

Gordon nods. ''Thanks allot for all this though, the books too.''

''Not to worry friend, knowledge seekers are always welcome, if you want to stop by just for a chat or have any questions feel free… Gordon? isn't it?''

''Yeah, that's it.''

''We both have very foreign names then!''

''So we do,'' Gordon smiles. ''Here's the money, I'll see you again soon, Filindril,'' Gordon pays his due and leaves.

''Goodbye!''

He dawdled back to his little shack to rest his books on his crooked desk. He was unsure if all these books he had mustered would have any information regarding what he sought, there must be something somewhere. What if people were just saying they don't know because they didn't want Gordon to leave? To use him? He stood there staring at the books and feeling the bag of gold in his pocket… ''Armour…'' he bolted straight back out and to the castle smithy by the barracks, a short walk from his shack. He sees Olm again, awake and staring into nothingness.

''Walker…'' He exhales pitifully in greeting as Gordon marches past.

Gordon stops in tracks. ''Olm…''

''How fares the day of Gordon Ard-Barker, hmm?''

''Fine… you?''

Olm scoffs. ''Yeah… been better… but you see how it is.''

''Hashna really gave you good kick, you took that well.''

''Takes a lot more than a kick from the gentle beast to break an urskull.''

''Brennus's kick to your leg put you on your arse pretty fast too,'' Gordon jests awkwardly.

''Go on, Walker. Get gone, leave me to my final hours in peace, just promise me one thing since this will probably be the last we speak.''

''What?''

''If… and I mean IF Darogoth win this, don't hurt my family, the Uldur Family… please… write to them, tell them I'm dead.''

''That's rich coming from you.''

Olm scoffs.

''Don't worry Olm, I have no intentions of harming innocent people.''

''Goodbye, Walker. Vistra guides your path,''

It was clear Olm had made peace with death. His face was so lifeless, his great voice now so monotone.

Gordon said nothing else and carried on his way. He spots the smith, Argus. He was in the middle of tempering iron.

''Ello there,'' Argus bleats gleefully.

''Hi, I've been told to get some armour fitted?''

''Have you now?! Any specifics?''

''Erm… I'm unsure.'' Gordon halted his request. ''I was given this gold for it by the high king.''

''Oh… let me see the gold.''

Gordon's eyebrow raises as he hands the bag over.

''Ah… this is the amount I charge for a standard oathsworn kit, you're oathsworn now?''

''Nope… but I've been given some sort of standing?'' Gordon shrugs.

Argus gives a lofty chuckle. ''Leave it to me, my friend. First let me take some measurements.''

Argus gets his measurements after poking around Gordon's physique. ''Stretch out your arms.''

Gordon Obeys.

''Now, legs apart, stand straight… right… I have what I need, you live in the little shack by the barracks don't you? I'll come by over the next week or so, shouldn't take too long, I have a few things already available that could work for your fitting, thankfully. I'll modify them and bring the full thing over to you, buckles, belts, cloak. I'll through in a few furs here and there for you to add yourself.''

''Oh… I need to buy a weapon also.''

''Of course, I'm guessing the high king gave you a specific amount again? Let me see.''

Gordon shows another bag of gold.

''Hmmm… this I can't quite tell… It's a lot for a sword… how about you pick one for yourself! There's quite the stock in here.''

Argus brings Gordon into his shop. Blades, axes, spears, maces galore mounted the walls and decorated the stands all around.

''A medium length blade you'll be wanting maybe? Not too long to halt your speed but long enough to keep someone at a distance, good for starting out, at least under your circumstances.

Go on, have a swing of a few that catch your eye, see how it feels for you,'' says Argus, mimicking a sword fighting stance.

Gordon ponders around the swords while Argus fumbles with a few bits of paper behind a counter. The swords all had very intrinsic and gorgeous designs etched on the hilts. Most of them in a pronged style, like most Darogothic swords. He picks a few up, weighing them in his arms trying to establish the differences.

Eventually one catches his eye, the blade was the same length as his entire arm, the hilt was bronze or at least looked bronze. It had a brown leather wrapping finely secured to the handle; the pommel pronged out like the nose of a beetle. It had a small boar engraved at the bottom of the blade near the reign guard. ''How about this one?''

''Ahh, good choice, I made that one about six months ago now, had a few interested in it, but no actual buyers as of yet.''

''Really? I think that's how long I've been here now,'' Gordon speaks as he admires the shine of the blade tip.

''Well, doesn't that seem fitting,'' smiles Argus

''Okay… how much?''

''Twenty gold.''

''I have enough in this pouch, I think?''

''Well, the high king wants you well kitted, ain't no finer smith than me in Carsinia, not even that old crone in the market can best my iron as much as he gloats that he can.''

Gordon chuckles.

''So... are you going to name it?'' Argus asks as he takes the coin from Gordon.

''Name it?''

''Most warriors who buy a dedicated weapon name them, it's a little tradition.''

''What do people name their weapons?''

''Everyone names them differently, it's quite a vast subject,'' Argus laughs. ''Let me think... Brennus named his sword 'Bleeder', Hashna's name was 'Artelius' after her late father. One fellow named his 'Shit Stabber' not even joking on that one.''

Gordon laughs and contemplates the possible name of his new blade. ''We both entered this world at the same time... that's something to go off. How about... Brother?''

''That's a great name!''

Gordon smiles as he admires his new sword.

''Here, the scabbard and a free belt. Fancy belt this is, designed it myself, a token of thanks I usually give to most who buy a weapon that expensive, go on... put it on!''

Gordon places the belt around his waist overlapping his tunic, fitting the scabbard in place. He then gently places Brother to rest in its new home, by his side.

''Now you're a real Darogothic warrior,'' Argus grins. ''If you need it sharpening or repairing or even altering, come straight to me and I'll sort you out.''

''Thank you for this, I'll see you soon, Argus.''

''Of course, I'll be in touch about the armour as soon as possible.''

Gordon leaves the smithy, the stride in his step signifying a small glimmer of pride as he struts back to his shack, hoisting his sword by his side. He felt quite proud of himself, but every time a positive thought entered his mind it would be stomped down by visions of death, the battle by the Sen, the burned bandit, the people of Seers Crossing. The images flash on and on, they take hold.

His breathing dips shallow and his chest tightens just as he reaches the door to his shack, another moment of desensitisation attacks. He backs away from the door and tries to ground himself. The images don't stop, he buries his hands into his face to catch himself. The world around him appeared to fuzz, screams of murder can be heard from the poor druids of Seers Crossing. Suddenly everything stops. A warmth flushes from his spine and into his stomach… he begins to breathe normally again.

Gordon finally grounds himself. He peers around, the people around him were going about their daily business as usual and hadn't seemed to notice the small breakdown that just occurred. As he peered around, he caught a glance of Olm, he was staring directly at him. Olm lifts his chin and frowns at Gordon in confusion.

Gordon rushes into his shack. He spends the rest of the day reading his new books and writing in his journal. He left the shack to get some food from the market, spending a few silvers on some street food, a boar wrap, pieces of shredded boar adorned in a flimsy bread, he returned to his shack to enjoy time alone, until…

Bang! Bang!

''Hey Walker? You alive?'' It was Brennus's voice.

''Aye, come in.''

Brennus barges in. ''We need to talk.''

''What is it?'' Gordon rises from his desk.

''Why the fuck was there still horse shit all over my section of the stable at this time of the day?'' Brennus yells, his rugged skin beginning to fuse red in anger.

A silence hovers over the two for a moment.

''The high-''

Brennus bursts into a howling laughter. ''I know! I know! Your face! You thought I was serious?!''

''Fuck's sake,'' Gordon slaps the palm of his hand over his face.

''Don't worry about any of that shit anymore, lad.'' Brennus pushes Gordon by the shoulder. ''You're a warrior now, and a well deserving one. You could probably learn a thing or two about self-control in the heat of battle though, but that's what I get told all the time still to this day, but… that's good enough for me. Your little bloodlust reminded me of myself back in my youth,'' Brennus clocks Gordon's scabbard still attached to his waist. ''What's this?! You bought a sword? Show me!''

''Yeah!'' Gordon produces his blade and hands it to Brennus, Brennus inspects it intently.

''Interesting… a fancy looking thing, isn't she? Bit too light weighted for myself, but I'll be damned, it's a fine piece of work. Good choice, she got a name?''

''I called it 'Brother' the smith told me he made it around the same time I came into this world, so I thought it would work.''

Brennus gives a friendly grunt. ''I like it… fitting,'' he points the sword at Gordon. ''Let's get fucking drunk.''

''I'm down!'' Replies Gordon, hastily.

Brennus hands the sword back. ''I have a few things to do around the barracks, but meet us over the tavern come sundown?''

''Sounds good.''

''See you soon, warrior,'' he smiles.

As the sun goes down marking the end of the day, Gordon readies himself for a night in the tavern with the oathsworn. As he leaves his shack, he is met with a light shower coming from the sunset strewn sky. He leans back inside and grabs a tatty cloak to shield him from the elements. As he makes his way into the market centre, the rain gets heavier, pelting down with quite the force.

He enters the Tavern in the market and is greeted with a loud cheer from a table in the back, about six of the oathsworn including Brennus, Hashna and Gaeliun, they look like they've already had quite a few drinks. The warmth of the tavern is pleasing, folk all over bearing hearty smiles, the scent a pungent mix of fruit and stout.

''Here he is!'' Belts Hashna, she presents a fresh tankard off the cluttered table to Gordon. ''For you, warrior!''

Brennus stands. ''Before we continue this night let's all make a toast!''

The table roars as Gordon stood awkwardly beside.

''Ah, there's no nee-''

''Gordon, I've known you since you entered this world. I've watched you grow from a lost little puppy ready to piss himself at the wind in the trees, into a man. A man of Darogoth! But then again, even when we first met you had that fire in you, you little bastard! He called me a cunt the moment we met!'' The table roars with laughter.

''Who doesn't?!'' Howls Gaeliun.

''But! But… we have grown quite well together haven't we, it's been a pleasure, Gordon. Whatever it is you do here in Altharn, know I'll be at your side,'' he fixes his slightly tipsy posture. ''To Gordon Ard-Barker, the walker of realms!''

The table cheers his name. Gordon looks down into his tankard at the brown froth sloshing around, thinking in the back of his mind how happy he is at this moment. To be appreciated by others in such a deep and endearing way, to feel proud of himself for all the impossible things he's accomplished. However, his thoughts become clouded. He dips his face into his tankard in respite, gulping down a ferocious amount of heavy stout to dull his entrenching anxiety.

Gordon's face folds at the taste. ''Fuck me, what is this?!'' He exclaims.

Hashna Laughs. ''That, my friend, is a proper drink. It's what will help grow that pathetic beard of yours.''

The table roared yet again as Gordon took a seat, the warriors around him patting his back, their drinks spilling all over the table as they frantically shuffled around, laughing and joking.

The tavern was in high spirits, for maybe the first time Gordon let himself go, he drank quickly and quite heavily. His personality really opened up this night as he allowed himself to relax, he never felt free in Altharn, he always felt the niggling constraint of being trapped.

Gordon was cracking jokes, making new friends and speaking to random locals, dancing, and showing his brethren in arms the love he always wanted to give them. He was always quite held back and would only let his true self out in small doses, but the longer he stayed, the more he opened up, and this night the people see a different side to him, the true Gordon.

Although intoxicated, Gordon was quite good at controlling his limit, he promptly stopped drinking as soon as he felt he had enough, however, the others wouldn't stop and became quite rowdy, and so Gordon joined in with the banter.

He truly felt like one of them. Being everyone's favourite man of the night was truly something, for a brief period he spoke with one woman. Betua the smith's daughter, her beauty caught his eye from the next table over, and as Darogothic tavern nights go, the tables intertwine and mingle often.

Her hair was fair and silky, her features sharp. The two found themselves chatting together often, with Betua naturally being quite infatuated by the mystery surrounding Gordon.

It was brief but Gordon felt something, attraction, and then, guilt.

Realising what he was doing he attempted to ease down conversing with Betua and distract himself with Brennus's drinking game everyone was ranting and raving over.

''Hey, Gordon,'' a young fruitful voice slur, Gaeliun. He led alongside Brennus during the skirmish at the Sen. Notably younger than most other oathsworn, despite this he was highly valued amongst the ranks. Especially by Brennus. ''That girl you've been talking with… Betua… she's pretty keen on you,'' he nudges with a mischievous grin.

Gordon gulps. ''Is she now?''

Gaeliun wraps his arm around Gordon's neck while balancing his tankard with the other. ''Not see the way she was playing with her hair whilst you were talking? The position of her feet?''

''Her what?''

''Go for her, friend! If anything will sooth you in this world, it's a fine woman such as her!'' Gaeliun kisses Gordons head.

Gordon glanced over to where Betua was standing, she was standing with two other women, Hashna and another oathsworn girl.

She glanced back and the two locked eyes briefly. He noticed something about her, she resembled Helen in many ways, the blonde hair, the facial structure, even her mannerisms. Gordon looks away anxiously. How drunk was he?

Gordon laughs and humours Gaeliun. ''Yeah… sure,'' he lied.

''That's my man! Gordon Ard-fucking Barker the Realm Walker! Bearer of fire! Defiler of women!'' Gaeliun lets go of Gordon's shoulder and stumbles over a stool, tripping over and falling face first into the floor, the whole tavern roars with laughter.

Betua catches his eye again, this time she gives a smile, she begins to approach.

''Well… looks like you've out drank one oathsworn,'' she remarks.

''Aye… so it would seem.''

''Now… how much can a man not of this world take?''

''Not much, I'll be honest I'm a slow drinker, I ease myself in.''

She gives a laugh, a cute laugh that sounded just like Helens, same tone, same pitch. ''A man who controls his drinking habits? You're definitely not from here.''

Gordon nervously laughs. ''I'm just going to get some fresh air, back soon.''

He hobbles out the front of the tavern, grabbing his wooden pipe and filling it to the brim, knocking himself off of the foundation posts and walls, stumbling around like a drunken fool. He looks over his pipe, the pipe Lucotorix gave him back when he arrived. ''I miss you man…'' he mumbles. As he fills his pipe, he realises how drunk he really is. ''Ok, NOW it's time to stop… I'm absolutely slaughtered,'' he thinks to himself, lighting his pipe with his magic.

He stares at the pouring rain thundering down outside the small thatch canopy he is standing under. The door to the tavern opens.

''Are you okay? Quite an abrupt exit…'' Betua intrudes.

''Oh… sorry… yeah… it's just… this world. It's a lot to take in sometimes. I needed a smoke to keep me settled, you know?''

''Of course, it must be truly something,'' she leans on the fencing next to him. ''But look at you… not even been here a year and you're already rubbing shoulders with the high king.''

Gordon smiles as he looks her in the eyes, she's intent on keeping eye contact. Hypnotised by her short gaze, he sees only Helen. The locked gaze pulls Betua closer. Gently linking his arm into hers.

''Oh, hello…'' Gordon says awkwardly.

Betua giggles, that laugh.

''Tell me of your world.''

Gordon loses balance and sways as he reaches for his phone, dragging Betua with him in his toxified stance.

He begins showing Betua pictures and videos he had saved on this phone. ''So that is called a car, it's like a carriage but doesn't need horses, you push a pedal and it moves.'' Gordon explains as he shows a video of him and his friends singing along together on a long drive to Scotland a few years back.

Betua is speechless at the device Gordon holds and the descriptions he gives of these otherworldly objects.

She squeezes his arm gently as she moves herself closer, unafraid of displaying her intentions.

Alarmed, Gordon makes an excuse to head inside in an attempt to lose Betua's interest without seeming too rude. He felt guilty… and she only made him think of Helen more.

The night carried on and eventually the tavern came to a close.

Stumbling home alongside the warriors in the heavy rain falling from the blackened sky produced many humorous results. Gordon fell face first in a large puddle of mud after wrestling with Hashna, the others also joined in, piling on top of each other until Gordon nearly passed out from lack of breath. They tricked Gaeliun into finding something that didn't even exist, only for him to be met with a flying kick straight into a market stall, toppling it over and smashing it to pieces. After a good laugh and a few strained moments of vomiting, they began to dance and sing in some of the market stalls.

They stopped once the town guard moved them along peacefully, after about an hour of fooling around, the rest of the warriors made their way to the barracks, the night drew to an end.

Gordon made it to his shack and gave himself a minute to feel the rain on his skin, he always enjoyed a good storm, they made him feel so alive.

He gave a large breath and exhaled out a lot of pent-up stress… as he turned to open his door, he caught a motion in his drunken vision, it was Olm, coughing. He was staring at the sky, watching the rain trickle upon his wounded skin from above, he was soaked to the bone, topless in nothing but trouser rags.

Olm catches Gordon staring upon him. ‘’Walker…’’ he feebly exhales, his voice drowned out by the hissing of the wind.

Gordon approaches in his drunken haze and grabs the chain that mounted Olm’s arms aloft to the post.

Using his magic, he sears the chain links with intense heat from his hands, breaking the chains and freeing Olm who collapses right to the floor from the strain.

‘’What are you doing?’’ Olm speaks through clenched teeth.

Gordon ignores him and instead lifts Olm up, rushing him to his shack as quickly as he can, falling down to his knees as the booze battles his vision, stepping on Olm’s feet multiple times before falling to the floor again.

He picks Olm up again and throws him into his shack, slamming the door shut. ''I'm freeing you.''

''I'll die anyway, it's over for me, you're acting foolish. I can't even walk properly, my legs still fucked.''

''No, I'm giving you a chance.''

Olm grunts.

Gordon rummages around his shack, he grabs a bundle of clothes and throws them to Olm alongside the half-eaten boar wrap from earlier. ''Eat,'' he demands.

Olm says nothing and snatches the wrap, forcing it down his gullet as quickly as he can. Gordon grabs his travel canteen and hands it to Olm. Olm takes it willingly and guzzles down as much water as he can in the moment. ''What now, Walker? My hands are still bound, how am I to leave?!'' Says Olm referring to his iron cuffs.

''If you're covered with a hood in the pissing rain, the guards will be none the wiser, I'll get the cuffs off now, just watch yourself.''

''What?!''

Gordon places his hands around the iron cuffs using his magic once again, accidentally burning Olm in the process as he slips from swaying to much in his drunken state.

''FUCK,'' Olm winces.

''Sorry!''

Olm uses the strength he has left to lift himself and change into the clothes Gordon gave him. ''Why are you doing this?''

''I know it's weird, but you're different… I can't watch you die; you have two little girls who want to see their dad return home….''

''You're insane.''

''You're welcome,'' Gordon slurs.

A strange silence fills the room.

He grabs Gordons hand, holding it tight, forcing him forward to his face. ''You'll regret this my friend… Thank you,'' the despair written upon his face still refuses to budge.

Olm pulls the large hood over his face and collects the small bag of provisions Gordon prepared.

''Goodluck,'' Gordon groans.

''And you… Walker,'' Olm leaves.

Gordon watches as Olm's silhouette hobbles out of sight and becomes fogged by the cloud of heavy rain.

He glances back to the post where Olm had been bound. ''Shit,'' he thought to himself as he rubbed his face that was gushing with rain water.

He scurries over to the post attempting to cover his tracks.

14: Moving Forward

Middlesbrough

Her world was empty, all happiness and hope had been sucked from her soul, she was left drained and grey, much like the skies that scour the north east.

She had slowly begun to tread upon a rigid path, careless and uninterested in the beauty of life that happened around her.

Without him, her world had crumbled, though she tried hard to remain vigilant.

It's been just over half a year, she was certain he was dead, the investigation had dug nothing up. Gordon had literally disappeared from the face of the Earth, no matter how much she wanted to believe he was still alive, she knew deep down, he can't be.

Six months and nothing, the longer time went on with no new news, the more the idea of settling on his death seemed to appeal to her. The biggest pain in all of this, was not knowing, she'd feel more grounded if she just knew, knew if he had passed by now, but no, she must suffer.

His disappearance had become viral, the constant sharing of his case on social media had made the rounds quickly, even prompting many people on YouTube and other social media platforms sharing their thoughts and ideas.

Helen was slumped in the living room with her laptop, watching the latest on her missing boyfriend.

''Good day to you my fellow mystery hunters, Derrick Withers here, and today we will be reviewing a rather recent unsolved case from the UK. A case that many have speculated on as of late, but I also want to bring more awareness to this case, because the earlier we cover this story, the more chance we have of finding this person. So, without further ado, let's begin. In December 2010, Gordon Barker of Middlesbrough UK, went missing without a trace, although there was a trace… but not the kind you'd expect. Gordon is a twenty-five-year-old man, an aspiring musician, a survivor of alcoholism, and an all-round genuine guy, he had great friends, and a loving family. So… what happened? Gordon was attending a night of drinking with his work colleagues the night he went missing. Now you might be thinking, survivor of alcoholism… drinking? Yes… Gordon had conquered his previous self-destructive habits and had been known to have it under control for many years. His known episode of alcohol abuse was brief, but we must take this into account when deciphering these kinds of cases, although he could in fact control his drinking it has nothing to do with why he's missing. Gordon left the social early and was last physically seen not five minutes from his home, it was here he was last seen… passing through a local park as seen here on the park's CCTV cameras, you can see him here, smoking a cigarette as he walks on through, completely normal stuff, right? But then… did you see it? A very faint shimmer of light, well Gordon certainly did. He went to investigate and was never seen again,'' the video gives silent eerie sound effects as spooky background music plays alongside the commentary. ''The widest and most controversial theory as to why Gordon disappeared is that he had been abducted… by UFO's. Now as crazy as that sounds, evidence on the scene does seem rather plausible, even his close friends that were interviewed also seem to speculate on the idea, but it's clear that they don't want to believe it as such. The police believe him to be and are still certain this may be the result of a kidnapping. After all, Middlesbrough is known to be in the top fifty of the UK's roughest towns, so not the safest place to live. The cigarette Gordon was smoking in the video was found and identified as his. But still to this day the shimmer of light still can't be identified. A headlight of a car? A Torch? Or… even a UFO. Very hard to digest, especially for his loved ones.''

''You're telling me…'' Helen sighs as she takes a sip of her coffee.

''The case has been on-going since then and nothing of value has been unearthed that directly leads to Gordon's whereabouts. We're going to take a deeper look into Gordon's life, his relationships and day to day life and see what we ourselves can dig out from this unsolved mystery.''

''Ugh, I've had enough,'' Helen slams shut her laptop.

She stares into the fireplace longingly for a few moments, nothing but the faint ring of her ears eloping with silence as she stares into space.

Helen's life had reverted to a stale existence.

She'd go to work, come home, drink, sleep and repeat. She wasn't abusing alcohol on a level that was rapidly degrading to her, but daily binge drinking wasn't exactly part of her personality either, nor was it good for her.

Her famous bubbly persona was a thing of the past and although she always tried to mask her misery, it never quite worked as well as she wanted it too. Her smoking habits increased, as did her drinking, self-isolation and a plethora of unhealthy life choices to boot. A careless attitude toward her wellbeing was slowly taking hold, she was hanging by a thread but her grip was firm.

She had gained a little weight over the past six months, her skin had become oily in appearance, her hair dye had all rooted out, revealing nothing but a faded colourful past. Despite this, her beauty still shone through.

She was depressed, though she fought hard.

Helen's dreamlike glare is interrupted by Emily's entrance as she storms into the living room.

''So, are you going to come tonight?'' She announces in hope.

''No.''

''Helen… come on. You can't live like this.''

''Emily, I don't want too.''

''Helen, you haven't left the house properly since… then. All you do is work and shut yourself at home, it's not good for you!''

''I know. Just let me deal with things my own way, okay?'' Helen bites back.

Emily sighs. ''Okay… fine… I just wanted you by my side tonight… I planned to go out for your sake, to get you out, you know I don't go out to these metal bars.''

Helen scrunches her eyes. She'd done nothing but palm away Emily's efforts for months, she felt bad for her friend who was just trying to help. ''Okay fine, I'll come.''

''Seriously?''

''Yes, but only for a bit. Then I want to come straight home. I swear to God Emily, if one person mentions Gordon at all tonight or makes a snide comment about how I've let myself go, I'm coming straight back fucking home.''

Emily stood with a small smile that slowly depleted, her eyes drop to the floor.

Helen rises. ''Emily… I'm sorry, I don't mean to-''

''I know Helen. I want to say I understand but… I don't. It's just hard seeing you like this.''

''Are Blood Winter playing?''

''No… I wouldn't do that to you.''

''Thank you,'' Helen scurries over, engulfing Emily in a lasting hug. ''You're the only person I can bloody trust…''

Emily gives a hopeful look of delight. ''Come on, let's get ready!''

The band were out this night enjoying a few of the other local musicians on the scene that were playing in town. They had done well for themself since Gordon's disappearance, they remained stable as a band and carried on with their weekly antics.

Unfortunately for them they did not play the big gig that was planned in Manchester, feeling too hard hit with the situation with Gordon they decided to pull out, however in recent weeks they did find a replacement.

After a lengthy run of auditions, they finally found the right person for the job, her name was Tasha, an old school friend of Jeb's, dark tanned skin and long black hair, baggy clothes with chains hanging all over the place, keen on alternative accessorising to say the least, she fit in quite well with the aesthetic of Blood Winter.

She was fully aware of Gordon and tread lightly with the band in that respect. She was in fact an old fan of the band and had frequented their gigs often, so she was already well averse in their music and to top it off, she was a damn good bassist.

Jeb, Dan, Pete, and Tasha were all together amongst the crowd, drinks in hand. A band had just finished a set and the room was now bearable to talk in.

''Did you see that video on YouTube that Derrek Withers did? He uploaded it earlier today!'' Announced Pete out of the blue.

''Yeah, I did….'' Jeb replies.

''Told you! Didn't I!''

''About the aliens and shit?'' Scoffs Dan.

''Yeah mate, aliens.''

Tasha's large black eye's jolted from side to side as the conversation jumped back and forth, awkwardly feeling absent from the conversation, she remained cool.

''Could be right. After all, nothing else has presented itself. I'm still with Pete on this,'' blurts Jeb.

''It's fucked up, but good to see his case getting some recognition though. But-''

''But what?'' Dan interrupts Pete.

Pete backs off a little, noticing Dan's change of stance. ''You know…''

''Stop talking about it now, yeah?'' Urges Dan.

''What are we supposed to do? Just forget?'' Pete stands his ground.

''Mate, not now.''

''Seriously?!''

''Look, we need to move on. All we can do is hope.''

''Hope!? Hope for what? Eh?'' Pete babbles sarcastically.

''That he's found and we get an answer, okay? Leave it at that.''

''But Da-''

''Shut the fuck up, Pete. I've heard enough,'' Dan barges forth squaring up to Pete's forehead.

Tasha stood in the middle of the argument casually sipping on her cider.

''Okay… okay… mate, calm down,'' Pete held up his hands in submission, he knew Dan was still hurting.

''Sorry Tash,'' Dan Apologises as he backs off from Pete.

''Guys, it's not a problem….'' she calmly replies.

''Pete… sorry mate, I'm so tired of thinking about it, about him, I don't want to sound like a prick, I'm just tired mate… I miss him, yeah? He's my best mate! And hearing all you lot talk about fucking aliens and shit… sounds like you're all taking the piss!''

''I get it man, alright? Just take it easy.''

''Oh shit!'' Jeb shouts. ''Look who it is… that's convenient.''

The group all turn to Jeb in confusion.

''It's fucking Helen!'' Jeb announces pointing out Helen who had just entered the bar alongside Emily.

''What? No way, I haven't seen her in months. We need to go see her… but before we do. DO NOT mention anything about Gordon unless she does, okay?'' Dan Orders.

Everyone agrees.

''Holy shit, Is that Emily she's with?'' Pete smirks.

‘’Yeah,’’ Jeb replies.

‘’My God, she’s so fucking hot,’’ adds Pete.

The group lead by Dan eagerly approaches Helen and Emily, elegantly swerving through the crowd of headbangers.

‘’Hel!’’ Dan shouts.

Helen turns to Dan, somewhat shielding herself upon seeing him.

‘’Long time no see….’’

‘’Yeah… sorry.’’

He places his hands in his back pockets. ‘’No, no… don’t apologise, love! It’s understandable.’’

Helen cracks an innocent smile as she peers off to the floor.

‘’Been keeping yourself busy?’’

‘’Too busy.’’

Jeb steps forward. ‘’Well, let's just have a drink and have a good night, yeah? It’s bloody good to see you again Hel, we’ve all missed you,’’ he leans in, putting his arm around her and kissing her on the forehead.

‘’I’ve missed all of you guys too, I just needed some space….’’

Jeb removes his arm from Helen’s shoulder. ‘’Let me buy you a drink! It’s been too long.’’

''Sure!''

''Hey Emily, how about I buy you one?'' Winks Pete.

''I'm fine, thanks,'' she turns to the bar away from the group, rolling her eyes at Helen.

Helen notices Tasha stood silently. Attempting to reignite her old self, she eagerly interacts. ''Hi… have we met?''

Before Tasha can even respond, Dan butts in. ''Yeah… Hel… she's….''

Helen's eyebrows raise.

''Our… bassist,'' he gulps.

''Oh, great!'' Helen chirps. ''Nice to meet you!''

Dan gives a sigh of relief.

''You too! What's your name again?'' Asks Tasha.

''Helen… Ignore Dan, I'm Gordon's girlfriend.''

''Oh….'' Tasha struggles to find an appropriate response.

''Look, don't worry, there's no beef or anything. The band needs to move on, we all do.''

Helen lunges forward giving Tasha a friendly hug whilst punching Dan in the stomach. ''You really think I'd be bothered Dan? Calm yourself down.''

Jeb returns to give Helen a gin and tonic. ''Here you go, love,'' he beams.

‘’Still haven’t forgotten my favourite drink?’’

‘’How could I!’’

‘’Thanks, Jeb.’’ Helen smiles.

The group caught up with one another up until the next band came on stage and blew everyone's ears out with a double bass of the drumkit and the thunder of the guitars.

Helen felt a weight lift off her shoulders, she thought being around the band would bring back old memories, memories that would upset her… it was almost as if she thought she was the only one suffering from the whole ordeal. However, she retreated to the toilets to gather herself, feeling a little overwhelmed by the social whirlwind.

Looking upon herself in the mirror, something she does daily, but never intently, she looks closer… she doesn’t recognise the woman looking back. Disgusted by what she sees that is staring back in the same disgust. She needs to revert, be healthy again, to pick herself up, she doesn't want to be consumed by grief. Although hard, she needs to move on.

A single tear escapes her eye, dragging her eyeliner with it. She watches as it trickles down her face, embracing the moment in full.

The door to the toilets creaks open.

‘’Helen?’’ Says Tasha.

Helen turns to Tasha, attempting to dry her eyes.

Noticing the tear and without a word, Tasha catches Helen in her arms.

''It's Okay,'' Tasha whispers with care. ''I'm sorry… I feel like I'm not making it any easier.''

''No! No! Don't be silly! You seem like a lovely girl, and you know, I can't wait to see you play! Please don't feel guilty, it's just a hard time for me, it's not you!''

''I know! I know…'' Tasha rubs Helen's back.

''This is the first time I've left the house… I'm a work in progress….'' Helen awkwardly laughs.

''And you're doing a great job! If I was in your shoes I'd still be hiding! If you need anything Helen… I'm here too. We can all be friends here.''

Helen nods frantically. ''I should get back to them, I want to have a good night.''

''You've got this, girl,'' Tasha smiles.

Emily bursts into the toilet. ''Oh my God! Please keep Pete away from me. I swear, I'm going to glass him in a minute!''

The girls share a unified laugh, a laugh that lifted Helen's spirit high.

15: The Spire of Oldwood

''The elves of The Glade have flourished in those mystical forests amongst their marble dwellings for as long as time can remember. Some of their stone that stands to this day in the fourth age has been there since the Gods' age and beyond.

The elves lived alongside Fanara herself, alone in The Glade, using Darogoth as their hunting grounds, their haven.

Elven society always resented man for taking Fanara's favour allowing them to settle the sacred lands, yet obeyed their God nonetheless and created an alliance with the new 'Ardites'.

The Ardites now had a crucial role on the continent of Uros, becoming the forefront of war in the conflict against Venethar's native beast folk, the Var'kesh. The conflict carried out for many years at a stalemate until the Kurians arrived ashore seeking new lands with Vistra at their front. Permanently wiping out the Var'kesh and solidifying an entire continent in an eloping of peace that would last for centuries.

Elves were the first known beings to follow Fanara's teachings, it is said Fanara herself was elven until she ascended to godhood, but those days are long forgotten. She herself would comment saying she was naught but a being of Altharn, a being blessed of the endless void.

Elven society is consistent in the way of the void, keen scholars of the skies, they're birth right and social hierarchy is structured by the patterning's of starlight. Those born under the constellation of Fanara's antlers are instantly granted a birth right status amongst scholars, elven druids who spend their entire life forcefully dedicated to the teachings of Fanara.

Where elves are specialists of the void and stars, the Ardites were at sowing the Altharn of its vast flora and producing incredible results of tinctures and ailments, they excelled at keeping Darogoth to remain the haven it always was, replenishing the destruction the Var'kesh wrought.

When Vistra arrived, the coincidence was uncanny. He was a man made of nothing but the void and stars, to look upon him was to look at the night sky. It was an instant attraction to the ways of the elves, and so when Vistra obliterated Ushkaru the Var'keshi God, the three Gods formed a bond unlike any other and the worship of the three Gods became equally apparent throughout the now three kingdoms of Uros.

Vistra teaches that fate is constant and never predicted. that the way of the void is concurrent and ever flowing forward and our actions only matter in the present. Likewise, Fanara would teach that the void was the maker of all things that exist. Vistra would preach about our actions and being a master of one's own fate, whereas Fanara would preach about the origins of life's purity and how sacred the void's creation is to us all, to conserve, to use, to waste and to repeat, which Vistra would comply with.

Iskarien however was a lot more straightforward. We never escape the embrace of death, so we in turn should welcome it, for death is life and life is death, all sewn together by the constructs of fate. This was the religious foundation of Uros, Cemented by its representatives. Fanara, Iskarien and Vistra. Life, death and everything in between.

Although elves preferably revere Fanara as do many Darogothians, that's not to say that some members of their society have had disagreements, elven history itself is bloody. Civil conflicts over worship have occurred in the past and many have been defiant and yet the Gods were equally forgiving of their rowdy children, showing love and compassion. Other Gods have come by with a blade pointed to Uros, yet all have failed. The bond of the alliance of the three kingdoms is paramount to the preservation of its lands.''

- *Falyth Alios - Curiosities of Uros, 4A 224.*

Brennus is sat eating his morning meal within the barracks, Carsinia's guard captain floats by, going about his daily business.

''Still no news on the urskull who escaped?'' Brennus asks the guard captain as he shovels a spoonful of porridge into his mouth.

''No… nothing at all. We're still looking into the faulty chains, but the men have been occupied these past few days with the trade festival kicking up a riot.''

''Fuck me… those chains weren't faulty; I attached that cunt to them myself! They were as tight as a deer's arse.''

‘’They were charred at the breaking point, if he broke free he must have had some help from someone… someone using fire perhaps?’’

‘’Fire?! It was fucking pissing down with rain that night, who’s going to be able to light a fucking fire in the rain?’’

‘’I’m not saying you’re at fault Brennus, I’m saying he must have had an accomplice….’’

‘’I don’t understand… he was our only prisoner from the skirmish.’’

The guard captain ponders a moment. ‘’Magic?’’

Brennus relaxes his spoon against his bowl. ‘’Has any of the war seers gone missing recently? Maybe one of them helped him escape and went with him? Are we dealing with a traitor in our own ranks? I bet he was spitting Kastrith’s nonsense at one of the mages.’’

‘’Not that we’re aware of but we’ll double check the war seers’ regiment for sure.’’

‘’Well hurry, I've sent out alerts to Mostos and Lunarum and neighbouring villages but my bet is he would traverse Fanara’s Forest out of sight. I’ve given his description, probably wearing Darogothic clothing by now, but his beard and accent will be enough of a giveaway,’’ Brennus sighs. ‘’I hope to fucking Fanara he hasn’t been told our movements in Glaen, this could fuck up everything.’’

‘’I know Brennus, we’ll find him!’’ The guard captain pats Brennus arm.

A thought springs to Brennus's mind, a worrisome thought. ''Magic… magic? No…'' he attempts to piece things together. ''His shack was close by… they did talk a lot on the cart… too friendly. Oh by the Gods, no….'' Brennus marches to Gordon's shack, his steps pounding with concern.

BANG! BANG! BANG! The door to Gordon's shack rattles.

''Gordon! Gordon!'' He knocks again, even harder. ''GORDON!!!''

A passing oathsworn, Unduren, walks by noticing a distressed Brennus. ''Looking for Gordon are you, Commander?''

''No, I'm just banging on his door and screaming his fucking name for the fun of it.''

Unduren laughs. ''He's training in the pit with Hashna, I've just come from there.''

''Thanks….''

The pit was a large underground structure built beneath the castle, where warriors and oathsworn of all ranks came to train, the grounds were incredibly expansive, spanning the entire foundations of Castle Carsinia. Inside, Gordon was sparring with Hashna.

''Gordon!''

Gordon turns to Brennus, taking a hit from Hashna's training sword to shoulder. ''Ow fuck!''

Hashna laughs. ''Yeah, try not to get distracted in the heat of a fight! Focus little Walker,''

''Gordon, we need to speak. Alone,'' The look on Brennus's face was alarming.

Hashna looks on to them both in concern as Gordon is taken forcibly aside by Brennus.

''Please be honest with me here, okay?'' He speaks, keeping his voice low.

''Okay…?''

''Did you free that Urskull that was chained by the barracks?''

Gordon gave a controlled gulp attempting not to appear suspicious. ''No, why would I?''

A breath of relief escapes Brennus. ''I know it's a stupid question but I have to ask. Your shack is close by, you would have seen him allot, his chains were likely tampered with by magic, I had to make sure… but, I trust you.''

''How can you determine it was magic? I thought they were rusty or something, it was raining hard that night and you know?''

''Because they were charred. Plus, one rainy night doesn't make something rust just like that… come on Walker, you're not that stupid.''

''Heh, yeah.''

''Well anyway, I reckon it was one of the war seers, the urskull most likely spouted some of Kastrith's bullshit and convinced someone to help him.''

''Sounds the most likely thing, yeah.''

''Okay... I'll leave you to your training, I've got to go, I'm making preparations with the high king about the moot on the Spire.''

''Okay, see you.''

Brennus gives a light jog out of the pit, returning to his duties as Gordon returns to Hashna.

''What was that about?'' She asks.

''About that urskull who escaped, they reckon he was aided by magic, so he needed to check with me.''

''Weird... I couldn't imagine why you of all people would want to free one of those responsible for the slaughter of Seers Crossing,'' scoffed Hashna. ''Anyway...'' she throws a punch to Gordons ribs.

''Fuck!'' Gordon jolts back, wincing.

''Never let your guard down! Need to work on your concentration!''

The two continue sparring for the remainder of the afternoon until the sun begins to set.

Arriving home, Gordon changes into some fresh clothes, he catches his reflection in the murky mirror stuffed away behind some clutter in the back of the shack, his pectorals were starting to show some definition, a six pack was in its early stages and his shoulders looked as if they had dropped and broadened outward, he was impressed.

After all he'd been through, his appearance was the last of his concern and he barely took much notice at all.

He'd never had a fine cut physique before, he was as average as they come with a very slight beer belly. The months of a proper diet and training was really paying off and doing wonders on his physical health.

After checking his topless self out, he looms into the mirror and focuses on his face. The scraggly beard he had grown out from months of not shaving was rather pitiful to look at, it was patchy and thin.

His head hair was quite greasy and unkept, the little blonde streak in his fringe beginning to fade out from lack of upkeep. He decided to try and work on himself a little, he grabs a small blade from the table and attempts to shape and clean up his beard, giving it a much-needed trim, he steps back, stroking his furry jawline. ''That'll do,'' he thought.

His attention is then brought upon his messy hair that dripped down his face from the sweat, he decides maybe it's time to tie it back, or cut it, after all it was long enough now, he could recall a few times his hair had brushed his eyes during training, and so with a makeshift hair tie he binds it back. He almost doesn't recognise himself. He looks, masculine.

The door knocks lightly.

‘’Hello?!’’ Gordon’s voice raises.

‘’It’s Argus… the smith, I have your armour,’’ muffled Argus’s voice from beyond the door.

Gordon jumps into a fresh white tunic and eagerly leaps to his door.

Argus stands there with a satisfied grin, both his hands holding a neat pile of leather, chainmail, belts and some tartan fabrics, on top of the neat pile rest his arm bracers and helmet.

The helmet's colour shimmering bright with a golden glow, the cheek guards decorated with beautiful patterned swirls, chiselled to perfection, on its tip a black horse hair plume drooped to the back for about half a metre in length.

The armour itself was relatively straight forward, chainmail with the strappings and an iron plating across the neckline with a clipping mechanism for a torc. It also had a chest boss, leather straps that would go over and under the arms with a circular plate in the middle that sat central to the chest, engraved into it was a symbol, a woman’s face that sprouted antlers.

Gordon stood in awe.

‘’Here you are!’’ Argus proudly presents. ‘’It's mostly representative of what the oathsworn wear in battle but I've made a few changes to your outfit that differs from theirs. I've given you a personal touch on the helmet with my own pattern design and also on the chest boss that goes over the chainmail. I've etched the symbol of Fanara, it represents Seers Crossing…

thought you might appreciate that. Now don't forget the torc hold by the shoulders on the clavicle plating, you just slide your torc into the fittings and clip it in place, stops your torc from moving around when you're in the thick of it, really simple, I'd stay and show you around it more, but I have to dash. Got some important work to do today. If you have any questions, I'm hoping your fellow brethren will aid you, but if you really need me, I'll be in the smithy. Good day, Gordon. Enjoy!''

As Argus leaves, a soldier from the castle catches Gordon before he shuts the door, ''Gordon… Realm Walker?''

''Yes?'' He answers back.

''A message from the high king, he wants you to meet with him at the stables in the morning. You're travelling to Glaen.''

''To Glaen?''

''Yes, to the Spire of Oldwood.''

''Oh… Okay. Thanks.''

The meeting at The Spire of Oldwood was to commence soon, where Gordon would finally meet the famed king of Venethar, the man behind all of Darogoth's concurrent pains, a man who could potentially have the answers Gordon seeks, Kastrith Mundur.

A nervous sensation washes into his stomach as he thinks more deeply upon what could transpire, he is straight away shuddered by the warmth of Camula's angelic embrace.

''Remember,'' her voice echoes in his mind.

He woke the next morning dripping with sweat, he'd tossed and turned all night, dreaming of home, of Helen.

He wipes himself down and puts on his torc, gets dressed and realises… maybe he should put his armour on.

He takes his torc back off and clips it in place upon the plating of his armour. After donning the leather chaps and the chainmail, he ties all the necessary components with belts and buckles, sliding into his bronze arm bracers. He then attaches the final piece, a thick green tartan cloak, the colours of the Drosii Clan.

He rests his blade, Brother, to his side. ''Okay… yeah… I think I'm ready? Am I late?'' It was always hard to tell the time without a clock.

Grabbing his helmet in a headlock he rushed out the door, a large mass of oathsworn and many strapping warriors were herded by the stables. Gordon marches over, confidence in stride.

Brennus clocks Gordon approaching. ''By Fanara, look at you… you're actually quite a handsome little bastard when you clean up properly.''

''Are we leaving soon?'' Asks Gordon bluntly.

''Yeah, just waiting on further orders, I was almost about to come and drag you out. Have you had any food?''

''No….''

''Get yourself to the mess hall, you're going to need it. It's a two-week journey to the Spire on horseback, and today's the day we're making the most tracks.''

Gordon obliges.

The castle grounds were bustling with activity. On the way to the mess hall, Gordon passed by Betua from the tavern, making a delivery for her father, Argus.

''Gordon! Oh, look at you! My father really did a good job with your kit!'' She looks him up and down with a flirtatious smile.

''Oh, hey Betua… yeah… your father, he did a great job! Can't stay, got to grab some food before we head out.''

''Of course, good luck… maybe I'll see you when you return?'' She asks in hope.

''Sure… why not… maybe we could… have a drink, or something?'' He panics as he pivots away from her. ''See you later!''

Betua carries on her business, as does Gordon, the hour passes and he returns to the stables with a full belly.

Vocorix arrives and barges through the men and women as he scours his horse, making sure his travel preparations are in place.

Brennus leads a horse to Gordon. ''Here, use her, she's a good one! She's Hashna's horse. She's not coming to the Spire but she allowed you to take her horse. Already packed with a sleeping roll and essentials.''

Gordon takes the reins from Brennus. ''Wow… thanks.''

''You remember our riding lessons?''

''Yeah, I should be fine....''

''Then mount up, lad!''

Every single warrior present amongst the castle grounds prepares to mount as they travel north to Glaen; thirty of his loyal oathsworn were alongside a handful of other notable warriors, a small force for a high target.

Vocorix orders all to mount up and make haste. The party carefully trot from the castle grounds through the rest of Carsinia and finally out of the main gates, galloping north.

From time to time, they would set up camp when needed, but the majority of the day was spent moving forward. They stopped at the city of Mostos for a day's break and to resupply.

Mostos was a relatively green city compared to Carsinia, many trees and plants alike painted the entire city as a beautiful picturesque metropolis, Gordon was again amazed by the many new sights he was seeing, unfortunately for him there was no time for sightseeing, the party promptly returned to horseback and made tracks, northward bound.

Many miles up from the city of Mostos was the border to Glaen, which they thundered through valiantly. By this point Gordon was chafing really badly from the amount of riding he was enduring, he'd developed some nasty blisters. Regardless, he pressed on.

The party would make one final halt at Illunon, a village just by Oldwood in Glaen that nestled by the base of the Spire, which could be seen from the village reaching up high and scraping the very skyline, an imposing sight to say the least.

Gordon visited the local druid for treatment of his riding sores and then had a small drink with the warriors in the tavern, making sure not to overdo it, one final moment of peace before the inevitable moot.

The next morning, they set out to make for the peak of this enormous mountain, leaving their horses hitched at Illunon and bringing an extra contingent of soldiers out of caution. There were multiple pathways to the summit, it was a common pilgrimage for those devoted to their Gods, for at the summit stood three shrines, one for Fanara, one for Iskarien and another for Vistra, all in their respective geographic locations, north, west and south, commemorating the day the Gods formed their pact together.

The party reaches the summit after hours of uphill tread.

Naturally, the Darogothian forces stand between the statues of Fanara and Iskarien.

''They aren't here yet?'' Brennus points out. ''I don't like this; the air is too quiet.''

''They'll arrive soon, we agreed to sunset this day. Order the warriors into a defensive formation, and Gordon… by me,'' Vocorix orders.

Gordon obeys and stands by Vocorix, he places on his helmet, strapping it firmly in place.

The sun begins sliding off the horizon, engulfing the world in a looming shroud as the darkness settles in on the worlds edge.

On the other side of the summit, five figures approach from the northeast, handling two captives as they made their way forward.

''That's them? Five of them? By Fanara, he's really showing his bollocks isn't he,'' remarks Brennus.

''Quiet,'' Vocorix barks, clearly conscious of Brennus's comment.

Kastrith approaches, standing to the side of Vistra's statue.

''That's him? Kastrith? The one with the mask?'' Gordon asks Vocorix.

''Yes… that's him,'' he puffs his bulbous nose.

There he stood, Kastrith Mundur. His appearance shadowed by his attire, a rich black cloth wrapped neatly around his head exposing his famed golden mask, it was like a turban topped with an iron cap with a fancy plume. The rest of his attire all matched up… layers of well fitted cloth with trimmed golden embroidery and pieces of armour plating woven within.

An eerie silence glides amidst the howling winds of the spire.

''Kastrith Mundur….'' Vocorix edges forward with a boisterous strut.

''Vocorix Fen-Drosii, it's been quite a while,'' Kastrith muffles as he edges forward, leaving his loyal guards behind.

''You've taken Shem from Glaen, we're here to discuss that and this conflict, what do you want from us?''

''You know what I want, but I might be able to compromise.''

''You know that can't happen. It's our way of life, you organised this meet to tell me what you've ordered of me for the past few years?'' Vocorix rests his hand on the hilt of his blade.

''Stay your hand High King, I want us to speak like true leaders. I'm also interested in your new friend…'' Kastrith stares at Gordon just a few feet away, his mask catching the final rays of the sunset. ''The lord of Shem will face their demise if you do not meet my terms,'' he signals the captives, their hands bound behind their backs. ''Abolish the druids, and this whole war ends now, it's that simple, Vocorix. Do not let your patriotic pride cost you the lives of your loyal lord and the people of Darogoth.''

Vocorix is left in a painful silence, his face clearly wrought with anger. ''You said you'd compromise with us here. You know the druids to be men and women of Fanara, not Darogoth, even you respect the lady of life.''

''Correct, that I do. But the druids are of Darogothic politics, though they act independently from you, they stir up all manner of heresy in their spiteful cauldrons, and you would allow it? Allow them in your holds? I do not respect the people who plot and avert the many from the father of fate. The druids have betrayed their own God and everything our beloved Fanara represents! Are these innocent lords to suffer because you won't punish those who betrayed our lady? Open your eyes Vocorix! Do Fanara's Justice, and Darogoth will be left to live as it will in Vistra's wake, that is my compromise.''

''Is this because of the realm walker?!''

''Speaking of which… come forward, Gordon.''

Surprised at Kastrith's knowledge of himself, Gordon steps out from Vocorix's side.

Kastrith scoffs. ''I see you've made him quite the Darogothian,'' Kastrith grabs an item from his pocket slowly. ''I believe this to be yours, Realm Walker,'' Kastrith throws Gordon's house keys to him, the keys he'd lost at Seers Crossing.

Then the most unexpected thing happens. Kastrith speaks to Gordon. but this time, differently.

''I know what you seek, I know what you need. I can give you this,'' Kastrith spoke, but the words were of Gordon's own tongue, English.

Gordon's eyes widened in utter shock. It was remarkable, how did Kastrith speak his language? Vocorix stares upon the two in confusion.

Gordon prepares himself to speak English for the first time in over half a year. ''How do you speak my language?''

''I am blessed by the power of the endless void, the power that you will need to return to your own realm. With that key I was able to pick at its foreign essence and use it to peer into your realm. You come from a beautiful, yet strange world. A self-destructive and Godless world that harbours no magic of its own, yet its inhabitants are rather similar to that of our beloved Altharn, a world dominated by only humans, wealth, and technological advance that no one of Altharn could ever truly comprehend.''

''You have the power to send me home?''

''Yes.''

Camula's voice breaks through to Gordon from within. ''He's lying.''

Gordon shakes his head.

''Come with me, Gordon. I promise you no harm. The attack on Seers Crossing was a mere act of caution from my side. We feared a great beast to enter our realm, not an innocent man. That is why we put the village to the torch, we were afraid, my people lived in fear! I protect my own! You appeared in the wrong place at the wrong time, a simple yet fatal… misunderstanding. The druids could have brought forth a being of unimaginable destruction, they knew that whatever came through the gate would pierce the veil and be drenched by the power of the Altharn, and thankfully you came forward. But WE did not know! Like Vocorix, I am a man of my people. You know this, I know you do, I'm not the villain he portrays me to be.''

Gordon felt heavy and confused, he noticed Vocorix staring intently at him, as if to expect to be told of what him and Kastrith were speaking of. Gordon wanted nothing more than to return home. He didn't trust Kastrith, but he spoke with a lot of sense and neutrality, something Gordon was not expecting.

He knew he needed the power of the endless void to return, but surely Kastrith had it? Why did Camula warn him? Gordon was strewn. Walk away with Kastrith and return home once and for all? Or was this all a ruse to have him killed?

Kastrith extends his hand. ''This isn't your fight Gordon, this isn't your world, let me send you back and correct the mistakes of the druids.''

Was this a euphemism? If Kastrith didn't possess such power, how could he know Gordon's language? know of his world? Gordon looked back to Brennus, then to Vocorix. He didn't know what to say.

''Kastrith, how can you prove this? If you can send me home. Do it, do it now.''

''It's not as simple as you may think.''

''Of course he would say that,'' Gordon thinks to himself.

''Peering into your world takes a fraction of said power. Is this not enough for you?''

''No… no it isn't.''

''So, you want to die alone in a world that's not your own?''

Gordon snaps. ''I don't fucking know! I want to go home, send me there now! What is it you need to do to send me home?! Eh? Or is this some fucking clever way of you saying you're actually going to take me away and slit my fucking throat?! SEND. ME. HOME!'' A tear streams down his face.

Kastrith gives a menacing laugh. ''I understand you need time to figure this out, my offer will remain open to you. I implore you Gordon, think on this,'' Kastrith stops speaking English and returns to speaking the common tongue of Urosi. ‘’Back to our business, Vocorix.’’

‘’What were you two speaking of?’’ He demands.

‘’Business between me and the realm walker is naught of your concern.’’

Vocorix grits his teeth.

‘’You want peace, you know what to do,’’ Kastrith adds.

‘’No.’’

‘’It’s all I ask.’’

‘’And what of your Venethari shamans?’’

‘’What of them?’’

‘’Won’t you banish them too?’’

‘’No, they have not committed atrocities against their Gods.’’

‘’Tell me Kastrith, what are these atrocities again?’’

‘’They speak of Vistra as if he were a villain grasping for power, they grow fearful of a God's long-awaited return and spread nothing but fear and hatred about him and myself, and then they threaten the safety of this entire world by bringing forth a being they weren’t even sure of into this world, knowing full well it would be drenched in the Altharn’s power. Do you have any idea what kind of beasts lurk the endless void Vocorix? Do you?’’

''The druids do not speak ill of Vistra, they revere him as they do Fanara. She is our culture, she granted us, the people of Darogoth the sacred haven as home, just as Vistra guided you to yours. The druids speak ill of you, Kastrith! You are the one spouting the lies and grasping for power! What happened to you, Kastrith?! What happened? Everyone knows it is impossible for the Gods to return. The Altharn has banished them forever.''

''That is a mere myth, Vistra stirs within me. So tell me… how did I achieve power such as this?''

''Gordon!'' Camula's voice shudders the walls of his mind, as it does the world moves slowly, his perception controlled. He watches as a purple glow illuminate from inside Kastrith's mask, his arm lifting to target Vocorix in a magical assault.

Kastrith sends forth a blast of purple flame, a blast unlike any other that dazzles with stars of the night sky, bound for Vocorix at unimaginable speed. Vocorix becomes blinded by the immense flash. Naturally his eyes closed, his subconscious had accepted death already within the fraction of a second.

Vocorix felt nothing.

He opened his eyes slowly… The inferno was a lofted in stasis before him, spitting out violently in all kinds of directions as it hissed and warped.

Gordon had caught the blast within his own magical force and was struggling to keep hold. The fire roared loudly, eruptions of searing heat escaping from all angles as Gordon's force was beginning to collapse.

‘’Fuck, Fuck! Fuck!!! He is strong,’’ Gordon’s inner voice screams. ‘’What do I do, I can’t hold this, I can’t fucking hold this!’’

Gordon, thinking on his feet, manages to divert the blast toward the sky, and sends his own force out toward Kastrith, Kastrith catches the force within his own power with ease and redirects it back to Gordon, grasping him in a levitated lock of magical pressure, crushing him in the air.

‘’Realm Walker… drenched by the Altharn….’’ he holds firmly onto Gordon as his attention returns to Vocorix.

The oathsworn charge forth, drawing their weapons, Vocorix signals them to halt.

‘’How about now… I’ll ask you one more time, High King.’’

Vocorix looks to Gordon, who was suffering as he choked, suspended in the air, spluttering in pain, his skin turning red as he is crushed by the pressure of Kastrith’s effortless magic.

‘’No.’’

Kastrith fires yet another blast to Vocorix intended to completely obliterate him without disturbance.

Gordon bursts his arm out with all the power he could muster and catches it yet again despite having his very being crushed, focusing even harder Gordon screams with the might of the Altharn, letting out an incredible pulse, knocking over all except Kastrith in a powerful shockwave that ripples through the summit, breaking him free from Kastrith’s grip. The three statues all fall to the ground, shattering on impact.

Gordon screams in agony as Kastrith rebounds the infernal blast, diverting it away and off the tip of the Spire.

As soon as Gordon's feet thud into the floor he jumped to an aggressive stance, his eyes glaring a purple hue, both his hands outstretched with the world's power itself pulsating around his palms as he pants excessively, ready for anything.

''You have much to learn,'' Kastrith remarks.

Vocorix signals Gordon to calm, Gordon Refuses, Brennus runs to Gordon's side.

''Walker, don't! All our lives are at stake here, you've seen what he can do.''

Gordon begins to take heed, panting away the exhaustion that rapidly engulfs.

''And so, the war continues, and the pact of our Gods, shattered to the floor by that which the druids brought forward....'' Kastrith walks off nodding to his guards holding the captives.

The guards slit the throats of the two captives. The lord and his wife, the lady of Shem fall to the floor from their knees as they gurgle desperately for the air that no longer reaches their lungs.

Gordon too falls to his knees in exhaustion.

Kastrith turns back to Vocorix. ''I'm ashamed of us both here on this day, Vocorix. Many thousands of years ago stood our three Gods, forming the bond that unified Uros, and here we stand severing it.'' Kastrith gloats as he watches the lord and lady of Shem succumb in a pool of blood.

''No! You fucking tyrant!'' Spits Vocorix. ''It was the elves broke that trust when they abandoned both our people!''

Kastrith takes a mental note of Gordon's exhaustion. ''Remember my offer, Gordon, you have until the dawn of the next season. If I hear nothing from you, or you decide to take the offensive on my people. Then you will become an enemy of Venethar,'' he says, speaking again in English. ''Ah yes, the elves... clever little bastards, aren't they? At least they do not interfere with Vistra's will, hmm?''

Gordon says nothing as he peers into the blackness of Kastrith's eye sockets, trying to find his eyes. Eyes which never looked back.

Kastrith turns away with his men and leaves, disappearing down the spire.

''Gordon...'' Vocorix murmurs.

Brennus lifts Gordon to his feet. ''You good?''

''Yeah... exhaustion... quite bad... I don't really know what happened, it just exploded... the power....''

''Take it easy, lad.''

''I need to train more with magic,'' Gordon remarks. ''Kastrith... he's... how am I able to compete with that?!''

''You did good! You saved the high king's life... twice!''

Gordon scoffs at Brennus's words.

16: Fen Craic

''The Bataari Dynasty came to an end in 3A 702, prompting the rise of the Mundur Dynasty with its first King, Algar Mundur.

It was Lord Algar of Dullskelle that led the rebellion against King Ulf Bataari in the great Venethari civil war, and so naturally Algar took his place, moving his family to Kasidor where they rule to this very day, and so goes the Mundur Dynasty.

King Algar Mundur, the liberator. 3A702 - 3A 723
Queen Helia Mundur. 3A 723 - 3A 755
King Val Mundur, the Innocent. 3A 755 - 3A 760
King Urgen Mundur 3A 760 - 3A 803
Queen Asataari Mundur, the fair. 3A 803 - 3A 830
King Ollur Mundur. 3A 830 - 3A 890
King Urgen 2nd Mundur. 3A 890 - 3A 943
Queen Danast Mundur. 3A 943 - 3A 999
King Bukhuul Mundur. 3A 999 - 4A 50
King Fenrith Mundur, the fierce. 4A 50 - 4A 95
Queen Julraia Mundur, the breathless. 4A 95 - 4A 98
Queen Dallia Mundur 4A 98 - 4A 134
Queen Esrie Mundur 4A 134 - 4A 160
Queen Eltai Mundur 4A 160 - 4A 192
King Argrith Mundur, the vengeful. 4A 192 - 4A 226
King Arkhuul Mundur. 4A 226 - 4A 259

King Veldon Mundur. 4A 259 - 4A 267
King Kastrith Mundur, the redeemer. 4A 267 - Present

In the early days of Mundur rule, there was a strict law that royalty could only form intimate relations with that of their own race and only to those of nobility in order to keep the Mundur rule firm and purely Venethari.

But under Danast's reign this rule changed, as she had always loved a particular Dakivan man long before her ascension to the throne, her father Urgen the 2nd, denied her of her desires, and so in spite as she came into rule, she altered the Venethari law with the majority of nobility backing her decision. She married one of the Pale Folk of Dakiva, Alkir Reinistad, a renown Dakivan warlord, adding the Dakivans to the Mundur bloodline.

From this time onward and seeing how foreign relations can strengthen the bond of those around them, Venethari royalty married whoever they desired, be they of nobility or not.

Mundur rule has always been known to be that of a peaceful one, conflict with other nations was quite a rarity and the people were relatively content with their Mundur rulers, but relations have always tilted back and forth with the Dakivans in particular.

One incident occurred during the rule of Queen Virnirak of Dakiva, who had falsely accused Queen Eltai of Venethar of laying with her favourite husband during a festival being held on Dakiva at the time. Without trial Virnirak had Eltai executed, and this brought forward the bloodiest war Mundur Dynasty had seen since the start of their rule. Eltai's eldest son, Argrith, then took to the throne, and all of Venethar to war.

A war that would be called off and back on many times during Argrith's reign, the war finally came to an end in his elder years, having captured the city of Neev in Dakiva and executing every member of Dakivan royalty present, and installing a new family to rule, thus earning the title 'the vengeful', for the vengeance of his mother's death was lifelong.

Argrith, having spent his entire life in conflict with Dakiva, finally passed away a year after peace had been made allowing his only child, Arkhuul to ascend to the throne of Venethar.

And with Arkhuul we reach more recent years.

Arkhuul's rule was one of peace, until he and his Mavrosi wife, Jenisir were assassinated in Darogoth after celebrating the coronation of Darogoth's new high king, a then sixteen-year-old Vocorix Fen-Drosii.

It was later discovered down the years that it wasn't just money hungry brigands, but the entire assassination was orchestrated by none other than Arkhuul's own son, Veldon.

Which brings us to Veldon's rule. Veldon must be the most hated ruler of all within the Mundur Dynasty if not all of Uros, he taxed his people into poverty, pressed the nerves of all nations with his erratic behaviour, and delivered the most executions any ruler had ever given on all of Uros combined.

When it was discovered that Arkhuul and Jenisir's assassination was of Veldon's doing, Arkhuul's youngest child,

Kastrith, took it upon himself to end Veldon's rule and his life, and so alongside his sister Tarna they both plotted their regicide.

In Venethari tradition the eldest child is the one to take the throne, this would mean Tarna was to now rule Venethar, but she nobly decided to pass on the throne to Kastrith due to his primary role in taking down their tyrannical brother, this was the first time in Mundur history a ruler has ever passed up the throne.

And so, the people cheer our king's name in delight. Kastrith, the redeemer! Long may he reign.''

- *Hyphal Taarkiman - Dynasties of Venethar - 4A 278*

''I don't understand,'' Gordon pleads. ''How do I return home?''

''You must remain calm,'' Camula's soothing voice echoes. ''You've been building yourself well.''

''All this time I believed Kastrith to be the one who harbours this power of the endless void.''

''It's not as simple as it seems.''

''What do you mean!?''

''When I left my body, I passed through the veil of worlds, the God's realms are infinitely attached and locked to Altharn by pocket dimensions, barriered away so they may never return, but there was something wrong. Vistra's' world lay dormant, I felt it myself when I was bound to the cradle in my passing. The others had an aura, a certain feeling that radiated from their presence… but Vistra's….'' Camula peers off into midnight void that surrounds her.

''Kastrith claims to be his vessel, is this proof Vistra is really returning?''

''I don't know Gordon, something is wrong. Kastrith doesn't hold Vistra's power, I sense something different in him.''

''So, what does he have?!''

''I'm unsure.''

''Is there no possible way for me to return?''

''You need to discover what is going on with Kastrith, we need to know the source of his power and its link to Vistra.''

''Is Kastrith somehow syphoning his power?''

''That would be impossible, there is no direct contact through the Gods' realms that are attached to the Altharn. At least not that I know of…''

''Then I need to find out what's going on… where should I start?'' A loud thud begins rumbling across the void of Gordon's mind. ''The fuck is that?'' It gets louder and more consistent.

''Stay strong, Gordon,'' Camula fades back into nothing.

Suddenly Gordon awakes abruptly to the sound of his shack door being struck.

''Who is it?'' Gordon shouts out sluggishly, still processing his awakening.

''It's…Vocorix, we should talk, Gordon.''

Gordon falls out of his bed and gets dressed as quickly as he can. ''Yeah? Sorry, was still sleeping.''

Vocorix laughs. ''At this time?''

Gordon finally opens the door. ''Yeah, it's been tough lately… besides, no training today.''

Vocorix nods his head in curiosity. ''A well-deserved rest… may I come in?''

Gordon welcomes Vocorix inside. ''What's the issue?''

''Forgive my informal visit, but I think we should talk… about what happened at the Spire.''

''Oh?''

''You saved my life, twice… despite me carelessly letting you fall into the grasps of that tyrannical bastard. I wanted to know if you understood why?''

''I was a little angry at first… but I've had time to think,'' Gordon glances off to his desk.

Vocorix gives a pitiful smile. ''It was nothing personal, and… I value you more than I ever could right now, I didn't know what to say to him… I'm a stubborn man, I know, but I couldn't let the hearts of millions sink by the orders of a single mad man, especially at the expense of just one. I… wanted to apologise, I thought I'd leave you alone for a few days to give you some space. You really displayed your power and commitment to us that day, can I ask now what it was Kastrith was saying to you in that… language?''

Gordon squints his eyes, still irritated by Vocorix. ''He told me he has the power to send me home, to leave this world and leave the issues between your kingdoms for you both to settle.''

''And… you said?''

''I declined. I didn't trust him.''

''Good, and you shouldn't. It looked like you were shouting at him at one point?''

Gordon looks off to the floor.

''Still want to go home, don't you?'' Vocorix adds.

''Of course I do… that's why I snapped at him… all my fear just left my body. I'm desperate… I need to find out what power Kastrith holds.''

''You think he really has the power to send you back?''

''No… maybe? But I have a feeling something is off about his 'power' whatever it is.

''Funny you mention that, we're trying to find out for ourselves, you know of his sister?''

Gordon cocks his head. ''Tarna? Isn't it?''

''Yes… Tarna Mundur, she escaped Kasidor not too long before you arrived in Altharn, she joined and heavily funded the rebellion against him, but their rebellion is in shambles from what we've heard of late. Upon our return to Carsinia I received a letter from her to smuggle her over the border, saying she had valuable information about Kastrith and his forces. Maybe she has the answers you seek?''

''She can be trusted? She is his sister....''

''She's leading an active rebellion, they captured the city of Antler just across the border, that's how she sent that message... but Kastrith's forces took it back, they've been roaming the borderlands of Venethar since, a small number of the Venethari rebellion want to cross our borders and recuperate their efforts, their struggling at the moment and need harbouring whilst they get back on their feet, but they don't know a way to cross the borders. We however do have a way, it's dangerous, and they wanted some... protection. A band of Venethari trotting through Darogoth isn't going to look good for the locals, they'll need escorting and someone with powerful magic to help them through our pass. Her forces are constantly moving, the last letter she sent to me said to send a party to find her and I know exactly who I need to do that.''

''You're sending me?''

''Yes... and we also have a very talented tracker, a woman by the name of Eithne, the best in all Darogoth, if anyone can find Tarna, it's her. She's based out in Vortighna, the capital of Fen.''

''So, you're sending me into Venethar?''

''Correct, but there's another thing we must discuss.''

''What?'' Gordon's face drops, he felt agitated, used.

''I have a reward for you. For saving my life… twice… and… for proving your loyalty to us,'' Vocorix sighs.

Gordon's face perks up a little. ''Oh, you do?''

''I'm giving you ownership of Fen Craic Keep in Fen. I'll also help you fund its restoration; it's been out of service for a while now and will need refurbishing, it sits by the Fen Lake, just a few miles north of Vortighna. You'll be working with the Governor of Fen and Lord of Vortighna, Gallus. So, this will suffice nicely. When you're ready, you'll set out in search for Tarna.''

''You're giving me a keep? As in?''

''Yes… I've ordered lords of Fen to provide you with a small number of soldiers to volunteer for your service whilst you get yourself on your feet. I'll provide you with a treasurer, and a druid when one becomes available. It shouldn't be too hard making an income from there, the lake is abundant with fish, and Fen Craic used to be a trading post long ago, maybe take advantage of that, but let the treasurer worry about that stuff. Oh, and the keep may have a bandit problem… a couple of low life smugglers have been seen using it as of late. So be careful on approach, I'll make sure to send a strong unit with you to wipe any threats out.''

''I… don't know what to say… thank you, High King.''

''About time you got out of this fucking shed,'' smiles Vocorix. ''It's time you learnt to lead warriors, use your power properly and really do Darogoth the service it needs. I promise I'll do all I can to help you find a way back to your home world.

It's not easy, and I won't lie, there has been no further progress. It's an impossible task and Daxos is old and frail, not as springy as she once was. If I were you, I'd just settle for the time being, but for your sake we won't give up on you, so long as you don't give up on us.''

''Okay,'' Gordon thinks for a minute, springing to hide his emotions. ''Wait… does this mean I'm becoming a… lord?''

''A minor one, yes. You're legitimised by your torc now, remember? You're the clan lord of your own clan now, and you'll be taking orders from Gallus Fen-Frenone, the Lord of Vortighna and Governor of Fen, he's a good man, to the very core.''

''What about you?''

''I give him orders,'' Vocorix laughs. ''Brennus will be accompanying you; he's going to be your master of arms and your oathsworn commander. You'll be telling him what to do now!''

''Thank you again, High King… I'll do my best.'' Gordon replies in angst, he wasn't confident about the whole ordeal but he was eternally grateful, dumbfounded, but grateful.

He had a goal now, find Tarna. If anyone had answers about the power Kastrith holds it surely was to be his sister, perhaps she even knew of a way for Gordon to return home.

With more gold to his name, his first big spend was of a noble steed. He spent a considerable amount of time at the stables trying to figure out which equine companion would be best for him. Eventually he grew impatient and opted for the most expensive horse he could find, he figured if he was to be travelling a lot he may as well get the most reliable horse he can, besides, he secretly always wanted his own horse.

She was stocky, quite large for a female. Brown with speckled white stains strewn across her body and a beautiful white stripe trickling down her face. Gordon thought of what he could call her.

''Epona. That's fitting… I know these people won't get it. But I don't think you could have a better name….'' he whispers to her, stroking her head gently.

For the first time Gordon had a few days spare, with no duties and no training or labour intensive work for a change, he decided to soak in the culture of Carsinia's city life before gathering his belongings, Epona and the essentials.

It was tough. With nothing to do he became cursed by overthinking and making himself upset. However, he found it a lot easier to find his feet, with a realistic goal and a solid direction and the ownership of his very own keep. Yes, things were starting to shape up for him.

Hashna was to remain in Carsinia, which saddened Gordon, she was like a big sister to him.

''I'm sure we'll see each other again soon enough! Make us proud. Do yourself proud,'' she punches his arm forcefully, proceeding with a tight bear hug. ''If you find a way home and are to leave us, promise you'll find me first, or at least write.''

''I promise, Hashna. Goodbye....'' Gordon returns a hard punch to Hashna's arm, she doesn't flinch.

The two share a smile of a potent friendship as Gordon climbs atop Epona, trotting off into the distance with new beginnings set on the horizon and hope wrapped across his heart.

Hashna watches on until Gordon and the party are completely out of sight, satisfied she grins.

Within the party many pack mules bearing supplies and materials travel onward to Fen Craic Keep.

Because of the large amount of supplies they carried it was estimated to take a few weeks to arrive at their destination. Travelling north west across the river Os, north beside the Ard Forest, and then finally west over the border to Fen, passing by the famed Bi Wood.

After four whole weeks of camping and travel, eventually Fen Craic came into sight, resting peacefully by the enormous Fen Lake, surrounded by strong fortified walls, as the party drew closer it became more obvious that the keep was in major degradation.

The walls were looking aged and nature had begun to engulf the weathered stone, weeds sprouted from below and within. Fen Craic had been out of operation for around thirty or so years, kept erected out of honour of its previous owner, it was apparently once a bustling fortified trading post and rest for travelling merchants, previously owned by a famed clan of Fen. The Dregenotix clan, now eradicated from the world.

The party approached the thick oaken the gates, the wood was clearly in rot, with one of the gates completely off its hinges, exposing the courtyard that appeared before them, suffocated by the overgrowth of the Altharn.

''Be careful, there might be a few squatters. But here's our new home, Walker,'' Brennus announces.

Gordon dismounts and draws his blade, warriors follow in his steps that carefully tread into the courtyard of Fen Craic, silent like the bloody aftermath of a vast battlefield. The party scoured around, entering the shattered buildings that encircled the courtyard, looking for any signs of habitation.

Nothing was found in the buildings tucked in the courtyard, nothing but crumbling stone with shards of wood that scattered the ground with every step, some of buildings had enormous holes in the roofing, one didn't even have a roof, nothing seemed suspicious, so the group continued onto the main keep down a central alleyway of stone buildings that guided the way up to some large steps, leading to the door of the main keep. They stood before the huge doors, they loomed at a great height, at least a little over ten feet, and they were barred shut.

Brennus pushes hard attempting to open the crooked doors. He gives in, bearing a jeering look. ''Something's blocking from the inside,'' he remarks. ''Looks like we have company… Gordon?''

''What?''

''Blow the fucking doors down. Warriors, at the ready!" Brennus shakes himself down as he adjusts his posture. ''Whoever is residing in Fen Craic, come out now and seek freedom! No harm will come to you unless you disobey,'' Brennus roars.

There is no response.

''In the name of High King Vocorix! Come out or we'll fucking force you out!''

Again, no response.

Gordon cocks his head. ''Brennus are you sure there-''

''You have ten seconds! Ten! Nine! Eight! Seven! Six…'' Brennus's patience runs thin. ''Fuck it, Gordon, now,'' he struts away from the doors, signalling Gordon forward by jabbing his thumb over his shoulder.

Gordon stumbles forward. ''Step back!!'' He brings his palm up toward the door.

BOOM!

The weather-worn doors tear away with immense force, flying from their hinges, bringing the makeshift barricades with them, debris spraying all over the inner halls from the awesome blast.

The warriors rush in, immediately forming a shield wall in front of Gordon.

As soon as the dust settled, they were met with a hail of arrows coming from behind more barricades further down the main hall. The warriors blocked the hail in a vigilant brace.

‘’PUSH!’’ Brennus yells at the top of his voice.

Everyone obeys, edging forward a few steps as they ducked behind their shields. ‘’BRACE!!’’ Again the warriors obey, dropping the tip of their shield to the floor and ducking behind.

Gordon, having no shield, shares Brennus’.

‘’We’re going to break their defence and give them one hard push. On my word, Walker, give them some fucking fire!’’ Brennus orders.

Gordon and Brennus push carefully to the front of the warriors. The sounds of arrows and other thrown objects smash against the shields in quick succession, a few arrowheads pierce through, protruding around the boss nearing Gordons face, causing him to jump in freight.

‘’NOW!’’ Brennus screams.

Gordon peers over the shield launching a ball of flame into the crowd of drawn bows.

As soon as the fireball connects with the floor it explodes, producing an ear bursting bang, sending flames abound into the enemy militia in a dazzling hail of inferno. As a devastating result, they scatter while some panic amidst the flames.

‘’Charge! Cut them down!’’ Shouts Brennus.

The warriors rush forward pushing out their massive shields in a terrifying stampede, overpowering and knocking the enemy into the ground.

The fighting ensued. One man charges forth to Gordon, screaming like a disgruntled boar. Gordon takes this opportunity and uses his magic to create a powerful force sending the man flying off to his side and cracking his skull off the cold stone pillars before he even had a chance to get into fighting distance. Gordon rushes over to him burying his sword into his neck, finishing him off, giving Brother his first taste of blood.

The brigands were bearing shoddy leathers, their weapons rusted and jagged, nothing compared to the craftsmanship of Darogoths finest. It was clear these were travelling folk. Their armament's spoke enough of their lifestyle, squatters who refused to coexist within civil boundaries.

A bloodlust engulfs Gordon as mental images flash throughout his mind, images of Helen's smile infuse a blood scorned rage as he puts men to the blade with the newly formed finesse he had acquired from months of intensive training, screaming viciously as he waves his sword arm around amongst his brethren in arms, determined he was.

In the corners of his tunnelled vision, Brennus can be seen smashing an opponent square in the jaw with his massive shield as he darts his blade into their belly, barking orders and screaming at the top of his lungs with the might of a fearless bear, warriors around him take heed, dashing to his orders.

Gordon utilises magical force to hold some in place as he effortlessly rammed his blade into them, others sent flying into the walls by the sheer force and more seared to the bone with flame, flame that was fuelled by the carnage of Seers Crossing, fuelled by his hope and despair.

Six of the militia perished before Gordon's magical might. The morale of the militia was wavering rapidly as they could do nothing but watch on in horror to the grandeur power Gordon had wrought upon them. Their formations in shambles, confused and terrified. Things were looking bad for the uninvited residents of Fen Craic; they tried to scurry out, being cut down one by one as they attempted to flee. An infestation of rats, effortlessly cleared out.

As soon as the initial conflict drew to an end, the entire party got to work. Scouring every nook and cranny for any more trouble, fixing and cleaning up the crucial parts of the keep. The party had their work cut out for them; it was going to take some time to restore Fen Craic to its former glory.

Brennus found a suitable holding and presented Gordon his new chambers. A large room that was in obvious habitation of the men who'd had just been slain.

The stone fireplace was out of use and blocked, the militia had created a shoddy bonfire in the middle of the room as a replacement. The entire room was cluttered and trashed, rags of clothing and animal remains cemented amongst the stone floor. Together the two gave an enormous sigh of exhaustion and began working on clearing all the mess, fixing the bed and laying down fresh bedding, repairing the bookshelves that sat in a nook where many books lay damaged, some of which were intact.

''Fuck… they were using these books for fire… glad they didn't use all of them, look at this collection!?'' Gordon stammers in excitement. He returns to his neutrality after realising his out of character excitement over some books, something he wouldn't usually become thrilled by.

In the main living space, there was a raised platform where a four-poster bed stood, from the bed a beautiful stone fireplace sat beside a battered liquor cabinet. The nook that was surrounded by bookshelves had a somewhat tattered desk, and at the end of the room was a hallway with a glass door leading to a balcony, overlooking the gorgeous Fen Lake with the city of Vortighna just in sight over the horizon.

Brennus and Gordon stand on the balcony, taking a quick break from labouring.

''They can't have been staying here permanently with Vortighna so close,'' scoffs Brennus. ''Fucking idiots.''

''Maybe they got too comfortable. Well, they're gone now,'' Gordon mutters.

''You okay?''

''Yeah. Still getting used to it....''

Brennus smiles. ''I'll leave you to soak in the new home, eh? Clearing that shit out was my day's work done, I'm glad my chambers aren't as fucked up as yours,'' he laughs.

''Yeah... that smell is still lingering though,'' Gordon remarks on the aroma of body odour and mould that coaxed the chambers.

Brennus pretends to regurgitate in jest. ''Right, I'm going to see how the others are getting on and get a report. I'll send you the details and you can write to the high king on what more needs doing and what we'll need,'' Brennus announces as he departs.

''Yeah, sure,'' Gordon inhales one last load of fresh air from the lake before re-entering the musky hum of his chambers.

Gordon walks around lighting the candles and torches with magic. He had his belongings dragged in and began unpacking as he cleaned.

He was fumbling around in the alcohol cabinet when he was interrupted by the sounds of footsteps walking toward his chambers from down the hall. The steps came to a halt at the open doorway to Gordon's chambers.

"Well, well… someone's doing well for themself," a familiar voice beckons from the doorway.

Gordon turns to the door and drops an entire bottle of mead in shock.

17: Friends in Fen

''Luke…'' Gordon stammers in total disbelief. ''Lu… Lucotorix, how?! How!?! You're alive!?'' He bolts toward him.

''Gordon!'' Lucotorix opens his arms wide.

The two run at each other, combining a loving embrace, the tightest hug Gordon had ever experienced in his life, no one from his home world had ever embraced him so intently. They both burst into a shower of tears, overjoyed.

''How!? How the fuck?! How? What?'' Gordon shrieks, jumbling his words as he attempts to dry his eyes on his chainmail bound sleeve.

''They took me away to Venethar, to be shipped off to Mavros Avir and be sold into slavery. A few of us managed to escape as the ship set sail… I swam back to shore with my hands still bound, I don't even know how I managed… only a few of us survived the swim,'' he looked off to the wall, reliving the tribulations he had experienced. He glances back to Gordon with a beaming smile. ''Enough about that, look at you! Your hair has grown! That armour?! And you have a torc?! The high king told me everything that you've done! I'm very proud of you, Gordon.''

''Fuck… I'm sorry Luke…'' Gordon's face drops hearing upon Lucotorix's story. ''Is that how you knew I was here? You mustn't have been far behind us?'' Gordon says as he swipes the broken glass with his boot.

Lucotorix adjusts his posture. ''Well, this is the fun part. So once I arrived at Carsinia I was told by the high king that you had departed a few days prior to my arrival, it wasn't hard to catch up… oh… and guess what….''

''What?''

He extends his arm in a cocky fashion. ''I'm your druid.''

''You're joking?!'' Gordon sings in relief. ''I can't believe this… this is amazing. I…'' tears refill Gordon's eyes. He pauses as an endearing thought crosses his mind. ''Oh… I have something for you actually… and yes there's a lot we need to catch up on too…'' Gordon digs around amongst one of his bags he was unpacking and pulls out a small wooden box his torc once sat in, for it now had another use. ''Close your eyes.''

Lucotorix obeys.

Gordon grabs what he needs from the box and produces it before him. ''Okay… now open them.''

As Lucotorix opens his eyes he is met with the torc of his late brother. He stands there speechless for a moment. ''Gordon… how did you get this?!'' He snatches the torc, holding it close to his chest, his eyes welling up once again.

''I went back to the village the day after the attack, Brennus was due to visit again and I knew I'd cross paths with him if I stayed at the village once the attackers fled,'' Gordon begins to turn pale as he recounts his tragic past at Seers Crossing. ''I burned them… I gathered them all up… put them all on a pyre… and I burned them. Brennus found me the next day.''

Lucotorix nods as he switches his glances from the torc to Gordon. He draws Gordon in for another consoling hug. ''You've really been through allot, friend. Well… we're here now, and we're back in this shit storm together, yeah?''

Gordon chuckles with watery eyes. ''Yeah….''

''We'll drink and talk together soon, right now there's a lot that needs doing round here, the high king has a load of supplies coming this way and wants me to give him the rundown on the specifics of the keep, plus I have some other things that need doing before the days end, and I also want to actually put my feet up and settle… it's been nonstop for me, friend.''

''Of course… I was about to do it myself… but hey, I'll let my druid do it,'' Gordon winks.

''Thank you, Gordon, for this,'' he holds up the torc of Orthunus and departs the chambers leaving Gordon standing in awe.

Lucotorix pokes his head back around the door frame. ''Let's smoke this evening?!''

''Definitely.''

Over the coming weeks Gordon and all now residing within Fen Craic had cleaned up the majority of the mess. They had dusted down all the webs and dirt, cleaned and repaired the furniture left behind by the squatters prior. All they had to do now was wait upon the delivery of supplies to make some finishing touches. Gordon and Lucotorix had a much needed catch up, they discussed and reminisced over their times in Seers Crossing and mourned together over the tragedy that befell them that fateful day.

Gordon was relieved to know he was alive, he still couldn't believe this was real, especially having Lucotorix just appear at his door so suddenly.

It was only a matter of time until a letter would come through from Vortighna from Lord Gallus Fen-Frenone. He was to visit in order to discuss the forthcomings of operations.

Gordon sat in his chambers at the desk, flicking through the many books and soaking in his now luxurious residence until being disturbed by a small knock at the door from Lucotorix.

''Gordon, Lord Gallus has arrived. Best come to the hall, I invited him in and he's waiting.''

Gordon made a quick check of his appearance before hurrying to the main hall.

Standing in the middle of the great hall and peering around in astonishment, was Gallus. Lord of Vortighna and Governor of Fen, Clan Lord of the Frenone clan. An aged man in his late forties, he had a prominent noble posture; and appeared quite fit within his slender frame, he had short grey hair that spiked upwards with a clay product, followed by the classic moustache which was notably shorter than most. He had one of the friendliest looking faces Gordon had laid eyes on. Gallus seemed to naturally beam a happy smile.

Gallus was accompanied by a large group of warriors. Their shields and clothing colours were very different from those Gordon was used to seeing, these shields were black on top and blue at the bottom. Three fish-like shapes representing the Frenone clan and two entangled trees representing the province of Fen.

‘’Ah! Is this he? The realm walker? I'm very excited to finally meet you, Ard-Barker, is it?" He announces as he pulls out his arm in greeting.

Gordon grabs his arm in response. ‘’It is, and you must be Gallus Fen-Frenone.’’

‘’That I am! It's good to finally see Fen Craic in operation again. We were going to bring it down all together and establish a fishing village. But now I have possibly one of the most powerful neighbours in Darogoth! Or so I hear,’’ he laughs. ‘’It's a very well-placed keep, do you not think? The lake is utterly stunning this time of year.’’

‘’It's really cosy, I love it. It beats living in an actual shed, that's for certain.’’

‘’Good to hear,’’ Gallus winks. ‘’Right, I would love to stay for pleasantries but I’m a very busy man, especially with the war and such. I suppose you'll want to know more about our little expedition into Venethar that we have planned in order to relocate Tarna Mundur.''

''Yes, I'm eager to make a start on that.''

Gallus gives a surprised look. ''Now… Tarna and her rebellion have been scattered all throughout the Borderlands in Venethar, last we heard they were around the edges of the Faceless Forest, but they've moved further north to keep patrols away from that part of the border, making it easier for us to get into Venethar.''

''How are we going to do that?''

''This may be the hard part; we need to cross the mountains. Now, there is a pass but it's not the Venethari we need to worry about.''

Gordon scrunches in confusion.

''It's the… faceless ones.''

''The, what?''

''Oh, fuck me,'' sighs Brennus, slapping his thick palm to his head.

''Yes… The creatures that reside in the mountains, that's why patrols are largely absent up that way on both sides of the pass… but it's our only way to get through if we are wanting to avoid Venethari detection.''

''What is a faceless one?''

''Ugly cunts, they have a large mouth and no face, they're quick and strong, and have these disgusting fucking elongated arms and legs,'' Brennus blurts. ''Tall as fuck as well.''

''Yes… thank you Oathsworn, for that… detailed description. Very awful creatures indeed, but from what I've heard of you, you have magic that can outshine even the most experienced mages and seers, yet you've been here just under a year now, give or take?'' Gallus smiles. '' Oh, another thing, you'll have the aid of our finest here to track down Tarna and sniff out any dangers ahead. She's the best tracker in all Darogoth! Gordon, meet Eithne Dun-Crannock,'' he proudly presents Eithne afront.

She was a proud standing woman of fiery red hair and smoky green eyes, with a face dotted with many freckles around her buttoned nose. Painted upon her cheeks were small blue swirls and patterns much like the many Gordon had seen throughout Darogoth. She was decorated in wolf pelts and the finest of leathers. She rested upon her spear with both hands as she stood silently, scanning him up and down, her face was an empty shell, shedding no emotion in her confident lean.

She gives a small nod in greeting. Gordon returns the nod out of respect.

''She's not much of a talker, her spear does most of that for her,'' laughs Gallus. ''I'm going to be leaving her and a small company of my loyal in your care who will accompany you to Venethar. Once Tarna and her party have been safely escorted into our lands, write to me and we'll continue from there.''

''Good, sounds good,'' Gordon eagerly agrees.

''I look forward to our future endeavours, oh and please provide a private living space for Eithne, she'll need her own lodging as she holds a lot of important information here and there… who's your master of arms here?''

''That would be me, Lord,'' Brennus steps forward, grasping his belt with his coarse hands. ''Former Oathsworn Commander to High King Vocorix and now Master of Arms and Oathsworn Commander at Fen Craic under Gordon Ard-Barker.''

''Is there enough space in the barracks here for all these warriors?''

''Should be… there's two barracks, very large.''

''Great, I'll leave you all to it, I just wanted to greet the realm walker for myself! I've got to travel to Ard and feast with the high king, and then on to Glaen, get to see the front lines for myself, those horse fanatics are really keeping the pressure on us in Glaen, we've withdrawn an army of thirty thousand in the east, Fanara preserve our sorry arses…. Good day everyone, and goodbye to you, Ard-Barker. A pleasure.'' Gallus leaves accompanied by his oathsworn, mounting his steed and galloping hastily through the gates while the rest of his warriors stay behind under Eithne's command.

''Disperse yourselves, make yourselves useful and aid Fen Craic's restoration. I'll notify you all when we are ready to leave for Venethar,'' Eithne announces calmly to her warriors in her raspy tone.

Gordon approaches sheepishly, feeling somewhat intimidated by her firm presence. ''Some of the guest rooms have been cleared out, they might need some work here and there but it's liveable,''

Eithne smirks with a silent spark of approval, she steps forward to follow.

Gordon leads Eithne on a silent and awkward walk to one of the guest chambers down the same hall as his.

''Hope this one is good enough for you,'' Gordon says as he pushes open the door to the chambers, revealing a bland, and somewhat empty room with only the basics, the room had been worked on well enough to live in, the furniture was still slightly dusty, some of it aged and worn but these things don't bother the hardy people of Dun.

Eithne dawdles in, her eyes darting around. After a few awkward seconds of Gordon standing by the door watching as she scours the chambers, she turns to him. ''Thank you,'' she says, her face still.

''If you need anything, I'm just over there,'' he gestures down the hall.

She lowers her head in response.

Leaving Eithne to her own devices Gordon returns to his chambers, soaking in the new life which he hadn't had time to do yet since so much work needed doing over the passing weeks, for the first time he didn't even seem to blink at the fact he'd killed again… was he getting used to it or was the yearning to return so prominently he just didn't care? He still even wondered if all this was even real, although that was something that consistently repeated within his mind, he'd always pinch himself and every time he'd always feel it. Yes, this was real.

Entering his chambers, he pours himself a cup of the left-over mead from the cabinet and prepares his pipe for a peaceful evening of relaxing and contemplation, sitting himself on his balcony and overlooking Lake Fen in the hazy sunset, flicking through his phone, peering at the same videos and pictures he constantly berates himself over.

The endless questions always presented itself, deep from the recesses of his mind. It poked and prodded his sanity, shaking it around like a ragged doll. ''Am I ever going to return home? They must think I'm dead… it's been so long… they'll definitely think I'm dead by now….''

This night Gordon had a little too much mead, feeling the burn of alcohol down his throat and the stale stench of his pipe, he'd stumble around erratically, mournfully yearning for home, crying out for his lost love.

The world would shift and morph the harder the grasp held, his heart would thud with fear, it was almost like sometimes he'd just forget what reality truly is. He felt trapped inside a locked box with no way out, Camula would always try, try to pry its fingers from his mind, she was never always successful however.

Gordon was never usually the type to become depressed or succumb to such darkness, he was the advocate for just 'getting on with it', but this night grasped tightly on his stability. Enough was enough, despite all the great things that had hurled his way, all he really wanted was to be home.

How would he do it? How could he end his life? Could he do it with magic? Jump from the balcony? No, although the thought crossed his mind, he was too fearful of such a permanent action, Gordon was determined to press on, he wanted to see this through, why was he even thinking like this?! Maybe the mead got to his head. He drenched himself with a water canteen and slumped by his bed, hanging his head low in a pitiful state as he swayed pathetically from side to side.

''It's not that bad… is it? Look at me… I'm the owner of a fucking castle mate… got money and shit… and magic!! Fucking magic!!'' He laughs hysterically. ''Beats work…'' he bellows a rumbling belch. ''Look… I just need to find that ticket home… Tarna… Kastrith? Maybe… but, but, but… look at these people, Luke, he's alive… he's alive! Brennus… Hashna… Gallus seems cool. Yeah, even that Eithne girl is alright, eh? They're good folk… I'm doing alright here, just… keep your head up G, we can do this,'' he waffles on to himself, until passing out by the side of his bed, blackened by the intoxicating ensemble of mead and smoke.

18: The Expedition

The day had arrived and it was time for the biggest journey Gordon was to take thus far. It was time to venture into enemy territory, into the Kingdom of Venethar.

The morning breeze was chilly, the air was fresh with the wind that guided the crispy scent of the lake into his open balcony. Fen Craic was awake and bustling, everyone was preparing for the coming venture.

Gordon was wide awake, unwilling to move from his large postered bed, allured by the warming comfort of such a blissful morning, and from fear of the cold.

He lights the fireplace from within his pelt quilts, allowing the gentle cackle of flames to spill a toasty warmth into the room.

His armour was displayed upon a stand by the door, he put it on piece by piece, tying his sword to his hip and holding his helmet firm to balance on his hip.

He marches down the corridor, making his way toward the kitchen where the cook would have morning meals prepared for the castle inhabitants; he didn't have a cook, so instead one of the loyal warriors volunteered for now.

Gordon grabs a typical morning meal, a broth of meat and vegetables, sometimes he'd crave the foods of his home world… but this was all he had and would have to make do. ''What do I have to complain about? For once in my life, I'm actually eating properly,'' he thought to himself as he brought his steaming bowl into the feasting hall.

A large table in the shape of a U surrounds a square hearth. Brennus, Eithne, Lucotorix and a few unfamiliar soldiers of prestigious ranking were already sitting, eating and chatting amongst themselves.

''Morning Gordon!'' Lucotorix greets.

Eithne turns to the doorway, watching Gordon take his seat, she cracks a half smile that lasted but a fraction of a second.

''Morning everyone, fuelling up for the day?'' Gordon takes his seat next to Lucotorix.

''Indeed, we shall set off as soon as possible. We have many tracks to make until we hit the border. We're going to stay the night at a fort just by the mountainside, Fort Fen Donaren! It's owned by Lord Ambunix Fen-Parvusii, me and him go way back actually,'' says Brennus.

''Sounds good,'' Gordon chirps as he digs into his food.

''I can definitely get used to this new life,'' smirks Brennus. ''This hall is grand.''

''It's quite something, I mean it's no shack… but it'll do,'' sniggers Gordon.

''Your accent is very peculiar,'' Eithne remarks. ''You really learned our language within just a few days?''

''Yeah,'' Gordon replies modestly.

Her eyebrows perk in surprise.

''It's quite complicated....'' he adds.

''Isn't life?''

Gordon scoffs in jest. ''Good point,'' he smirks as he takes another mouthful of his broth.

Lucotorix rises, collecting his empty bowl. ''The high king has a lot of deliveries to arrive here while you're gone, when you return, we'll have more building supplies and a few more members to staff the keep and help run the place. I'll get the courtyard set up for a market so travelling merchants can stop by, after all it was a trade post... I'll add a small trade tax until the treasurer explores our options and decides otherwise.''

''Good luck, the sooner this place is self-sufficient, the better,'' muffles Brennus with a mouthful of food. ''Right, I'm done,'' he swallows. ''I'll go pack some dried meat and order the warriors to prepare the horses. Shall we ride for, say, a few hours? Before midday?''

Gordon looks around. ''You're asking me?''

''Well, yes....''

Gordon's eyes darted from side to side. ''Erm... Yeah.''

''You'll get used to it,'' Brennus chuckles.

''I'll prepare the warriors of Fen,'' Eithne rises.

''Come... my Lord,'' laughs Lucotorix.

Gordon slaps the back of his head playfully. ''Eh, I've only just sat down!''

Catching a glimpse of Gordons armour, Lucotorix notices something. ''No herb bags? Did you learn nothing when living amongst us?''

''Oh no… I just haven't got one on my armour, I don't wear it for battle, I still have it though.''

''Keep it on you. Especially if you're venturing behind the border, I have some fresh dry moss I picked out yesterday, I'll give you it. Venethar also has many useful ingredients within its great steppes. I can pack a small book for you from my personal collection about foraging in the Steppes if you like?''

''Thanks, Luke,'' smiles Gordon. ''I'll make sure to take note. You take care while we're gone, yeah?''

''As always, my friend, be careful beyond the border.''

With breakfast out of the way and preparations assembled, Gordon mounted his steed, double checking his strappings and belts were secure and ready to go.

The entire party patiently waits around for orders as Gordon stalls.

''After you, Brennus,'' Gordon announces, trotting up beside him.

Brennus cracks a smile from the side of his mouth. ''We move north, to Fort Fen Donaren! On me!''

The party roars out of the keep and into the wilds of Darogoth, thirty strong galloping with great haste as they stampede northward bound.

All they had to do was find Tarna Mundur, sister to Kastrith. By aiding the rebellion, Darogoth gained insight and a powerful ally and Gordon may finally get the answers he'd sought since his arrival; he was as eager as ever.

Something felt right about this endeavour, Gordon had an inkling that soon he would be home, or at the very least have a more straightened path to follow. He could Imagine it now as he gripped his reins, arching forward, galloping freely through the evergreen glow that is Darogoth. Daydreaming of returning home and watching the world flicker in that instance as it did when he arrived, embracing Helen so tightly that they can barely breathe, telling her of all the crazy experiences he's had to endure just to be back in her arms, the look on everyone's face when he appears out of the blue having been gone for long, calling his mother to assure her that he's okay. Wild thoughts of freedom stormed Gordon's hopeful mind, he was raring to see this through, no matter what it took.

A long week of travelling would eventually bring them to Fort Fen Donaren. A heavily fortified bastion that stood before the mountainous mass of the great border. There they were welcomed by lord Ambunix Fen-Parvusii; a childhood friend and cousin of Brennus. A friendly yet stern man with a fearsome reputation as a once ferocious warrior. Another of Darogoth's high society, keen to meet the newly famed realm walker.

Ambunix was already awaiting the party by his gates upon hearing of their approach.

‘’Welcome, welcome! Finally, the realm walker arrives at my humble keep!’’ He bellows loudly, arms wide open, his large belly protruding through his bright blue tunic.

Ambunix was a large man, his shoulders were ever so broad and his limbs thick, filled with fat, all of which bolstered his imposing build, his grey beard was exceptionally long and matted, he clearly hadn’t washed it for quite some time.

‘’Brennus my friend! It's been far to fucking long! By Iskarien’s bony thighs, you've aged well!’’

Brennus dismounts his horse eagerly and approaches his old friend, the two burly bastards embrace one another, hitting and patting each other down as they grunted and snorted like two playful piglets.

‘’Ambunix, I see the boars have been breeding aplenty on this side of Darogoth!’’ Brennus howls.

‘’Still a cheeky little fucker, aren't you?’’ His belly wobbles as he laughs, ‘’And here we have Eithne Dun-Crannock, a pleasure! Good to see you again my dear!’’ He turns to Gordon. ‘’Come, Realm Walker… Gordon, isn't it? Gordon Ard-Barker. My, my… you've settled well, haven't you? Brennus told me all about you in his letters. Welcome to Fort Fen Donaren, the front-line bastion of the north western border to Venethar, and the hold that stops the faceless from streaming into Fen. Come, I'll show you all to your quarters and then we'll get acquainted, yes?’’

Everyone gabbers amongst themselves as Ambunix guides them all to their temporary lodgings.

This fort was significantly larger than Fen Craic. It seemed a lot bleaker also, with a notable eerie tone to it that clamped the dry stone, clearly it was in operation for more practical purposes, but once inside the great fort itself the interior well outshined the battered walls with beautiful woodwork and artistry, gilded seams upon every fabric in view, statues and busts of legends past.

In the evening, Ambunix hosted the leading members of the party to drink with him, his family and associates within the great hall of Fen Donaren.

Whilst all stood around the large hearth sipping all manners of beverage and basking in the warmth of the fire, Ambunix takes his time to properly speak with Gordon.

‘’So then, have you dealt with them before?’’ He asks.

‘’The Venethari? Yeah.’’

‘’No, no… the faceless,’’ he dips his bushy chin in concern, his fat rolls compiling together.

Gordon takes a nervous sip of his tankard. ‘’No….’’

‘’My advice… Realm Walker, and listen carefully. They're fast… every step you take in the mountains must be a step of caution… you must always be one step ahead, they mimic human voices to lure you out, but if you listen carefully, you'll notice there's nothing human about the way they wail, they’ll torture you with their screams, horrible things, but don’t just think they’ll only try to lure you out, oh no, they’ll stalk you and pounce the moment you let our guard down in their territory, when you camp at night order up some sleeping shifts to keep an eye out.''

Gordon stares on at the floor, trying to picture such a creature, taken back by Ambunix's warning. ''Thank you… I've yet to receive proper advice about dealing with these… things,'' Gordon says, his Earthly mind still naturally stubborn to such mythos.

Eithne, standing nearby, joins in on the conversation. ''Don't forget about their senses… they may not have eyes, but they have orifices for ears and a nose, they say even the skin around their head is just one big sensory gland, their senses are sharp, very sharp. They'll sniff us out before we can sniff them, that much is certain.''

''That's sure something coming from her, boy, trust me,'' Ambunix comments on Eithne's reputation.

''Wonderful, you two are really filling me with confidence here.''

''Worry not,'' Eithne says as she takes a delicate sip of her drink.

Ambunix gives a snorty giggle. ''I haven't gotten to the best bit yet, they're cautious of fire, they're not completely afraid like a wolf or such a creature, but they're cautious of it and try their best to work around it, you'll be lucky if they avoid you completely. If you ask me, you're the perfect man for the job, Gordon.''

‘’They may be fierce but they’re also quite clumsy, don’t let that make you underestimate them though, never underestimate your enemy,’’ Eithne adds.

‘’Aye, Brennus constantly tells me that,’’ laughs Gordon, shaking away the entrenching anxiety. ‘’Speaking of… where is he? I swear he was just over there a minute ago,’’ he points to a table where he last saw Brennus tearing into a boar's leg.

‘’He left with Ambunix’s sister-in-law,’’ Eithne smirks.

‘’He fucking what?! Elladane? Really?’’

‘’Yep.’’

Ambunix sighs heavily. ‘’She does have a type….’’

‘’Burly blondes with too much testosterone?’’ Says Eithne.

‘’Hmm…’’ A mischievous grin washes out the surprise in Ambunix’s face. ‘’I’ll return shortly,’’ he pats both Eithne and Gordon on the arm before barging past them, knocking them both aside with his bulbous frame.

Gordon and Eithne look at one another, sharing a unified chuckle. A silence then drowned the two, Gordon decided to break the ice.

‘’So, you’re from Dun? That would be the only place I’ve not set foot on in Darogoth now….’’

‘’Yeah,’’ she grips her tankard with both hands. ‘’It’s peaceful, too peaceful.’’

‘’How so?’’

''Well, Fen and Glaen share Venethar's border, so allot of the conflict in Darogoth's lands tend to happen more commonly here, so this is where the work is.''

''Are you some sort of mercenary?''

''No, I was a scout for the army of Omock in Dun, but I decided I wanted to get around more, so… I transferred to Fen, worked for a few minor lords here and there until I got some recognition, and now I'm the scout captain of Vortighna under Gallus.''

''Wow, nice. Looking forward to seeing how you do it,'' Gordon gives a nervous laugh. ''So, what's Dun like?''

''Dun is just crags and mountains…'' she stops and looks him directly in his eyes, narrowing onto him like a wolf on prey. ''Tell me of your world.''

Gordon gives a breathy sigh. ''My world is… different, very different. I come from a world of technology and science, a world with no Gods or magic… my world seems to move faster than its people… and sometimes, it's quite scary.''

''No Gods? Maybe you had Gods long ago, like us? And no magic? I'm no magic user, but even that sounds unbelievable. The world itself is magic, how do you think life exists?''

''Well… some people believe in Gods, but there's no proof they are real or even existed at all, that's how I see it at least, I think the people of my world believe in Gods for comfort, as nobody knows what happens when we die, that's my guess…

most of the things I've experienced on Altharn are just superstitious… at least on Earth it is.''

''Earth, is that your home? So, Earth is a home to humans?''

''That's its name, assuming I'm on a different planet… yeah, I suppose so… we don't have any other beings like us… just us and… animals? I guess. Here, I'll show you a piece of my world. This is one of the only things that came with me when I arrived here, I can show you my world with it.''

Eithne looks on eagerly as Gordon presents his phone, he turns it on and the screen brightens in front of her, she pivots her torso backward in caution as her eyes fixate.

Gordon shows her pictures of his world, the massive buildings of concrete, the roads, cars, technology, and the people.

Eithne's jaw drops. ''How is that possible? Little paintings?''

''Look, I'll show you how it works,'' he turns on the camera and snaps a shot of him and a confused Eithne and shows her the picture.

''That thing literally captured this moment?! Like a painting? But instantly?!'' She gawks.

''Yep, where I'm from, everyone has these. They're called 'phones' and you can speak to other people from any distance with them. They take pictures, record sound, you can store music in it, all sorts….''

‘’Any distance?! You can speak to your people now? And music?! How do you put music into it? Music is but sound….’’ Eithne is clearly baffled.

‘’No… that only works in my home world… I've tried countless times to reach my family from here… there’s no signal, and signal is only present on my world.’’

‘’But surely this ‘signal’ is just your Earth word for magic? That’s the essence of the power? Like Altharn’s magic is to the seers?’’

‘’Hah, you have a good point… but nope. It’s science, it’s just very complex technology, all built with materials and stuff. You know, it never gets easier explaining this stuff to your people.’’

‘’Sounds like a form of magic to me,’’ Eithne gives a long stare as she ponders the device gormlessly. ‘’I dread to think what weapons of war you have in such a world.’’

‘’Awful ones, we don’t use swords or anything like that, we use guns.’’

‘’Guns?’’

‘’It's like a ranged weapon that kills anything in front of it instantly with the press of a button.’’

Eithne’s brows raise with concern.

‘’We also have these huge containers we call bombs, some of them are big enough to wipe an entire country of life.’’

‘’Is your world not devastated by the scars of war?’’

‘’You could say there’s been a few that have done that, but it’s politics, all complex and shit… I don’t know, I’m not involved… even I hate my own world at times.’’

Eithne gives a pitiful grunt. ‘’And you miss it?’’

‘’Yeah, yeah, I do, I lost everything, literally, everything. My family, friends… my home….’’

‘’You also gained a lot from what I hear, you came as nothing and now you have that which most people could only dream of. Magical ability… a fancy castle… wealth.’’

‘’I know, I think about that all the time… I wasn't even wealthy in my home world… it’s too weird… but losing what I already had… it’s….’’

‘’I can understand,’’ she smiles in pity. ‘’Family and loved ones are much more than material wealth, especially in a world you don’t belong.’’

Gordon returns the smile. ‘’I’m focused on the now, that’s all that matters. Pissing and moaning isn’t solving anything, I’ll find my way back… somehow.’’

‘’Good, best of luck to you.’’

‘’I have a feeling Tarna might have a lead though.’’

‘’Only one way to find out.’’

‘’Exactly.’’

Excessive cheering rattled the great hall, Ambunix had thrown a drunken Brennus into the hall, diving upon him in a fiery brawl.

Shocked at first, Gordon jumped forward in concern only to realise both men had ridiculous smiles brandishing their faces, they were laughing as they punched one another, rolling around like teenage boys.

''Men...'' Eithne scoffs. ''They love parading their masculinity, especially around others.''

''If Hashna was here, she'd knock both their heads together no problem,'' Gordon adds. ''He better not get too hurt... we've got to pass the mountains tomorrow.''

''He'll be fine, it's not like another blow to the head can make him any thicker,'' Eithne smiles.

Gordon shrugs as he watches on, gulping down the remainder of his drink. The fighting soon stops with the two laughing in hysterics.

''I'm assuming this is normal?'' Gordon asks.

''To a degree,'' Eithne responds.

As the fight came to a stop, Gordon joined in socialising with the Parvusii clan. He became quite the celebrity amongst them as they all would ask the countless many questions regarding his home world. It started to become tiresome but Gordon found himself enjoying the moment, soaking up this newfound celebrity status amongst these people, he didn't really feel very awkward anymore and his social standing definitely helped propel him forward.

Gordon embraced the night in full, for tomorrow, the true journey begins.

19: Screams of the Mountains

Gordon stood in the mists of the park, the light behind that brought him to Altharn shimmered violently as it imploded upon itself, vanishing from existence. As the light dispersed, his eyes adjusted to the darkness. In front of him stood Helen, all on her own, tears filling her eyes.

''Gordon!!'' She runs full speed toward him, almost knocking him to the ground. ''Where have you been?! We all thought you were dead!'' She cries hysterically.

''You wouldn't believe me if I told you… I've been through some crazy shit, but never mind that. I'm here with you now and you're not going to lose me again!''

Helen tightens her hold on Gordon, squeezing him with her unconditional love. ''I lost you. I lost everything!!''

''I know! So did I! Come on, let's go home and grab a drink, yeah? I'll tell you everything.''

She nods erratically as the tears stream down her face, dragging her make up with them, she pulls away to get a view of the man she'd lost so long ago. ''I can't believe you're alive, you're actually alive!''

''Yeah, I'm alive,'' he sighs, allowing all the worry and pain to release its long and tiresome burden. ''That light behind me, it was like some kind of wormhole. I got taken to a world of magic and druids… I had to live with them and train with them. It was… surreal."

''I was about to ask about the weird clothes…'' she laughs as she wipes away a tear. ''You look silly, and you need a haircut, and a shave!''

''Really? I was beginning to think it suited me!'' Laughs Gordon.

''You do look quite rugged, but I want my Gordon back.''

''Well, I'll shave up and get back to looking normal again!''

''We need to tell everyone! You have no idea how hard we've searched for you!''

As they approach their front door, they give one last hold of each other before entering their humble home.

''I love you,'' Helen cries.

''I love you too, Hel.'' Gordon returns, tearing up. ''Come on, let's-''

Suddenly his front door opens on its own. Startled by this, he looks on to find Camula standing there, her arms folded, a concerning look washes her angelic face.

''Camula?! Haru es vulos?'' Gordon speaks out.

Gordon springs up out of his slumber sweating and panting. ''How?! No! Helen? Where… no….'' he takes a minute to gather himself, he looks around.

He's still in Altharn, in his chambers in Fen Donaren no doubt, it was all a dream. ''Fucking hell…'' he pants as he gives himself a minute to recuperate.

He gets out of bed and prepares for the day, donning his armaments and fastening his sword in place.

The band of Fen Craic were to venture into enemy territory, but first they must cross the treacherous mountains that divide the border between Darogoth and Venethar, it is said these mountains are home to many dangers, dangers such as the faceless ones, humanoid like creatures that stalk the upper crags. He had full trust in his team and although he was a little nervous, the magic always nurtured his confidence.

''Good bye, Brennus. It's been good seeing you again after all these years. I'll visit you in Fen Craic soon enough, if the war allows it,'' says Ambunix with a porky grin.

Gordon raises a proud posture atop Epona. ''You're always welcome to Fen Craic, Lord Ambunix. Thank you for having us.''

''Tell Elladane to wait for me,'' Brennus smirks.

Ambunix delivers a warming smile to Gordon before turning back to Brennus. ''Fuck off, you.''

The two laugh wholesomely as they part ways, Gordon's party venture out further north, up a rugged pathway leading on into a valley that guide their way upward, deep into the crags of the mountains.

Palettes of grey stone and dirt begin to surround them, large pointed boulders and rocks begin to loom over them like that of beastly claws ready to snatch them up in a deadly clasp, a most crooked path, a path not forged by man, but by nature itself. The atmosphere grew drearier the more they tread onward and up, the small talk of all the warriors lessened as the air engulfed them in uncertainty.

''We should dismount and take this part of the journey on foot, the crags here are too narrow, and we don't want to be mounted anymore until we reach the other side of these mountains,'' Eithne suggests as she drops from her horse, spear in hand.

Everyone obeys and follows Eithne's lead as they guide their horses onward through a water-logged track from the morning's light drizzle, the terrain swilled in dirt and stone, shining in the midday sun.

The sun stretched out the shadows of the mountains as the cold air began to bite harder, they were all adorned in extra furs, ready to brace the elements of the north. They had abandoned their tartan and colours, making it somewhat harder to be identified in enemy lands.

Eventually after hours of mountaineering, they had reached the peaks of the upper crags, and looking back behind them all, provided a glorious sight, the green blanket of Darogoth stretching out for many miles, they stopped for a moment to take it in.

Nothing but the howling of the wind could be heard whipping their hair vigorously. Eithne led ahead, confident she could keep the party on their toes when the need arises, constantly on the lookout to sniff out any danger that dared come their way.

''It's beautiful up here,'' Gordon remarks, peering around in awe.

''Too quiet for me,'' says Brennus ''How are we, warriors?!''

The warriors give a small positive cheer.

''Good! I must say, it's not every day you see a sight as grand as that…'' Brennus comments on the glorious view of the landscape soon to be left behind.

''You've never been to the mountains before?'' Asks Gordon.

''Never. No-one does, there's only two safe passages through the mountains and ours is the Evercrag Pass… not so safe anymore now….''

''What about the other?''

''That one lies west of Venethar to The Glade… and those fucking elves will have nothing to do with the war, they won't allow us to even enter, nor will they allow Venethar.''

''Shame… could of made this journey allot easier by the sounds of it.''

''Tell me about it, Walker…''

Eithne comes to a sudden halt, using her spear to blockade the party.

''Eithne?'' Brennus asks.

''We're being watched,'' she mutters.

''What? Where?'' Says Gordon, surprised. He darts his head around; nothing is to be seen.

''Wait,'' she orders.

''How ca-'' Brennus asks but is quickly shot down by Eithne.

''Shh!'' She tilts her head to the sky, attempting to listen carefully to what the wind carries.

Nothing sounded obvious to be cause for concern.

''Draw your weapons,'' she says, her voice sharp.

The entire party unsheathe their blades and begin huddling together.

''Forward then?'' Gordon asks.

Eithne gives a nod as she steadies her pace, edging forward.

The party carries on, their heads jerking to every crevice in sight.

''Help me!'' A voice screeches from beyond the crags in the distance.

''Here we go,'' Eithne sighs.

''Help!!'' It shouts again. ''My Leg!''

''That's a faceless?'' Gordon asks quietly.

Brennus nods.

''Please!'' The voice shrieks.

Ambunix's words echo in Gordons' head. He was right, there was something not quite human about it despite how human it actually sounded, he readied his casting hand igniting a small flame ready for combat.

''Help!!''

''What do we do, Eithne?'' Asks Gordon.

''Everyone, get behind me. Brennus, manage them from there, get the horses to the back and Gordon, bring that flame to me,'' she orders. ''We must keep moving.''

''Okay,'' Brennus replies as he positions himself with the warriors. ''At the ready!''

Gordon stands in a moment of disbelief and fear, unknown what to expect. Peering around the crags, he gives a nervous gulp.

''Walker…?'' Brennus gives a breathy whisper.

Gordon looks back to Brennus who signals him to move forward to Eithne's side with a nod of his head. Gordon edges himself cautiously to her as he pans around the crags, his breathing turns heavy.

''Help me!'' The screams were a lot closer, the group snapped to attention like frightened cats.

''Ignore it. Come,'' she orders again.

Eithne was the only one not showing any degree of fear, she did not flinch at mere sounds and nor did she tremble, she was

Darogoth's most renowned and decorated scout, her talent as a tracker stems from the days of her youth, she would hunt with her father daily for skins and hide, he was a warrior as well as a tanner and taught her well and she herself was a natural, the people of her home village would joke, referring to her as the 'wolf girl' as she would spend days living in the forests of Dun, stalking her prey and moving with the wildlife, all to keep her family fed and stocked, for her scent was never off course, her eyes bound by the hunt, her face as still as the leaves, for to remain neutral was to remain strong, to never reveal your true motives was to always remain victorious. What was it that made Eithne so stern? So unhinged? Nobody knew.

The group move in a tight formation leading their horses behind with Gordon and Eithne affront, pacing slowly.

A faint noise of pebbles scattering from above pricks Eithne's well attuned ears. Her head snaps immediately to the source of the noise. She caught sight of a grey body swiftly whip behind the endless rocky abyss. She says nothing as she pushes Gordon back with the shaft of her spear, her head fixated on the rocks above. The air grows silent, the wind settles its blow.

''Keep your focus on our left fl-'' Before Eithne can issue her command, a great lengthy beast pounces from a nook, diving upon an unsuspecting warrior in rapid speed and tearing into his neck, swinging its head side to side, ripping out his throat with ease.

The warrior gives a blood curdling scream as he holds his spurting neck in fatal agony, screaming for the life that drained from him that soon turned into a gargle, drowning in his own blood. The horses whinny in fright rearing around in total panic.

''Keep hold of them fucking horses and keep them out of the way!'' Brennus shouts.

The faceless creature had vanished just as quickly as it had pounced, back to the rocks before anyone could react. It stood above, revealing its gruesome self to its victims, looming over them in a sinister stance.

As Gordon turned to face the distress, his stomach dropped at the sight of such a horrific looking creature. It was immensely grotesque, the stuff of nightmares. Standing over them all at seven feet tall above the rocks, its arms down to its knees, long sharp claws, its skin grey, its body frail and twisted, it's rib cage protruding through its chest and then there was its face, its face… nothing but a wide slit at the base of its head for a mouth. It opened up its frothing hole, displaying a hellish array of razored teeth that spiralled down to the back of its throat, decorated in a fresh paint of its victim's blood. It stood proud of its murderous accomplishment, flailing its arms and howling to the sky.

As Gordon gawked upon such a disgusting beast, he noticed in the corner of his eye a horse escaping, running away back from where they had come. It was jumped and taken to the ground by another beast in the distance, ferociously mauled to death with no remorse.

Gordon had to give up a few precious seconds to take in what had just happened, the warriors huddling tightly as the faceless beast drools and snorts violently, flailing its head all around as it screams its ghastly cry of victory.

Gordon, thinking on his feet sent a flame bound for the creature, it slipped away before the impact, scurrying back behind the rocks with impressive speed, like that of a timid spider.

''Fuck… fuck!'' Gordon yells.

''Gordon! BEHIND YOU!'' Eithne yells as she positions her spear, sliding her feet firm to the ground.

Gordon turns to see a faceless charging him from a front about to leap into the air, another one was standing off to the side in clear view, fiendishly awaiting an advantage.

He stops it in its tracks with his magic and slams it into the cold ground, incapacitating it briefly. He then sends out a blaze to the other in order to disperse it. Eithne plunges her spear as quickly as she can into the downed creature before it can regain its stance.

The creature that jumped out of the way of Gordon's flammable strike, leapt to a tall rock and sprang to another, and then to Gordon. Before it could land upon him, he ejected another fearsome pulse of force, sending it back into a large protruding boulder.

Gordon charges forward, seeing his chance and thrusting his sword into the creature's skull as hard as he could. ''Shit!!'' He yells. He gives a moment to stare upon the monstrosity, its veins bulging in and out of its head as blood spills from its wound. ''Where's the other?!'' He tears his blade from the faceless skull, his heart pounding, his skin flushing a ghostly white.

''We don't know!!'' Brennus shouts back.

An eerie gurgle can be heard from both sides of the small valley. Brother begins trembling in Gordons unsteady hand.

''There's about three more of them!'' Eithne announces.

''Seriously!?'' Gordon gives a sturdy stance, brandishing Brother outward in guard, ready for the unknown, sucking in a great inhalation of fear up through his nose and pushing out his chest.

''Please!'' A voice shrieks from afar. ''Gordon!!''

''What?!'' Gordon retracts.

''Gordon, please!''

''Don't listen to it!'' Eithne nudges him with her pommel.

''But how?!''

''It doesn't matter! They'll play their games, we need to find better ground, we can't defend ourselves well enough in this tight valley, if we stay here, they'll pick us apart!''

''You heard the girl! Keep fucking moving!'' Brennus orders. ''Tight formation, I want a full circle, shields up!''

''Gordon, me and you to the middle of the circle, we'll move from there.''

Gordon nods.

Eithne and Gordon enter the circle of warriors, peering around above them as the entire party shimmy through the valley, step by step. The faceless had retreated and the screams were further afield, but oh did they wail.

Gordon looks to the poor helpless warrior who lost his life to the creature, watching as they step over his convulsing body, leaving him to his death, to rot on the mountain alone. It felt wrong, very wrong.

Slowly but surely the party presses forward and the wails eventually fade out.

''Sounds like they've gone....'' Gordon mumbles silently.

''They'll stalk us till the end, they'll attack when we least expect it, they know they have a fight on their hands and they're going to keep trying, stay alert.''

''Can we not just mount up and get out of here fast?'' Asks Gordon.

''No, if they jump while we are mounted, we'll be an easier target, there's not enough room for the horses to gallop around. The terrain ahead is treacherous; we need to guide in with caution,'' Eithne replies.

''Okay... let's carry on then.''

The party moves forward, every now and then the harrowing screams echo in the distance. They would pierce their hearts and shake their fearful minds, sometimes they were close, as if the faceless were just around the corner, other times far away and sometimes no sounds at all, nothing but the wind rippling through the pockets of the crags. The party could never identify how close the beasts truly were, Eithne listened carefully, but even she, the famed scout, felt at a loss at times, however she was certain they were stalking, running back and forth to the party to cause disarray, keeping them on their toes, keeping the fear fresh in their bodies, whittling them down from within.

Eventually Eithne locates a well defendable spot to set up a small camp. They brought the horses in, tucking them into a tight corner away from potential danger and set up torches to last through the coming night.

''What if they come in the night.'' Gordon speaks out as he prepares his bedroll.

''They will.... '' replies Brennus.

Gordon nods anxiously. ''How long till we get out of here?''

''I'm unsure... but faceless territory will string out beyond the mountains, hence the name of the forest we will exit into.''

''The name?''

''Faceless Forest.''

''Oh, for fuck's sake,'' Gordon shakes his head.

Gordon unravels and flaps his bedroll to the floor, watching around in angst as the shadows grow longer with the descent of the sun.

''Does Ambunix deal with these things often?'' Gordon asks Brennus as he unpacks some of his provisions from Epona's bags.

Brennus marches some firewood over to the pit the warriors had assembled. ''Not really,'' he huffs as he drops a full bundle of wood, ''But Fen Donaren has its occasional sighting and the odd trespasser so to speak, it's why Fen Donaren was erected in the first place, to eradicate them and push them further to the mountains, ever since then Darogoth has barely had to worry about them. They're creepy little fuckers, Walker. Ambunix told me that one time they had five of them fucking things stand over a hill overlooking Fen Donaren, they stood there for five days, they didn't move, they just stood there… staring, staring with no eyes.''

''Horrible fucking things…''

''Yeah?'' Brennus scoffs. ''They have nests all over, they tend to be in small packs of about seven or ten or so, all the nests they made in Darogoth are gone, the only ones that remain are among here.''

''Why not exterminate them completely?''

''I don't know, free border patrol?'' Brennus sniggers. ''As horrible as they are, in times like these they're quite useful in that respect, stops the horse fuckers crossing the mountains at least,'' Brennus guides his arm to the fire pit. ''Walker?'' He gestures.

Gordon lights the fire, taking a seat on the dusty floor, basking in its warmth as he nibbles at a piece of dried meat. ''So, how do you know Ambunix so well?''

''Ah, we're cousins, his mother was my aunt, she was of my clan until she joined the Parvusii's and moved over to Fen.''

''Ah, okay… you're of Ard though, yeah?''

''Yeah, I was born in Ard, in Datulauni, a village east of Mostos, but I lived much of my childhood in Westwatch just west of Fen Donaren for a while, so I saw a lot of Ambunix. Was always quite jealous of him as lad, him being brought up by a noble clan, the lords of Fen Donaren and some of the villages too. Our clan were mostly carpenters and sheep farmers, only my uncle Galvatorix was anything to sniff at, he was a warrior, a real warrior… he became an oathsworn for the high king, I wanted that prestige myself, to bring my clans name forward, so I begged him to take me on as his ward,'' Brennus chuckles.

''And then you became the oathsworn commander for the high king, sounds like you did pretty well for yourself if you ask me.''

''Aye, took many years to climb that ladder, and now I'm stuck with you,'' Brennus howls. ''What about you? Didn't you mention you were some kind of bard?''

Gordon laughs. ''Yeah, you could say that, I played an instrument with a band… a bass guitar it's called.''

Brennus shrugs his shoulders.

Gordon takes out his phone and shows Brennus a picture a photographer once took at one of his gigs. ''That's a bass guitar.''

''What the fuck, it's like some kind of lyre?''

''Definitely not a lyre….''

''Help me! Help! The beasts! They're coming!'' A voice in the distance shouts. The camp all rise to their feet and dart around, weapons unsheathe in unison.

Just as the atmosphere was beginning to pick up, their morale took a nose dive upon hearing the horrid wails once again.

''It's them again… cunts.'' Brennus peers around, his blade extended. ''Stand down everyone, stand down, but stay vigilant!'' He calls out.

''We need to get out of here… how the hell are we going to sleep with all that?''

''I don't know, Walker, but by Fanara we'll pull through.''

As the darkness crept in, their sanity stood firm on a narrow step. They slept in small shifts, whilst half would keep a watchful eye amidst the darkness, for death could come swiftly by the faceless beasts of the mountains. Every warrior slept with a blade in their hands, some didn't even sleep at all.

The passing wind carried upon it the howls of the faceless, frightening all who were awake and keeping many from entering a much-needed rest. Although the noises scratched at their minds, to their surprise… no ill came to them this night.

Morning came, many of the party sleep deprived, but all were raring to go. Gordon did not sleep well at all, he felt the burden in his bones, his eyes carrying red bags. Regardless, he powered on, eager to leave the mind-numbing hell of the mountains.

There was a different atmosphere amongst the party, an atmosphere of dread. A dullness of morale, the screams sucked every inch of hope from their souls, they moved on and on silently, listening out for the next howl and wail of the creatures that stalked.

All they wanted to do was leave, Venethar was close but still so far away, one night was one too many, but with every step they took, was a step closer to leaving this all behind, and so they pressed on. For many more nights they'd spend, tortured by the everlasting screams of the mountains.

''YYEEERRRAAGGGHHH!'' A high-pitched monstrous scream nearby tears through the blackness of the night.

''Everyone up! There's another one close by!'' One of the warriors screams at the top of his lungs.

Without hesitation everyone scurried from their bedrolls, the fearful pants of the party drown the silence of the night, their breath visible floating amidst the torchlight.

Eithne's head snaps to a disturbance. ''Behind the rubble,'' she turns to Gordon, giving him a subtle nod.

Gordon already knows what to do and sends a flare upwards and behind, directing it to the creature laying behind the rubble, a direct hit.

The creature cries out, smothered in searing flames, exposing itself to the party. A brazened warrior steps out, lunging his blade deep into its ribs as it succumbs to his fiery demise.

''Get back!'' Eithne orders.

Another faceless emerges from the darkness and pounces onto Brennus, knocking him to the floor, he takes cover behind his shield that is pressed against his body as he attempts to avoid the deadly swings of its sharp claws, he rolls the creature to the floor, pressing down and keeping it firmly in place, half the warriors jump away, looking upon the ugly fiend that was pinned to the ground.

As they disperse themselves to give Brennus room, ready to give a fatal stab in aid, they become under full blown attack. Faceless ones, one after the other, fly out of the darkness, diving and screaming. ripping and slashing ferociously into the party.

Brennus digs the creature in the ribs with his sword, it screeches in pain as it flails its claws desperately to break free from Brennus's fatal hold, he delivers more stabs, this time into its head, its desperate thrashing comes to a halt as it succumbs to its wounds. He rises to see his warriors desperately trying to fight back against thc swift and terrifying beasts.

He ran to the aid of one of his sisters in arms, she was becoming overpowered as she staggered about ducking behind her shield, unable to find her footing to react back.

Just before Brennus can be of aid, the creature brings itself to all fours and charges her, bashing her into another creature nearby, it grabs her by the head, slamming her face into the floor with unbelievable speed, before tearing into her neck, its mouth of daggers cutting and tearing the flesh with ease, it grabs the poor woman and drags her off into the darkness.

He shakes his head in anger and sadness, knowing he could have saved her. He gives a mighty roar as he charges on into the struggling crowd, the warriors were holding out fiercely but it was clear some of them were holding back in fear. Brennus gives a mighty slice to one's bony leg as it attempts to ravage one of his comrades, severing it completely. The warrior reacts quickly, slamming the rim of his massive shield into its neck as it falls to the floor and driving his blade into its bulbous head.

Brennus looks to Gordon, Gordon was burning as many as he could, the beasts were nimble and he was struggling to get a hit.

‘’Form up! Form up!’’ Screams Brennus. ‘’We need vision, Gordon!? Get us some light out here for fucks sake!’’

All the warriors present huddle back together forming a shield wall that faced the entrenching darkness.

Gordon sends a ball of light toward the sky, illuminating the entire area. The warrior smothered in her own blood lay lifelessly in front of one of the creatures as it wails with half of the woman's face dangling from its mouth.

Gordon, with his force, pulls the creature toward him and extends his sword, impaling it through the gut; the party gives aid with their blades to be sure of its demise.

‘’They’ve retreated again….’’ says Eithne.

‘’That’s two we’ve lost here!! Fucking two! What the fuck are you all doing?! Pick yourselves up, you pack of cunts!’’ Brennus shouts, his face blistering with anger. ‘’How do you think we're going to make it back? Keep on your fucking toes, we’re warriors of Darogoth! Fucking act like it! All of you turned your back on those cunts when I got brought down, and that alone could have had us all killed! See how they pounce?! How they wait for the right moment!? Stay fucking vigilant!’’ He storms back to the fire pit and passes Gordon. ‘’Good work, you should have already had the light up, use your common-sense lad,'' he slaps his arm as he barges past, knocking him aside with his broad frame.

Gordon looks to Eithne, she delivers a nod of respect.

As the sun stretched out over the horizon burning away the fear of the night, they set off once again trekking through the crags, manoeuvring the crevices, guiding the horses and climbing the narrow slopes.

They worked incredibly hard to keep the horses as safe as they could, unfortunately a few fell victim to the beasts as they pressed on, they knew that once they were in Venethar, a few warriors were going to need to share their mounts.

By midday they finally come down from the mountain and into Venethar, entering the Faceless Forest.

The faceless that reside in the forest do not hunt in packs as they do in the mountains and tend to be more evasive, being away from their nests. They would find the faceless alone, the creatures only seemed to stalk and watch, they didn't dare attack, the party had no trouble passing through The Faceless Forest, a relief felt by every waking soul, but they mustn't let their guard down.

Brennus's anger picked at Gordon, he felt responsible for the deaths of those brave souls, if only he had just sent his light out as soon as the attack started, that woman might still be standing by their side.

''Focus,'' Camula whispers

20: The Borderlands

Venethar, a prodigious expanse of northern Uros, A land of great rocky plains and lush pine forests alike, It's Fauna beastly and large, Its palette a fusion of greys and greens. A land settled by the semi-nomadic Venethari.

The air was more frigid and colder than that of Darogoth, The scents spacious and fresh. Large droves of snow bound peaks could be seen in the horizon to the north reaching up and touching the clouds, and to the east, the enormous city of Antler, nestled atop a sturdy cliff overlooking the great Borderlands Steppe.

This was The Borderlands, the western territory of Venethar that bordered The Glade to the west and Darogoth to the south, hence its namesake.

''Here we are, and there's Antler in the distance,'' Brennus points out as he guzzles down on his canteen.

''That's Antler? Where the rebellion was routed from?'' Gordon asks.

''Yep… Antler is the main staple for their movements on the front lines for the moment, bolstering the Evercrag Pass, giving them easier access into Glaen, so we best be staying well clear of it,'' Brennus reattaches his canteen to his belt. ''What say you, Eithne?''

‘’I say it’s high time we made tracks, last we heard, the rebellion was encamped within the ruins of V’tar when they were driven from Antler, that’s our next stop. It’s doubtful they’ll still be there, but I’m sure we’ll pick up their trail.’’

The party all mount up and begin trotting north east, gazing on at the expanse of the open steppe, not a soul in sight, it was freeing being away from the mountains, a sense of relief like no other.

‘’V’tar… strange name,’’ Gordon comments.

‘’V’tar was an old Var’kesh city back in the Gods' age, it was their capital I believe,’’ replies Brennus

‘’The Var’kesh? I've read about them, the horned folk?’’

‘’Maniacal bastards they were, they all fled to an island far away once the Venethari arrived and all of Uros smashed them into the ground thousands of years ago. They keep to themselves nowadays, but I know there’s a Var’keshi man living in Glaen who was actually granted a torc, he serves one of the lords there. Other than him, you don’t usually see any. Well… I’ve never seen one anyway.’’

‘’Wasikala Glaen-Fur’rok’’ Eithne blurts.

‘’Hmmm?’’

‘’He’s the head steward in Pathririi, don’t think he’d still be there with the invasion force coming down harder than a stampede of oxen.’’

‘’How do you know him?’’ Brennus asks.

''I don't.''

''You scare me, woman.''

Eithne gives a satisfied grin. ''He was exiled by the Var'kesh for showing sympathies of the banished Gods, he came to Glaen and began work... took a while until he was able to settle, he even cut off his horns to prove his loyalty.''

''I wonder what else you know....''

''About what?''

''I don't know, me?'' Brennus gestures.

''Brennus Ard-Renirios, former Oathsworn Commander to High King Vocorix. Now? Oathsworn and Master of Arms to Gordon Ard-Barker at the behest of the high king. Your salary even got reduced, so I'm quite impressed at your enthusiasm given your track record.''

Brennus frowns, staring into space as his horse sways him side to side. ''How do you know that?!''

''Knowledge is my work,'' she glances back as she rides ahead.

''You never told me you're getting paid less, that's cute,'' sniggers Gordon.

''Fuck off, Walker,'' he sneers. ''Vocorix won't be paying me a damn thing once Fen Craic is on its feet, that's on you,'' he glances off. ''Well, whoever the fucking treasurer is anyway.''

Gordon gave a satisfied smile, his content washing over him being free from the screams. It truly was a breath of fresh air, almost as if no dangers could come to him in such a beautiful landscape. He straightens his posture giving his back a satisfying crack as he stares onward, watching Eithne's burning red pony tail bounce around glamorously as she trots ahead.

Brennus brings his horse closer to Gordon and digs him in his ribs. ''Enjoying the view?'' He jests.

''Yeah… Venethar is just gorgeous… It's like it just goes on forever.''

''It sure is, isn't it. Shame it's full of cunts.''

''Shit… look over there….'' Gordon remarks being distracted by a herd of bison gathering by a nearby lake.

''Ah yeah, big fucking cows,'' he mumbles, disinterested.

''Maybe we should hunt a few for food, and their hides.''

''No, we're here on business and we have plenty of provisions, we can't just walk on into Venethar and leave a trial for ourselves.'' Brennus laughs.

''They're so big!''

Brennus rolls his eye. ''Wait till you see the sabre cats, if we see any at all of course, doubtful one would come near us with a party this size.''

More days of long travel ensued and thankfully no unwanted surprises, although pleased he was finally travelling peacefully, and actually being able to have a somewhat stable sleep whenever they would camp, he found himself thinking back on the creatures of the mountains often, the deaths of those who fell so easily in such a horrific way, images that would surge through his mind attempting to send him into a blind panic, but every time they tried, Camula was there to ward them off, giving Gordons' head a shake from within his very being.

''Focus,'' she would always say, ''You must press on,'' words he'd find himself saying too.

The ruins of V'tar are now in clear sight. Its walls crumbled to the floor, most of its buildings nothing but a collection of rubble. It was impossible to even make out the architecture. The city stood atop a small hill in the middle of the ginormous steppe.

''There could be anyone up there. Hitch the horses in the forest to the south, we'll approach on foot and keep the horses out of the way,'' Brennus orders.

''Good thinking,'' says Gordon.

''Best hope we don't get caught in between without our horses,'' Eithne remarks. ''But I agree.''

The group dismount and hitch up, trekking on foot toward V'tar.

Upon reaching the raised hill they poke around discreetly. No signs of habitation or anyone nearby.

‘’Look for signs of camp. A recent one,’’ says Eithne.

The group scour around and inside the many crumbled buildings, looking for anything that might lead them to information regarding Tarna and the rebellion.

Eithne stops in her tracks as she spots something on the floor. Bread crumbs, fresh bread crumbs.

‘’There are people here,’’ she says calmly in confidence.

‘’Where?’’ Gordon asks.

‘’I'm not sure just yet. We need to gather up and lay low, we can’t risk getting into a fight. Something tells me we’re not the only ones seeking Tarna Mundur.’’

‘’You sure they couldn't be from the rebellion?’’

‘’Could be, but they would have left this place ages ago, this isn’t stale enough, surely the rebels would be more careful than this.’’

‘’What should we do?’’

‘’I’m going to scout ahead, stay with the others and stay quiet.’’

Gordon without question marches off to find the others scattered around nearby, clutching his hilt in anticipation, beginning to feel very wary of the danger he could be in.

Eithne carried on further throughout the ruins, searching frantically for people she was sure were still around.

As she carefully treads upon a large fragmented house, she hears muffled voices coming from a large room dugout underground, beneath a blanket of rubble.

‘’That's what I said, north. If they seek refuge in The Glade, they'll just be thrown back into Venethar, they're not stupid. We’re wasting time,’’ The gruff voice echoed.

Eithne jumps behind a nearby wall tilting her ear to the dingy stairwell.

‘’So, what now… should we try further south? There are a few buildings that are more sheltered out that way.’’

‘’Try the old matriarch's hall? It's big enough but it's too obvious a place to stay. They wouldn't camp down in the main point of V'tar surely? Even Tarna isn’t that dumb,’’ the voices emerge as people. Two of them, soldiers of Venethar, laced head to toe in scaled armour, trimmed with fur.

Eithne sees her chance and pivots around the wall, driving her spear through one man's helmetless face from behind with scrupulous poise, the tip of her spear exiting through his mouth.

The other soldier jumps away startled as he produces his axe and shield. ‘’Fuck!’’

‘’Drop your weapon!’’ Eithne orders, ripping her spear from the dead man’s head.

‘’Fucking bitch!’’ He charges her with his shield placed neatly across his vitals, ready with his axe. She shuffles away just in time and gives a responsive counter thrust, he blocks efficiently as he turns back to face her, forcing her back and pressuring her stance as he delivers a relentless and skilful assault. Despite Eithne's speed and elegance, his strength was proving a worthy challenge.

The party could hear the faint sounds of the fight and rushed over as quickly as they could, surrounding the two with their weapons drawn.

The soldier notices the warriors rush to Eithne's aid. Knowing he had no chance of victory he threw his weapons to the ground in submission. ''I yield! I'm clearly outmatched now, eh?!'' He spits to the floor.

He takes note of everyone's subtle appearance. The men's moustaches and the fair hair of the women. ''Warriors of Darogoth so it would seem, eh? What are you doing here? What do you want?"

''We'll ask the questions. Why are you here?'' Eithne heaves.

''Clearing out a nest of bandits,'' The soldiers' confidence in defeat was remarkable, his voice didn't even shake upon his words.

''Liar,'' she snaps, pressing the tip of her spear into the man's genitals.

''Woah! Okay… okay, easy, easy… I'm tasked to find the remains of an active rebellion, so yeah… a nest of bandits.''

''What have you found?'' Brennus reveals himself from the crowd of warriors, holding his blade up to the man's neck in an unnervingly casual fashion.

Brennus's towering presence begins to unsettle the man. ''We're... unsure... we haven't found anything solid just yet.''

Brennus looms his battle-hardened face over the soldier. ''I don't believe you,'' his deep voice rattled the very air as he pressed his blade's edge gently into his neck.

Feeling the intensity of Brennus' frightening presence and the sharpness of his blade, digging into his throat, the man begins to crack. ''I'm telling the truth... I... I don't know! We're still looking for signs of their camp. All we know is that after they were driven from Antler, they recuperated here in V'tar, we've split off our hunting party looking for clues, I haven't found anything yet!''

''How many of you?'' Gordon blurts out.

''About fifty or sixty or so? The majority are split up in the northern sections.''

''We're done here,'' says Brennus, sliding his sword deep into the man's throat.

The soldier gasps in shock and for air, spluttering and groaning as he drops to the floor, his throat irrigating a fountain of blood.

Gordon looks away from the chilling sight.

''Brennus?!'' Eithne barks.

''What? He would've only squealed if we let him go.''

Eithne tilts her head in regrettable agreement. ''True....''

''So, we have a large party of Venethari that outnumber us? Great, how are we going to do this now?'' Gordon moans.

''Hide these bodies, they'll notice some of their men are missing eventually, especially that one, he wasn't your average soldier, nor was he an urskull, but still, should take them longer to prepare to leave, we need to find something before they do and get a head start,'' says Eithne.

''And all without the Venethari finding out we're here…'' replies Brennus, cleaning his sword upon the body of the man he just maimed.

''I can scout the north of V'tar and keep out of sight, if you stick together and remain in the south, you're less likely to be noticed,'' Eithne suggests modestly.

Brennus gives an agreeable nod. ''Fine… doesn't look like we have many options. We'll hunker down somewhere safe… if you get spotted, retreat toward us by those two buildings down that alley over there… looks to be a good ambush point. We may be outnumbered but if we get the jump on them, we'll have a slight advantage. Plus… we have a Gordon,'' he thinks for a minute. ''They must have their horses nearby? We could probably fuck with them too. Is anyone one willing to volunteer to find the Venethari horses? I'm… not the stealthiest. ''

One of the warriors' steps forward without hesitation. A slender man who held the weight of a shady past, outshined by his service to Darogoth. Black of hair, his braids poking out from under his helmet. A soldier of Carsinia, now of Fen Craic. His name, Nurinien Ard-Durisios. ''I will, Commander.''

''Excellent, Nurinien. Are you sure you're up for this?''

''Of course, stealth was my specialty before joining the army.''

''Dare I ask why?'' Brennus gives a menacing chuckle. ''Mind you, I have heard good things in your reports, so don't let us down now, lad.''

''I won't, Commander,'' Nurinien bows his head as he begins tying his large shield to his back.

Eithne's attention draws to Nurinien. ''Check the eastern side of the ruins, the old main gateway was around that area and it's likely where the Venethari entered if they came from The Heart or Vul March, especially with a party that large.''

Nurinien gives a silent nod.

''Goodluck to you both, if you're not back by sunset, we'll send a search,'' Gordon adds.

''It's settled then,'' says Brennus.

The group split off and go their separate ways, Gordon and Brennus bring the warriors and nestle down out of sight whilst Eithne prowls into the northern section of the city weaving between the never-ending rubble of V'tar, searching every nook and cranny for any signs of the rebels.

Nurinien headed out toward the eastern gateway in search of the Venethari horses and with luck he found them.

A horde of Equine hitched all around, huddled together off the main gate just as Eithne predicted, but there was a slight issue. A small lookout was placed by the horses, two men sat on some broken stone beams facing out toward where Nurinien was crouched, eating and laughing, enjoying their free time.

Nurinien decided to take a longer route around the outside to flank them, climbing through tattered windows of crumbling houses right by the horses, every step he took he took with each careful breath, so as not to alert the guards, or the horses.

He now found himself behind the guards, watching and waiting, plotting every inch he made.

After a brief contemplation, sprawled out on the dusty floor, tucking himself away, he knew what to do, it seemed to be the only thing he could do.

Nurinien moved back away and took off his shield, undid his straps and removed his chainmail and other armaments until he was wearing nothing but his tunic and breeches, placing them on the ground carefully and quietly. He gave himself time to mentally prepare until he felt the time was right.

One of the guards was propped upon the makeshift seat, sharpening his sword with a rough whetstone. He carried a horn that was attached to his belt, this was the one to target.

After finishing and inspecting his sword he sheathed his blade back into its scabbard.

Nurinien saw his chance. He crept slowly behind a small stone wall, the only obstacle between him and the guards, traversing it with care. He draws his blade and scurries along silently.

He took one last deep breath, and as quickly as he could wrapped his forearm around one of the guards' heads, yanking him backward from his seat and placing the edge of his blade across his throat. To Nuriniens' pleasure the Guard was now caught in his grip.

''Now shut the fuck up and listen to me,'' Nurinien spits through his gritted teeth.

The other guard goes to grab the hilt of his weapon as he raises to his feet.

''One word comes out of your fucking mouth and I'll slit this cunts throat.''

The guard stands in silence, frozen. His hand tremors atop his hilt.

''You, remove that horn and throw it behind me,'' he orders his hostage. ''And you, drop your weapon and no one gets hurt, okay?''

''Who are you? What do you want?'' The guard whispers calmly.

''Do as I fucking tell you,'' Nurinien Barks through his clenched jaw.

The guard obeys, slowly drawing his curved blade and resting it gently to the floor. Nurinien drags the other man with him as he scoots toward the grounded blade, feeling the heavy breath and sweat dripping from the head of the man in his arms.

Nurinien signals the guard to move up against the wall. ‘’Now, take the armour off.’’

‘’What?’’

‘’Do it!’’ He draws blood from his hostage as he gives a forceful slice.

Nurinien’s hostage muffles in pain.

The guard obeys, removing his scaled plate.

‘’Right, this is what is going to happen now,’’ Nurinien kicks the sword out of reach.

The guard adjacent to Nurinien watches as his sword clinks across the chalky floor and is then unexpectedly met with a nimble slice to his throat from Nurinien’s clever positioning. After slicing the man's throat, he gives an assuring thrust into his unarmoured belly for good measure, all while having tight hold on his hostage.

The man in Nurinien’s arms begins flailing frantically at the sight of his brother in arms burying himself into the wall, sliding down it as blood erupted from his wounds, finally flopping to the ground as his strength waned.

The hostage bites into Nurinien’s arm as hard as he can, desperate to free himself. Nurinien perseveres with the struggle and digs his sword into the man's ribs as he screams in the lower recesses of his throat to dull the pain of the bite, attempting to muffle away any noise.

Nurinien took on the pain incredibly well which only clamped down harder when his hostage was met with the kiss of Nurinien's sword. In a ferocious fit of pain infused rage Nurinien delivers a flurry of mortal stabs, eventually releasing the man's jaws that clamped down on his arm. He falls silent, consumed by Iskarien's shadow, the sweet release of death.

After dealing with both guards Nurinien staggers away in pain, almost falling over a multitude of debris that cluttered the floor, his arm was bleeding deep from the bite, he tore some pieces of cloth from the guards under armour and tightly wrapped it around his arm, he would tend to his wound later.

Now he needed to deal with the horses, he combined the reins of every horse present as quickly as he could, tangled them all together and led them out into the steppe. He then launched a stray brick to startle them, and all together they scurry off into the wilderness; how far they would run he didn't know, but he needed to get away as fast as he could.

His heart was pounding the entire time, unknowing when an enemy soldier would return and catch him in the act, he hurried himself, gearing back up and making his way back to the others.

''Nurinien has returned!'' A warrior points, watching as Nurinien approaches the hideout sluggishly, feeling a little light headed.

Brennus rushes out to him. ''How did it go?''

''Done,'' he replies.

''Good work! You look quite pale... what happened?''

''They had two men posted by the horses, killed them both, took a bite in the arm from one of them, it's pretty bad. Anyway, I tied the horses together with their reins, they're galloping off into the plains as we speak. Not sure how far they went, but should give us time to get ahead of the Venethari.''

''Excellent! A bite?! I won't ask... go to Gordon, he trained with the druids, he can help clean the wound and fix you up a bit,'' Brennus gives a hard pat to Nurinien's back, knocking him onwards into Gordons direction.

Gordon sat Nurinien to the floor as he inspected his wound. ''That's nasty... you said they bit you?''

''Had one of them in a lock, he got a little upset when I killed his friend.''

''That's really deep, I won't be able to construct it for you, but I can stop it from getting worse... that will no doubt get infected if you leave it.'' Gordon pulls a face of disgust looking upon Nurinien's arm, torn and bloody. ''Must hurt... Jesus...''

''What, who? Yeah, it hurts now, quite bad actually, getting a little tight....''

''Looks like you've lost quite a bit of blood, I'm not surprised, that guy must have been biting for his life. Let's get this sorted,'' Gordon prepares the paste in his travel pot just the way he learned from the druids in Seers Crossing, he cleans the wound of fresh blood and dirt, he cleans it thoroughly and applies the paste, dressing the wound with fresh bandages. ''There you go, you should be fine… you have rust for the pain?''

''Yeah, I have some in my pack.''

''Don't overdo it with the rust, we need everyone sharp for this expedition. Here, get some food down you,'' Gordon hands Nurinien some provisions and water

''Thank you, Lord Barker,'' Nurinien smiles. ''Have you seen any Venethari whilst you've been hiding out here?''

Dumbfounded by Nurinien's comment on his title, Gordon gives his head a slight shake, returning to the conversation. ''Yeah… they seem to be in groups of two or three and spreading out to cover ground, we've not had any confrontations though, one group got close but we decided not to attack.''

''I hope Eithne gets back soon, we need to leave this place,'' Nurinien adds.

''Seems to be a common phrase no matter where we go… I know, I'm a little worried for her, but sunset is still a few hours away. At least we're not stuck in the mountains again.''

''Don't remind me… I don't think I'd ever been awake so long in all my life. Wait, how are our horses?!''

''I'm assuming they're fine… we sent someone over there not too long ago to check up on them.''

''Fuck, this whole thing… I've never done anything like it before… I've seen battle… but never anything as… intense as this. We still have so far to go.''

''You're doing a great job, man. You've done enough, you take it easy, yeah? We'll take this whole venture one step at a time and we'll be back before you know it.''

''I hope so, I was just getting used to the comfort of Fen Craic,'' Nurinien titters.

Hours go by, the wait itself was becoming tiresome being stuck inside the rotting shell of an ancient building. Gordon rises and begins preparing his pipe until being interrupted by a cross-armed Brennus.

''Gordon, don't bother. If anyone sees smoke, they'll investigate, stay down, stay quiet, stop doing shit that will get us killed,'' Brennus chuckles.

''Fuck's sake… I'm dying for a smoke.''

''We need to leave!'' Shouts Eithne as she barges in. Everyone jumps in shock.

''Fuck, woman! What is it?'' Brennus jolts.

''I'll explain later, we need to leave, now!''

Everyone gets up and begins pouring from the building and out of V'tar as quickly as they can to their horses, stealth was no longer an option as Eithne rushed them along.

Everyone wrestled with the reins of their horses.

''Eithne, now's a good time to tell us where we are going?!'' Brennus shouts.

''West.''

''You found a solid trail to follow?'' Gordon asks.

''You could say that… but the Venethari know they're not alone. We just have to move quickly.''

''Right… everyone you heard the girl, let's go!'' Brennus rears his horse and twirls his blade in the air, signalling the others to move.

They gallop out of the small forest on the edge of the steppe and back into the plains storming around the perimeter of V'tar behind a large treeline, shadowing themselves out of view, onwards west.

''What did you find?'' Asks Gordon, as he fights his balance atop Epona.

''The Venethari found them first, I was nearby when one of them found a hidden encampment in the underground sections, he was alone so I killed him and had a closer look myself, but I had to leave fast, others were approaching. Meaning, they found his body and are aware they're not alone.''

''Why couldn't the rebels just meet us where we entered Venethar?''

''Because they're being hunted. They need to be on the move and they've taken heavy losses since losing Antler to Kastrith, if they strayed around the border long enough, they'd be tracked down easily. Tarna has a heavy price on her head.''

''Do they not have any other allies they can call on for aid?''

‘’They did, but were betrayed in Antler. They’re roaming the lands attempting to find somewhere to stand against Kastrith’s forces and keep out of their way at the same time.’’

Eithne slows the pace of her horse, veering off and intently inspecting the ground, she appears to be following something. Disturbed ground? Markings? Gordon peered over in interest but saw nothing.

‘’We’ll make camp in Danerath Forest, it’s getting late,’’ Eithne shouted at the party. ‘’Slow your pace for now, I’ll find us a safe place to camp, just keep heading directly west, I’ll find you,’’ she thunders ahead without saying another word.

‘’Is now a good time to smoke?’’ Gordon smirks.

Brennus laughs.

‘’I can’t believe we got out of there… on second thought I can’t believe we passed the mountains….’’ Gordon lights his pipe.

‘’It’s been a rough one… don’t get too complacent, and don’t overthink things, Gordon. The mountains are past us now, as is V’tar. Focus on what we’re doing now, I feel we’re getting close, just hope the horse fuckers don’t catch up anytime soon,’’ Brennus swivels his head behind him, checking the horizon. ‘’You’re doing well, Gordon. You’re keeping yourself well collected so far, keep it up lad.’’

‘’I hope they’re experienced fishers; they're going to have their work cut out for them unravelling those reins,’’ Nurinien laughs.

Eithne returns an hour later. ''Follow me,'' she orders as she rides past the party leading them into the depths of Danerath forest, weaving through the enormous pines, traversing the wavy terrain, eventually presenting them a fold of boulders nestled within an overgrown grotto, a small crevice lead into the fold, revealing a small cave deep inside.

The entrance was too small for the horses but with Gordon at hand to shift one of the boulders and expand the way in, they didn't have a problem squeezing them in, as cramped as it was.

Gordon moves the enormous boulder back behind them, pushing it a little more to completely seal the entrance, he creates a ball of light that hovers in the centre, illuminating the cave, the party now felt safe and secure. Finally, they might get a proper night's rest, without the fear of waking to drawn weapons and blood curdling screams.

And rest they did.

In the early hours of the next morning before the daylight could bless the lands, everyone was back to packing and preparing to leave, hoping to make good distance while they still had the cover of darkness. Continuing westward from where they left off.

''How long can we continue Eithne? Where are we going?'' Brennus asks sternly.

''West.''

''I know that! But where in the west? We'll end up in The Glade before long, there's no chance they've gone there, The

Glade will send them back into Venethar. You know, because of the pact!?''

''It's not so simple Brennus, it...'' Eithne suddenly falls silent as she becomes lost in her thoughts. ''Keep heading this way. I'm falling back, I need to check our behinds.''

''Eithne?!''

Without responding, she rears her horse and gallops away.

''Where is she going now?'' Asks Gordon.

''Checking our behinds?'' Brennus shrugs. ''I don't know I'm assuming she's making sure where not being followed.''

''She seems agitated. She's doing a good job though by the looks of it though.''

''She takes her work very seriously... just do as she says.''

Eithne returns hastily within minutes. ''Move! Move!''

''What now?!'' Brennus moans.

''They're on our trail.''

''HOW?!''

''I don't know, they obviously countered our meagre pranks.''

''How far away?!''

''Not far, they're making up for lost time. I don't even think they've slept? We can try and lose them in the treeline at the north end of Danerath, we're much smaller than they are... I'm expecting the rebels to be somewhere around the forest or at least have been through it but we need to cross the middle plains first into the other half.''

''Well, there's my lunch spoiled,'' Brennus tightens his grip on his reins. ''Yargh! Come, full speed!'' He barks.

The party breaks back through the forest, weaving around endless trees until coming out into another large plain, they cross as quickly as they can, their heads on a consistent swivel.

A familiar noise can be heard from Gordon's past, a thunder like no other. The whole party halted and froze to look into the direction of the thunder down the valley to the south, dust can be seen spewing from the ground as the sun rises, giving the horizon the appearance of an oncoming sandstorm. It was the Venethari, charging forth with malicious intent.

''Fuck,'' Brennus sighs.

''Up the rise into the trees! Go! Go!'' Eithne screams.

Brennus holds back. ''We're going to have to fight them!''

''We can't! We're outnumbered and against their horse archers we may as well end our own lives now, we need to run!'' Eithne argues.

''Run where, woman?! They'll follow! You can't outrun Venethari cavalry! They'll run us into the fucking ground!''

''We need to keep moving, if we enter the forest, we can move through it faster.''

''They won't stop! I'd rather die fighting than die running!''

''How thick is your skull, Brennus?!''

''I like you woman, but we have to stand our ground! We haven't got a choice!''

''We can at least carry on so we can figure out what else to do!''

''By the time we think of anything they'll catch up, they're not stupid! They'll surround the perimeter of the forest and take us down. If we dismount now and form a shield wall, Gordon ca-''

''Shut the fuck up! Both of you!'' Gordon yells. ''Either way, fighting them here isn't going to go down well. Move up the rise and into the trees, THEN we can turn and fight them, if we can limit the movement of their horses we stand a better chance, you said it yourself, Darogoth has the best infantry in Uros, we need to force them to our level. Set up an ambush!''

''Wow....'' Brennus was lost for words, impressed by Gordon's sudden change in character and tactical intellect.

Eithne nods. ''Every second we waste, they draw closer! Come on!''

The party galloped up the rocky rise just enough for the horses to tread upward without falling back, already this piece of land formed a slight terrain advantage. Once they were up, they dismounted their horses, returning to the little hill and hiding amongst the trees. Gordon shifted a felled trunk to the edge.

They waited anxiously as the thunder of the cavalry drew closer and closer; their backs pressed firmly against the pine trunks.

The noise sends Gordon into a freight, it was just like reliving Seers Crossing all over again, the louder it got the more it wrapped around his mind, consuming his hearing, feeding off his fear, the thunder grew louder and louder, drawing closer and closer, his heart kickstarts a fearsome beat, a beat he could feel within his throat, pulsating rapidly with terror and uncertainty.

The thundering stopped before the rise, Gordon's eyes snapped shut. The Venethari sent they're Cavalry two ways out in a pinscher manoeuvre whilst a central unit pressed forward slowly up the hill, following the party.

''Bastards,'' Brennus spits as he peers from the shadows.

The party allowed the central unit to pass them.

"ATTACK!" Screams Brennus, his neck veins bulging profusely as he sprang out with his sword drawn in both hands, severing the legs of a trotting horse with all his might, bringing it and its rider to the ground.

Gordon opens his eyes and draws in his magic, pivoting around the tree trunk and sending out a burning explosion of fiery death, engulfing multiple riders at once as they're blown from their steeds, man and horse alike screaming in agony.

The rest of the party charge in to face the heat of battle.

Many of the riders began dismounting. The remainder of the Venethari who had looped around return on horseback, bows drawn.

''Shields up!! Take the grounded ones!'' Brennus shouts.

Gordon sends soldier after soldier aloft with force; over and over again and finishing them with fatal strikes. He cries a woeful screech of battle, echoing through the forest. He pulls a tree right from its roots launching it toward the mounted archers on the perimeter to keep them busy and to halt the endless hail of arrows, completely burying three riders under the trunk of crushing death. This wears Gordon down tremendously from pushing out so much magic in such a short burst of time.

The warriors of Fen almost stopped in their tracks at such a sight, they'd seen him use magic before, but never at such a magnitude.

He got a little over confident in the heat of it this time round and was now beginning to feel the magicka exhaustion weigh on him just as the fight broke out.

He pulled himself up and readied his blade, this time he was not going to be using magic to fight. He'd already downed a good number, his confidence stood strong.

The fighting roared on and Gordon shared the shield of Nurinien as he ducked for cover from more arrows. A good portion of Venethari were taken down but many still stood, still outnumbering the Darogothians. Their horse archers were having a hard time with their aim amongst the trees having to stop in little clearings to shoot efficiently.

The party was being pushed on the defensive, warriors fell to the floor succumbing to many arrow wounds, one arrow whistled by striking Eithne's calf, bringing her to the ground.

Gordon had to do something, the arrows were tilting the tide of battle in Venethari favour, he rose from behind Nurinien's shield and created a magical barrier, stretching across the entire fight, arrows that struck the barrier started floating in mid-air, just like they would if they flew into water, slowing down rapidly to a halt. ''Attack now while the barrier is up!'' Gordon winces as he fights with his magic.

The horse archers seeing this began to dismount and draw their weapons.

A soldier sees Eithne downed to the floor and readies himself to finish her off as she crawls desperately to safety.

Gordon springs forward disregarding his own safety, dropping the barrier, allowing a few stray arrows to zip by as he runs forth.

With brother in hand, he deflects the blow of Eithne's attacker, staggering him and his exhausted self. As Gordon grasps his balance, he brings an overhead swing to the soldier that becomes blocked instantly. The soldier pushes Gordon off and fixes his stance, following up with a responsive swing. Gordon ducks and slices the man's unarmoured legs, driving his blade down the attacker's clavicle, feeling the restriction of the soldiers' ribs, Gordon forces the blade in harder, the bones snap and crack inside, the soldier drops his sword and hunches forward lifelessly.

With his foot, Gordon pushes the corpse of the soldier backward, releasing his blade and rushing to Eithne's aid.

With all the strength he had left, he tosses her over his shoulders as he removes her from the field of battle, bringing her to safety behind a collection of rocks.

Two men take notice and follow Gordon, he soon realises he's been targeted and turns back to them, forcing one of them into a sturdy pine, face first. Gordon drops Eithne to the floor, the other soldier rushes him with the thrust of a lengthy spear.

Gordon slows his perception, grasping the spear and bringing his sword tip directly to the kidneys, he pushes the spearman to the floor and then rushes off to deliver a few stabs of assurance to the one who had come head first with the tree, flailing his sword arm back and forth all over his body, making sure he was nothing but dead.

As quickly as he can he returns to Eithne's side. Collapsing to the floor due to his waning strength that his magic seeped upon.

''Gordon! Get up!'' Eithne shouts.

He pants excessively as his arms tremble, rising himself to slump by Eithne's side. After catching his breath and re-tuning his vision, he inspects her wound.

She was lucky, for it had only penetrated her flesh.

''Okay, fuck… Luke told me about these… you… you know what I'm going to do here don't you?''

''Yes,'' she grabs a stick from the floor, placing it in her mouth. ''Do it.''

Gordon pushes the arrow through Eithne's leg, popping it out to the other side. Eithne screams at the top of her lungs, her agony muffled by the stick.

He splashes her wound with a water skin, and bandages her up, with his travel pot on his horse he had no way of making a paste and now was not the time.

''You won't be able to walk, will you?'' He sways slightly from dizziness.

''No, but I'm not going to die like this,'' she forces herself up, reaching onto Gordons shoulder. ''What's going on over there?''

Gordon takes hold of her and the two limp around the rocks, only to see the warriors surrounded and in a circle formation all with their shields up, the Venethari were taking swings at them and laughing amongst themselves. The archers aim for within the circle, taking pot shots at the defeated Darogothians.

''Shit… what do we do now?'' Gordon asks.

''Your call, I'd prefer to die fighting.''

Gordons heart sank. Was this it? Has it all come down to this? Eithne's words seem to resonate something within, the thought of dying with honour, to die trying. There was something eternally peaceful about it, especially in this moment.

After a short lapse in his thoughts, Gordon gives Eithne a nod of confidence. He had lost himself, the fear of death, gone.

He supports Eithne to her feet, grappling her arm around his shoulders as she positions her spear with the other. The two shuffle forward, toward the ongoing hostility.

‘’HEY! Come and fucking have me, you cunts!’’ Gordon screams at the top of his lungs.

The archers are the first to respond, all of them turn to Gordon and Eithne and draw back as one.

The urskull bursts into menacing laughter as he orders his archers to let loose their arrows.

The arrows release. Eithne tenses up as they fly toward them, until the hail before them halted in mid-air.

Another barrier Gordon had erected rippled elegantly with the air, tightly holding the arrows stationary, Gordon drops the barrier hunching over in exhaust.

‘’Charge them!! That's the realm walker, take him out!" The urskull howls.

Almost all the soldiers divert their attention to Gordon and charge ruthlessly; he flings some away, slapping them away like mere flies as Eithne thrusts her nimble spear fighting off all who dared come near.

‘’BREAK!!’’ Brennus shrieks from within the beaten formation.

The warriors of Darogoth give a unified chant as the circle explodes with the wrath of their morale, shields charging forth, bashing down the archers.

One archer fires a well targeted arrow, screeching past the warrior's charge, clipping right in between the eyes of Nurinien who couldn't raise his shield on time. Falling back into the battle torn mud, his life, forfeit.

As the fighting carries on, Gordon is at breaking point. He drops to his knees as he attempts to hold himself and the attackers off with a barrage of flame. His vision begins to blur, his hearing begins to water out, and in the corner of his blurry vision, he spots a more harrowing sight.

More Venethari, more archers and a fierce vanguard charging through the forest onto his fellow warriors.

His life begins to flash before his eyes.

Watching his favourite cartoon as a toddler, sitting on the sofa, with no troubles to burden him and his innocent existence. The look on his mother's face when he won an award at school for his hard work. His first kiss with a girl in high school. His dad wiping away his tears after losing his first love. Comforting his dad, the day his mother left him. The night his grandfather died right before his eyes, bound to a hospital bed. The many times he got drunk with Dan in his flat and laughed the night away. The day he first plucked the strings of his first ever own bass guitar. His first gig with the band. The day he met Helen.

More images cycle through his dying mind as a fatal charge of screaming warriors run directly for him and Eithne, all of it moving in the slowest motion.

The light. Looking around upon Fanara's Cradle as he entered the world, never to return home. Parinos's embrace when he woke up from night terrors. Foraging with Lucotorix and Orthunus. The raid of Seers Crossing. Fighting alongside Brennus by the river Sen. Training with Hashna in the pit. His first kill. Seeing Lucotorix at his door after believing he was dead. Daxos, placing the torc around his neck and feeling its girthy weight.

A dreaded blackness consumes.

Gordon collapses to the floor, Eithne catches him as the two fall together.

21: A Soul Scorned

''Walker! Walker!... Gordon!'' Brennus groans. ''You're awake! By Fanara… this…'' he takes a moment to catch his breath, coughing and spluttering. ''This… this is Tarna Mundur.''

Gordon lifts his head slowly, feeling nauseous. ''Tarna? Tarna….'' her silhouette is nothing but a blurry mess in his weakened state.

''Realm Walker… what a display. That was a sight for song, so it was. We found you all in the nick of time,'' her voice soft, decorated with a thick accent.

Gordon focuses his eyes as he feels himself easing to normality, looking upon the beautiful Tarna Mundur. Her hair tied back into an elegant bun, black as the void itself, her features are sharp and long. She didn't look much like a princess, donning leathers of battle with a fur trimmed overcoat, but nor did she look much of a warrior either. Despite this, the majesty of her graceful stance was very clear.

''Fuck… ing… hell…'' Gordon's head flops back to the floor.

Tarna smiles, a glint shimmers in her dark black eyes. ''I'll let you rest. We'll take you all to our encampment, we have plenty of food for you all to share,'' she marches away, back to her loyal soldiers.

''Can you stand?'' Says Brennus.

''I thought we… we were dead, I…'' Gordon mumbles.

''Take it easy, Walker. We're alive, only just… how fair you, Eithne?''

Eithne laid aside Gordon, supported by her forearms, groping her spear tightly, coated in the spray of enemy blood. ''I'm fine.''

Brennus helps them both to their feet, supporting Gordon in one arm and Eithne in the other. ''Look at the state of you two. Come, let's get out of here.''

The area was pitted with death, many of Darogoth's fine warriors lay lifeless within churned mud. Puddles of blood coagulated with the dirt; arrows stuck firmly within the sludge as well as the many bodies. Although Gordon had seen battle before, the scene was unlike anything he'd witnessed prior.

He passes Nurinien's corpse, a single arrow sticks out from his head, his eyes still as they stare off to the sky.

Many of the horses had perished and were smothered into the dirt along with everyone else. Some were still out in the distance, hitched further out to the trees, even some of the Venethari horses still stood strong. Gordon scans around hoping to the Gods that Epona was safe, he couldn't see her anywhere, even where he left her.

''Where's Epona?!'' He cries out in concern.

He then spots her a little way off, peacefully gnawing on a stray patch of grass, away from the battle site. ''Oh, thank fuck, she's okay.''

‘’You’re lucky, those bastards took mine out, Fanara rest his little hooves,’’ Brennus sighs as he props Eithne atop her horse. ‘’I’ll take one of theirs, always wanted a pure bred Venethari Steppe.’’

‘’Eithne, are you going to be able to ride with that leg?’’ Gordon asks.

She says nothing as she nods, clearly exasperated.

‘’Hey…’’ Brennus calls out. ‘’I know how they caught up to us so quickly….’’

‘’Oh yeah?’’

‘’They’ve cut off all the reins of all their horses… I’ll have to get some fixed on, let’s gather all the ones that are still alive, the rebels could make use of them at least.’’

After gathering themselves and accounting for what little remains of the party, they follow the rebels just hours away to where they were camped.

Small yurts were dotted around surrounded by sharp chiselled barricades; it appeared as if they had been settled here for some time. Tarna wastes no time bringing Gordon and Brennus into her personal yurt.

‘’Good to meet you both, I'm hoping to be escorted across the border since I'm quite a high target here in Venethar. I have much information regarding my brother and his armies.’’

''Good, are you able to provide some arms for the journey back? We've lost many on our way here. We've been reduced to only eight now,'' Brennus mutters, dipping his head in respect of the fallen.

''Of course, of course. I can only imagine the perils you all endured wandering into enemy lands. Would you both care for a drink?''

''I'm fine, thank you,'' says Gordon.

''Very much so… Your Grace, thank you,'' Brennus adds.

''Please, I won't be using my titles of high nobility any longer, for they have been stripped of me. That and holding the Mundur name only carries with it a pain that only haunts my existence these days.''

''Apologies.''

''It's not a problem… erm?'' She replies, insinuating a name from Brennus.

''Brennus Ard-Renirios, Oathsworn Commander to Gordon Ard-Barker and Master of Arms for Fen Craic.''

Tarna smiles in greeting. ''Wow… Ard-Barker? And the owner of a keep? Darogoth is really putting you to use, aren't they?'' She smirks.

Gordon composes himself. ''A pleasure, Tarna. What can you tell us of Kastrith?''

''Wow, straight to the point, so he is. I like it.'' She clears her throat. ''His 'situation' is a lot deeper than you may assume. Although, there's a slight truth to his claims.''

''You're fucking joking with me? He's actually the vessel of Vistra? Vistra is to return? How is this possible?'' Brennus blurts.

''Please, do listen carefully... No... Vistra is not returning... at least not as himself. It's not how you think. Today's concerns actually trace back, all the way to the Gods' age, before the banishment,'' she realigns her posture as she takes a seat at her table, signalling Brennus and Gordon to join her. ''Before the Gods were banished, Vistra tore out a piece of his ethereal being from himself and buried it deep within The Heart, eastern Venethar. His intention was to use it to see if he could break through the void to return to Altharn using his connection to his torn away soul. My elder brother Veldon was newly crowned king at the time the location was discovered and wanted to use it to solidify himself as Venethar's immortal leader under the name of Vistra, for 'Fate had guided him' to such a find,'' she scoffs. ''Both Kastrith and myself knew this would be devastating to the kingdom, if not the world. We had no idea the magnitude of power or what it could be capable of. So, we hired The Black Stag mercenaries from Darogoth to intercept Veldon's attempts to retrieve the soul. The operation was successful, and the soul alongside the rock it was infused with was brought before Kastrith, myself and Hyphal, our court wizard. I still remember the glow it shone when I laid my eyes upon it... It was dying, I can't explain... but we just knew... Hyphal suggested that because it had been separated from Vistra's being for so long it was withering away over time, Kastrith made an innocent mistake when handling it and… this caused the soul to leach onto Kastriths' lifeforce, using him as a catalyst for its own growth. Life energy and void magic are very intertwined with each other, this is why he has the powers he has now. It was an incredibly slow process, we didn't even think anything had happened for years… until it was too late, but there's more,'' she takes a sip of her drink before continuing.

Gordon leans forward in anticipation.

''Vistra never returned. If this was his doing, it hasn't worked. Not in the four thousand years he's been gone. This soul has changed Kastrith, he was sweet and loyal to his cause, much like our father. The man that Kastrith is now is not Kastrith and nor is it Vistra. Our scholars and shamans along with Hyphal claim it gained its own sentience after being separated from the God entity for so long and is using Kastrith as a host to grow itself. We discovered Kastrith can somehow leach into the barrier of Vistra's Realm using the soul and is seeping energy from our beloved God using its natural connection to him. In short, Vistra has unintentionally birthed a godlike being that is now consuming him.''

''What the fuck?'' Brennus says, his jaw hanging from his mouth.

''But I thought there was no direct contact through the realms attached to the Altharn… does this mean Kastrith wasn't lying about sending me home? He offered to send me back home when we met upon the Spire of Oldwood….''

''Although he holds a part of Vistra, no, he cannot, Vistra is a fully fledged God, a being of the void with all its power. This soul that is growing within my brother is but a sapling of such power and is trying to ascend to Vistra's level by consuming him entirely, because eventually it will be capable of doing so. If he could break through the void, he would have sent you home there and then when he offered, regardless of what you said, it would have been easier to dispose of you that way. The soul has created something of itself and isn't powerful enough to completely withhold the true magic of the void. However, the Altharn blocks Vistra from reaching out, but it can reach him… to a degree. Who's to say our God isn't already dead….''

''So Kastrith can't send me home? This is really baffling…''

''I don't think you quite understand. It's allot to take in…. ''

Brennus places his hand on Gordons shoulder.

Tarna takes note of Brennus' support. ''If he can break through the endless void as void magic can, he hasn't found out how to… If he did, he would of brought forth a being of his own, and this world would surely suffer.''

''Explains why he could speak my language, and describe my world to me.''

''Magic is also the forefront of illusion, Gordon. You should know this.''

''How can I find a way back to my own realm?! I don't understand….''

''When you came here the druids used Fanara's Cradle, Fanara built that place and imbued it herself, nurturing her magic, altering it so that it settled peacefully within the Altharn. Vistra didn’t imbue his magic into anything, he merely tore a part of himself that withered over time in a desperate attempt to evade the approaching banishment. He thought that by separating his physical form he’d possibly find a loop around the banishment. I know… it’s complicated,’’ she gives a pitiful sigh. ‘’I’m no master of magic, I've only learned so much since being around Kastrith ever since he consumed the soul all those years ago. Hyphal is the one we all learned from when it came to such things, him and the shamans of fate revealed much about Kastrith.’’

‘’Could he help me?!’’

‘’He could… he’s very knowledgeable of the Gods and their ways. But… he’s loyal to Kastrith, so he is. In fact, it was he who betrayed my trust, that spineless bastard. He’s the reason I fled Kasidor,’’ Tarna leans herself toward Gordon. ‘’Look… If you want to return to your realm, you need the magic that flows with the endless void. The same type of magic that was dormant within Fanara’s Cradle.’’

‘’Yeah, magic of the Gods, I know… but where can I find it?! I was sure that Kastrith would have it or at least have a lead, or something!’’

‘’I’m sorry Gordon, I know of no such item or place where this king of magic resides. We didn’t even know Fanara’s Cradle existed, let alone what it was capable of until news of your arrival.’’

‘’I guess I'm stuck here then… I don't know anymore…’’ Gordon rises from his seat. ‘’I need some air… and a smoke. Maybe a drink too actually….’’

‘’Guard!’’ Tarna claps her hands twice. ‘’Get Gordon a drink of mead,’’ Tarna orders.

A guard rushes around the tent, he pours Gordon a tankard of mead and hands it to him.

‘’Oh… thank you and you, Tarna.’’

‘’Hold your head high, Realm Walker.’’

Gordon leaves without saying another word, his face nothing but disdain.

‘’Poor soul,’’ she purses her bottom lip in pity. ‘’Being torn from your home and brought to a completely different realm must be ever so painful and draining on one's mind… how does he fare?’’

‘’Over time he whines less about it. I think he’s sick of whining himself, but he has every reason too. He's a good lad, he was very certain that you would have the answers for him.’’

‘’Well… I'm deeply sorry I couldn't provide him with what he wanted to hear, truly,’’ she gives a sorrowful smile. ‘’Right, onto our business then. I have information regarding all the movements of the campaign Kastrith is leading into Glaen, he’s trying to convince Mavros Avir to join the fight and bring Darogoth to its knees with as little bloodshed as possible. They’ve been bringing in mercenaries from Kuria into the fight too. Kastrith is adamant on bolstering his numbers, he wants this war to end a quickly as possible.’’

‘’He’s in for a struggle, thinking Darogoth will just surrender being outnumbered, well then, we need to bolster ours too, we've no choice. I'll send word to the high king about calling on allies… if this is going to become a full-scale war, then so be it…."

"Who would you suggest? Obviously, The Glade is out of the question."

"Dakiva? Aventium? Maybe even the Var'keshi… I don't know… this stuff isn't usually my line of work."

"Dakiva is probably your best bet, Aventium have their own troubles with Deep Swamp and Murk, and the Var'kesh… you'd be a fool to think they'd associate with anyone who helped kill their God."

"They seriously have a seven-thousand-year-old grudge?"

Tarna shrugs sarcastically.

"Well anyway, we need to get you into Darogoth, who's going to be leading the rebellion, you have a second?"

"Thornus will be leading the rebellion in my absence, I trust him with my life. We've found a location in the Valley of the Lost for us to permanently set up, they'll be moving there shortly and we can establish stronger communications between our nations smuggling letters to a runner I have in The Glade."

Brennus scrunches his face as he leans forward. "Thornus? That's quite a familiar name…."

"That's because he is of Darogoth. Thornus Glaen-Caerwen, it's a long story, but he saved my life."

''How? Wouldn't he have been persecuted as a Darogothian in Venethar?''

''Like I said, It's a long story....''

Looking around and watching his own warriors mingle with members of the Venethari rebellion. A strange sensation of peace settled amongst the air.

It was definitely strange being amongst the people he'd been fighting against, but it was also nice to get a closer look at them.

Like the Darogothians, the Venethari were hardy people, not as tall in stature so to say, but they oozed a certain resilience. They were folk of darker hair and massively extravagant beards, he didn't see many women in their ranks as he had done the Darogothians, but every single warrior carried a small recurve bow alongside their trusted melee weapon. Their armour and dress were quite pleasing to gawk upon, neatly scaled plates stitched atop leather, trimmed and coated with the fur of bison, bears or sabre cats, their helmets consisting of fur trimmed iron caps.

He lit his pipe, and took a swig from his tankard as he dawdled over to a lowly tree, placing himself at its base, his eyes welling at the frustration that boiled deep within.

''Fucking shit... I don't think I'm getting back... I... can't be stuck? I don't know...'' he mumbles. ''Fuck this shit.''

''Gordon?'' Eithne speaks out softly as she hovels above him.

''Eithne?! Fucking hell, you need to stop doing that,'' he jumps as he wipes his face down.

''Are you okay?''

''Yeah.''

''Clearly….'' Eithne jests.

''I… I'm not going home.''

''How do you know that?'' She slumps down to his side, carefully keeping her injured leg elevated away from the ground.

''Your leg… have you had it seen to?''

''Not yet.''

''Here, let me prepare a paste so it can heal properly at least,'' Gordon gets up and grabs his pot, lighting a small fire in front of them to prepare the paste.

''Okay… so, why are you so glum?''

Gordon gives a heavy sigh. ''Tarna explained it all to me, about Kastrith, his powers, everything, and she's right… if Kastrith really could send me back he would have done it himself at the Spire of Oldwood, he wouldn't of even asked me.''

''I'm sorry.''

Gordon shrugs as he mixes the paste, taking a final gulp of his tankard of mead.

She stares upon him in concern. ''I… wanted to thank you. I would have died out there.''

''You're welcome,'' he smiles. ''Okay, take of that bandage''

Gordon smothers the paste into her wound and reapplies a fresh bandage. ''There… done,''

She exhales the pain as he finishes up. ''Thank you… I'll leave you be, you need some time,'' she smiles as she struggles to raise herself up, Gordon takes her arms, lifting her to her feet.

''You shouldn't be walking around on that.''

''I'll be fine.''

Eithne limps away to her bedroll nearby, Gordon watches her for a moment before returning to his thoughts, thoughts that he was sick of thinking about.

Two days were spent with the rebels of Venethar, but time moves on and so must they, the rebels planned to travel to a more secure location within the Valley of the Lost, it was also Tarna's time to move on too, to join with the party and make their way back into Darogoth.

The next morning everyone prepares for the long-awaited journey back. Although everyone was eager to return home, they weren't too enthusiastic about crossing through the mountains again.

Tarna marched around the camp barking orders here and there as she gathered her belongings to soldiers who were to reinforce the newly formed party, as she finished up preparing her horse, she said her final goodbyes to Thornus who was to remain and take lead of the entire rebellion.

Thornus was a rugged man with a troubled past. Standing at six feet with thick messy brown hair and a scraggly beard, he consoled Tarna like a lover, how he'd come into Tarna's presence at such high regard was baffling for the warriors of Darogoth. No-one had really spoken to him since being within the rebellion's care, he stayed well out of the way of any Darogothian and showed no interest in speaking with anyone who wasn't part of the rebellion, keeping mostly to himself during the stay of Gordon and the others.

Tarna wraps her arms around Thornus' neck. ''I'm unsure when I'll return… but keep the fight alive here in Venethar, keep our people safe. Until Darogoth decide to push, stay out of my brothers grasp.''

''Of course, my love. Please be careful, I hope you return to us soon… your people need you more than I.''

''So they believe… we shall see what transpires. Goodbye, Thornus.''

''Goodbye, Tarna….'' a look of sorrow drowns Thornus' face.

The newly formed party sit idly by as Tarna and Thornus share a kiss.

Although many were deeply curious about their relationship. The time to press on and out of enemy territory was now.

The party mustered themselves up and made for their long journey back to Darogoth, now accompanied by Tarna Mundur and some her soldiers to bolster their numbers through the mountains, though travelling through Venethar, the only souls they would come across were that of roaming farmers and merchants who wouldn't even question the party and its motives, nor did they recognise their princess, shadowed in cloak and rags.

Venethar's patrols and military presence was clearly focused elsewhere, being so scarce, the fear of running into someone was always a concern, but no ill would present itself on their swift journey through the steppes.

They of course encountered a large number of faceless that would wail throughout the day and night, stalking them in the shadows and across the crags, the life of one unfortunate victim fell to the creatures on the journey back. Although one was lost, they made it past much more safely than their previous attempt, having more numbers to bulk their safety.

Being yet again sleep deprived by the howls and screams of the night, the party pressed ever onwards. Their hearts filled with security and joy as the choking green of Darogoth presents itself before them.

The expedition was a success.

22: Trust

‘’Welcome back, I see we have visitors!’’ Lucotorix shouts in relief as he welcomes everyone at the gates of Fen Craic.

Lucotorix then noticed the Darogothic side of the expedition was tragically allot less than it was before they left.

‘’Hi, Luke,’’ Gordon says as he jumps down from Epona. ‘’My fucking thighs are chaffing so badly; I think I’m bleeding actually….’’

‘’How did it go?’’

‘’Tough… very tough… we lost many on our part, some good warriors too… but we did it. There’s Tarna,’’ Gordon points to the group of Venethari, peering around in curiosity.

‘’Wow… I never thought we’d have the pleasure of housing foreign royalty within these walls, let alone royalty of Venethar, especially in times like these. I’m sorry the journey was hard, I'm glad you're safe, friend,’’ he gives a consoling smile.

Gordon and Lucotorix fuse their forearms together in greet. ‘’Oh… there’s someone here for you, they came about two days ago.’’

‘’They?’’

‘’Over there by the tavern, they’ve just came out, probably heard you’ve returned,’’ Lucotorix gestures towards the tavern in the courtyard. There stood a man, a woman and two young girls.

‘’I don’t recognise them….’’ Gordon shrugs.

‘’Ah, I don’t know then, go and see what they want. I best get back to work, a lot of supplies came through and we’re just organising what needs to be where.’’

‘’I suppose. Oh, wait, Luke. Eithne will need her leg seeing too, she got pretty badly injured.’’

‘’Not a problem! I’ll go see to her first then, see you soon.’’

Gordon looked back over toward the tavern, the man’s stare was intense, he and the people with him just stood there, staring.

‘’Huh?’’ Gordon inspects them more closely. The stranger begins approaching.

‘’Realm Walker… It’s been a while,’’ he speaks out.

Gordon was still trying to work out who he was until…

‘’Olm? What….’’

‘’Look… I need your help… my family… I smuggled them out of Venethar for their safety. I’ve defected. ‘’

‘’Olm… I don’t know what to say….’’

‘’I heard you owned this keep; thought you might help me out. I know, I know… I owe you my life. But I might just have something to make up for it. There’s a plan in motion right now that threatens Vortighna, I have all the information you need and

I'll get to that, but listen, my wife here Ilda, is a blacksmith, we noticed your little smithy hasn't been worked on yet… if you would have me, I'll fight for you and my wife will start work for you right away. Please… I know you're a man of honour.''

''Please, we're desperate, we just want to keep our girls safe,'' Ilda jumps in.

''But….''

Brennus struts by.

After taking a glance to Gordon he notices something about the people Gordon was speaking to, he stops in his tracks to gain a closer look. The style of their clothes, the dull colours, the fur trimmings, no torcs, Venethari. He decides to approach with curiosity.

Gordon notices Brennus approaching with a chewed-up face as he inspects Olm and his family.

Before Gordon can even open his mouth Brennus pipes up. ''You're that urskull?! You little cunt Gordon, you lied to me? You freed him?''

Realising there was no way around Brennus, Gordon gives in to honesty. ''Yeah.''

''Why?! Are you fucking bent in the head?''

''Why kill him?! He gave you everything you needed and asked for without hesitation, he complied with you and in return you sentenced him to death? It's wrong.''

''You don't know these people, Gordon. You don't know this world!''

''Brennus!'' Gordon takes a second to calm himself before losing his temper. ''Hear him out.''

Brennus rests his hand on his hilt. ''Go on then Urskull, you have five minutes to tell why I shouldn't stick my blade in your cunt throat.''

''I returned to Venethar, to my position. Urskull Fenrith, the other urskull behind the attack on Seers Crossing is backing an operation that will devastate Vortighna to make it easier to counter you, Gordon. Word travels fast you see. They've captured trading ships from Dakiva and are loading them with soldiers and weapons of war. They're going to hide in them and attack Vortighna from the inside, all while Fenrith sneaks in a ground unit that's going to run in the while the gates are open.''

''Stolen trade vessels from Dakiva? That's an act of war. Venethar aren't even at war with Dakiva,'' Brennus spits at Olms feet.

''I know. But Kastrith is adamant Dakiva would join Darogoth's side in the future, so he decided to get one over on you all by pulling this stunt off, there's also has a small fleet preparing to storm through once the city is taken to get to Fen Craic using the river.''

''I'm struggling to believe whether it's you or him that's the stupid one. Or both?''

''I swear it's the truth. Mavros Avir have recently agreed to a military alliance and will be joining them in the coming war.''

''If this 'attack' is a lie and some sort of ruse, I'll fucking hang you by your own innards, horse fucker.'' Brennus threatens.

''I've brought my family, why would I bring my family into a place that could put them in danger! My wife is a skilled blacksmith and my eldest daughter is training too. I needed to get them out of Venethar, I smuggled them on a war vessel bound for Shem, we've been through a lot to get here. I have defected, Oathsworn.''

''I don't like this,'' Brennus storms off toward the keep.

Gordon hangs his head in shame. ''We've lost a lot of good folk the past few days. We've had a rough journey into Venethar ourselves… It's been very difficult; I'm sure Brennus is just feeling sore from the losses.''

''Don't feel you need to apologise for him, I remember that brute from Carsinia,'' something catches Olm's attention. ''Is that… that's Princess Tarna?! well… this is very interesting. I haven't seen her since she fled Kasidor.''

''You know her?''

''Of course, she's Princess of Venethar. She may recognise me from Kasidor, she may not. It's good to see her alive and well, she's a smart woman, you know. She played Kastrith at his own games many a time and got away with it.''

''That's good to hear… I can see a lot of work has been done to our keep since we've been gone, the smithy is still empty. For now… take refuge here with us. I can't promise you anything so far though….''

''I know my arrival will upset some, but I can't thank you enough for providing me and my family with safety.''

''Thank you for the warning… if what you say is true.''

Gordon returns to the keep and calls for Brennus to meet him in his chambers in an attempt to settle some past mistakes.

Brennus barges in. ''I'm still pissed off with you for lying to me.''

''Brennus, I'm sorry, okay?''

Brennus strikes his finger onto Gordon's nose. ''Sorry?! Sorry isn't good enough, you can't free the enemy from us like this! You could be putting yourself and innocent people in danger! Do you have any idea what Vocorix would have done to you if he found out you did this?! Do you have any idea how fucking bad this really is?! It's treason, Gordon!''

''It was unjust, Brennus. He was cooperative and gave you everything you asked for, he barley even needed torturing!''

''Yeah? And what do you think he'll give the enemy if we're to get captured? He's not trustworthy. He tore through our sacred grounds and cut down our druids! Druids who raised you!''

''He doesn't agree with Kastrith's rule.''

''He's an urskull. They're high-ranking officers and he was an urskull for Kastrith, personally. Look, he claims that a Dakivan trade vessel is housing an army of Venethari soldiers and they'll attack Vortighna's port. For all we know it's a ruse, it'll force us to attack an innocent merchant vessel and Dakiva will not ally with us for the coming battles. It's the perfect plan. All they need to do is to get someone to give you false information, someone who you're fucking soft on, and now it's our entire nation who looks the cunt, all thanks to you.''

''Shit... I... never thought of it like that.''

''Exactly. I say kill him now and toss his family into the wilderness, you may be a lord now, Walker. But that doesn't give you free reign to make stupid fucking decisions.''

''I did this before I was given Fen Craic... anyway, we have to act on this, we should allow the trade vessel to port but we can't attack it, if it's filled with Venethari soldiers, then we can attack! Get the guards in Vortighna ready for the worst. If not, he lied to us... well... I'll leave Olm's fate to you. Evacuate the people from the port... we can at least be prepared for this.''

''That I can agree with. Oh... and by the way,'' Brennus punches Gordon square in the face, his head snaps back with the force of the blow. ''Don't fucking lie to me again.''

''Fuck, man.''

He then grasps Gordon with a bear hug. ''You're like the little brother I never had. But this is serious, we should make it to Vortighna as soon as we can, we're leaving tomorrow.''

''Ahh, we only just got here....''

''Hey, this is your fucking fault, Walker!''

''If Olm is telling the truth, it won't be! It would be a fucking miracle!''

''We'll see... he can stay in that smithy. I don't want his wife working on our gear just yet and I'm posting a watch on them, all hours of the day.''

''Fair enough,'' Gordon says as he rubs his face, sore from the blow.

''I'll inform Eithne. After all, Vortighna is her home.''

''She's not exactly in the right condition to fight.''

''She won't be fighting. You will,'' Brennus leaves Gordons chambers promptly.

Gordon pours himself a heavy stout from the new barrels installed in his chambers and goes to the study corner and slumps in his desk, still feeling the burn of Brennus's blow, his jaw felt like it had clocked out of place.

He takes a drink as he silently thinks about all he's been through in the time he's been here. Seers Crossing, the raid, training with the oathsworn, the first taste of battle by the river Sen, receiving his torc, The Spire of Oldwood.

He looks back on how much he himself has changed in this time. How his fears subside with such ease compared to how it was back then, his eagerness and willpower, and even his physique and appearance. His hair is now quite long, the blonde dye in the front of his hair had faded out, his beard became bushy again. A thought struck his mind.

He rose from his seat carrying his drink and made his way to the mirror by his bed. He decided to have a shave, he shaved his chin and his cheeks down to the root. Leaving only a moustache, the high fashion of Darogoth. He smiles at himself as he peers into the mirror, giving a small chuckle.

His new moustache drooped all the way down to his jaw line, like those American bikers or even a younger version of Lemmy Killmister, it made him feel quite masculine, Gordon was quite fond of it. He liked the people of Darogoth, this made him feel a little bit more connected. He was proud of himself and all he had accomplished, that much was certain. But he still wasn't home.

Knock Knock Knock

''Hello?'' He called out to his chamber door.

''It's Tarna, may we speak?''

Gordon double takes his appearance, making sure he's presentable enough and rushes to his door. ''Good evening,'' He greets.

''Ah. you're really growing with the Darogothians hmm? It suits you,'' she comments on his facial hair.

He gives a nervous chuckle. ''Come in, would you like a drink?''

''Why not!? Thank the Gods we're out of all of that.''

Gordon approaches his cabinet. ''What do you drink?''

''You have wine?''

''Yeah actually, there's a bottle in the rack here… that's been sat there since we occupied this place.''

''Wonderful. I'm tired of mead, thank you, Gordon.''

Gordon pours and passes her a silvered goblet. ''So… is everything okay, come have a seat.''

The two sit adjacent to each other on cushioned chairs by the fireplace.

''I'm just curious about you, I thought it would be proper of me to spend time with the famed realm walker, I want to get to know you and I wanted to thank you personally for escorting me to Darogoth.''

''It's not a problem. I don't mean to sound awful, but I'm not doing any of this for anyone but myself. My goal is to return home.''

''I can sympathise with you. I'm very sorry I could not provide you with the answers to your plight.''

''It's okay, I shouldn't be so hopeful about my situation, but I've been here long enough to know that.''

''The pain must be quite unbearable, is it not?''

''To a degree… I'm surrounded by great people, that's always helped,'' Gordon looks up into Tarnas dark eyes. ''Tarna… you lived with Kastrith whilst he was consumed by this… soul?''

''Yes… he's been its host for fifteen years now.''

''At what point did you decide to join the rebellion?''

''The day he killed my lover and our family friend.''

''Oh shit… I'm sorry… I thought you and Thornus….''

''Thornus is another story, a recent one. In short, he helped me escape Kasidor and our relationship has flourished since. Years ago, I was swooning over one of the urskulls, his name was Leithur, fate shone upon me as he was also interested, we started a relationship but Kastrith disapproved. By this point into Kastrith's rule he had begun to lose his mind and said I should marry into a foreign nation to increase standings, which is completely not what Venethari royalty do, at least not anymore. We've always been free to marry who we wish. Kastrith changed over the years due to the soul. Granted, me and Hyphal always knew, but we never even really learned what was going on until it was too late. We thought it could be a good thing and that Kastrith could be blessed…. Anyway, Kastrith found out that me and Leithur hadn't separated on his orders and slew him and our family friend who stood up for me, the Warlord, Fjorn. Kastrith killed him as he held back the guards, buying me time to get out… he was a lifelong friend of my father and our family. Served us since he was a teenage boy. Forty years he served the Mundur Dynasty. He was killed by the very family he swore to protect,'' she pauses as she stares longingly into the goblet of wine.

''That's awful…. Hey, he died doing what he swore to do, I can't believe Kastrith just snapped like that. You mentioned he used to be different?''

‘’Yes. He was a lovable man, the people loved him, we all loved him. He was gentle and caring. When our brother Veldon became king, Kastrith always stood by my side when I questioned Veldon’s ways. Now, he was a bastard of a man, always had been… but alas, look where we are now. Fate works in mysterious ways.’’

‘’I’m sorry Tarna, you’ve clearly been through allot.’’

‘’As have you, yes?’’

‘’Yeah… I've never really seen much death until I came here, I never held a sword before. I got taken away from my family, friends and girlfriend, they all probably think I'm dead now. Once I arrived, I got taken care of by the arch druid of Seers Crossing until the Venethari… sorry, no offence…’’

‘’None taken, go on?’’

‘’They came, they slaughtered the village, everyone. Orthunus… Parinos… they were helping me, they raised me, they held my hand in this world, and they got put down, just like that.’’

‘’And now look at you. Thanks to these people, their deaths were not in vain, you’ve become a brave young man, a powerful one too. You’re the lord of this keep, you have warriors who’ll die for you, people who believe in you, be proud, Gordon.’’

Gordon gives a soft smile. ‘’It’s just too unbelievable… this life… it all happened so quickly. I was nothing back home.’’

''And now you're everything to Darogoth. I hope the best for you and your endeavours here, however long you do stay, I do hope you find your way home.''

Gordon becomes somewhat distracted by her intimidating beauty. ''Tarna… I'd be nothing without the drenching of magic. It's not all me, if I didn't have this magic, I'd be dead.''

She edges forward to him. ''Yes, yes, it is all you. You make your choices. This is what Vistra teaches, your fate is yours to mould from the fabrics of the void, your place in this world is significant no matter who or what you are, just as much as you are insignificant. You shape this world simply by existing, like you without magic what would I be without my family name, hmm? Many of us are given things by the majesty of fate that we do not ask for and some of us are lucky enough to have the good side of it, this is the balance of the world. The Altharn drenched you! You walked into our realm and you become the person you are today, using that power and sculpting yourself by your own choices. All this here? Is entirely down to you,'' she extends her arms out, gesturing the keep. ''Never reflect on yourself so negatively, Gordon. Appreciate what you have and use it for what you believe in.''

Gordon sits silenced by Tarna's powerful words. ''Thank you.''

''Just telling you what you need to hear,'' she smiles.

''I'm unsure what to do with myself, but I've kind of thrown myself into the middle of this conflict now.''

''Don't think badly of it, you're in the right league, Kastrith is a tyrannical bastard and needs silencing. Well… he isn't, that thing is… that thing that took away my beloved little brother.''

''I suppose…''

Tarna takes a delicate sip of her wine. ''I heard today you freed an urskull and he's warning of an impending attack on Vortighna?''

''Yeah… Olm, he said he worked in Kasidor? Do you know him?''

''Heard the name, I never spoke much with him, but he was a good soldier from what I heard.''

''Do you know if what he says is true?''

''I've been running from my brother for too long now, I couldn't tell you what he's planning as of now, I only know what my sources tell me, and I've not heard of this 'plan'. I think what you want to ask me is, should you trust him? And the answer is no, it was foolish of you to free him.''

Gordon looks down in embarrassment.

''Regardless, the news is out, you must take the correct precautions with Olm, go to Vortighna and prepare. Do not attack those ships under any circumstances, approach this delicately.''

''Yeah, that's what I said. He also mentioned something about an alliance with Mavros Avir?''

''Good, then we'll get to the bottom of all this in due time,'' she gives a half smile. ''I knew Kastrith was in talks of an alliance just weeks ago, so that of which Olm speaks of, is actually true.''

''Hmmm... then maybe he is telling the truth.''

''Or maybe he's telling a small truth to fabricate a big lie.''

''Ugh, fuck's sake,'' Gordon rubs his eyes.

''You have allot to amend, it's been a pleasure to be in your company Gordon, but I must make new preparations with my men now that you are unable to escort us to Carsinia, I do hope you can provide some of your warriors to us so we don't get hounded by locale? For the morrow we make for Carsinia and you go to Vortighna. I wish you the best of travels. Vistra guide you, Gordon.''

''And you.''

Gordon see's Tarna out of his chambers, returning to his desk, drinking until he is tipsy. He would not drink too much this night, Tarna's words echoed in his mind over and over again, he decided to get an early night, for tomorrow he would ride to Vortighna.

Gordon wakes, the time for yet another journey is now. Vortighna only sat a few kilometres south of Fen Craic, so at least it wouldn't be too long this time.

He finishes up his morning routine, then onward to the courtyard, where he would order half of the Garrison of Fen Craic to prepare for travel to Vortighna. He approaches the smithy; Olm is leaving the building just as Gordon approaches.

‘’Olm,’’ Gordon calls out.

‘’Gordon?’’

‘’We're moving to Vortighna, you're coming.’’

‘’Okay… let me change into my travel gear.’’

‘’Hey you! Urskull,’’ Brennus shouts from a distance as he makes his way toward Olm and Gordon. ‘’You’re coming and if I find out you're lying, I get to be the one to gut you,’’ he turns to Gordon. ‘’Take his weapons. I don’t want him armed until we know what’s going on.’’

‘’Can I at least say goodbye to my family?!’’

‘’Of course,’’ Gordon allows.

Brennus sizes Olm up and down before scoffing at him and storming off.

Gordon turns and leaves with Brennus, as they wait for their warriors to prepare, they spot Tarna with her soldiers making their own preparations.

Gordon kindly approaches. ‘’Well, it was nice to meet you, Tarna. Thank you, for everything. Half of my garrison will escort you to Carsinia, while the rest accompany me.’’

‘’I’m sure we’ll meet again, Gordon. You’ll be hearing from your high king soon enough,’’ She mounts her elegant black steed gracefully. ‘’Goodluck in Vortighna, Vistra guide you, farewell,'' The Venethari rebellion cantered peacefully away from Fen Craic and off into the deep forests surrounding.

And as for Gordon, the short journey to Vortighna was now underway.

Upon reaching the gates of Vortighna the party thunder through and up to the castle urgently to get the news to Gallus, Eithne is the first to barge in accompanied by Gordon, Brennus and a painful hobble. Gallus was already giving court upon his throne as they entered.

''So then, you'll be fined for theft, and therefore- What in the… Eithne?'' Gallus rises from his great oaken throne.

''Gallus, we have urgent news.''

''You're wounded….''

''We need to speak… in private.''

''Fine. I'll deal with him later,'' Gallus orders the guards to take away the petty thief that was receiving his judgement.

''What happened, Eithne? You're hurt.''

''Yes Gallus, a minor flesh wound, we need to speak.''

Gallus guides Eithne and Gordon to his chambers, he slams the door behind him. ''What is going on? Were you successful?''

''Yes, Tarna is making her way to Carsinia as we speak,'' Gordon pauses for second. ''Are you due a trade with Dakiva anytime soon?''

''Yes, not expected for a few days or so… why?''

''We may have some information that those vessels are part of an attack on Vortighna from Venethar.''

''What? How?!'' Gallus frowns, compressing his ageing wrinkles.

''Gordon…'' Eithne indicates.

Gordon sighs. ''I have information that may or may not be true. But we can't take any risks, so I came to you directly with as many warriors as I can to aid you. So, Venethar may have captured some Dakivan trade vessels and filled them with their own soldiers.''

''Why would Kastrith attack and steal Dakivan ships? It's nonsense, those two are currently in a non-aggression.''

''Or… it could be a ploy to get us to attack Dakiva blindly on false information.''

''I see…'' Gallus rubs his stubbled chin. ''Where did you acquire such information?''

Gordon gulps. ''A Venethari urskull… he sought refuge with me after I… freed him from captivity in Carsinia.''

Gallus narrows his beady eyes. ''You freed an urskull from captivity?''

''Yes… he smuggled his way into Darogoth and sought me out claiming to have deserted Venethar.''

Gallus's eyebrows lower in concern. ''Eithne?''

Eithne nods. ''We should take precaution, we have the urskull with us now.''

''Bring him here.''

Eithne sends for Olm, within minutes he is marched into the chambers by Brennus, now standing before Gallus.

Olm stands there, brave and silent.

''Urskull… Is what you claim true?''

''Yes.''

''Now, how were you informed?''

''I returned to Venethar after the walker freed me, I was put back into service alongside Urskull Fenrith. He is the main orchestrator on this attack, I was to assist him.''

''And you just decided to come and tell us?''

''I've deserted, Lord. I never agreed with Kastrith's ways and over time I found myself questioning what I'm fighting for anymore… he's an unstable man, not fit for rule. He's torn the ancient bond between our nations and this cuts deep into the people of Venethar, people like me. Not only this, I couldn't find it in me to bring harm to the man who spared my life and allowed my children to keep their father, we know Vistra won't return and we know that standing against such heresy is paramount in returning to peacetimes, I was planning on seeking out the rebels, but my family would have been in too much danger within Venethar, so I followed my orders and got on a warship bound for Shem in Glaen which is under Venethari occupation. I managed to smuggle my family in as servants. The best chance for my family is away from Venethar, so I came to the man who spared my life and gave me a chance. I only wish for my family to be safe.''

Gallus scowls at Olm's words. ''We'll see,'' he turns back to Gordon. ''Away with the urskull.'' He spits. ''Gordon… why did you free this man?''

''It was in my early days here; I can only blame my lack of sense and experience for the world.''

''I'm not sure that is a valid excuse… but who am I to judge how people do things in your own world? Fair enough… let's hope this urskull is telling the truth for your sake. I do hope you were duly punished for such wild disobedience.''

''Brennus has given me a heavy enough punishment I believe….''

''Good. Next time you have an objection against something you have disbelief in, I suggest you speak your mind before acting upon it, or speak to those around you for support, communication is key, Gordon. Although I'm sure by now you know this. Nevertheless, this act of 'kindness' may have just saved our arses.''

''I know Gallus, I'm sorry,'' Gordon sighs.

''When the ships arrive, I'll gather the warriors and evacuate the port,'' Gallus' face snaps out of disappointment and into intrigue. ''Now, tell me about your journey?''

''It was a success… at great cost of many good warriors' lives.''

''I see… I'm sorry to hear, what kind of trouble did you encounter?''

''The expected mostly… the faceless did a good job at weakening us, they took a few lives with them also but we managed to fend them off. Once in Venethar, Eithne guided us to V'tar, where we found a significantly larger Venethari party also hunting Tarna down. We dealt with them well, found a lead before they did and sabotaged their horses. But as fate would have it, they caught our trail and caught up with us. We lured them into some forest to give ourselves a slight advantage. We fought well, but then they overpowered us as we began losing warriors. We must have been outnumbered, what? Five to one? Anyway, we reorganised ourselves and pushed them back one last time and then the rebellion found us and finished the job.''

''My word… that must have been a fearsome fight?''

Eithne shuffles herself in and adds to the report. ''Gordon's magic truly is something. He saved my life as I took an arrow to the leg and was taken out of the fight, I was quite impressed. Our warriors fought well and hard that day, my Lord.''

''Fanara rest them, well done to you all.''

''The journey back was a lot calmer. In fact, the lack of enemy patrols was quite alarming,'' she adds

''Well, what's done is done and we have succeeded. Now we have a new issue to attend to. Gordon, make yourself and your warriors comfortable within Vortighna for the time being. We'll begin strategizing for what may come.''

Gordon and those accompanying him stay within Vortighna, resting their weary selves and savouring their form for the day the ships were to port.

Vortighna, much like Carsinia, was a bustling metropolis, being one of the four major cities that governed Darogoth as a whole. Megaliths of ancient devotion and statues of sung heroes of times past scatter throughout the city, Vortighna is also home to the largest constructed port in all of Uros, being at the forefront of sea-based trade. Where most of Darogoth's cuisine is centred around boars, red meats and vegetables, Fen and Vortighna's staple diet is that of seafood, mass harvested within the Silent Sea, bulked by the river Bi that runs through the entire province and beyond, making food for the people of Fen easily accessible.

Word finally arrived that two Dakivan trade vessels were sailing in by the coast on the border of The Glade. As soon as the message came by, Gallus had Vortighna solidified under total lockdown.

Gallus donned his lordly armour, an Iron breastplate with the symbol of Fen, two entwined trees engraved across the chest, his helm sprouted an elaborate plume topped with an ornament of a fish.

The port was evacuated and many warriors surrounded the perimeter, barricading all ways in and out.

''And shut the main gates! We don't want a surprise from the supposed unit hiding on the outside, I want a steady watch on the walls!'' Gallus orders.

Gordon, now kitted for battle, arrives in port with Brennus and their own handful of warriors.

''So, what now, Lord Gallus? We just wait in port until they arrive?'' Asks Brennus.

''Precisely,'' Gallus replies sternly. ''The vessels were spotted northward near the Gladian shores, they shouldn't be long now.''

Brennus turns to Olm who was being forcibly ushered around. ''Let's see what the day brings shall we?''

Olm glances back at Brennus giving an expressionless look, staring him directly into his only eye.

''I hope you're not lying Olm,'' Gordon expresses. ''For your family's sake. I'll see they are removed from Darogoth safely, that I can promise. But for you… you'll be in his hands,'' he gestures to Brennus who stood with a narrow eye.

Brennus heads off to reorganise his warrior's formation around the port, Gordon thinks back on Olms words from the day he freed him. 'You'll regret this'.

''Olm… tell me now, is this real?''

''Yes.''

''Because if it isn't....''

''By Vistra, it is! Just… wait and see.''

The ships appear upon the horizon, two Dakivan merchant vessels. Large thick sails as well as an enormous hull, carved out of dark Dakivan wood. The ships grow slowly in size as they approach.

Gallus steps forward. ''Prepare yourselves for the unknown! Gordon, by the dock. If you can set these ships alight once we confirm an attack it'll be less of a headache to deal with as they pour out. I want a wall of warriors blocking the docks to stop them spilling out!'' Shouts Gallus. ''And you, Urskull, with me.''

''Lord Gallus, I insist… let him stand with me,'' Brennus offers.

''Fine, just keep a close eye on him.''

''Oh, I will.''

Eithne arrives at the port, geared up and ready for battle.

''Eithne? What are you doing here?'' Gallus blurts in shock.

''Protecting my home.''

''No Eithne, you need to keep recovering.''

''I can walk…''

''I don't care, I order you to return to your home.''

''Gallus…''

''Now! This is not ideal in your condition, please....'' he begs.

Eithne gives a huff as she storms off past the barricades, loitering on the perimeter.

The ships dock into port, an anticipating silence fills the air.

Gallus inspects the helm intently. ''The helmsman... he's definitely Dakivan....''

The man at the helm was that of a typical Dakivan man, thick wraps of polar furs, his hood was down revealing his face, naturally narrowed and thin eyes that combat the blinding snow, his skin was exceptionally pale, as Dakivan skin was, even the crew members on the top deck were clearly Dakivan, going about their work normally, nothing seemed suspicious.

Brennus brings his blade to Olm's neck.

''Wait...'' Olm winces. ''Wait....''

''What?! Wait for what?'' Brennus speaks through gritted teeth.

''You there! Helmsman,'' Gallus calls out.

The man at the helm, looks to Gallus.

''What say you of this vessel?''

''This is just our regular trade import?'' He speaks out, calmly.

''Oh, you fucked up,'' Brennus whispers to Olm.

‘’I swear by Vistra’s name those ships are loaded with soldiers! Think for a second, that helmsman is scared for his life, they’ll kill him if mutters a wrong word.’’

Brennus considers Olms words, his grasp tightening.

‘’I’ll go check it out,’’ Gordon offers. ‘’I’ll keep myself safe with magic, at least until I can get off the ship as soon as I see the danger.’’

‘’No… they’ll be aware we already know, they’ll try and ambush you. I’m not risking you like that,’’ replies Gallus. ‘’Helmsman! I’m ordering you to disembark this vessel.’’

The Helmsman hesitates to move for a few seconds, but then slowly begins making his way to the gangplank that was placed down for him.

As he makes his way down the steps from the helm, he suddenly breaks into a sprint, running for the gangplank.

An arrow shoots from aboard, striking the helmsman in the back, he stumbles and falls off the gangplank and into the water below.

‘’Gordon! Set it ablaze!’’

‘’What about the crew?!?’’

Swarms of Venethari begin to pour out from all kinds of spaces amongst the vessel, jumping to the lower docks and the water, they huddle to the top deck creating a defensive formation with their shields, frantically swamping the area.

‘’Gordon, NOW! Archers, line up! Warriors, get stuck in!’’

Gordon sends a wind of fire bound for the ship, roaring fiercely as it engulfs all within its way, he catches many in the blaze, but not enough as they all pour out frantically, some just simply diving to the water to extinguish themselves and then climbing to the lower level of the docks below where they found cover.

On the other ship adjacent, Venethari attempted a push, fighting with the warriors blocking the way, Gordon ran over to set it ablaze.

''Forward! Don't let them pass!'' Brennus screams. Before running off into the fight, Brennus stops and signals his men to Olm. ''Give him his axe, let's see how loyal he really is,'' he orders one of the warriors carrying Olms' large bearded axe. ''You three'' he points to some nearby warriors. ''Follow the urskull, if he turns on us, fucking kill him,'' he orders.

Olm takes his axe proudly, bearing an intensive snarl, eager to prove himself.

Brennus runs to the dock's edge watching Venethari climb upward hiding in the crevices. The docks of Vortighna were very complex and built with multiple levels that lead all around, making it easy for the Venethari to manoeuvre, but their fates were already sealed, for Olm had single-handedly toppled the entire plan. Fate would have it that Iskariens' shadow is cast upon the Venethari this day, and with no escape.

A hand grips the ropes to the upper dock, before the Brennus can react and before the soldier can solidify their climb, Olm's axe comes slicing through his wrist with tremendous force, severing the hand. The soldier screams, falling to the consuming waves.

Brennus looks to Olm, giving him a small nod of approval.

Olm charges off toward the frontline to assist the blockade, his war cry shattering the hearts of his former companions as he slices through their ranks.

Gordon stands at the docks edge, throwing his flame upon the men below taking cover, catching them off one by one until an unknown magical force tears him aside, throwing him off the entire platform. He drops his blade as he plummets into the water.

Gordon was now in serious danger, the weight of his armour was making it difficult for him to swim, he managed to grab onto a large wooden support beam, clasping onto it with his life. A ball of fire comes screaming towards him from underneath the dock on a lower platform, he defuses it just in time.

A battlemage stands with two other soldiers hunched under the dock; he sends forth another ball of fire. Again, Gordon defuses it.

Gordon was stuck in a fatal predicament; the beam was too difficult to climb whilst under fire.

The battlemage of Venethar draws in all his focus, dispatching a thundering wave of force, smashing the beam entirely, Gordon plummets back into the water, along with the entire dock and all soldiers standing on it, including Olm and the enemy, they all crash into the engulfing waves below.

Wooden debris showers over and all around him as it topples down, taking a hefty bashing from a large plank, pushing him further underwater.

Everyone in the water was splashing about frantically, many began ferociously fighting amongst the lapping waves in a bid to survive, others struggled to swim encumbered by their armour, succumbing to the depths.

''The water....'' Camula whispers. Straight away, he knew what to do.

His eyes imbue the purple hue, and he explodes out of the water like a geyser firing into the sky. Using his magic, he stands atop the gushing pulse of water beneath him. He propels his arms forward sending forth an incredible collection of water pressure toward the battlemage and the two soldiers. The battle mage erects a magical barrier around himself, as the oncoming storm crashes into the barrier like an angry hurricane, but the warriors beside him were exposed, slamming backward into the wall behind them, the mage continues to hold his magical shield with all his mental might.

Gordon pushes his arcane prowess even harder as he screams aloud, the mage manages to keep holding out.

Gordon snaps his arms behind himself, projecting straight toward the mage, crashing into him.

Gordon picks himself up quickly and pummels the battlemage over and over again with a barrage of punches, he then slams his palms down onto the mages face and seers it fiercely with the burn of fire.

''Argh!'' The mage screams as his face sears to the bone.

One of the warriors gets up and takes a swing to Gordon, he quickly rolls off the mage's body but the blow of the soldier's weapon catches Gordon's torso, luckily his armour cushioned the blow, the pain was heavy and hard.

He uses magic to trip the legs of the soldier upward, slapping him to the ground. Gordon picks up the short sword of the mage which was sheathed amongst his scabbard, he runs to the grounded man, swift fully kicking his sword from his hand as he raises it to defend himself. Gordon viciously slices at him until he moves no more.

Once finished with them both he knew only one remained. The soldier was still sitting by the wall mildly injured from the water pressure Gordon had blown onto him, he was breathing heavily, gawking upon Gordon in fearful awe. ''Please....'' he whimpered.

Gordon ignored the plea, gritting his teeth and holding him in place, he stuck the blade in the soldier's neck, pressing it further in. As the soldier's life ceases from his body he stares Gordon dead in the eyes, Gordon's enraged state fades as he looks upon the pure terror within the soldiers' eyes, he stumbles back from the man, a wave of guilt floods him. ''Fuck... this isn't me... no....'' he drops the man to the floor.

Gordon falls to his knees, panting erratically. ''I'm sorry, fuck! What the fuck am I doing?!'' He wails.

He hits himself in the head. ''No! He would have killed you!'' He stumbles around for a moment. ''No, he was pleading for his life, he was terrified! He was just following orders....''

''Pull yourself together, get out!'' Camula shrieks.

A warm flood shudders down his spine as Camula sends forth her comfort. Manically, he tries to reject it, flinging himself to the wall in despair, pulling at his hair and scratching at his own face. ''What the fuck are you doing?!'' He shouts to himself. ''People are dying! We need to fight, fight for Helen, to get back home! Remember home?!''

All of a sudden, his mind snaps back to reality as Camula soothes him once again, without further thought, he rushes to the edge of the lower dock, watching on as a mass of warriors frantically splash around and stab each other, the water turning red with blood. The fight within the waves was an utter mess.

He watched on as they all struggled for their lives, he caught a glimpse of Olm burying his axe into the shoulders of a Venethari, ripping right through their leather pauldrons.

Although he felt slightly weakened, he was strong enough to carry on and extended his arms, using his magic to lift the Darogothians one by one from the water, pulling them out and to safety by his side. He was unable to save a few as the fighting consumed them... brutally chopped by the blades of the enemy.

He felt comfortable leaving Olm amongst the Venethari while he lifted out his fellow Darogothians, Olm was a seriously formidable warrior, even in the swallowing of water, his display of strength was impeccable. Finally, Gordon picks Olm from the water flinging him beside him and the others.

''Archers! Archers! The water!! Now! Knock and loose!'' Gordon screams at the top of his lungs with all the breath he had left.

Within seconds the archer's line themselves by the dock and fire into the water. The Venethari struggle and attempt to climb out, grasping onto anything to keep them afloat and would shield them from the barrage of arrows.

''Up to the top of the docks, now! Go! Go!'' Gordon orders.

''That's twice you saved me now,'' Olm splutters.

Gordon says nothing, burdened by his emotions.

The group ran upwards to the top deck, the vessel beside them burned valiantly, blistering the air as one of the masts collapsed on itself, falling into the water atop the many bodies that lifelessly bobbed on the surface.

Only one ship remained and it was in good control by Vortighna's forces.

Once Gallus saw the warriors emerge from the lower docks, he made the final order. ''Everyone, to the eastern dock now!''

Everyone swarmed the final ship, Olm eager and pumped of adrenaline, jumped right into the action upfront, swinging his massive axe into the bellies of the enemy.

Within minutes, the remaining Venethari surrendered. Raising their arms to the air and dropping their weapons. A decisive victory for Darogoth.

This wasn't enough for Gallus. ''They would have slain innocent men, raped innocent women, and the children? I dare not think what they'd do to our children… they would have brought suffering and pain to the everyday folk of Vortighna. Merchants, smiths, craftsmen, farmers, children… I have no care for those who wish ill on my people. Kill them all.''

The warriors cut the throats of the remaining Venethari under Gallus's orders.

''Well, well… you were right all along Urskull. Your name?''

''Olm, Olm Uldur.''

''Well done, Olm. You really made yourself known.'' Gallus says with a frown.

''Just like he made himself known when he the ordered the deaths of innocent druids?'' Brennus scoffs.

''Oathsworn Brennus, still yourself. If it were not for this man, the people of Vortighna would be cut down by Venethari means. I'd say he's earned a degree of gratitude; do you not think?''

Olm steps forward. ''Brennus… I didn't kill any druids in that raid. Urskull Fenrith did though… he killed the druids. I merely rode into the village looking for a supposed other worldly beast as I was instructed to, I don't bring my fucking weapon down on those who do not fight,'' he bites back in defence. ''Speaking of

Fenrith, he should be on the outside… if you want to take revenge for Seers Crossing, go and hunt him down!''

''Oh I will… ''

''It was my job Brennus, just like being oathsworn is yours. They were my orders. Why do you think I'm here now, slaying my own?! I've deserted. Fuck the king, he's a fucking lunatic.''

Brennus stood silent, and somewhat impressed. ''Fine… if I ever find out you're messing with us, I swear by Fanara, I'll piss on your fucking corpse,'' he squares up to Olm's face pressing his bulging nose against his. Olm does not budge, standing his ground as he stares back into Brennus's eye of fury.

''Enough, Oathsworn!'' Gallus shouts. ''An issue still remains, as Olm mentioned, the urskull behind the attack is still lurking, we still have a large unit of Venethari hidden in the Forest of Askelix waiting to attack. I can only assume they'd be gone by now knowing their plan has been foiled. A foolish suicide mission such as this could only be effective if executed perfectly.''

''We need to chase them down,'' Brennus replies

''A bold move by Kastrith, an even bolder one by the soldiers,'' Gordon expresses.

''I'll have Eithne's second scout Askelix whilst she's in recovery,'' Gallus announces

''What about the fleet? What if they send forth a full-scale attack? Surely they wouldn't back down now just because their initial plan failed? And why would they hijack these vessels? Does Kastrith not care for foreign relations?'' Gordon asks.

Gallus turns to Gordon, placing his hand on his shoulder. ''Venethar has never really had a good relationship with Dakiva. Kastrith probably expected us to call on Dakiva for military aid, so he probably expected them to turn on him anyway,'' Gallus pauses. ''We'll keep the port locked down until we know what's going on, we'll send out the fastest ship we have to scout the seas,'' Gallus shudders. ''I don't like this war. I can't say I'm fond of any war, but this one… this one has a strange air about it… It's erratic, unpredictable… yet paced and silent, striking us in the sides when we least expect it. Only the Gods know what we're in for.''

''Agreed…'' Brennus responds. ''But by Fanara, we'll fight it.''

''Oathsworn of Vortighna! Return to the castle. Guards, I want patrols heavy on the port!'' Gallus orders. ''I'll go find Eithne's second, thank you all. We made a quick victory here today,'' he gives a sorrowed smile. ''We can handle the rest from here, Gordon. You may make your way back to Fen Craic if you wish. You've done enough, get yourself some well-deserved rest,'' Gallus grasps Gordon's arm in respect.

''Well done out there,'' Eithne approaches from nearby.

''Where were you?'' Gordon asks.

''Gallus ordered me to stay out of the fighting, I stood nearby in case I was needed. Quite a show you put on….''

''How's the leg?''

''It's healing, I should be back on my feet properly soon.''

''Quite literally.''

Eithne gives a soft smile. ''I am, sort of… we've had quite the adventure the past few weeks, it's been an honour.''

''And you, Eithne.''

She lowers her head in respect.

Gordon couldn't stop thinking of the poor soldier's plea's as he drove a blade through his throat, it reminded him of Orthunus's face they day he was taken, it was exactly like his, utterly drenched with terror, he could see the inner child crying for his mother just by peering upon his innocent eyes.

He felt evil, disgusting. He shook his head so many times on the journey back to Fen Craic he gave himself a headache.

The gates of Fen Craic open upon return.

''Fancy a drink?'' Brennus asks as he hitches his horse in the stable.

''Definitely,'' Gordon responds.

''I love how you have a fully functional tavern before a working smithy,'' Olm sniggers.

''Priorities Urskull, priorities,'' says Brennus. ''Urskull?''

''Hmm?'' Olm grunts.

''Join us, will you? Let me buy you a drink, It's the least I can do after… all of that. This doesn't mean I fucking like you though.''

''There we go Brennus, not that hard, is it?'' Gordon adds.

''Shut the fuck up, Walker.''

''Yeah… I'll join, why the change of tone?'' Olm replies.

''I've been thinking about your words on our way here, I would have probably done the same thing.''

''You know… I understand your distrust in me. I'd be the same if I were you.''

''Enemy or no, you still lead the attack on our most sacred grounds, I cannot ever forgive you for that, know this, Urskull,'' Brennus hacks up a clump of phlegm, spitting it out to the floor. ''But… you did well out there. Just know I've always got my eye on you.''

''The working one? I hope so, otherwise you'd be blind,'' Olm sniggers.

''Don't push your fucking luck.''

The three three fall gleefully into the shoddy little tavern, it's small, dainty and is almost already full with warriors. Lucotorix catches word of their return and joins them in the tavern.

''Gordon! Good news,'' Lucotorix announces as he takes his seat.

''Oh?''

''We have received even more supplies from Carsinia and the treasurer will arrive in the coming days. The folk here have been fishing in the lake, hunting and foraging nearby. We're quite fortunate to have an abundance of food. One of the warriors has given up his blade entirely to cook and manage the kitchens in the keep; he requested one of the chambers to stay in. So, I made the decision to accept it, if that's okay?''

''Of course, it's an important job. If he works in the keep makes sense for him to live there.''

''All repairs to the smithy have been made, Olm's family are happily settled in now and are already working hard.''

''Ahh good! I'll go to them shortly,'' says Olm.

''And one more thing, the high king has requested you create a crest to represent your clan.''

''What?''

''You're a Clan Lord, with no symbol or representation of your standing here in Darogoth.''

''It's just me though… I don't have family here.''

''Anyone can join your clan, they have to formally leave their old one and perform the joining ritual though…''

''Okay… but why would I want anyone to join my… 'clan' I'm not even planning to stay here long.''

''You don't. The point is that you are the lord of Fen Craic. Only clan lords can own land in Darogoth, this is just to settle the laws of the land.''

''Just humour it, Walker,'' laughs Brennus.

''Oh, okay… what should I use as a crest?''

''Well, Gallus' clan is Frenone, he has three fish that form a circle… Vocorix's Clan is Drosii and he has four horses that entwine together,'' says Lucotorix, gripping his tankard. ''Allot of Clan Lords suggest something and have their druids make it for them.''

Gordon gives a moment to think, he thinks about things that are dear to him and that could work for his crest, and then it comes to him. ''Well… everyone seems to use animals, how about a white wolf's head for mine, maybe?''

''That's oddly specific,'' Brennus adds.

''It was the logo for my band back home. It was a white wolf with blood dripping from its mouth, it was fucking cool.''

Lucotorix blinks in disbelief. ''Well, not every clan uses animals, the Parvusii clan has two spears resting against a torc! But living things usually represent life, and life… Fanara! I can help with that, there is a clan in Dun who uses a wolf, but not a wolf head… hopefully that won't complicate things, I may need to skip out the blood… anything else notable about it?''

''It was facing forward? Erm… snarling?''

''Okay… I'll see what I can come up with for you. Then once we're all done, we can get it painted onto the shields and draped around the keep.''

''Cool!''

''What colour should represent your clan?''

''Red! Since you're not letting me have blood.''

Lucotorix gives a bellied laugh. ''Okay, okay it shall be done soon enough. So, since you're now a clan of Fen, the shields will be repainted, the province symbol will be at the bottom of the shield, and yours will be at the top, like all clans have their shields. The banners and drapery will all just be of your symbolism though.''

''And the Fen symbol is the two trees, yeah? It represents the Bi-Wood.''

''Correct!''

''So, is that all the keep business taken care of then?'' Brennus remarks.

''For now.''

''Good, now back to relaxing, what a fucking eventful time we've had, eh?''

''Yeah… I can't believe we even survived,'' Gordon blows a sigh of relief. ''If the rebellion hadn't found us, we would have been dead… for real.''

‘’Thank the scout girl for that, she tracked them down like a sabre cat on prey. She works in weird ways… but it gets the job done.’’

‘’Yeah….’’

23: Making a Stand

Altharn, Fen, 4AB 284

Time flows ever onwards.

The white wolf banner of Gordon Ard-Barker flutters vigilantly in the gentle breeze of Fen Craic, a wolf's head in the form of swirls and knots nesting in blood red fabric just as he'd requested so long ago.

As the months came and went, Gordon's hope of returning withers with every passing day, he adopted the life of these people, became one of them, and for him, he was okay with this, the people respected him, he was something in Altharn, and nothing back home, but Helen, his friends and family were everything. However drastic and different his two lives were, the end goal remains unscathed, return home.

Every evening he would flick through the library of his chambers that was left by the previous owner many years ago, he'd trip to Vortighna and purchase more books and scrolls there too, frantically searching the lore of Altharn for any signs of the magic of the Gods, just as he had done since the day he arrived, his enthusiasm for this had whittled down due to the long stretch of time he'd been in Altharn, and would take a more relaxed attitude toward it. How long had Gordon resided with Altharn?

Two years by now? Maybe more, it definitely felt like more, he had completely lost track of Earthen time. He tried many times to work out how long it had been but never seemed to feel correct in his calculations. Altharn's days and nights always felt a little longer and never really matched up, the seasons were also exceptionally longer, usually lasting around six months or so, a while back he made a conscious decision to forget about how long he was here, in hopes of stabilising his mental health and as a result, he'd never be able to keep track of time.

Fen Craic was a bustling fort now in perfect operation. The gates were always open, the treasurer Pelix Ard-Brinante would call the shots on Fen Craics' upkeep, the wealth and how it was distributed to the staff and warriors.

Just as it was previously, it became a merchant hub, the tavern became an inn and the many stalls in the court would have merchants trading with each other and the inhabitants of the keep, Pelix decided keep the tax on trade small, a smaller tax than that of places such as Vortighna making it much more profitable for travelling merchants between provinces and cities.

With Fen Craic being situated by the enormous Fen Lake, the small dock was reconstructed and the warriors would occasionally go out on small fishing boats, harvesting the waters for a fresh supply. Gordon especially enjoyed this, the peaceful aura of the lake was calming to him, he always wanted to go fishing back home but never really pursued it. He spent more time fishing than he did in his library some days.

Olm's wife Ilda was hard at work, making repairs to armours, weapons and tools of the like, with the help of her eldest daughter

Ymitre and of course Olm when he wasn't on duty. Ilda gifted Gordon a metal wolf plaque as a token of thanks for harbouring the family and he displayed it proudly above his fireplace in his chambers.

The endless passive aggression between Olm and Brennus never seemed to end, eventually Olm just stopped biting back and took it on the chin, Brennus would always find some way to shoot a snide remark toward Olm despite clearly having a small amount of respect for him, much of the keep just believed Brennus to be jealous of Olm, Olm was like a more level headed version of Brennus and many believed Brennus knew his flaws. Regardless, Brennus was a man of honour and pious, he managed the warriors of the keep remarkably and even formed an oathsworn force in the name of Gordon. Picking out the most dedicated warriors to fight for Gordon's cause and training them up in typical hardcore oathsworn fashion, despite his qualms with Olm, he singled him out to become oathsworn, bringing Olm under the fold of the most dedicated and loyal fighters of Darogoth and Olm took the oathsworn pledge without hesitation.

At first it was suggested to Brennus by Lucotorix and initially he brushed it off, but over the days he would ponder on the idea, watching as Olm and Gordon's friendship bloomed more and more, noting the hard work Olm did around the keep, the amount of food he would go out and forage, the training he excelled at, the work his family put in around the forge and the respect the other warriors grew for him and his family. Although Olm was not of Darogoth, he displayed the utmost loyalty to Gordon, and so Brennus made him oathsworn. Increasing his pay and donning him in the classic plated and chain garb, the only difference between Olm and the other oathsworn of Fen Craic was that Olm had an unusually strange relationship with his axe, it was well known he would sleep with it, although this may stem from his Venethari nationality, as nomads were known to do such things in their days of travel to feel safer. Most Darogothians favoured a sword or spear with a large oval shield, but Olm was comfortable with his large two-handed bearded axe, Ilda altered his armour to be more lightweight for him, making his axe swinging much more feasible.

Fen Craic was alive, Gordon's income was no longer coming from Vocorix, he had developed strong bonds with the people he met and was flourishing.

The war with Darogoth and Venethar was slow and ongoing. After Vortighna, Gordon's unit was kept out of the majority of the fighting, despite the odd skirmish here and there they'd be called forward too, usually around the edges of Glaen.

The struggle was becoming all too real, Kastrith was fighting the war on many fronts, not only was he swatting away at the rebels, led by Thornus who was ambushing supply lines and keeping the strain tight on Venethar, but Dakiva had joined the fray on Darogoth's side and began launching small raids on the northern shores and backing the rebels.

Glaen had been the main focus for the conflict and had now fallen almost completely into Venethar's hands, spare the odd village and town still putting up resistance. Many of the people of Glaen fled to Ard, Dun and Fen, many of which actually journeyed to Fen Craic in hopes of fighting for Gordon, knowing of his famed magical prowess in battle. Fen Craic now was unable to house any more arms, Gordon now had a small army at his disposal.

Gordon was never sent to the front lines to defend Glaen, usually being ordered to smaller conflicts, he thought he was being purposely kept away for his inexperience, even though that didn't really make much sense considering he'd been thrown into the thick of it since his arrival. Either way, new plans were made, and Gordon would find himself at the centre of it all.

Gordon stands within his own void, before him the white silhouette of Camula.

''I've read so many books, I've learned so much about the Gods, what they did when they walked this land, what they left behind before they disappeared, I found nothing that could lead to the magic of the endless void. Nothing....''

''These kinds of relics are kept secret for a reason.''

''Is the answer in Darogoth? In Uros? Would I need to look elsewhere?''

''Perhaps, but Darogoth has need of you, you must keep fighting.''

''Camula, it's been far too long. I can't keep doing this, it'll be my birthday again sometime soon... that's another year....''

''I know there's something in your heart that can settle your troubled soul.''

''No.''

‘’I feel the contrast, despite all the hardships you’ve faced, you’ve never felt more alive.’’

Gordon scoffs. ‘’Yeah…’’ A thought crosses his mind. ‘’If I found a way home, what would happen? Would I keep my magic? Would you stay with me?’’

‘’I don’t know, but if you settle your heart, maybe then you’ll find the answer to returning home.’’

‘’That’s such a fucking cliche thing to say….’’

‘’Gordon….’’ Camula whispers abrasively.

‘’Maybe if we win the war, I could fuse my own magic with Kastrith’s… he's the only thing that comes close to the magic I need. I’m unsure how, but… maybe my connection to Earth and his connection to Vistra… the magics combined might just do it!?’’

‘’That I can’t answer.’’

‘’It’s worth a try… especially if that’s my only option.’’

‘’Don’t stop searching and don’t forget how far you’ve come here in Altharn, don’t forget those who’ve supported you, raised you, and fought for you, I know Altharn isn’t your world. But you live and fight for it as if it were.’’

‘’I live and fight because I have too, I haven’t exactly got a choice… otherwise, what’s the point?’’

‘’Exactly.’’

The world begins to shudder around him. The rumbling grows stronger and stronger.

''But do you think I-''

Gordon awakes abruptly from the hideout of his mind.

His chamber door shakes from a vigorous knock.

''Gordon, you in there?'' Lucotorix shouts from the other side.

''Ye-Yeah,'' he groans.

''May I come in?''

''Let me get some pants on at least.''

''You're still in bed at this time?!''

Gordon rolls out slipping into some chequered trousers he had on the previous day.

''Yeah? What's the issue?'' Gordon asks, rubbing his eyes.

''Letter from the high king.''

''Oh, shit,'' Gordon takes the letter from Lucotorix. ''Smoke?'' He asks.

''Always.''

The two make their way to the balcony, alighting their pipes and soaking in the glorious view.

''So, are you going to read it?!''

''Yeah… yeah, just give me a moment to wake up.''

Lucotorix laughs. ''You're really getting used to it now, eh?''

Gordons eyes widened to Lucotorix as he took a hit from his pipe.

''What?''

''Nothing.'' Gordon exhales. ''You're right, I need to sharpen up a little. It's just the past few weeks I've actually been able to get proper full night's sleep. It's just been nice having that kind of peace.''

''Oh, you're not having those crazy dreams anymore?''

''They're becoming less frequent, but they still prop up often.''

''Well, it's nice to see you more relaxed, by Fanara I remember the first night we had you. You were a complete mess!''

Gordon gives a modest smirk. ''Yeah….''

''You've done well Gordon, I'm proud of you. Parinos would be proud too.''

''I hope so, Luke… I've decided to dedicate myself to this, we need to win this war.''

''You've always been dedicated have you not? I know you're desperate to get back home but you've always had that little fire for us all.''

''I live to survive, I'm fortunate to have this magic and I'm fortunate to be where I am, I know this. But returning home is clearly unreachable, isn't it? I've always known it… but the answer will come when it comes. I need to focus; I live here now and have done for what? Two years now? If the day ever comes, I get to return, then so be it.''

Lucotorix cocks his head in surprise. ''Now that's the mindset of a true druid.''

The two share a bonding smile.

''I best open this letter, I'm going to guess Vocorix is finally planning on marching into Glaen.''

''Most likely, he'll want to rush in there before Mavros Avir join the fray and start landing.''

''But Dakiva agreed to a military alliance with us, didn't they? I thought it was agreed they'd defend our shores?''

''Indeed. But the Mavrosi are not a nation to underestimate, Mavros Avir is huge, twice the size of Darogoth, the same size as all of Uros in fact and thrice the population, Dakiva may be larger than Darogoth, but it's freezing terrain limit's them as a nation and won't be enough.''

Gordon ponders for a moment. ''Then we clearly need more allies.''

''Yeah… I hope by Fanara that the high king is working on that.''

''I fucking hope so… one ally that doesn't even equal the population of Fen alone isn't exactly going to cut it….''

Lucotorix's face dims to a glum expression. ''What else does it say?''

''Say's lords of Fen will gather and march into western Glaen, whilst Ard and Dun will become the main bulk, forcing through the south. He's expecting Venethar will likely target the army that I'm accompanying… he reckons keeping Fen separate and smaller will throw them off.''

''Is he an idiot?''

''What do you mean?''

''Venethar will know you'll be joining with Fen's part, you're a lord here.''

''Wait… he wants me and my garrison to separate and join Ard and Dun at some point to keep Venethar on their toes, hasn't said when…'' Gordon points to the letter showing Lucotorix. ''He'll send a messenger across with more information as we gain access into Glaen.''

''Okay that's not entirely terrible I suppose… he seems to think this entire campaign is reliant on where you will be… which is understandable, but Kastrith will know this.''

Gordon continues reading as he balances his pipe in his mouth. ''Dakivan ships will be massing along Glaen's coast to defend the borders and block any reinforcements coming in from the sea.''

''This is going to be a campaign spoken through ages, we have to beat them back.''

''Venethar are massing forces around Glaen, says they're preparing a full-scale invasion to topple into Ard.''

''No. This is too straight forward… they wouldn't brute force us like this, every conflict Venethar have ever been in they never brute force their opponent, they've always performed some outrageous strategy that puts them on top, they must have something else up their sleeve.''

''Maybe Kastrith is overconfident.''

''Maybe so, the attack on Vortighna said enough about that…'' Lucotorix rests his chin into his hand as he ponders the possible outcomes. ''They're allied with Mavros… they'll use Mavros' Navy no doubt, hmmm,'' Lucotorix gives a hard thought. ''What if the Mavrosi invade Dun? Dun is well out of the way of the fighting, if that were struck whilst all of Darogoth's armies are in the north, including Dun's, it would be the perfect plan to execute, especially if Dakiva are only watching the eastern shores of Glaen?''

''Fuck… yeah? You should have been a strategist,'' laughs Gordon.

''I'm a druid, we're taught such things, it's our job.''

''Wouldn't Vocorix take that into account? He seems to be a good high king in my eyes.''

''Vocorix… he's a just enough man, just careless in my opinion… If he hasn't considered the safety of Dun during this campaign, he's a bigger idiot than I initially thought. He'd be literally leaving the doors of invasion wide open for Mavros Avir… what kind of high king leaves that kind of opportunity open to the enemy? It's a damn good thing Darogoth has its druids.''

''Maybe I should write to him about this?''

''Would be wise of you.''

Gordon wastes no time in rushing to his desk to grab a quill and whisk out a letter for the high king, calling for one of his soldiers to dispatch as soon as possible.

''When is the campaign to begin?'' Lucotorix asks, approaching Gordon's study.

''I'm unsure, he said Gallus will be notifying the Lords of Fen when we are to leave.''

''Well, let's hope Vocorix is still in Carsinia when your message arrives…'' a thought pierces Lucotorix's head. ''Shit, I need to gather some ingredients, we're going to need a large supply if we're going on a campaign. Join me in the forest if you wish? Like old times?'' He adds.

Gordon gives a soft smile. ''Maybe… I have a lot to think about.''

''Well don't think too much, you know it isn't good for you.''

''Yeah,'' Gordon snorts.

Lucotorix leaves the chambers, rushing out in preparation for a long forage.

Gordon looks at the two banners that loomed over and beside his bed. Blood red, white wolf.

Blood Winter. One of their songs begins playing in his head... It's almost as if his lifestyle had evolved in some weird way, like an alternative reality. He sat at his desk, appreciating the banners and the memories of his old passion for music, a passion that seemed to only be a distant memory now.

He still feels dumbfounded by Altharn, even after all this time.

He reminisces about his childhood, his old dreams. He was a lovable, hyper and very optimistic child, his parents took great care of him until they split when he entered his teenage years. He became quite a mischievous boy in school, getting in trouble allot. As a teenager he would begin expressing himself with black clothing, chains, tattoos, smoking and drinking, he joined a band, he went to college to study music, attempting to keep his life on some straight path that would stop him from spiralling out of control. As an adult he ended up working in bars, serving drinks and playing gigs. He met Helen, they moved in together, he lost his job and then began working as a shelf stacker at a local supermarket and now?

The Lord of Fen Craic, Clan Lord of the Barker Clan, with many taking up the blade in his name, a renowned magic user, fearsome in battle. This was one hell of a contrast.

He would always wonder what his folk back home thought of him to this day, did they truly believe him to be dead? Would they be looking for him still even after all this time? Did Helen class herself as single now? Would she have a new boyfriend?

How did his mother feel? The same kinds of mind-numbing thought's that had attacked his sanity every day since his arrival.

''Push harder,'' he whispers to himself. ''Push.''

On a grey and dreary day, the sky spits down a light drizzle. Autumn was nearing its end in Altharn, and the end of Autumn was usually quite dull, ready to draw in the freezing winds of winter just a month or so away. A messenger from Vortighna arrives, delivering a sealed letter to Gordon, who at the time was helping untie a load of fishing nets that had been tangled up in a fishing trip.

He takes the letter from the messenger, drying off his hands before opening it carefully.

''Gordon Ard-Barker of Fen Craic.

The call to arms is upon the people of Fen, let us stand together and repel the enemy from our lands in Glaen, let this be the last time the borders be broken by the hordes of Venethar and show them the true power of Darogoth's might. We must turn the tides of this war and take back Glaen, the lives and homes of many depend on this. Darogoth needs you.

You will meet the campaign on the northern banks of the river Bi, east of Denunnos. We will amass all the Lords of Fen and march eastward into the Oldwood of Glaen. Once there, we will be establishing a new forward base in Oldwood where we will march north to retake the city of Northus.

The high king's army accompanied by those of Dun will be gathering in the only city left in Glaen under Darogoth rule, the city of Ollus. They will be bolstering the defence with their massive force.

The Venethari have split, as they themselves are bolstering in order to march south, leaving Northus with very little guard, but to our knowledge are still using Northus as a supply front connecting it to Antler in The Borderlands. We must eliminate their supplies. But with you at our sides we are confident.

Once we have taken Northus we are to exterminate and or capture all Venethari within the walls and establish a military front within the city, once done, our task is to locate the Venethari forces and unveil their movements and cut off the route of their main reinforcements, that being the Evercrag Pass. You will be accompanying Fen, until further notice.

Allow yourself and your garrison a week to prepare, whilst I establish other means of work to support the campaign.

I look forward to fighting by your side yet again, Gordon.

Gallus Fen-Frenone, Lord of Vortighna and Governor of Fen.''

Gordon places the letter in the pocket of his scraggly fishing jacket, thanking the messenger. ''We'll be there,'' he says as he returns to untangling the nets, once done he excuses himself back to the keep. It was time to prepare.

Only a handful would remain to man the gates of Fen Craic, Lucotorix stays behind to take charge of things along with the staff.

Olm enters his home, Ilda, Ymitre and his youngest daughter Helia stood in their living quarters, all consoling their loving father, saying their goodbyes.

''Vistra be with you, father,'' Ymitre expresses sadly, a small tear escaping her big brown eyes. ''Please come home safe.''

Olm bends down to her stroking her cheek with his thumb. ''I always come home safe, my girl.''

''It's different now, Olm,'' says Ilda. ''You're fighting our own… It doesn't feel right.''

''And fighting for Kastrith does? Look, it is what it is. We're safe, that's all that matters my love,'' he kisses Ymitre on the forehead as he rises to his wife.

''I know, be careful Olm, I love you,'' Ilda pleads.

''I love you too,'' he says to Ilda as he ruffles Helia's hair. ''And you be a good girl now, no teasing your mother while I'm gone, okay?'' He says to his youngest, Helia

''Yes, father,'' Helia squeaks innocently.

Olm picks Helia up in his giant arms, embracing her one last time.

Ilda and Olm share a kiss and a longing embrace, he then departs, heading toward the stable.

The army was ready, a small but strong four hundred stood under the banner of Gordon Ard-Barker. oathsworn, melee Infantry, the painted faithful, archers, spearmen and a small unit of melee cavalry, and even some dreaded black tusk war boars, A type of boar native to Darogoth, exceptionally large and can even be ridden. The only thing Gordon was missing that he truly wanted by his side, were charioteers.

Supply wagons equipped with tents, food and other necessities finished packing, the army began their move, slowly but surely following the river Bi for many miles northward, right up to the border of Glaen and Fen.

Marching the river banks Gordon would frequently look back behind him as he trots gracefully upon his horse, admiring the beauty of his small army bearing his wicked banner of the white wolf.

''I can't believe I'm leading an army to battle. This is… I don't even have words.''

''You sound like a fucking teenager,'' Brennus laughs.

''Fuck off,'' Gordon returns the banter.

Brennus sneers. ''Well, just wait until we get to the main camp, every lord in Fen and their own will be there.''

''How many are estimated?''

''I reckon about a hundred thousand, Ard and Dun's armies will be larger, probably around three hundred thousand.''

''We're really throwing that many people into Glaen?''

''We're not fucking around anymore, Walker. We've been skirmishing and fighting in Glaen for a while now. We've had talks, ceasefires... back and forths... and now we've had enough, they need to be kicked out of Glaen so we can take back our side of Evercrag Pass, otherwise this war will end quickly in their favour.''

''I hope Vocorix got my letter, I wrote to him suggesting he should bolster Dun's defence while the bulk is in Glaen.''

''Good shout, you're probably right, but with luck Dakiva can pull their weight well on the seas, even if a Mavrosi armada tries to loop around to Dun. They're fearsome in naval warfare. There's a reason Dakiva has never been conquered or invaded before.''

''Really?''

''Yeah, they're damn good in those ships of theirs,'' something catches Brennus's eye in the distance, he squints as he peers onward. ''I think we've arrived, Walker. There's a lot of smoke in the distance.''

The army paced their way toward the smoke, as they got closer it became clear it was a war camp, the armies of Fen were present.

Travel tents dotted around all over with multiple fire pits spewing smoke into the air. Warriors of all kinds drinking and going about their work, the neighing of thousands of horses and chatter of tens of thousands of hardy men and women.

Gordon strut onward, passing the barricades proudly as he and his small army bear the white wolf banner.

''Where do we go?'' Gordon asks.

''Find Gallus, look for his banner, he'll tell us where to set up our part of the camp. I'm guessing we won't be here long, looks like half of Fen is already here.''

The warriors he passed on his way all looked upon his banner in awe, they all knew who this was, this was the banner of the famed realm walker. Many knew of Gordon's exploits and his new found reputation, Gordon noted that few would scowl at him, some even spitting upon the floor. ''This is weird, doesn't look like some of them seem too happy to see me…''

''You're an outsider who's risen to lordship within such a short time. Those cunts are just jealous, don't worry yourself with the opinions of lesser folk, you do what you need to do.''

Although taken back by the sudden disdain from the random common folk, he soon lets it pass and focuses on finding where to go.

''Ah, there's Gallus's banner, that didn't take too long,'' Gordon spots the tri-fish banner of the Frenone clan.

Gallus see's Gordon and his army arrive, he welcomes them with open arms. ''You've arrived! Good to see, and look at this… all these are yours, eh?'' He remarks on the number of Gordon's loyal warriors.

''We've had many refugees of Glaen come to Fen Craic.''

''Good to see the people of Glaen taking up the fight!'' He smiles proudly. ''Great, well if you don't mind setting up a temporary encampment next to the Alios clan by the eastern side, you'll want to keep an eye out for the green and brown banner with two boars eating an apple on it, and then place your banners by your camp so we know you're accounted for. We're hoping to move as soon as possible within the next few days, we're just waiting on a few more lords. Relax yourselves while you're here, we've a long road ahead.''

''Of course, Gallus. Good to see you again.''

''And you, Gordon!''

Gordon catches Eithne in the corner of his eye, leaning deviously against a tree trunk by her tent intently watching around as if sniffing out prey. He gives a subtle nod of greeting from atop his horse, she responds with a cunning smile.

He directs his horse eastward further through the masses of warriors and nobility, looking for the Alios clan; eventually they find the banner brandishing two boars with the apple and set up camp on a nearby clearing.

They get a large fire going as they prop up their tents.

''How are you feeling, Walker?'' Asks Brennus slumping himself beside Gordon on a rugged log.

''Fine… strangely.'' Gordon replies, staring at the boar skewered on the spit above the fire.

''Why strange?''

‘’I usually have a little bit of anxiety before I know there’s going to be fighting, but I feel nothing.’’

‘’Probably getting used to it.’’

‘’No, Brennus. I feel numb, I feel like-’’

‘’A killer,’’ Brennus interrupts. ‘’When I was a lad, after my first few battles I felt exactly the same, after a while the numbing evolves and becomes part of your nature, you learn that this is what we’re supposed to do, protect ourselves, the ones we love, your way of life.’’

‘’I’ve never been a fighter.’’

‘’So, you keep reminding me, but now look at you.’’

Gordon purses his lips as he stares onward hypnotically into the campfire leaning over his log stool. ‘’Still fucks me up, all this.’’

‘’Yeah… I can imagine…’’ Brennus says, rolling his eye and peering up to the moonlit sky appreciating the beauty of the moon as he gives a sigh of contempt, he then returns his sight to the horizon. ‘’Is that Eithne?’’

Gordon pulls out of his trance, frisking around. ‘’Where?’’

Brennus bursts out in a giant laugh. ‘’Why so paranoid? I’m joking….’’

‘’Dick head.’’

‘’You like her, eh? I knew you had an eye for her, I don’t blame you, she's a pretty woman. Scary… but pretty.’’

''No, I mean, yeah, she's pretty but… I have a girlfriend back home. It's not a crime to appreciate other people's looks, is it? Yeah, she's alright.''

''Walker… it's been a long time, and like you said to me before, she's probably moved on by now.''

''I don't know, I don't even know if I'm even truly alive….''

Brennus slaps Gordon's face. ''Feel that?''

''Ow you cunt! Yes!''

''Then you're not dead. You're here, Walker. So, do as you will, want my advice? Chase some tail, might relieve some of that pent up stress of yours,'' he pats Gordon's chest. ''She's a fine woman, not my type personally, but she's nice,'' Brennus rises from his seat, stretching out his arms.

''You have a type? I thought you were the kind of guy to just fuck anything. A woman of this world wouldn't be interested in me anyway, it's almost like… bestiality or some shit.''

Brennus breaks his stretch off with laughter. ''Oh Walker, you can be funny! Have you not seen the way she looks at you? Compare that with the way she looks at others. Plus, she barely speaks to anyone, but apparently you two have had lots to talk about,'' he gives a humorous gesture with his hands. ''Open your eyes, you little fuck,'' he smiles.

''She looks like she wants to rip out my jugular sometimes.''

''Probably does,'' Brennus grins. ''Right, I'm getting an early sleep, I'm fucked… good night.''

''See you,'' Gordon chuckles.

Gordon stayed put, staring on into the fire. He began meditating, allowing the flow of magic to pulsate around his very form, feeling the power in every waking muscle and freeing it into the atmosphere, testing the boundaries of his willpower, strengthening his hold. After a few hours, he moved on to his tent and slept the night away.

After a few idle days mingling around the campsite with the neighbouring lords, the time to march had come, eastward bound to set up a forward base within Glaen.

Vocorix had sent his orders, the armies of Fen were to retake Northus. Ard and Dun would operate out of Ollus, and would split off to protect neighbouring villages from raids, assisting the remaining settlements of Glaen that remained under Darogoth control.

The main Venethari force was yet to be found and their movements determined, before setting out to siege Northus, Gallus ordered Eithne that very task, and so she left with a small party of scouts, deeper into enemy territory.

Gallus was determined not to use siege weapons to destroy the walls and gates of Northus, for innocent Darogothians still walked its streets under Venethari oppression, Gallus didn't want to risk taking the lives of innocents.

According to reports, only a small defence remained to keep watch. Gallus saw this as an opportunity, but for how long and why there was a small defence, Gallus could only guess.

He wanted to take a subtle approach. The lords of Fen had gathered in Gallus's tent discussing possible strategies.

''If we could get a small number in, maybe we could open the gates and have the rest of us rush in. They won't be aware of us just yet, but time is of the essence, no doubt Venethari scouts will spot us soon enough,'' suggests Gallus.

''How do we get inside? Do you propose we use ladders?'' Says Ambunix.

''In the dead of night? With Gordon in there the chances of success would be a lot higher,'' replies Contelios, Lord of Westwatch.

''Agreed, but still too dangerous… how can we make it more… subtle?'' Gallus responds, brushing his chin with the palm of his hand.

''What other choices do we have for a subtle approach? We could spend weeks building siege towers but I don't think we have the time and we don't know if the main force is to return,'' Says Orgeirios, Lord of Elra.

Gallus scrunches his face in thought. ''We'd waste a lot of resources and warriors with siege towers… my scouts will report the movements of the main force. Until they return, we don't know anything, what we do know is that the city is lacking a proper defence right now, we don't have the time to consider structures that would take weeks. What do we all think to climbing the walls with a small party at night.''

''Northus sits on the river Bi? Could we not get someone in that way?'' Ambunix suggests. ''Propping a ladder against its walls is too risky. We don't have a clear view of the guards, we'd be taking blind guesses of where to assemble the ladders, and not only that we need to approach unseen.

''Eithne reported the river gates were shut tight at the sides, and yes… you're correct… it is very risky, but with an operation like this what isn't going to be risky?''

''But those gates are significantly less reinforced than the main gates, yes?'' Replies Ambunix

''I could heat the metal with magic and break it open,'' says Gordon.

''And you could do that… silently?'' Asks Gallus.

''Yeah….''

''Those gates would take considerable heat… are you sure you have the power to maintain such magic?''

''Yes….''

''What am I saying, of course you do… would it exhaust much of you though?''

''I should be fine. Do we have mages? War seers with us?''

''Yes.''

''Then send me two war seers for support and a few warriors who can stay low.''

Gallus sways his cheeks for a moment until addressing the tent. ''Lords of Fen?''

''Aye!'' They all chant.

''We haven't got much fucking choice really, have we? I have faith in the realm walker!'' Ambunix booms.

''They could even steal and don some Venethari armour once inside if they're capable,'' Mentions Orgeirios, adjusting her posture in resonance with the war council.

''Good point. If it helps them get to the gatehouse faster, of course. But the more they kill, the more at risk they are of being caught,'' Gallus remarks.

''If we catch a soldier on their own, I'm sure we can persuade them to give me their armour,'' Gordon smirks.

''Would make this entire thing a lot easier for you, but don't make that your priority, stay hidden and get that gate open, once it's opened the rest of us will storm the gates,'' Gallus advises.

Gordon nods in agreement.

Gallus stares toward the door of the tent, noticing the rain starting to pick up outside. ''Would you go tonight?''

''Yeah....''

''Good... we'll get everyone ready, break through the river gates, open the main gate, and we'll rush in. Hold them off as long as you can and if you run into trouble, we'll be with you as soon as we can.''

Everyone left Gallus's war tent and immediately began preparations, Gordon was supplied with two support mages, or war seers as they are known in Darogoth, mages of druidic background, and three warriors all equipped lightly.

All that remained was for the sun to set, the rain got heavier, filling the sky with an endless hail. This aided the operation greatly, making it much harder to see at night and muffling the noises that usually amplify through the night time silence, many believed it was a gift from the Altharn itself, a sign.

''You know me, Walker. All that sneaking around isn't quite my forte, be careful in there,'' Brennus approaches, giving Gordon some final words of confidence.

''Thanks, I'll manage....''

''You'll be fine! Go now, the rain is heavy and the mist of the rainfall is strong, this is perfect!''

''Right... let's go!'' Gordon shouts to his newly given companions. ''Down the bank, lay low by the river!''

The group gave a light jog toward the river bank to stay out of sight, keeping themselves low, ducking down the banks, veiled by the heavy rain. They tried hard to get a view of the walls of Northus to see if they could spot the guards, it was almost impossible to see anything, so surely the guards won't be able to see them either.

The mud of the banks encumbered their pace, squelching and grasping at their feet as they soldiered through the rain forged bog as quickly as they could to reach the river gate, the gate was massive, stretching almost half the width of the Bi, they all stood aside for a moment, wondering where to begin.

Gordon picked out the right corner and approached with caution, submerging half of himself within the river. The gate was as thick as two stone walls plastered together, he glanced at the war seers, their faces folded in pessimism.

Gordon wastes no more time, he places his hands around one of the thick iron segments, squeezing hard and focusing on the flow of his magic, weaving the ethereal flow into his hands, sizzling the metal as his heat begins to build. The rain was extinguishing his heat, and the gate was in no way showing any signs of damage just yet. He pushed harder and harder, matching his power to the thickness of the metal, and fighting the encumbering drench of rainfall. Eventually a molten glow began to shine out as steam spewed rapidly, the war seers joined in, flowing their magic to Gordon, stabilising his own.

Gordon had to produce extra strain on his arcane abilities to muffle out the loud sizzling and creaking of the gate as the metal weakened, combining this with protecting himself against the heat… it took a lot of effort.

They pushed harder and harder, the molten glow now a gleaming yellow, it began to budge and bend. Gordon pulled as hard as he could, snapping the piece of metal in half, and pushing as much of it out the way as he could.

‘’Argh!’’ He winces as he flaps his hands from the pain.

''Can you continue, Lord?'' Says Drellix, a war seer that was assisting. A druid becoming a war seer was regarded as one of the most honourable achievements druids could make. Donning the classic and notable uniform of the war seer regiment, a chainmail hauberk with plated shoulders, all cleverly sewn in with the classic druidic white robes, shortened at the knees for practical purposes. He sheltered his head with his white hood, leaving his crystal blue eyes and freshly shaven face the only notable features of his appearance not shadowed away.

''Yeah… we've got to get a few more of these bars to break and bend and we should be able to make a space to climb through, how are you?''

''I'm fine, Lord. I'm not tiring yet.''

''Good. Again, this one here.''

The seers and Gordon continue to work slowly but surely through the giant gate to create an entrance point, after a good while of stress and strain, they finally achieve success.

''Your willpower is astounding, it's true what they say, and to see it for myself…'' says Drellix, lost for words, slouched over with his hands to his thighs. ''I mean… throwing a ball of fire is lightly burdening to a developed mage, but to hold such power for extended time and not only that, but fighting with this rain too…''

''Let's waste no time, when you're ready,'' Gordon replies abruptly.

''Apologies... let's go, Lord,'' he picks himself up, straightening his back.

''Men, you ready?'' Gordon asks the three warriors waiting patiently by the wall.

''Aye,'' they all whisper together.

Gordon squeezes through first, lowering his body and checking the perimeter of the river gates, the others follow on, slowly creeping through.

The rain was pounding with tremendous force, coming down so hard it felt like pins jabbing at their skin.

The group crept inward weaving around the houses of the residential section of Northus, nestling amongst the drooping thatch roofs, this section looked rather depraved in general, the houses more primitive, similar to those of Seers Crossing but even more simple looking. The stone work was shoddy, almost like someone had just dumped down a pile of rocks and placed some thatch above it. Houses across the river were more large, well rounded and intricate in their architecture, with looming canopies and their own personal gardens, so far, no guards were in sight. They made their way up from the river docks and into the edges of the market district of Northus, they still had not seen any guards.

''Where are the guards?'' Whispers Toccus, a warrior bearing a lengthy dagger in one hand and a jagged axe on his hip. He was one of the painted faithful. Warriors so dedicated to battle that they had their torsos completely exposed and smeared in blue paint, bearing only their torc. They rely completely on speed and ferocity in battle, and are usually pumped full of rust. He had short brown curly hair and a typically oversized moustache.

‘’Maybe they’re only stationed on the walls? The rest will be using the barracks and the tavern no doubt,’’ Gordon replies.

‘’There are some stairs to the walls just over there,’’ Drellix notes. ‘’It should loop around to the gatehouse.’’

The men bend down low and rush to the stairs, ducking low and taking a speedier approach as the rain fall shadowed their movements.

Toccus decides to crawl ahead in prone to take a look upon the wall, a Venethari guard almost catches sight of him as he patrols the wall, the guards sight blinded by his cloak which he had folded over his head to shelter against the rain.

Toccus lays low, watching the guard until his back is turned. He gets up and crouches his way toward the guard, driving his dagger through the side of the guard's neck, while giving one hard chop to the waist with his axe.

As the guard drops, Toccus signals to Gordon and the others.

The group pressed on up to the first tower on the southern wall, inside they could hear the talks and laughter of more guards underneath the shelter.

‘’What do we do now?!’’ Asks Toccus.

‘’Seers… with me, let’s make this quick, one big push from the three of us.’’

The seers nod and follow on.

The three approach the tower. ''On my count, we burst in, and use force to throw them all down, or even out the nooks, okay?''

They nod again.

''Three, two, one....''

Gordon gives a mighty kick, smashing the door open and revealing their identity, they all rush in. The guards all look to each other in confusion at first, but then all rise in aggression.

Before they can even draw their weapons Gordon and the seers magic combined, explodes forward a massive shock wave, sending all of the guards flying backward, four of which flew directly off the tower through the nooks and to their agonising deaths below. The two remaining who had smashed into the reinforced beams were quickly stabbed down.

''That was a lot louder than I was hoping for… shit,'' sighs Gordon. ''We have to move now, I can see the gatehouse, it's our next stop, quickly!''

''At least they didn't sound the alarm!'' Drellix pants as he runs off with Gordon, followed by the rest.

''Quickly, all of you through here!'' Gordon bursts through the gatehouse doors, undenounced to him it was full of guards taking shelter from the rain, allot more than he could have expected, two of which were about to open the door to investigate the noise from the tower.

''Fuck.''

The guards draw their weapons. Gordon slows his perception and sends forth another shockwave pushing them all out of his way, the fighting ensues as the team all storm in.

He drew Brother from his scabbard preparing him to taste the blood of the Venethari, instantly slashing a guard's unarmoured legs as he made his way up from the floor, finishing him off, burying his face with fire.

As Gordon bravely takes on the majority of guards eager to surround him, the others take advantage, thrusting, slashing and countering with all their skill.

Toccus darts up the stairs of the gate house trying to slip past the fighting to open the gate.

Once up top he finds a lonely Venethari, watching the handle to the gate locking mechanism, the two share a glance until Toccus charges him with his axe. The guard holds his blade out in defence and manoeuvres around Toccus, carefully parrying away the speedy and vigorous slashes, after a successful chambering he gives a well-directed lunge to Toccus' exposed belly. Fortunately, Toccus was swift enough to pivot out of the way, catching the guard's sword arm; with his dagger, he then brought forward his serrated axe, chopping multiple fingers in one hefty swing.

The guard was now completely incapacitated, kneeling to the floor in submission, holding onto his gored hand in agony. Toccus gives a deadly flurry with his axe, hacking the life away from the guard in a vicious and merciless onslaught. Once the guard was dealt with, he unlocked the gate and ran back down the stairs to the second load of locks that sat upon the gate itself.

''They're taking a while. Is the gate open yet?'' Gallus asks.

''I can't see my Lord. The rain, it's too heavy,'' says one of Gallus's oathsworn in concern.

''Send a runner. Now! They are not to return until that gate is visibly open.''

''Of course.''

Gordon took a few cuts around his body facing multiple attackers. He slowed his perception, blocking every swing coming his way in many directions, a feat observed in real time was absolutely morale hindering for the Venethari.

He gives a punch to one's face, stabs another in the thigh, draws his blade from the thigh to deflect an incoming blow toward his head, the metals clink as they connect in rapid succession. He slides down the enemy blade with his own, parrying the blow away and bringing his hilt upward, jamming the pronged cross guard into one's eye. Gordon yanks his sword back, strafing backwards to give himself some space.

The others had taken into the fight well, the seers were not using their magic in fear of exhaustion, the men were outnumbered but were holding off as best they possibly could. Toccus releases the lock and successfully opens the gate, diving straight back into the fight, jumping on the back of an enemy and stabbing him relentlessly to the floor, screaming wildly like a disgruntled boar.

In a matter of moments, a loud roar rumbles from outside, it was the army of Fen charging the gates, thousands upon thousands tearing through to liberate their city of Glaen.

As soon as the Venethari realised what was happening, they instantly dropped their weapons in surrender, shouting out loud, pleading for their lives, holding their hands above their heads.

The barracks from within the city erupted in panic and many Venethari rushed to the gates in defence, many even attempted to flee the city.

''All Venethari will perish within Northus this night!'' Cries Toccus.

''These ones have surrendered,'' Gordon remarks awkwardly.

Toccus ignores Gordon, driving his dagger into the eyes of a vulnerable soldier, he screams at the top of his lungs in sheer anguish.

''What the fuck are you doing!?!'' Gordon shouts, furious at such malice.

Toccus, consumed by his thirst, takes his dagger to another surrendered Venethari.

Gordon subdues Toccus to his knees using magic.

''Let me kill them! Let me kill them! My Mother! My Sister! My fucking Father, dead! You fucking rats! I'll feast on your fucking corpse, horse fuckers!'' Toccus spits ferociously as he thrashes around on the floor, attempting break from Gordon's magical grip.

''Calm down!''

''Have you lost your family to these bastards?!?! No! They've taken my family. My home!''

''I lost everything, Toccus! Because of Darogoth!''

Toccus stops thrashing around and comes to a still. He pauses and stares Gordon square in the eyes, realising what he meant by his stern words. ''Lord?''

''I lost everything and everyone I ever knew and loved, all because of Darogoth. Yet here I am fighting for you and your people with my life,'' Gordon throws Toccus off to the side. ''So, get the fuck up, and listen to my orders! You will not kill these who've surrendered!''

Toccus rises promptly, lowering his head. ''Forgive me, Lord. I'm stricken with grief. These monsters… My Family, I'm of Glaen… I….'' he begins to visibly tremble with embarrassment and shame.

Gordon scrunches his eyes tightly at himself, lacking the confidence in the authority he was laying down. ''Forgiven, bind the captives. I don't want any of you joining the fight in the city. We've all done enough, I'm… sorry, Toccus.''

''Walker!'' The door bursts open and right off its hinges.

It's Brennus, with a face drenched in rain and blood. ''I knew you could do it! Well done to you men as well! Very tough work! I'm impressed!!'' He beams with excitement.

''Are you okay?'' Groans Gordon.

''Am I okay?! Ha! Are you okay?! We've just taken Northus back with barley any fucking effort!''

''You're welcome,'' says Gordon sarcastically.

''I know I know! It was all down to you brave fuckers here! Well done men, well done!'' He claps. ''Let's get down to the tavern for a little celebration! The women will be more than happy to greet their liberators!'' He bellows as he bursts out of the room as quickly as he entered.

Gordon gives Toccus a friendly pat to the back as he leaves with Brennus.

''Lord… Gordon,'' Drellix approaches off from the side.

''Yeah?''

''You may not remember me, but I remember you. I was going to say something earlier, but thought it was best to leave it until we had finished our business here.''

''What is it?''

''I was at Seers Crossing… I survived by playing dead, a horse even trampled on my legs whilst I lay on the floor, breaking every bone in my strong leg here, yet by the grace of Fanara, I stayed silent through all that agony… I managed to crawl all the way to the nearest village.''

''By Fanara….'' Gordon extends his hand in greeting, bringing Drellix in for a manly greet.

''You've grown so much… I remember the night you arrived; you woke half the village.''

Gordon gives an awkward smile. ‘’Ha… Sorry.’’

‘’You should be proud of yourself.’’

‘’Thank you, Drellix. Where are you living now?’’

‘’After Seers Crossing, I went to Lunarum for a year to train as a war seer once my leg healed up, then moved to Westwatch working under Lord Contelios Fen-Dellen.’’

‘’Amazing, I'm glad you survived… It truly was a tragedy, unlike anything I've ever experienced, it still shakes me to the core to this very day. Do you know of any others who made it out?’’

‘’Indeed… those kinds of events haunt you till the end of time so they say, my friend Sheilen got out, she still resides in Lunarum… but other than her, you’re the only person I’ve known to escape.’’ Drellix exclaims as he lowers his hood, revealing his ginger locks all braided back in a fine and noble fashion.

‘’Did you know Lucotorix?’’

‘’The arch druid's apprentice? Yeah, everyone knew him.’’

‘’He’s alive. He’s my druid in Fen Craic!’’

‘’You’re serious?!’’

‘’I’m serious,’’ Gordon nods enthusiastically.

‘’I must come and visit sometime. How did he get out!?!’’

‘’He got captured and was sold to Mavrosi slave traders, he managed to join an escape plan with some other captives and got out.’’

''Unbelievable... of course Lucotorix got away! He was always slipping and sliding out of trouble!'' Drellix laughs. ''Gordon... come, let's share a drink.''

''Aye! Let's!''

Gordon and Drellix make their way to the tavern of Northus celebrating its liberation with the others and the locals.

A great and victorious first step into the campaign.

The captives are bound and thrown to the dungeons, the entire army move their supplies into Northus and immediately station themselves inside, bolstering the garrison. The city celebrates its liberation wildly, as if it were their final days on Altharn.

After the first night Gordon mostly reframed from attending so many celebrations in fear of the battles that lay ahead, wondering what was to happen next. He had suffered many bruises and bumps to his body due to the collision of weapons against his armour, his torso was covered in injuries of all shapes and sizes, with a large black bruise stretching over his shoulder and under his ribs. The pain was almost unbearable whenever he inhaled a breath of air, he wondered how much this would affect him and how long for, and even more so, how much more could he take?

It was relieving to meet Drellix, a former druid of Seers Crossing, they had a lot to share with each other. Their knowledge of herblore, their mutual relations with the people they both knew. Gordon didn't recognise Drellix but looking upon Drellix's youthful and freshened smile it shimmered nothing but the signs of freedom and virtue, leashing back one of the many demons that thrashed within Gordon's soul.

The army of Fen would wait in Northus until news of the success reached the high king.

In their time waiting, Eithne returned. She reported that Venethar were massing within and around Pathirii, another Darogothic city under Venethari control. A huge force was also due to travel through the Evercrag Pass and join up with the invasion, they suspected Northus would be placed under siege.

News also arrived that Dakivan ships had encountered a small fleet from Mavros Avir, attempting to disembark on the southern shores of Dun. It turns out Lucotorix was right all along.

Days later a messenger arrived from Vocorix, instructing Fen to leave behind a strong force within Northus to secure a garrison and make their way to the north of Northwood, to block out the Evercrag Pass and halt enemy reinforcements.

The plan was to meet Venethar on the move as they made their way back toward Northus. to isolate their forces and close in on what's remaining in Glaen. Vocorix insisted that all forces surround the Northwood and catch the enemy on ground that Darogoth knew they could fight efficiently in. Fen would enter from the north after securing Evercrag pass. Ard would loop around to Northus and attack from the west and Dun would watch Pathirii from afar and in turn loop around to the south of Northwood.

Communication is key to Darogoth's success, there had been no word of Kastrith's whereabouts or even if he was to join the battle. Vocorix was adamant in his vigilance, this battle could end everything, or it could do nothing, Kastrith was not a predictable man.

24: Northwood

The armies that remained of Glaen marched throughout the lands, retaking settlements lost, besieging forts and facing the bloodiest of skirmishes. All out fighting was in full swing across the province of Glaen, the land itself suffered greatly under the struggle of the two kingdoms, tugging the ropes of war.

Sadly, those who suffered the most in such trying times would always be the common folk, losing their homes, their families, and even their lives, caught in the crossfire of conflict.

At the siege of Fort Glaen Carrick in the east, the Governor of Glaen, Trabelos Glaen-Fern, had lost his life and was executed upon defeat. The forces of Darogoth began their movements, ready to take the frontal force of the main horde, all armies were now attempting to retreat from the fighting in order to get a strong foothold for the main horde. This meant sacrificing a lot of retaken land in order for the battle to shift more favourably, but was it really a sound strategy?

Forces of Fen made their way to the Evercrag Pass, leaving Ambunix and his garrison to stand in wait, watching out for enemy reinforcements whilst they locate the horde within Northwood.

Eithne returns to Gallus after scouting ahead. ''We have a tribe of trolls lurking just a few miles ahead, we need to divert.''

‘’Trolls?’’ Gordon exclaims.

‘’Yeah, you don’t fuck with trolls. They fuck with you,’’ says Brennus.

‘’But surely an army as big as ours can handle a few trolls….’’

‘’That’s not the point. They’d devastate a good number of us and create too much of a commotion. A commotion we can’t afford to let happen; do you have any idea how thick a troll's hide is? Let's hope we don’t find out… they like to play with their food,’’ he adds

Gordon and Brennus listen in on Eithne’s report to Gallus.

‘’We can’t step any further forward south; they could have gotten a scent for me.’’

‘’That’s not good… this could ruin everything,’’ Gallus ponders for a moment as he sits atop his horse. ‘’Fine, we'll take the eastern route, but we’ll have to return south as soon as possible.’’

Eithne nods, returning to her posting ahead of the army.

And so, Fen diverted, a lengthy journey eastward through the Northwood, until being halted again a few miles into the dense forest.

The entire Venethari camp had been found and were settled within, Eithne brought Gallus, Gordon, and some other notable officials forward to view from a hillside vantage point.

It was hard to see so far away and with so many trees blocking the view, but smoke was clear in the tree lines and they could faintly make out yurts, travel tents and soldiers alike. The more they looked on, the bigger the force of the Venethari appeared.

''Why have they come this way? And why have they stopped here?'' Asks Gallus.

''It looks like they're going to instead march north, toward Evercrag? I'm certain they're trying to find a way to collect us all together at the pass, don't know why though… not sure I want to find out either,'' Eithne proposes.

''You're right, something is very off about this. Well… that's cause for concern,'' Gallus responds.

''What do we do? Dun and Ard should be near… but not near enough… what are your orders?'' Eithne asks.

Gallus pauses, angst and dread showering his thoughts. ''I don't know… surely the others will recognise their change of movements? Maybe we try and lure them… throw them off somehow?''

''I have an idea…'' Gordon interrupts.

''Gordon?''

''Yeah… it's a little crazy, so bear with me.''

''What is it?'' Gallus narrows his beady eyes.

''Those trolls, what If I lured them through the forest and into their camp?''

‘’You’d sooner find an arrow in between your eyes,’’ Eithne scoffs.

‘’But I have magic, I could use magic to shield myself and storm through the camp and the trolls could do the hard work.’’

‘’Gordon….’’ Eithne sighs.

‘’Nonsense, its suicide,’’ Gallus adds.

‘’If we can’t afford to have the trolls attack us, then surely, it’s the same for them, especially if they’re not expecting it.’’

Eithne rolls her eyes. ‘’And then they will chase you down. They’re not stupid, they’ll see a man bearing the armour of Darogoth and point their arrows accordingly, and they’ll know exactly who you are if you go about displaying such magic. You may have power, but performing heroics as reckless as this would just get you killed?!’’

‘’Aye… and we can use that to our advantage.’’

Gallus approaches Gordon, suppressing his bushy brows. ‘’What?!’’

‘’Set up an ambush!’’ Gordon flails his hands.

Gallus envisions Gordon’s request. ‘’It could work… still Gordon, this is madness?!’’

‘’Think about it, the trolls will create a great distraction. All I need to do is run through and get out as quickly as I can, and with the magic I have, I can do that. Isn’t this what I’m for? If you’re going to rip me from my home world, at least use me efficiently! We’ll take down a large quantity of them without risking our own. If I can execute this just right, we'll have the best advantage over them possible, especially if the other forces join in, clamping them down in the Northwood, we'll have them in the palm of our hands!''

''That is actually rather plausible... if it works.''

Eithne steps up to Gordon. ''One arrow, that's all it takes. One arrow planted into you or your horse... if they take down your horse you're dead, even if you do manage to kill many on your own, at least until you become exhausted. Why would you risk yourself so carelessly after all you're seeking to accomplish?''

Gordon's face drops into a neutral state. ''Dying like this doesn't sound too bad.''

''What are you saying?'' Gallus snaps.

''Just let me do this, Gallus.''

Gallus stares into Gordons soft blue eyes, noticing a trauma that haunts his once innocent being. There was a peculiar glaze over Gordon's eyes, a haunting presence.

''I can't believe I'm even considering this...'' Gallus scoffs at himself. ''Devastating the enemy as much as we can right now would really waver their entire invasion... if we're going to do this, we need to do it properly.''

''Gallus?!'' Eithne jumps but is interrupted by Gordon.

''Eithne,'' Gordon silences her.

She stares at him in utter bewilderment. ''You want to die?''

''No… but this world is not my own.''

''But-''

''But nothing, you don't understand. You know nothing of my home or where I've come from, you and everyone else only tell me how lucky I am to be away from that. I get it! Okay I g-''

''Enough! Bickering like children, pathetic. We have an invasion on our hands, I've made my decision, it's time to leave before we're scouted. I need to inform the high king of what's now transpiring, I'll let him know we'll be the first to face the horde. If we are to act, we need to act now.''

The sun begins to set. It was time to put the new plan in motion.

Although initially perplexed at the extravagant tactic, Brennus and Olm bravely offered to ride by Gordon's side in support. They both took hold the largest shields they could wield, mounting the sturdiest horses available and reinforced their already heavy-duty armours.

Drellix also offered to ride with them, wielding magical support from behind, to which they agreed. With Gordon affront, two heavies either side with large shields and Drellix at the rear, they felt their adrenaline surge at the thought, inspiring a motivation amongst themselves.

And so, the four separated from camp, travelling back in search of the beasts of Northwood.

Brennus is the first to sniff them out from a distance, quite literally. ''There they are, ugly cunts,'' he says after following a pungent stench of mould and rot accompanied by the feral sounds of grunts and beastly natter.

They peek out their heads, weaving around the tree trunks atop their horses trying to get a decent view from afar. The trolls hadn't noticed them yet as they potter around going about their beastly business, building shelters and preparing food, a herd of deer were piled up on the floor, many of them bearing no skin at all, their raw skins being used by the trolls to create their shelters. They were viscous and eerie looking things. Like giant gorillas with mossy green matted fur, their arms elongated at twice the length of their legs. They were well stocked with pounds upon pounds of muscle and the worst part was their concave faces. Angry looking beasts with flattened nostrils that wheezed and flared, their ivory tusks protruding from their mouth, and two large bulging black eyes, like that of a spider. The sight of such creatures sent shivers through all men, except Gordon, a strange aura filled Gordon this day.

''How are you expecting to get the entire tribe to chase you down?'' Whispers Olm, nervously stroking the reigns of his mount.

''If he kills one of their young, that should piss them off enough,'' suggests Drellix.

Gordon's feet thump upon the dry floor as he dismounts, taking a closer look.

''Well, that's fucking dark,'' Brennus Scoffs in jest.

''They're trolls, they do worse to our people, if anything were to stop future generations being picked apart by these monsters,'' Drellix replies.

''Fair point.''

''There!'' Shrieks Gordon.

Without hesitation he drags the young troll by the force of magic, the innocent beast frantically kicks and flails as it attempts to wriggle free, squealing out for the protection of its guardians. Gordon reveals himself from the bushes making sure its tribe watches on as he skewers it in the head with his blade. It wails desperately in its nasally tone as it fights for its life, the squeal of the infant troll was deafening to say the least, like a mix of a dying pig and a cat in heat.

An urge deep inside fuelled Gordon against any remorse for the young creature. His fears subsided, his care non-existent, the monstrous trolls before him didn't shake a single hair upon his body. His face is void of all but fury and hopelessness.

A mighty roar unlike any other ruptured through the trees.

''Could of gave us a fucking warning, Walker!'' Brennus shouts as he rears his horse ready to flee.

Gordon darts back to Epona, his blood pumping with adrenaline as he jumps atop her saddle frantically beating her with his heels to gallop as fast as she could.

The trolls make way with impeccable speed. A speed Gordon may have underestimated greatly.

They gallop frantically for miles as they flee the pursuing beasts. The trolls didn't give up, tearing up the very ground in a relentless and bloodthirsty rage.

Gordon gave a small blast of magic from time to time to keep the trolls invested in the chase, they made their way toward the Venethari encampment, the time was now.

A Venethari soldier sat by a campfire roasting some pheasant on a spit, turning it gently as he sipped back the nourishing gulps of water from his leatherbound canteen, blissfully unaware of the carnage racing forth to shatter his reality.

The ground began to quake. ''The fuck is that?'' He pricks his ears to a rumbling noise in the distance.

He dawdles a few yards away, to the opening of the camp, drawing his recurve bow, peering out to the forest now swallowed by the shadow of the setting sun.

Bursting from the tree line arrives Gordon, Brennus, Olm and Drellix, and an entire herd of ferocious beasts, ripping trees from the very roots of the ground as they propel their momentum forward in chase.

''What!?! The fu- lads! Lads!'' He scurries back into camp. ''On your feet! Enemy incoming!!'' The soldier screams.

Gordon's eyes flash purple as he surges his magicka to an astronomical level, arching forward within his saddle, charging through the entrance of the encampment. Propelling out a shield of force ahead of him, blowing away everything in his path of arcane destruction, deflecting the many projectiles that now fired his way by the many defenders scurrying for their lives. Remnants of barricades, tents, and all kinds of debris scattered all around as they hurl out from the mighty explosion of Gordon's magically surged charge.

They smash through the camp and the trolls follow on as planned. Instantly the Venethari react in panic, throwing javelins, axes, arrows, all of which bounce away as Gordon charges on.

The trolls pour into the camp, consuming all in their path of brutality, sending soldiers bound for the skies, and tearing down yurts. The longer the chase went on the more the trolls became distracted as they were attacked by the Venethari in a desperate attempt to get the situation under control.

Absolute chaos was running rampant, the matriarch however wasn't giving up with Gordon firmly in her sights, the taste of revenge foaming at her snarled mouth. Further they galloped into the camp, soldier and worker alike diving out of the way and fleeing from the carnage trampling through, Gordon's magic stayed ever vigilant as he pushed and pushed.

Eventually the matriarch began to slow, and became consumed by a mass of soldiers attacking, she held her ground, ready to take as many lives with her as possible, Brennus looked on behind as she smashed them into the ground with ease, throwing and bashing the enemy like simple playthings, tearing the bodies of entire soldiers in half until succumbing to her many injuries, sustained by barrages of arrows.

The camp was turning into a complete wreck, at least this part of it was, so far so good.

All that remained now was to escape as quickly as possible but their estimations were correct, a small unit of cavalrymen had rounded up and were now bound for them, taking chase. Horse archers fired onward from behind, Drellix deflected from the back but was now becoming exhausted by the magicka he was producing, keeping a supportive link onto Gordon as well as keeping his rear safe from arrow fire. Olm and Brennus fell back to match Drellix's pace, providing extra cover with their shields as Gordon storms on ahead.

Drellix was becoming gaunt in the face, his arms shaking with weakness.

''Drellix! Stop using your magic to support me, I can feel you disconnecting! Don't pass out on us here!'' Gordon shouts behind himself. ''I've got this! Olm, Brennus, keep him covered! We're getting the fuck out!''

It was a sight unlike any other, an unstoppable force, trampling its way to victory.

The cavalry starts gaining on them, eager to end the chaos.

Gordon locates a way out and leaps into the forest opening with due haste, his sight starting to blur.

The cavalry behind was gaining fast, drawing and firing over and over again, the arrows rebounding, they were not giving up, and knew Drellix would have to give in to exhaustion soon.

''We're not going to make it! We need to break out!'' Olm Screams, noticing his horse tiring from the weight of reinforced armour.

''Push!!'' Gordon yells back ''Come on, girl!'' He pats Epona's girthy neck.

They steer off into a forested clearing. As the Venethari charge after them they are met with a sudden halt. A large strew of rope and knot emerges from the ground lifting into the air from the shadows of the treeline.

The horsemen fall into the coarse rope netting, crashing into each other and tumbling all around as the netting breaks from the sheer force, tripping up more coming in for the chase.

From the shadows of the treeline charges the vengeful might of Darogoth.

Gordon halts his horse and watches on as many grounded horsemen are stabbed to death, piled upon by a flurry of hearty warriors. The bloodcurdling neighs of downed horses drowning out the mighty war cries of Darogoth's ravenous onslaught.

Gordon steps down from his horse and collapses to the floor in exhaustion, struggling to breathe. A figure looms over Gordon's pitiful breathless state.

''You're a fucking lunatic,'' says Eithne.

''Oi…'' he pants. ''I… fuck…ing… did it….''

She holds out her hand, as Gordon grabs it as she yanks him toward her. He stumbles and hunches over her shoulder as he makes his way to his feet.

Brennus, Olm and Drellix all come and give Gordon a well-deserved pat on the back and do the same to each other, they themselves couldn’t quite believe what they had just accomplished.

Gordon tears away from Eithne as he stabilises his balance and catches his breath.

‘’This fight’s only just begun!’’ Cries Olm.

Brennus draws his trusty blade. ‘’Are you ready to stick it to some Venethari, Urskull?’’

‘’Always,’’ Olm nods.

Brennus takes Gordon's side. ‘’Gordon, how are you doing?’’

In response to Brennus’s words, Gordon draws his sword. ‘’I’ll be fine.’’

‘’Drellix?’’

‘’I’m good!’’

‘’Eithne?’’

She nods.

Gordon straightens himself out and cracks his neck, scowling with malice and riling himself up like a rabid dog. The images, the feelings, everything he’d done, everything he’d lost, everything he’d endured surges throughout his soul. He was more eager than ever to see this through to the very end. Too willingly take the stand and finally stare death right into its face.

‘’Loose the black tusks!’’ Gallus orders.

A beast master sets out his massive black tusk boars, the merciless breed of boar, five times the size and mass of a regular common swine, charging straight for the camp lines, squealing and grunting in their fear inducing pitch, the vanguard of the assault whilst the warriors finish off the ambushed cavalry.

Gallus waits for the boars to approach their target, as they ramp up the chaos on the front line. ''Chariots! Now!''

The chariots thunder down a rickety hill from within the treeline, ready to set the stage and make way for the oncoming battle.

''Now! Warriors of Darogoth, In the name of the high king, and by the grace of Fanara, Take back our lands!'' Gallus cheers heroically, raising his sword to the air as his cloak ripples against the wind.

The carnyx bellows the horns of war, signifying the start of a mighty stampede.

''Tear these cunts apart!!'' Brennus screams.

They join the fray, warriors sprinting down into the encampment, running alongside each other in unison, their hearts beating in rhythm to the drums of war, screaming at the top of their lungs. Their faces donned in blue; their spirits as high as the Spire of Oldwood itself.

Helen sat at her dresser, applying her makeup and bouncing about to her favourite songs, readying herself for a night on the town, whilst Gordon charged into the jaws of death.

As she swipes her brush across her soft pale skin, Gordon tears into the flesh of his enemies.

Helen picks up her ringing phone. ‘’Be ready in about an hour? Are you still coming to mine beforehand?’’

Gordon shrieks in the midst of battle, his vocal cords tearing bloody at the force of is cry.

The heat of the fight purged deep into the drawing night.

A blow comes from two Venethari, both of them blocked by the spear of Eithne, her grace unmatched as she spins and swipes at her opponents. Olm caves in the skull of one as she trips up the other, planting her blade directly into their neck.

Gordon and Brennus stood side by side, taking on every enemy that dared enter they’re blood-drenched sight. The screeches of the night echoed ever vastly, the sounds of cries, pain and roars alike. The clanking of metal, the cut of flesh, the end of life, the beginning of a new hope.

Ard joined the battle. Vocorix rode in above his white steed donned in a muscular gilded plate body, glimmering in the blood red night, Dun arrived in from the south, it was now or never.

Olm’s axe becomes wedged in a man's chest, as he yanks it out, he is met with a terrifyingly familiar voice.

‘’Look who it is! It’s the fucking TRAITOR!’’

Olm's head snapped toward the voice and there he stood in the famed uniform of the urskull. Segmented plated leather, the chain veiled helmet, Urskull Fenrith.

''Olm?!? WHY?'' He shouts in wrath.

Olm says nothing, hesitating to lift his axe to meet his old friend.

''Fucking scum!'' Fenrith lifts his rounded shield, smashing it into Olms' head.

Olm regains his balance before tripping up. Preparing his axe for an overhead blow, quickly parried by Fenrith.

Olm's massive frame doesn't budge from the parry, he brings his axe pommel back upward, striking Fenrith's chain veiled neck.

Fenrith slashes furiously with vigour and finesse with his curved sword. Olm blocks as much as he can, catches his blade and parries it out the way, greeting Fenrith with a vicious headbutt that connects both their helmets. Fenrith staggers downward and rises quickly, returning with a brutal uppercut from his shield, clipping Olm's hands, disarming his beloved axe. With poise, Fenrith reaches down below, slashing through Olm's ankle.

Olm falls to the floor in agony.

Fenrith raises his sword to the sky, readying to bring it down and end Olm's life. ''Thought I'd get more of a fight from you, Olm. I'm disappointed. You foolish bastard, may Iskarien drown you in-''

The sound of ripping flesh tears into Fenrith's armpit. He drops his blade in agony, turning to find Brennus who had stuck his sword deep into his armpit while his sword arm was held high.

He bashes him with his great shield, bringing Fenrith to submission on the muddy ground.

Fenrith attempts to gain some distance from Brennus, but Brennus simply drives his sword into his Fenrith's calf as he tries to spring back up, protruding all the way into the ground itself.

Brennus kicks Olms' axe toward him. Olm rolls over to grab his axe. ''You Darogothians, always saving my fucking arse.''

''Care to do the honours… Urskull?'' Brennus smirks.

Olm rises to his good foot with the help of Brennus. ''He's not worth my time.''

''Fucking traitor! Fucking COWARD!'' Fenrith screams.

Brennus plants his blade into the eyeholes of Fenrith's visor. ''Whiney little cunt, that's for the druids of Seers Crossing.''

''Thanks,'' Olm nods, patting Brennus's back as he arches over in pain from his wounded ankle.

''Get yourself to safety, Olm.''

''Just give me a one-handed weapon, fuck my axe.''

''Your funeral,'' Brennus says as he passes him Fenrith's sword.

As Olm attempts to move onward, he is stopped by the bleeding pain of his ankle. ''Fuck!''

''Just get back to camp!''

''I'm oathsworn! I WILL fight!'' Olm shouts.

''You do you, Oathsworn,'' Brennus smiles and charges off back into the fray, catching up with Gordon and running forward together with their warriors into the inner parts of the Venethari camp, following on as the enemy retreated to the centre.

''Ballista!'' A warrior screams, running away to cover in safety.

A giant ballista bolt, the size of a pike, fires from ahead, soaring past Gordon and skewering Brennus to the ground with an intense thud, completely obliterating all of his armour and padding with the sheer force.

''BRENNUS!'' Gordon screams in horror, his voice cracking from the pressure, molecules of blood kissing the air as it escapes his dry throat.

Brennus' mouth begins spewing with blood as he jolts back and forth in shock.

''BRENNUS! BRENNUS!'' Gordon cries, stumbling over to him.

Brennus splutters, struggling to get air as he chokes upon his own blood that rapidly pooled over himself.

Another bolt fires, taking out a multitude of nearby warriors, it screeches through the air ending with the screams of its victims.

''No! No! I'm getting this out! I'll heal you; I'll try magic!!'' Gordon flails around in desperation, staring upon the massive bolt in horror that held Brennus firmly to the ground. He places his palm on Brennus's shoulder, shaking him in desperation with no idea what to do.

''FUCK OFF!! I'm done! By Fanara,'' he spurts out a large clump of blood, spraying onto Gordon's face. ''Don't be a stupid cunt,'' He gives Gordon a sharp kick with all the strength he could muster, wincing in anguish, holding on tight to the fatal bolt protruding from his abdomen.

Gordon falls back from Brennus's kick. The ballista shoots another bolt, Gordon gets up and dives out of the way crouching behind a shattered yurt.

The Venethari had barricaded themselves in the centre of their camp, taking a final stand, firing their siege weapons into the forces of Darogoth. Ballista's, catapults. They were giving everything they had.

Gordon takes one last look at Brennus as he lay dying on the floor. Brennus looks to the sky, his life fading from his eye.

A silence washes over Gordon as he stares upon his dying brother, the sounds of war muffled out of his focus, a silence that suddenly becomes shattered by a scream. Gordon screams so loud it ripples the very fabric in the air, deafening all those nearby. His eyes explode with a magical fury unlike any other.

Gordon runs to the frontal centre of the camp where the Venethari gathered, desperately placing barricades and shooting relentlessly toward the forces of Darogoth.

Ballista bolts fly out toward him, he stops them and propels them off into the distance, he conjures down a heavy rain of fire atop the entire perimeter of the camp's centre stage of destruction, whilst simultaneously forming a protective barrier around himself, and sending forth the most incredible wind of fire that had ever burst from his hand. The weather becomes erratic as he flicks and flails his other hand, conducting the eradication of all life by the force of the Altharn itself within the concentrated area.

A storm swirls high above, crackling the sky with thunder and lightning, Infernal rains pour down upon the enemy, the wind and force of gravity become so intertwined all manner of objects are propelling and whistling all around, smashing into soldiers and obliterating everything within the area, lighting strikes and heat incinerates. The fire that spewed from his palm glows a boiling white, melting and searing all. His screams a deafening shock wave, bursting out like the beating heart of his very being.

The world begins to shift and warp all around him, the world gives an eerie shudder, flashing and stretching, until Gordon hits the floor, engulfed by the blackest of sights.

25: Allure of the Altharn

His eyes slowly open, the blur subsiding. A woman of golden locks can be seen tinkering with a large object by his side.

''Oh my God! Gordon! Gordon!'' Helen jerks in astonishment upon noticing the motion of his head.

''What?! Where?'' His vision begins to clear, he is home in his bed. He takes a hard blink of disbelief as he peers around. He is weak, he hadn't used his body in such a long time he could barely lift anything beyond a few inches, he was bed bound. It was a bizarre feeling, no matter how hard he tried, he couldn't lift his arm, despite feeling that he could.

Helen leaps forward to him wrapping her arms around his neck. ''I love you so much, I can't believe this! Finally! Everyone's going to be so happy to know you're awake!''

''I don't understand!? How am I here?'' He notices a strange machine by his bedside, after a little subconscious deciphering, he realises it's a life support machine, and it's attached to him.

''What do you mean?'' Helen replies. ''Look Gordon, you've been in a coma for a very long time, okay? I know you might be a little woozy, just take it easy babe,'' she says as she combs her hand through his hair.

''I was fighting, Brennus… he… I blacked out, the magic?!''

''What?''

''So, this is it? I was right? I was dead? No, in a coma?!''

''Yes Gordon, just sit back I'll go and grab you some food!'' She says with a relieving smile.

''Is this a joke?! No! It was real! I remember feeling him slap me!? The things I felt, they were real!''

''Gordon? Calm down, okay? I'm here, it's going to be okay, you've obviously had some crazy dream whilst you were out. But you're back, with me!''

Gordon didn't understand how to feel anymore, it was almost like he wanted to back in Altharn, after all this, fighting to return home, he was baffled, confused, even more so than before. The scars of battle, the trauma, the pain, the love and the sense of pride he had as he built his life, it all still remained in his soul, and just like that, he had lost it all over again.

''Helen, you don't understand, it was real, it must have been! I can even speak their language!''

''What are you talking about?''

''Ek felion hynwrath telithrio hynwreion.''

Helen pauses. ''I need to ring the doctor… they'll want to see you now you're awake,'' she says with a berated smile as she takes out her phone and hurries into the next room.

Gordon's hearing begins to ring loudly with a horrid screech. His eyesight returns to a blurry state becoming filled with a yellow haze as he jolts himself forward with little strength he had, blood rushing to his head. He pulls away the sheets as he begins to endure a panic attack.

As he unveils his naked body, he sees nothing but skin and bone, all his natural fats had but vanished, withered away like some deteriorating corpse, except he wasn't a corpse, he was very much alive.

He panics even more, accelerated by the sight of his frail body. Before he can even try to stand the world around shudders again, the fabric of reality morphs violently.

''Stay calm,'' Camula's voice echoes. ''Fight.''

''What's going on?!''

Camula's silhouette materialises at the foot of his bed as the space around becomes engulfed by black matter.

''Take hold within, This… this….''

''What?!''

Her angelic voice breaks off into the recess of nothing. ''Persist….''

The world shimmers yet again.

His bed vanishes into thin air, forcing him to plunge downward into nothing.

Gordon's body reforges back into the stout man he was, his muscles morph back into shape as he falls amidst the void, as he descends, he notices the blackness around him begin to resemble the deep recesses of space, as stars begin appearing and forming all around him.

Stone columns and other pieces of intricate structures float around him as his fall is halted by an unknown force.

Colours of a solaris origin paint the world around him, dotted with stars and nebulas. Platforms of land appear in the distance with large otherworldly ruins atop, floating in the essence of nothing.

He hears a voice crying out, but he can't make out the words as it cuts out. Large purple storms of magical matter spray across the land forms rapidly like crashing waves.

An ethereal quake shudders his naked body. He feels a presence and its tears of pain within the air. He feels sad and lost, just like the voice that desperately tries to reach him. Gordon wiggles around in zero gravity, trying to stabilise his orientation.

''Help!'' He calls out.

The voice responds, but the words are unclear. It was unnaturally deep and angelic, echoing throughout.

Gordon begins falling again, the stars in the sky flickering around him becoming brighter and brighter, vibrating so hard it starts to blind his sight, until exploding silently into a white light of devastation, drowning all around.

The flash finally dims and Gordon finds himself lying on solid ground, back at the battlefield of Northwood. He looms above Brennus's body that was impaled by the giant bolt, his blood dry like paint. A grey mist chokes the land, he steps back in horror and stumbles over something on the ground, he looks to see what he tripped up on and jumps out of his skin.

It was Parinos, lying there mangled and broken, his chest caved inward, dead.

Gordon's head darts about, he can barely see six feet ahead due to the thickness of the mist, as he carefully treads around he makes another disturbing discovery.

Orthunus, the arrow poking from his neck, his face decayed with his jawbone on show. Insects burrowed within his eye sockets, consuming what was left of him.

Gordon buries his head in his hands.

The mist begins to subside, he notices the brigands that tried to rob him in Seers Crossing, they lie just a way off from Orthunus, soaked in blood that had dried up, one of them totally charred by flame.

He looks back to Brennus. ''What is this?'' His voice shakes in a frightened whisper.

No response, nothing but the howl of the wind.

''You're not from Darogoth are you?!'' A gritty voice speaks from behind.

Gordon turns to see the bandit, his first kill standing there with his face charred and broken.

''Fuck off,'' Gordon jumps. ''Fuck off!''

''No,'' he eerily responds, a chunk of charred flesh falls from his face, bursting on impact with the floor into a strange black soot, vanishing completely.

''What is this? You're dead, I killed you….''

The brigand laughs manically. The mist clears and more of the dead surround him.

''HELEN!?'' He shrieks. ''No this isn't real.''

He darts around in fright, seeing more familiar faces. Eithne, Vocorix, Gallus, Hashna, Olm, Dan, Pete, Jeb. His mother and father.

''No… they're not dead!''

''All that lives, is dead,'' the bandit speaks with a deathly murmur, his arm falls away from his body, his head follows and explodes into a black ash that plumes from the ground up.

The world shudders once more under Gordons tears of sorrow as he kneels down smothering his face into his hands.

''It's going to be okay,'' a sweet youthful voice soothes the pain. A voice so harmonic it plucked at the strings of his very existence.

Gordon looks up to see a young woman clad in noble silks, a fur shawl with a red tartan overlay. She donned the Torc of Unity that rested upon her delicate collar, her hair golden brown, her eyes as green as the leaves that fell around them both, her beauty unmatched.

The bodies around him, gone, nothing but beautiful trees.

‘’Who are you?’’ Gordon asks.

The woman says nothing. She just stood there, smiling. It was warming and Gordon felt nothing but comfort and harmony as he peered into her eyes.

‘’Hello?’’ He asks again politely.

A man clad in chainmail appears at her side, seemingly from nowhere.

He himself was very handsome. Lucious brown hair that was platted on both sides, a short moustache and green grassy eyes just like the woman.

Something was very off about these two, something that Gordon wanted to believe was wrong but he couldn’t help but feel comforted and smitten in their presence, all his fears subsiding.

They both approach him slowly, Gordon stands firm.

The man edges forward, his eyes filling with tears as he gives a humble smile. He embraces Gordon, holding him tight, Gordon responds the same.

A rush of love and happiness flushes every inch of his body.

The woman approaches and joins in. As soon as the woman lets go of Gordon, she makes her way to his side as she begins to cry.

‘’What’s wrong? What’s going on?’’ Gordon asks.

Arrows appear from thin air and strike the armoured man piercing his armour as if it were as weak as paper. He reacts to the impacts as his body spasms with pain, his skin erodes flaking off and away into the air, leaving nothing but a skeletal corpse in shattered armour.

Gordon takes a minute to take in what he had just witnessed.

Before he can say anything the woman ages rapidly before him, growing wrinkles, her hair greys, her height shrinks and finally she collapses to the floor withering into a skeleton. The leaves around him turn red like blood and then the void consumes yet again. Except this time, differently.

The trunks of the trees form into marble stone, the leaves turn black and drip with an oily substance as dark as the night itself.

The floor reforms into a black stone, a floor so polished that he can see his own reflection staring back as watches on.

Whilst glaring into the floor his ears are met with the screams of children, the cries of babies and deathly groans of men and women alike.

He covers his ears, overwhelmed by the screams and cries.

''You,'' a voice tears through his body.

The voice that pierced his frame had a foul stench that followed. The stench of death and rot.

something catches his eye in the distance, another woman, walking toward him.

Upon closer inspection, he becomes very unnerved and weary. This woman was half naked in nothing but black rags and a pronged golden tiara that rested atop her head. Half of her body was exposed by bones; her leg and feet were skeletal as well as her entire arm. The skin that was left on her body was as unnaturally white just like the marble tree trunks that surrounded him. Her eyes are also white, nothing but white. She was freakishly beautiful with her elegant black hair that rustled within the winds of woe.

''No,'' she speaks out, her voice angelic and beautiful, yet fouled with rot.

Gordon stands speechless.

''Do not succumb.''

''I....'' Gordon stammers.

''Awaken, and live.''

Gordon wakes panting as he always did after such vivid dreams, but more so than usual, this string of dreams had left him in a bed roll laden with sweat, totally drenched.

He was badly dehydrated, his tongue sticking to the roof of his mouth. He scans around, his instincts lead him to search for water, he notices he is in a war tent, his armour stripped of him.

His canteen was just by his bedroll along with some of his gear, he snatched it up, taking a tremendous and satisfying gulp, hydration flushes his head.

He is in pain, his body aches, he feels groggy and lethargic, coated in large bruises all over, black and blue. He'd pushed himself so much he had induced a side effect of magical exhaustion, and had endured its sickness. He felt truly battered, like he had been hit by a truck.

He pulls himself up with his arms slowly, the pains shooting and flaring all over him. He notices the midday sun glow through the tent fabric, he starts feeling disoriented, his concept of time lost to him more than ever before.

He remembers what had happened, memories of the bolt splitting through Brennus mail, pinning him to the ground, the bravery in facing death as he accepted his fate. Gordon had lost his closest friend, his brother in arms.

The initial shock of it all had overridden his emotions, they tried to shake free of the shackles that were placed, but he was numb.

He slowly rises from his bedroll, looking for any food that might be lying around the tent, he only sees his belongings and his roll, he scratches his head in confusion.

The tent's flaps are pushed aside as Hashna peers in.

Gordon looks to her as he stands there in nothing but his breeches. She stands with a proud look sweeping her stoic face. She marches up to him, his eyes explode in a fountain of tears as his emotions break free at the sight of her.

''Hashna! Brennus....'' Gordon whimpers.

''I know, I know,'' she consoles him. The two embellish a moment of mourning. ''We did it, Gordon. Glaen is ours once again.''

''He was like a brother to me, Hashna.''

''Brennus would be proud of you for what you did. You decimated the entire force that killed so many of our warriors, his death was not in vain. The Altharn took his soul and fuelled yours to save Glaen!''

Gordon pulls away, wiping his tears and nodding his head erratically. ''I can't believe it… he's… gone.''

Hashna places her hand on his shoulder. ''We'll mourn him together, Walker. Other than the obvious, how are you? You fainted after that little demonstration of carnage.''

''I feel ill, tired, achy, shit. I've missed you, Hashna. What happened? How long have I been out?''

''Likewise, Walker. It's been a long time… you've been out a few days, come and get some food, you must be starving.''

''A few days?!?'' Gordon lunges forward in surprise, hurting his ribs that were badly bruised. ''Fuck!''

''Take it easy little warrior! Look at you…'' she remarks his injured frame. ''You really dove deep into the thick of it, eh?''

''You're telling me…'' Gordon responds. ''Oh shit, hang on-''

He jolts forward again, vomiting all over the floor.

Hashna supports his back. ''You're sick? All this stress and pain, all that magic....''

''Oh, fucking hell!'' He gags.

''Come on, come on… let's get some nutrients down you!''

The army was still stationed in Glaen whilst they picked up the pieces that Venethar had thrown to the floor, liberation and support efforts for the province very much under way.

Gordon throws on a tunic, trousers and some leather boots as he and Hashna leave the tent.

Warriors all over turn to face Gordon and all give a unified silence. Gordon felt awkward as the crowd of brazen warriors stared upon him silently.

They begin to clap, which turns into a loud applause.

''Hail the realm walker!'' One of the warriors shouts with valour and hope.

More warriors gather to Gordon's side as they chant and applaud.

Gordon didn't know how to respond, especially in the state he was in, clung to Hashna's hip as she carefully ferried him through.

''Hail the realm walker!'' They cheered with relief in their faces. ''Hail the realm walker!''

Gordon stood in awe as the warriors cheered on. Gallus notices the chanting and comes to join in, his face beaming with glee, revealing all his wrinkles.

Eithne stood by Gallus's side mimicking the words quietly.

As they all calmed their chanting, Gordon was gifted with an entire boar leg from one warrior and a tankard of mead by another. ''For you, Realm Walker, the Keeper of Fanara's Will!''

Gordon felt overwhelmed by the many acts of kindness swamping him, but smiled it off nevertheless.

As quickly as he could, he demolished the boar leg as Hashna aided him down to a rugged log rolled out by the fire pit.

''This is… I don't even words….'' Gordon gasps as he tears into the boar.

''You deserve it,'' Hashna smiles.

''Gordon,'' Eithne calls to him from behind as she approaches, her hands held behind her back.

Gordon rises from his seat to greet her, wincing from his bruised ribs with a mouth full of roasted boar. ''Eithne.'' He mumbles.

''Well done.''

''Thanks.''

''I… have something for you.''

His eyebrows perk.

Eithne hands him Brennus's torc. ''I took it from his body when the battle was won, you were out… and thought you'd appreciate this, to remember him.''

Gordon holds the torc gently in his hand, he looks upon it intently, disheartened and still in disbelief. Looking upon the torc of his fallen brother, the reality of it all comes streaming in, his eyes well up.

He grabs her by the waist, pulling her in for a tight squeeze. She wraps her arms around his neck.

''Thank you, thank you,'' he whispers into her ear softly. ''Where is he?'' He asks as he pulls back from her.

''Vocorix's army has picked him up… they've… already given him to the Gods.''

''What!?'' His stomach folds.

''You were out for days, Gordon. I'm sorry. I knew you'd be upset by this so I took his torc for you.''

Gordon glances off to the floor in sadness. ''Thank you, Eithne. This… this really means allot to me,'' he says, giving a mournful smile.

Gordon returns to his seat, staring upon Brennus's torc. Hashna leans in to look upon it as Eithne takes a seat beside him.

''How's Olm?'' Gordon asks.

''You mean that urskull you freed?'' Hashna kisses her teeth. ''He's fine, he's with the druids right now, a few flesh wounds,'' she replies.

''Good… yeah about that… don't worry, Brennus already gave me a 'talking' too….'' Gordon smiles. ''So, what of Kastrith in all of this?''

Hashna Scoffs. ''I bet he did… but it is what it is, he's proven himself from what I've heard, and Kastrith wasn't present, we have information across the border that he was preparing to move with the gryphon riders and were to meet us at Evercrag Pass… but apparently, he didn't even show up. This was after you fell unconscious.''

''The what?''

''Gryphon riders. People that ride gryphons?''

''Gryphons?''

''Yes. Giant birds that inhabit The Heart of Venethar. They're ferocious beasts. It's always custom that the monarchs of Venethar learn to ride them.''

Gordon leans onto his knees in interest. ''Why've I never heard of this?''

''They're rarely deployed. It's more of a ceremonial or traditional thing nowadays. Gryphons are small in number. Before Kastrith, Arkhuul, his father was preparing conservational efforts for them.''

''Wow,'' Gordon picks up his mead, guzzling down half the tankard.

Hashna laughs. ''Always something new to learn here, Walker.''

''It's great to see you again, Hashna,'' he smiles. ''I didn't see you in the battle....''

''And you, my friend!'' She punches his arm. He retracts in response to his already injured body. ''Fuck, sorry....''

''Argh!'' He grits his teeth. ''It's fine... you were saying?''

''I was with Ard's forces of course, was by Vocorix's side the whole time, being his oathsworn and all that... I was hoping to run into you. But then I saw that crazy storm in the distance and I knew exactly what was going on.''

''Yeah....''

''Quite the sight... I must say,'' she exclaims.

''So, these gryphon riders were to join Venethar in the fight?''

''Yes, but we sent the main invasion force into the ground before that could happen.''

''Fuck's sake.''

''What's the matter?''

''If we waited a little longer, we could have gotten hold of Kastrith.''

''No Gordon, if we waited a little longer we would have lost the entire war and as mighty as your magic is, I don't think you're ready for what that bastard is capable of, you've not seen what he did before your arrival... this wasn't the right time to engage a man like him.''

''Really?''

''Also, you've not seen a gryphon before, have you?'' She laughs. ''I don't mean to insult you Walker, but caution and preparation is how we're going to win this war, even with your magic.''

''She's right Gordon… I know I was wrong to doubt your plan and although it worked… Kastrith is something else entirely,'' Eithne adds as she sat sharpening her skinning knife.

Gordon gives a heavy breath as he gulps down the remaining mead. ''So, what now?''

''We go home, we're finished here. Vocorix came to visit you when you were out, he was thankful you were alive, but he had to leave. He's in Northus for the moment, figuring out what to do with Tarna and supporting the rebellion to keep Venethar on their toes. Glaen's inhabitants will return and all provinces will provide a stronger defence to secure it for the future,'' Hashna's eyes fall back into her head. ''Just like in the days of old, Glaen becomes the frontline of battle… It's going to be tough, but until we know what to do next I guess we just drink!'' She bellows.

''I'd like to go home.''

''Home?'' Hashna asks, noticing a strange vibe in Gordon's tone.

''Fen Craic,'' says Gordon.

Eithne smiles. ''How are you feeling?''

''I don't really want to talk about it. Brennus… he was everything to me here… everything.''

Eithne lowers her head in respect. ''Whenever you're ready we can go to Gallus and get moving.''

''Yeah. Let's go, Olm will need proper rest at the keep. At least his family will be happy to see him alive at least,'' Gordon rises from his seat giving a careful stretch of his sore and tight muscles. ''Hashna, it's been great to see you again, I'm going to visit Carsinia to come see you, once I've rested.''

''I'm coming with you,'' she responds.

''Huh?''

''Vocorix released me of my oath at my request to come with you… if you wish it, of course.''

''I'd love nothing more,'' Gordon beams. ''Hashna Dun-Cruvax, will you swear oath to me, to clan Barker?''

''Formal, like a true lord! You've come a long way since I last saw you. Of course, I'll swear an oath to you,'' she rises and joins her arm with his.

''I… need an oathsworn commander… and master of arms for Fen Craic,'' his mouth sinks at the words. ''I couldn't think of anyone more qualified and trustworthy than you, would you accept?''

''Yes, my Lord.''

''Fuck off, you don't need to call me that.''

Hashna smiles. ''Ok, Walker.'

And so, the battle of Northwood had been won by the forces of Darogoth, by clever tactics, brute infantry strength and the power of the realm walker.

Many of Darogoth perished that fateful night, warriors such as Brennus Ard-Renerios. This cut Gordon deeper than anything he had ever experienced in his life; he was so numb by Brennus's death his face had become void of all emotions from that day onward.

Gordon was always a reactive sort of person, his face always had something to it, even when idle, but this was no longer the case, he'd seen too much, far too much death.

The death of his brother in arms had stricken the remaining innocence of Gordon's soul. He was a husk of his former self and although he didn't quite believe it, so much stronger because of it.

Camula always had a strange influence on his soul, guiding him from within, savouring his gut and soothing the trauma as she flushed through his spine and speaking through his subconscious where she could reach him. Without Camula, Gordon would have surely perished in this brutal yet beautiful world.

After finally reaching Fen Craic the army of clan Barker returns, they are met by Lucotorix and the Garrison soldiers upon entering. Lucotorix noticed straight away that Brennus was nowhere to be seen and Hashna was clearly here to take his place, a look of concern swamps his face and despite the knowledge, he masks well.

''Welcome back everyone, I've heard fantastic news!''

''Well, you haven't heard what I have to say have you?''

''Gordon?''

''Brennus is dead.''

''I'm sorry… Gordon, truly. I find it hard to believe a battle-hardened veteran such as him to be one to fall in battle. But it seems fitting for him, he died by his oath. That's what all the oathsworn swear to do, be happy for him, Gordon. He fulfilled his oath.''

Gordon says nothing, raising his eyebrow to Lucotorix's words. He gives a gentle nod and marches off to the keep.

Upon reaching the keep the guards opened the large double doors into the main hall, down the wooden framed and cobblestone hall stood his clan throne. A larger than average wooden chair, laden in furs upon a raised step from the floor.

Gordon approaches the throne and begins shifting around a few nails that were already embedded in the wooden frames, pulling them out with his magic. He mounts Brennus's torc on the wall behind and above the throne.

He takes a step back to appreciate it. A single tear trickles from his eye. ''Get this fucking armour off me!'' He vigorously yanks at his chainmail and belts. removing it all completely and slamming it all to the ground in a burst of stress, marching off to his chambers.

A knock at his chamber door startles him.

''What?''

''It's Lucotorix, are you okay?''

''Leave me alone, Luke. I need some time.''

''Of course,'' his voice muffled from behind the door, his steps can be heard as he dawdled away.

Instantly Gordon prepares a pipe and heads to his balcony to smoke, punching the wall on the way out in anger, cutting open his knuckles and almost breaking his hand.

He drops his pipe and punches the wall again using magic. He punches over and over, breaking the thick stone outer layer tearing some of the masonry off that fell to the floor. ''FUCK!''

It was really beginning to sink in now that he was back at Fen Craic without Brennus.

The days that followed were anything but restful on the mind. Gordon hid away, residing in his chambers, playing on his phone, smoking and drinking, wishing he was back home, falling into a pit of utter and complete despair.

Anyone who dared bother him was verbally abused and turned away… even Hashna who he'd not seen in such a long time got nothing from him. But Hashna knew, she knew he was in pain.

He'd only ever come out to eat, even then he ignored the guards and castle staff who greeted him in passing.

Until a letter arrived.

''Gordon?'' Lucotorix shouts from outside the chamber doors.

''What?'' Gordon blurts bluntly from inside.

''A letter from Gallus, not sure what it's about. Looks important….'' Lucotorix slides the letter under the door.

Gordon takes the letter.

''Can I please come in? We don't have to talk about… you know… I just want to see you, Gordon. I'm worried about you, many of us are. I'm not just your druid, I'm your friend. Okay?'' Lucotorix was beginning to get impatient.

Gordon ignores him as he reads the letter from Gallus. He was inviting Gordon to a celebratory feast at Vortighna. A formal feast for all the lords of Fen for their efforts in the war.

''You can't live like this Gor-.''

''Argh!'' He pulls at his hair in frustration. ''I don't care, I lost my brother out there!''

''Gordon, stop it! Listen to yourself! Do you think you're the only person who lost someone in Glaen? How do you think I felt when my little brother was killed right in front of me?! I carried on, for him! And you should too! I've just had to send out letters to warriors' families who were stationed here in Fen Craic that they're beloved son or daughter is dead! Come on now, you're a lord! You're a good man Gordon and I know you're stronger than this! Let me in and let's have a smoke or something. Okay?!''

''Fucking hell, fine,'' Gordon rips open the door.

''Erm… yes… good,'' Lucotorix responds awkwardly.

''I'm sorry,'' he sighs, running his hand through his dishevelled hair.

''We understand, okay? Now get your pipe,'' Lucotorix rushes Gordon to his balcony.

The two appear over the beautiful scenic view of Fen Lake, signs of Gordon's carelessness and despair were very present, his chambers were a mess, bottles and cups laden all over, especially around the balcony.

''So, what did the letter say? If you don't mind me prying.''

''Gallus invited me to a feast.''

''I thought it might be that… those kinds of feasts are traditional after a victory such as that. You have to go! You need to get out. Go mingle with the other higher ups. Let them feed your ego, let your hair down!''

''Ugh… I don't know, would you come with me?''

''What?! I'm a druid Gordon. Druids are forbidden to drink with lords.''

''You drink with me all the time?!''

''Yeah… but no one has to know that, do they?''

''Why is that anyway?''

''If we are to advise efficiently, we are to be sober when the lords are drunk, so that no decisions are made in 'foul' mind.''

''Fuck… and I got stuck with you?'' Gordon gives a pitiful laugh. ''Well… I can't go on my own… I mean I could… I just feel like I'd be a bit awkward, not feeling myself lately and stuff….''

''Hmmm, maybe Gallus would make an exception for you, since you're the only blood member of your own clan….''

''I mean… I can't wallow around like this I know, even I'm getting sick of myself now. I'm just… Just trying to process everything,'' he screws his face around as he fights with himself. ''Ah… fuck it… I'll go… I'll go alone, it'll probably push me to be social and do social shit, suppose keeping busy will help?'' He moans, uninspired.

Lucotorix wraps his arm around Gordon's neck. ''There we go! That's the spirit, you are right, just remember what I said, he died doing what he did best, he died a true oathsworn, for you. Make him proud Gordon, go out there do what you need to do, for him!''

Gordon gives a heavy snort. ''Yeah… I know… I'll try my best. I've never had a formal feast in Darogoth before… what's so different from a normal feast?''

''Ha. Well, you need some fancy clothes… I mean, no offence but you need some rich linens, silks. you know what I mean? The good stuff! Not the commoner's tunics and scruffy trousers with a half-tattered belt that all stinks of fish because someone doesn't know how to clean his clothes properly....'' says Lucotorix with a mischievous grin.

Gordon scoffs. ''Alright, alright... I've seen enough Darogothic nobles to know how they dress, and give me a break man! I've been feeling like shit!''

''You know I'm only joking,'' he pats down his arm.'' You'll be okay! I'm sure the tailor in Vortighna can help you out.''

''So, is that it... I just dress fancy?''

''Yeah, basically. There's usually a bard or two, lots of free food decorating the entire hall and enough booze to drown the kingdom.''

''Fair enough... well, it's in a few days, so I'll go to Vortighna for the day and sort some clothes out with the tailor.''

''You'll naturally be staying overnight,'' Lucotorix says as he attempts to relight his pipe.

''Huh?''

''Yes, the feasts last all through the day and the night and the day after that! You'll be given a guest bedchamber. It's a good thing that governing cities have huge fuck off castles.''

Gordon giggles.

''First time I've seen you smile in a while,'' Lucotorix remarks.

''It's just that you don't sound right when you swear. It's funny, especially when you copy the way I do it.''

''Fuck fuck fuck.''

''Shut the fuck up,'' laughs Gordon.

''Would be wise to bathe before you leave by the way.''

''What are you trying to say?''

''Your body odour is quite offensive.''

''I know, yeah… fair enough.''

''I'll leave you be… it's been good talking. You know where I am if you need me, okay? ''

Tears brace in Gordon's eyes. ''Yeah.''

Upon Lucotorix leaving his chambers Gordon took a deep long breath, inhaling all his festering emotions and exhaling a future of hope. He had no idea what was to come of him, the place he was or where he'd end up.

He peers out to Lake Fen and takes one last hit of his pipe, watching as the calm lake glimmers in the sunlight, the tranquillity soothing his tired soul.

''Onwards,'' Camula echoed.

After taking much needed care for himself, bathing and scrubbing and trimming, he cuts off all his now matted hair, back to the short length it was when he arrived, but keeping hold of the moustache, he embellished his hair with a white clay, spiking it up, quite like how he used to before he arrived, he felt himself again, spikey hair was Gordon's hair.

And so alone he ventured to Vortighna, a short horse ride following the Fen Lake out and down along the riverside.

Upon arriving through the gates, he could already see the people of Vortighna in festive spirit, everyone had drinks in their hand and smiles on their faces, singing songs from times of old and dancing in the cobbled streets.

There were decorations and tables erected all over the main market square, boar, venison, and beef being roasted outdoors. Merchants, farmers, fisherfolk, warriors, guards, carpenters, stone masons, tanners, hunters, craftsmen, people of all backgrounds together drinking and celebrating the victory Darogoth had won.

Gordon hitches his horse and seeks out the nearest tailor, spotting one on the edge of the market, down a tight alley of triangulated homes, its shop sign swaying in the breeze. ''*Threads of Fen.*''

He enters to find a jolly woman already working with some fabrics laid out on a table as she sips a goblet of wine on the side.

''Hello! Welcome!'' The shop owner cheers, placing her goblet out of sight upon noticing his entry, clearly enjoying the festive atmosphere.

''Hi… I need some decent… clothes?'' Gordon spoke sheepishly.

The woman giggles. ''Of course! It is a grand feast after all! Where is it, we are having a party tonight?''

''The castle, with Lord Gallus.''

The woman's laid back demeanour changes instantly. ''OH. Well, I can definitely help you out there! Are you a lord of Fen? A member of one of the great clans? Or just filthy rich?'' She cheers.

''Yes... Ard-Barker.''

Her eyes widen as a large smile slowly stretches the entirety of her face. ''Well, well... what a pleasure to have you come to me for some finery.''

Gordon gives an awkward smirk.

''How about something like this?'' She leads him to a corner in the shop where presumably the more expensive garments reside. She presents him with a high-quality leather overcoat belted at the waist, decorated in stitched loopy patterns and a golden embroidery at the trim. A fine linen laced up green tunic and a smart pair of heeled boots and a pair of tan trousers stitched to perfection. ''It's not the most colourful, but definitely something to get the ladies turning their heads!''

''Sure... I'll try it on?''

''Of course... usually lords send an order through and it takes me a few days to prepare such work... but... I could make a few adjustments to it for a better fit, I'll do the best I can on such notice.''

''Okay... I didn't even think about it like that... in that case I'll take it if you can tailor it to me?''

''That's my job! We may be here a little while....''

The tailor begins to fit the clothes onto him, stitching here and there, tightening and loosening different parts.

After a few hours he was dressed up and ready to party.

''Marvellous, Lord Gordon. You look very presentable!''

''Do I?''

''Here,'' she shows him to a mirror.

''Ahh, yeah, I like it actually...'' he responds positively, Gordon had never really bothered with fine clothing before. ''Thank you!'' He pays the woman her due and a little extra for her quick assistance with the fitting. Feeling much more confident he leaves and makes for the castle immediately.

In a lofty strut toward the castle, he approaches the main gate, the guards see him in, the doors open to the foyer of the castle where a steward stood, greeting all into the castle. ''Ah greetings! Barker, isn't it? I remember your face.''

''Yeah.''

''Good! Lord Gallus will be happy to see you! Let me get the door for you,'' the steward pushed on the large double doors revealing the main hall, decorated elaborately with many flora dipping down from the upper balcony and stone and pillars that gracefully directed the visitors to the throne of Vortighna, many iron braziers stood symmetrically aside each pillar, lighting the way.

Around the entirety of the castle all nobles, aristocrats and people of power alike from all of Fen festered within, chattering and laughing amongst themselves.

Gordon dawdled onward, scouring the place, laughter, music and all manner of peaceful sounds echoed the great halls of Castle Vortighna. Seeing everyone's high spirits made him wish Brennus was by his side enjoying the victory with him, his face reduced back to its glum state.

He felt quite lost, unknowing what to do. He couldn't see Gallus anywhere, he noticed a few familiar faces from the campaign around, he gave them a nod and a simple hello but he didn't feel comfortable having a conversation with anyone right now, so he wandered around in search of something to drink to loosen up a little.

He enters the dining hall, in its centre a ginormous hearth cooks a massive array of food, surrounded by the finest quality crafted wooden tables he'd ever seen, even fancier than that of Carsinia.

People were scattered all over the room, upon tables, in chairs, many others danced to the melodies of a band that were staged in a corner. It was a freeing environment.

He spotted the mead barrels all stacked together over by the garden door where people were filling their cups and tankards, so Gordon helped himself.

After filling his tankard, he immediately takes an eager sip, followed by a sigh of discontent.

‘’Hello you,’’ a voice startles him.

He turns around to see Eithne.

Before he could even respond to her, he becomes stunned by her appearance, this may be the first time Gordon ever laid eyes on her when she wasn’t donning her leathers of battle.

her hair was free, drooping over her shoulders and down her back, of course it still had all manners of braids and beads as it always had done. She wore a white dress that gracefully complimented her delicate curves, a blue tartan shawl that wrapped at her neck with a golden broach in the shape of a little bear, golden bracelets and armlets decorated the entirety of her arms alongside many blue painted swirls, her eyes were even lined with a black makeup.

‘’Eithne… Fuck… you need to stop doing that,’’ he laughs nervously.

‘’Are you okay?’’ She responds with a perched brow.

‘’Yes… you… you look amazing.’’

She tilts her head like a puppy. ‘’Thank you. I was about to say the same to you, you dress up very nicely, you look very handsome, you cut your hair?! It really suits you.’’

Gordon gives a warming grin as he takes in her compliment. ‘’Where is everyone?’’

Eithne gives a light chuckle. ''Here?'' She gestures with her hands across the hall. ''Gallus is in the cellar, looking for some kind of wine for his wife, and everyone else… is-'' she interrupts herself, cocking her head as she gives a cunning smile. ''You come alone?''

''Yeah.''

''Shame, then again, I suppose that's the downside of being the only member of your clan.''

''What of your clan? Are they here?'' Gordon asks.

''My clan is of Dun and they are not nobles, my clan are but humble tanners. But I do see Gallus and his family as my own these days… they take good care of me.''

''Do you miss your clan?''

''Yeah. I try to see them as much as I can, but with the war I haven't seen my mother and father for a few years. I write to them often.''

Gordon perches his behind upon the table. ''Let's hope we can both see our families soon enough, eh?''

Eithne gives a pitiful smile for Gordon. ''Yeah….''

''Hey, you haven't got a drink, want me to get you one?'' Gordon offers.

''The barrel is right there… but sure, you can get me a drink if you want too?''

Gordon takes one of the tankards from the table and pours Eithne a mead. ''There we go.''

''Thanks, I'll come find you soon, I promised Olio I'd get him a drink.''

''Olio?''

''Gallus's son, he's just become old enough that Gallus promised him he could have his first drink today, but he's too shy to show himself, thinks the other Lords with mock him, he's a sweet boy, reminds me of my younger brother back home.''

Perplexed, Gordon moves aside from the barrel. ''Of course! Sure, yeah....''

Eithne takes her mead and gets a drink for Olio and swiftly moves away giving Gordon a confusing glance as she walks off into the crowd and out of sight.

Gordon slaps himself across the head as he rubs his eyes. ''Fucking hell,'' he groans.

''Barker!''

Gordon turns to see Ambunix signalling him over.

He felt relieved to see Ambunix, he liked him allot, but he knew he would start talking about Brennus, he felt quite reluctant to go over, but he swallowed his emotions knowing this man was also deeply close to Brennus.

''By the Gods! It's good to see you again!'' Ambunix roars.

''And you, Ambunix. How are you?''

''Fucked… after losing Brennus… it's been hard. He and I were like brothers. We grew up together as lads we did!'' Ambunix says in a softer tone.

''Likewise… he had the same effect on me, it's been… tough.''

''Of course! He practically brought you up so I hear, been at each other's side since you arrived! My deepest sympathies for you, Walker. But let us celebrate his life. Let us drink to that mean old cunt, let us drink to his victories! He was a legend of a man he was!'' Ambunix signals to clink his tankard with Gordon's.

The word 'walker' repeated in Gordons' head. The word Brennus and Hashna always used to refer to him by. Many people used it, but it sat with Brennus better.

Gordon clinked Ambunix's tankard. ''To Brennus Ard-Renarios, fucking legend.''

''That's it! May Fanara rest his soul, for he died a true oathsworn, so he did!'' He shouts out to the hall; he was clearly quite tipsy. ''Come here you! You're a fucking good man you are!'' He embraces Gordon, giving him a tight bear hug, cutting off his breath. ''I saw it all Gordon, when me and my garrison arrived just as the battle ended, I saw him die, and then… and then I saw you. The storm, the magic… how you reduced all the Venethari to nothing but fucking dust! Oh, Walker, I'll sing songs about that day until Iskarien finally decides to smother me in my sleep! Brennus would be bent over sucking on the tits of Fanara herself if he saw what you did!''

''I think he did actually....'' Gordon adds.

''Then by Iskariens mucky minge, what a sight to see before you die!''

Gordon gave a small chuckle at Ambunix's vulgarness, it was just like Brennus, there was no wonder they were so close.

''A pleasure to meet you Walker, Gordon.'' A man stood by Ambunix who had watched on as the two conversed. ''I'm Abanistix Fen-Drosii''

Gordon cocks his head. ''Drosii? Same clan as Vocorix?''

''That's correct, our clan is Fen based primarily, Vocorix is my older brother, I'm Lord of Denunnos. I saw you briefly on the battlefield and have heard much about you.''

Now that he mentioned it, Abanistix resembled Vocorix facially, except younger. He had a freshly shaven head and a mighty red beard that rested beneath his crooked nose. He was a lot skinnier than Vocorix in comparison.

''A pleasure!'' Says Gordon, offering his arm in greeting.

''Glad to see you joining the feast! What are you drinking?''

''Erm... mead?''

''From the barrels over there?'' He points behind Gordon.

''Yes....''

''Try the brown ale in the Larder behind the cask of chouchen, it's kept away for a reason!'' He howls.

''Strong?'' Gordon asks

''Strong?'' Ambunix roars. ''It's enough to knock out a fucking horse!''

''Have you had some, Ambunix?'' Gordon chuckles.

''I've had about three mugs,'' he grins, displaying his glazy eyes. ''There's definitely something special in it,'' he winks.

''I'll be sure to check it out.''

''My sister is here and would love to meet you, Gordon!'' Says Abanistix eagerly. ''Hold on I'll get her!''

''No, no… it's okay, I'm…'' Gordon trips on his words.

Abanistix becomes slightly concerned by Gordon's denial.

''I'm just a little… erm… overwhelmed… you know? With the battle and people always giving me a bit of attention… Brennus… and stuff… you understand? I just want to keep it a little quiet tonight. I just want to settle a little first… I know it's a feast. I just want to avoid the fuss… I'm not of this… world… you know?'' Gordon trips on his words.

Abanistix glances off to Ambunix in concern. ''Gordon, of course… you need but say. My apologies, I didn't mean to offend you.''

''No offence at all! I'll be sure to swing by later and greet her. It's been great to meet you, I just need some air now I think?''

''That's fine by me my good man, come find us soon though, Walker! I dare you to try and outdrink me! You may be the master of magic, and my brother the high king of Darogoth, but I'm the King of all ales!''

''Are you fuck!'' Ambunix bloats, punching Abanistix in his gut.

''Definitely, Abanistix.'' Gordon gives a wink in jest.

Gordon excuses himself, it was strange, after he got into the new fancy clothes, he felt a wave of confidence hit him, he almost felt, normal? But as soon as he entered the castle, he felt like he'd just re-emerged into Altharn all over again, anxious and abhorrent.

He wandered off into the beautiful garden of the castle that veered off from the dining hall, leaning over a stone wall that peered over a well sized pond, casually sipping his tankard as he pondered on in his moment of peace, allowing the mead to burn away at his anxieties.

He hears footsteps approaching him from behind. He scrunches his eyes in disappointment just wanting to be left alone, so he turns around to address the person approaching only to find it was Eithne, coming his way.

''Look I just- hey!''

''Gordon, I thought you would be mingling all through the night.''

Gordon gives a heavy sigh as he turns back around, peering out into the garden allowing Eithne to join him. ''I needed some air, struggling a little with the attention. It's weird… I feel so alone again, I wish I could have brought Hashna, or Lucotorix.''

''Well… I'm here with you.''

Gordon scoffs. ''You are,'' he takes another sip and places his tankard on the wall, returning to looming over the pond. ''I'm glad actually… I enjoy your company.''

Eithne gives a smile as she tilts her head to him. ''And I enjoy yours, I like you, Gordon,'' she says bluntly.

Gordon slowly turns his head in confusion, becoming lost in her evergreen eyes.

A strange aura fills a connection between them both, the kind of silence that spoke much of the moment. He gives a gulp of uncertainty, feeling the silence stretch out for longer than it should. Her words had a force behind them, a meaning.

A mutual glance that touched the moment brought them closer, Eithne inches herself toward him, gently kissing his lips, testing his reaction.

Gordon backs off instantly. ''Shit….''

Eithne retracts herself, holding herself firm.

Noticing Eithne's steps, Gordon shakes his head vigorously, peering back to the pond. He then darts over to her, placing his hand on her waist, gently pulling her into him, the two share a glance of emotional consent.

She places her hand on his chest giving the smile that revealed her deepest desires. He felt for the first time he was looking upon the true Eithne. He fell deep into her alluring eyes, moving his head closer to hers, basking within the warmth of her soft freckled skin, her aura pulsating with a passion he too desired. He guides his lips into hers.

All of his worries dispersed, all his insecurities vanished, his cares no longer mattered, his sorrows no longer held him prisoner by the weighted ball and chain. Everything he ever wanted was right here in this moment, with Eithne. It was almost as if everything had changed in those precious minutes, sealed by the kiss he and Eithne shared. A kiss that moved him unlike any other.

''I wanted this....'' Gordon confesses.

''Good.''

''I tried to tell myself I didn't, but I remember the moment I saw you leaning on your spear, looking at me like... that. Like you wanted to kill me, I could have sworn you were weary of me.''

''No... I found myself drawn to you. You're true to yourself, and you're true to those around you, you are nothing but you and... I want you.''

''Smile at me again the way you did before we kissed, because it was the most beautiful fucking thing I've ever seen.''

She smiles softly, grabbing his head and forcing a kiss upon him.

She remembers something, something she was certain would hinder their affections. ''Gordon... what of your home?''

Gordon gives a heavy sigh.

Eithne glances off in a brief moment of sadness.

''I'm here and there's no way back.''

''We don't know that.''

''Well for what it is… I'm still here and have been for about two years now. I've accepted that now… It's been hard, but when I was out after the battle, I had the most immersive dream… I dreamt I woke up back in my own realm and all this wasn't even real, and the only thing I felt… was that I wanted to return, to Altharn.''

''Don't pursue me if you want to go back, Gordon.''

Gordon sternly locks his eyes with hers. ''This is my home.''

''Are you sure? You seemed homesick before Northwood.''

''Eithne, my time here has been nothing but the highest highs, and the lowest of lows… when I arrived, I was so lost, my only goal was to return to my old home, but over the years I built this life, and I found it hard to accept, but after Northwood… I can't even explain. My old life is gone, Eithne. I live in the now, because if I carry on searching for a way home, will I even have a life to live? I'm here now, here with you.''

Gordons eyes reflected the truth pouring from his heart. Eithne was a master of catching out liars, and with Gordon she felt safe.

''Okay, Gordon,'' she smiles just before melting Gordon's face as he allows himself to become stunned by her beauty.

''Eithne, you are something else. This moment here? I have no words.''

''You had a woman back home, how does this affect that?''

''I've been gone for so long, they would have believed me to be dead a long time ago, it's time for me and my life to move on, I remember when we went to Venethar, I remember finding myself watching you by the campfire, that's when I truly started questioning everything, after all, you're a woman of Darogoth, why would a woman of this world find interest in me? But it was that moment I realised my old life was becoming nothing but a memory to me… it was hard… I was scared. I've accepted Helen may have moved on, and I hope she does, I hope she finds someone who can treat her right.''

''I trust you… you have a purity about you unlike others,'' she takes hold of his coarse hand. ''Yes, I suppose it is quite… strange. You're of another world, but people have relations with elves and that's never been frowned upon… is that so different when you're so human?''

''I don't know, fuck it,'' Gordon replies.

The two share another kiss and turn back to the wall overlooking the pond, leaning upon one another, arm in arm.

''It's crazy…'' she whispers. ''But I like it.''

''Me too… do you think this war will be over soon?'' Gordon asks.

She rests her head on his shoulder. ''I don't know, maybe. I wasn't very confident about it all before I heard of you, especially with what Kastrith is capable of… it made me feel uneasy, unsafe… like the world was due for a terrible change, a change we couldn't control. Your arrival and cooperation has filled the hearts of many with morale and hope. The common folk, you know what they call you? They name you the keeper of Fanara's will.''

''Let's savour this moment, I know my part in this war isn't over.''

''I know….'' Eithne sighs.

''What's next do you think?''

Eithne places her tongue on her cheek. ''I don't know, but whatever it is. I hope we're in it together.''

26: Regicide

Gordon spent the night with Eithne, he joined her in her humble home in Vortighna. A night of passion and love.

The morning arrives with an unusual disturbance at Eithne's door.

Bang! Bang!

Eithne and Gordon were sitting, having breakfast together, curious to who it could possibly be.

''Ugh… probably Ambunix to poke fun at us I bet…'' she rolls her eyes as she approaches her door, opening it, only to find a total stranger, a man of Dun.

He had a rough and dirty face, a large muscular man hailing from the mountain tribes of Dun. This was apparent through his appearance and more specifically his hair, it was shaved to the scalp leaving a long tuft on his crown with many braids buried within, a common practise of the crag folk. Something was very off about him, he was heavily travel worn, his face bore a look of concern and angst. Eithne takes a defensive stance and she holds firm on her door. ''Who are you?'' She says, her demeanour snapping.

''My apologies for disturbing you, Is the… realm walker with you?''

She narrows her eyes in suspicion. ''I'll ask again, who are you?''

''Wait, Eithne…'' Gordon approaches, peering over her shoulder. He doesn't recognise the man standing before them. ''Yeah… okay, who are you? How did you find me?'' Gordon starts feeling slightly uneasy.

''Let me reframe, my name is Valmaros Dun-Taranos. I'm a former member of the Black Stag… I have a lot to tell you, Gordon. I've been searching for you… I arrived back in Darogoth after the battle of Northwood took place, and knew I'd find you in Vortighna for the feasts… I was informed you were with the tracker, so I sought you out. May we speak… in private if you will?'' Valmaros explains, swaying his square jaw in anticipation.

Gordon looks to Eithne. ''Somethings off… I'll go speak with him; I'll return to you soon, okay?''

''Be careful,'' she says as she leans into her door frame. Watching as Gordon and Valmaros walk away out of sight.

Valmaros leads Gordon into a dingy alley, Gordon starts becoming weary and prepares himself to cast, stopping Valmaros from proceeding further. ''Wait right there…'' Gordon orders. ''I'm not going any further, why have you been looking for me? I have no idea who you are? You said you're a Black Stag, the mercenaries of Shem? How did you find out where I was? If you're here to kill me, you can certainly try,'' Gordon arches out his hand, swilling it with energy.

''No! I'm not here to harm you! I want to help! I'm not even armed! Do you even know what the Black Stags do? Look, I am or at least I was part of that organisation… I'm going to tell you everything, but I need to be cautious. One of the guards gave me your location… with a small bribe….'' Valmaros raises his hands in submission.

''So, what is it? What's with all the cloak and dagger? I don't quite like being taken out of sight by a stranger.''

''I'm sorry, you don't deserve to feel so unsafe… I know this looks suspicious! But there is quite a lot to explain and I want to be away from prying ears, so… I'll try as best I can.'' Valmaros takes a deep breath as he peers around making sure no one is around. ''Many years ago now, I joined the Black Stags, one of my contracts was from a man named Hyphal Taarkiman, of Venethar.''

''Hyphal? The name rings a bell….'' Gordon defuses his magic.

''Yes, he's the court wizard of Kasidor. Back then Veldon Mundur was King, and word about the supposed location of Vistra's' torn soul had been revealed, and Veldon wanted it. So Hyphal reached out to us to intercept at the Mundur family's request. We accepted the contract, me and my comrade, Faalwyn. It was an Illegal contract too… we took it up before the overseers got wind of it, the pay-out was too good to turn down,'' he shifts his bloodshot eyes off to the side in remorse.

''Faalwyn?''

''You might know him now as Faalwyn Khan. He's king of Aventium or 'Khan' as they call it. Although, back then he had no idea he was to be the Khan, he was a secret heir, you see? But that's another story. Anyway, Faalwyn also became a Black Stag when he immigrated here from Aventium. We took up the contract, hired a few extra lackeys and got the job done before Veldon could march his elites in. We got very clear instructions by Hyphal on how to transport the 'soul' and so we obeyed. And… well… look how that turned out,'' Valmaros sniffs as he peers around once again in paranoia.

''I sort of already knew that, Tarna Mundur explained it all to me. So, you're one of the mercenaries who did the deed then, what's your point?''

''Look, people can't know who it was that started this whole thing, keep your voice down! but there's more… Faalwyn and I… we were close friends in the Black Stag days, until he got shifted away back to Aventium. I've been doing my own research ever since I heard about Kastrith's claims to godhood, to clear my name, to fix what I started. I've spent years upon years, searching… and… I found something that only someone with magic like yours could be capable of wielding, something to use and put an end to all this. I found something that withholds the magic of the endless void.''

Gordon's eyes widened in shock.

''With your power, you can use this magic to restrict the soul's grip on Kastrith and send it back through the void, back to Vistra himself! But you'll need help! I have something here that can see the unseeable. It was a torc forged by Iskarien in the days of old. Now don't ask me how I acquired this, I'm not proud of it, but here it is, The Bone Torc. When you wear this torc and use magic, it is said you can see the realms of the Gods in the sky…

Iskarien had it made to send sacrifices to her realm before she was banished,'' Valmaros pats on a shoddy rucksack he had attached to his back. ''It doesn't hold the same magic as the void, but what it does do is help us direct Vistra's soul back to him, into his own realm! Using this with the void magic that I discovered should get the job done….''

Valmaros' words rattle Gordons' head. ''What?!? Wait, so… this void magic… where is it? Where?''

''It's in Murk, A country far south of Aventium. I'll keep it short and sweet, but the Murkith God, Sin Fan Rok, was slain in the Gods Age and his people created a monument out of his corpse. You see, before he died, he imbued a tree with his magic, but was slain before he could do whatever it was, he was going to do… I don't know the full details because I don't speak Murkish, but the people tended to the tree, worshipping it as they did him and over time the tree consumed his corpse, not many people know that it still contains a God's magic, even though he's been long dead. The Murkith keep to themselves away from the diplomacy of the great kingdoms of Uros and Loria, not only that, but Murk is inhospitable, you can barely breathe in the place without ingesting toxic fumes from the deadly vegetation that grows there. I found this out after journeying to Aventium to appeal to Faalwyn myself, but the guards wouldn't let me get anywhere near him no matter how hard I tried. I've been through allot to get the information I have, Realm Walker. With your help you might be able to request a proper audience with Faalwyn and maybe get Darogoth another ally in this war while we're at it. Aventium's laws are very strict with their Khan's, they barely ever even address their own people due to fear of Murkith assassinations, they're firm on keeping the Khan bloodline pure and forever ongoing, it's not going to be easy but I know this is going to work! It has too.''

Gordon stands almost speechless. ''What the fuck. Why haven't you gone to the high king?''

''I can't… you could say it was me and Faalwyn who stoked the fire of this entire war, that we're responsible for everything. After all, we took on an illegal contract… I need the support of someone with standing and power, someone like you. The people would lynch us if they knew what we had done. I know Faalwyn cares too, but he feels he can ignore it, now that he's Khan of Aventium… I haven't heard anything from him despite my efforts, he refuses to look back! He's ashamed! If only I could speak with him, just once.''

''You were just doing your job though?! If Veldon got hold of the soul, surely things would be so much worse? Especially from what I've heard of him.''

''Your words speak the truth, but it was still an illegal act. Will you help me? I need your support to bring this to the high king, and I need you to pique the curiosity of Aventium and end their neutrality on this war. Maybe with all this information gathered, I can fix what I started, and if Vistra's fate still has it in for me to be executed, then so be it, but by Fanara, I must fix this,'' Valmaros Pleads, anguish ladens his tiresome face.

''Magic of the endless void…'' Gordon whispers to himself. ''After all this time….'' Gordon becomes conflicted.

Eastern Ard, Darogoth.

Within the recess of Sprig's Grove, a small and secluded little forest in the eastern Ard peninsula, south west of the city Oriaxos. Tarna and her most loyal had assembled their yurts, living like the days of the old Venethari, out in the wilderness, taming the lands. Except, these were the lands of Darogoth.

Tarna was not a warrior, she may know her way round a bow like most Venethari, but she had never drawn back its strings and ended a life, the only strings that Tarna drew back and let loose her grasp were those of the lyre, she adored music, she could be seen dipping her very essence within the tunes and melodies, even in the most uncertain of times, like now, as she sat back in her own personal yurt around the fire, strumming upon her lyre as she always had done.

She was away from her people; her rich and lavish lifestyle was a thing of the past. Being a once proud member of the Mundur dynasty she revelled in her ancestors' stories, those of nomads, strong and hard, the masters of the land, so living as such did not rub her the wrong way, she didn't as much yearn to drink the finest of wines, or wear the most glamourous of silks as she did when she first fled Kasidor, she'd grown now to love the ways of old, she felt at peace.

She smiled to herself as she continued to glide her fingers across her most beloved of instruments, in her own personal celebration of Darogoth's victory over Kastrith.

''You're Grace?'' A hollow voice called from outside.

Tarna places her lyre gently aside, leaving her yurt to confront the voice.

''What have I told you all about addressing me as such? I am royalty no longer; I am but a symbol of our cause.''

''Apologies… Tarna,'' her loyal guard mutters, still struggling to address her so casually. ''We have a situation.''

''Oh?''

''You might want to prepare yourself.''

''Out with it.''

The guard bobs his head to the camp's centre.

Laying down to the ground was her runner that would frequent journeys through The Glade, passing messages of great importance between the rebellion and her post in Darogoth.

His face blank as he straddled himself upon all fours, dipping his head in submission, awaiting Tarna's presence. Right before him was a wooden crate he had brought through.

''Uldreth… what ails you?''

''Tarna… Tarna… my Lady….'' his bottom lip tremors as his voice shakes in sadness.

''Uldreth, you're frightening me.''

''Our cause… my Lady, It's over. They found us, they… they….''

‘’This can’t be! How?! Thornus… is Thornus okay?’’ She starts pacing, her steps replicating her fear.

Uldreth forcefully shuts his eyes tight as he shakes his head, puffing out his bulbous nostrils.

‘’No! No!’’ She erupts in a flood of tears.

‘’Kastrith, he attacked us, he himself rode in on the back of a gryphon and slaughtered us all within minutes. They spared me and ordered to deliver you….’’

‘’What?! Deliver me what?!’’

Uldreth holds his hand out, gesturing to the crate he had brought with him.

Tarna wastes no time in storming over to crate and wedging it open herself.

To her horror, there sat the severed head of Thornus Glaen-Caerwen.

The rebellion had been utterly crushed.

Carsinia, Ard, Darogoth

In the dead of night, and after days of celebrations, Vocorix is woken by a loud crashing sound, accompanied by muffled shouting and screams of his guard and oathsworn.

He disregarded the disturbances as a dream, as he was half asleep, until a louder and more terrifying beastly screech and a rumble that shook the entire castle wedged open his weary eyes. His queen Geldra also awakens, disturbed by the sounds.

''What was that, a quake?'' Geldra speaks out in her sleepy tone.

''I don't know… I'm going to see the guards now,'' he jumps up, dresses and makes his way toward the commotion in the distance, it was coming from the great hall. The longer it went on the more it stoked his concerns, something was wrong.

His guards were nowhere to be seen as he made his way through the castle, Vocorix grew more and more worried. He gives a brisker pace, storming down the corridors that echo with uncertainty, the sounds getting louder, screams, smashes, and the clanging of metal, his walk turns into a run.

He burst open a side door leading to the great hall, and to his surprise, a pride of mounted gryphons had torn through the castle, reaping the guards with their terrifying beaks and ferocious talons, leaping about the great hall and smashing all in their wake as they squawked and screeched.

One of the riders donned a golden mask, it was him, Kastrith Mundur himself.

They barge on through, pushing back the defence of Castle Carsinia, Vocorix can do nothing but watch on as his guards are shredded before him, mutilated like playthings as the gryphons volley them about the hall, one of the gryphons sustains enough injuries in the fight and becomes downed, its rider swamped by guards.

Kastrith takes note of Vocorix's presence, he carelessly dismounts his dreadful beast, making his way to Vocorix with casual steps.

Guards upon guards pour into the room in a state of emergency, all of them swatted aside by Kastrith's terrible magic, smashing them into the castle interior with ease. Others were torn limb from limb as the massive gryphons engulfed them whole and shook them around viciously, clamped within their freakish beaks.

Kastrith had erected a great barrier of arcane fire upon the crumbled entrance, halting any further advance from outside the castle.

Vocorix watched on in horror, speechless in fright.

''Vocorix!'' Kastrith shouts from beyond the chaos as he makes his way forward. ''Good of you to join us, I was just about to request an audience with you,'' he halts a charging guard, slamming him to the floor belly first. He stamps his boot onto the guards back forcing him down into the stone floor, and with his hands conjures up a harrowing energy, pulling the guards head upward until snapping his neck and severing his head completely, displaying the ferocity of his power before Vocorix.

''What!? What!?''

Kastrith catches the guard's head, throwing it off to the side and cleaning his bloodied black gloves upon the cloth of his armoured robes. ''Surprised, are we? Just look how easily I forced my way into your court, shameful. I have come to deliver a message, personally.''

Vocorix struggles to focus. ''Kastrith what are you doing? For the love of our Gods what are you doing?!''

The fighting in the hall had come to an eerie halt as the guards either fled, or died.

''You're not the only one with reckless tricks up their sleeves that can turn the tide of battle. You think your victory in Glaen will halt us, halt Vistra? Think again, heathen.''

He reaches out his arm taking a firm hold of Vocorix, encasing him within his magical grasp, raising him from where he stood and into the air.

''What is it you hold most dear, Vocorix Fen-Drosii? Your kingdom, or your family?'' Kastrith tightens his squeeze.

''I... can't... you....'' Vocorix struggles to get out a breath, let alone speak.

Kastrith slams him to the floor, breaking his knees with the sheer force, as well as cracking the very stone beneath him. He rises him up again and slams him back down, shattering his pelvis.

''Stop it! Stop it!'' Geldra shrieks as she scurries into the room upon hearing the commotion.

''What is it, you hold most dear, High King?'' he loosens his grasp on Vocorix, allowing him to speak, keeping him firmly suspended from the ground.

Vocorix gasps for the air he desperately needs. The agony of the blows leaves him completely incapacitated and mangled beyond recovery, he look's Kastrith dead into the eyeholes of his reflective mask that shimmer that purple light. ''Family,'' he coughs out.

''How noble… now why is it so hard for you to heed my words?''

''Geldra, get out!'' Vocorix strains.

''Quiet!'' The rage of his voice changed into a dark and voided tone, speaking through the magic, humming throughout his presence. ''I'm not finished. Now, your family can't be that important, can they? Especially if you keep being so persistent, interfering with Vistra's return, why do you wish to hinder your God, Vocorix. Why do you only seek to stop him?!''

Kastrith nods his head to one of his gryphon riders who had all but dismounted, watching on as their king manhandled the now feeble Vocorix.

A gryphon rider skewers Geldra from behind with his sword, her gasp silent, frozen still by the cold blade that sliced through her back and protruded from her front. The rider yanks out his blade and Geldra drops to her knees as she watches her own blood pool out from her stomach. She gives a lasting look to her broken husband, her face as white as snow.

With her final breath she lets out a blood curdling scream. Falling to the floor as she begins to lose consciousness, and her life.

Vocorix cries in a fit of rage bound in air, forcefully angled by Kastrith to watch on as his queen's life slips away right before him.

''What say you now? High King.''

''You… you… fucking…'' Vocorix pants in a state of rage. ''BASTARD! BASTARD!!''

Kastrith scoffs. ''You're not even worthy to die by the hand of Vistra,'' he flings Vocorix to the centre of the hall, and snaps his fingers.

As Vocorix thuds into the cold hard floor, he is met with the sight of Kastrith's gryphon, looming over him with a terrible hunger festering its large black eyes.

It snatches him by his head and flails him from side to side, snapping shut its beak upon his torso and separating it from the rest of his body, mauling him to death and engulfing the remains.

''And so, ends the reign of Vocorix Fen-Drosii, no doubt another pitiful bastard will take your place… but I'm sure after receiving this… message, the next will be more coherent with Vistra's will.''

Kastrith and the remaining riders mount back up, flying off into the night, for what their intentions were, only Vistra truly knows.

To be continued...